UNDERCITY

CATHERINE ASARO

UNDERCITY

This is a work of fiction. All the characters and events portrayed in this book are fictional, and any resemblance to real people or incidents is purely coincidental.

A Baen Books Original

Baen Publishing Enterprises
P.O. Box 1403
Riverdale, NY 10471
www.baen.com

ISBN: 978-1-4767-8141-9

Cover art by Alan Pollack

First Baen paperback printing, May 2016

Library of Congress Control Number: 2014034534

Distributed by Simon & Schuster
1230 Avenue of the Americas
New York, NY 10020

Pages by Joy Freeman (www.pagesbyjoy.com)
Printed in the United States of America

This book is dedicated to Quantum and Angel
Who allow me to adore their esteemed Catness

ACKNOWLEDGMENTS

I gratefully acknowledge the
following people for their invaluable input:

the Aly Parsons writing group: Aly Parsons, Bob Chase, Charles Gannon, Carolyn Ives Gilman, John Hemry, J. G. Huckenpöler, Simcha Kuritzky, Mike LaViolette, Bud Sparhawk, Connie Warner, and Al Warner;

Lina Perez and Kate Dolan;

all the Baen team, including my publisher Toni Weisskopf, my editor Tony Daniel, also Danielle Turner, Joy Freeman, Hank Davis, Marla Ainspan, and all the other great people who did such a fine job making this book possible;

the folks at Spectrum Literary Agency, including my agent Eleanor Wood, Kris Bell, and Justin Bell; and my publicist Binnie Syril Braunstein.

A special thanks to my husband, John Cannizzo and my daughter Cathy, for their love and support.

BOOK I

The City of Cries

1

The Offer

The flycar picked me up at midnight.

Black and rounded for stealth, the vehicle had no markings. I recognized the model, a Sleeker, the type of transportation only the wealthiest could afford—or the most criminal. If my client hadn't told me to expect the car, I wouldn't have gone near that lethal beauty. I just wished I knew who the hell had hired me.

The Sleeker waited on the roof of the building where I lived. As I approached, an oval of light shimmered in its hull. A molecular airlock. Why? A vehicle needed that much protection only if it intended to go high into the atmosphere. We could be headed anywhere on the planet.

I had no wish to leave town. I had a good setup here in Selei City on the world Parthonia, the capital of an empire, jewel of the Skolian Imperialate. Droop-willows lined graceful boulevards and shaded mansions under a pale blue sky. It was far different from the city where I had spent my girlhood, a place of red deserts and parched seas.

The luminous oval on the flycar faded into an open hatchway. A man stood there, tall and rangy, wearing a black jumpsuit that resembled a uniform, but with no insignia to indicate who or what he served. He looked efficient. Too efficient. It made me appreciate the bulk of the EM pulse gun hidden in a shoulder holster under my black leather jacket.

Normally I wasn't one to attribute details of clothing to the way people looked at you, but this stranger definitely watched me with a hooded gaze. I couldn't read anything from his expression. As I reached the vehicle, he moved aside to let me step into its cabin. I didn't like it. If I boarded, gods only knew where I would end up. However, this request for my services had come with a voucher worth more than the total income for every job I'd done this last year. I'd already verified the credit. And that was purportedly only the first payment. Of course I'd accepted the job.

However, certain types of clients didn't like questions. If I asked too many, this pilot would leave. Without me. Credits gone. No job. I could walk away from this, but I needed the money. I didn't even have enough to pay the next installment on my office loan.

And I had to admit it: I was curious.

I boarded the Sleeker.

Selei City spread out below the tower. The landing pad on my building was high enough that individual skyscrapers and magrails of the metropolis weren't visible, just a wash of sparkling lights. I reclined in a seat with smart upholstery that adjusted to ease my tensed muscles with a finesse that only the most expensive furniture could manage.

It didn't help.

I was the only passenger. The cabin had ten seats, five on my side separated by a few steps from five on the other side. The white carpet glinted as if it were dusted with holographic diamonds. Who knew, maybe they were real gems.

Flycars usually had a pilot and copilot's seat in the main cabin. This one had a cockpit. The membrane separating it from the cabin irised open for the pilot and he left it that way. Everything looked normal when he slid into his seat—until a silver exoskeleton snapped around his body. If that mesh worked like the ones I knew, it was jacking prongs into his body, linking the flycar to his internal biomech web, which would include a spinal node with as much processing capability as a starship. Few people carried such webs inside their bodies, only military officers, the exorbitantly wealthy—and those who worked for the most notorious criminal lords.

"Hey," I said.

The pilot looked back at me. "Yes?"

"I was wondering what to call you."

"Ro."

I waited. "Just Ro?"

He regarded me with his unreadable dark eyes. "Just Ro." His face remained impassive. "You had better web in, ma'am."

Ma'am. A polite crook? Interesting. I asked, "Where're we headed?"

No answer. I hadn't expected one. Nothing in the message delivered to my office this afternoon had hinted at my destination. The recording had been verbal only, with no signature, just that huge sum of credit that transferred to my account as soon as I accepted the job.

I pulled the safety mesh around my body. I was a slender woman, more muscle than softness, and the webbing had to tighten from whoever had used it before me.

"Ready?" the pilot asked. He was intent on his controls, and it took me a moment to realize he had spoken to me rather than to the flycar.

"Ready," I said.

With no warning, g-forces slammed me into the seat like a giant invisible hand. The chair did its best to compensate, but nothing could gentle a kick that big. A noise rumbled through the vehicle that I wouldn't have believed if I hadn't heard it. Rockets had just fired. This "flycar" was a damn spaceship.

The pressure built until black spots filled my vision. The webbing pushed against my body, countering the effects, but I still felt dizzy. Pinwheels spiraled in my vision and bile rose in my throat.

As soon as the pressure eased, I said, "Where the hell are we going?"

"Best relax," the pilot said. "We'll be a few hours."

I didn't know how fast we were traveling, but given that rocket blast, we had to be moving at a good clip. We were still accelerating, less than before, but enough to feel the effects. A few hours of this could take us deep into the solar system.

I regarded him uneasily. "I don't suppose this flycar has inversion capability?" It was halfway to a joke. Starships went into inversion to circumvent the speed of light, which meant they could end up anywhere in space, light-years from here. A vehicle would only need such engines if it were leaving the Parthonia planetary system, which of course we weren't going to do.

The pilot looked back at me. "We invert in six minutes."

Flaming hell.

II

The Study

In eons past, the Vanished Sea had rolled its waves on the world Raylicon. Now only a desert remained where those great breakers had once crashed on the shore. The empty sea basin stretched out in a mottled red and blue expanse to the horizon. The City of Cries stood on the shore of that long-vanished ocean. I knew that desert. I knew that city. I had grown up in Cries and lived here later as an adult.

I had never intended to return.

The Sleeker hummed through the night, banking over Cries, a chrome and crystal city that glinted in the desert. I could just make out the ruins of the ancient city farther along the shore, the original Cries, which my ancestors had built five thousand years ago. Beyond them, the pitted ruins of ancient starships hulked on the shore of the Vanished Sea, their hulls dulled over the millennia. They were shrines, enigmatic reminders that humanity hadn't originated here on Raylicon, but on a blue-green world across the galaxy.

Earth.

It was the home we never knew, a legend grown misty with time until my ancestors called it a myth. Six thousand years ago, an unknown race of beings had kidnapped humans from Earth, left them on Raylicon, and disappeared with no explanation. Had a disaster killed them before they completed whatever they began with their captive humans? We never knew. They left my ancestors here with nothing.

Primitive, terrified, and confused, those lost humans had struggled to survive. Their kidnappers left behind only those ruined starships. However, those ships contained the library of a starfaring race, and desperation drove my ancestors to learn those records. The library contained no history of the ships, but they detailed eerie sciences unlike anything we used today. Although it took centuries, my ancestors learned enough to develop star travel and went in search of their lost home. They never found the birthplace of humanity, but they built the Ruby Empire, an interstellar civilization that spread its colonies across the stars.

That was five thousand years ago. Built on poorly understood technology and plagued by volatile politics, the empire soon collapsed. The ensuing Dark Age lasted four millennia, but we did finally regain the stars. We split into two empires then: the Eubian Traders, who based their economy on the sale of human beings, and my people, the Skolian Imperialate. Eventually our siblings on Earth also developed space travel. They had a real shock when they reached the stars and found us already here, building gargantuan and bellicose empires.

I had left all that history behind when I left Raylicon. Yet here I was, back home. The flyer soared into the mountains. We landed on the roof of a solitary building high among the peaks. The crenellations bordering the roof were carved into mythical beasts, their fangs and horns sharp. Onion towers topped with golden spires loomed above the flycar, reaching into a sky brilliant with stars. I took a good long look through my portal, and sweat trickled down my neck despite the climate-controlled cabin.

As I released my webbing, the pilot left the cockpit. I wished I could place his background. He had the black hair, smooth skin, and the tilted eyes of Raylican nobility, but that made no sense. A nobleman wouldn't work as a private pilot no matter how upscale the transportation.

The noble Houses traced their heritage back to the Ruby Empire. In this modern age, an elected Assembly ruled the Imperialate, and the Houses no longer held the power they wielded five millennia ago. The days when warlike matriarchs had kept their men in seclusion were gone; now both women and men held positions of authority. The Houses kept to themselves in their rarified universe and would never bring in a stranger to deal with their problems, especially not a commoner. Especially not me. So who else could afford this place? A crime boss. No wonder she had been cagey about her identity. She wouldn't be the first underworld mogul to cover her operation with a phony aristocratic sheen.

As I disembarked, warm breezes ruffled my hair around my shoulders, sending black strands across my cheeks. When I worked, I pulled back my hair, but in Selei City I had become used to letting it fall free. Not here. I clicked a band around the tresses, keeping them away from my face.

Seven years had passed since I breathed the parched air of Raylicon. All that time in the gentle atmosphere of Selei City had spoiled me; the air here felt hot and astringent. It smelled dusty. Fortunately, the nanomeds in my body could deal with the differences. They also gave me the health and appearance of a woman in my late twenties, though I was well into my forties.

"This way," the pilot said behind me.

Ho! My reflexes took over and I spun around, ready to strike. Although I stopped in time, the pilot had already raised his fists. He was unnaturally fast, another indication he carried biomech inside his body. Its system would include high-pressure biohydraulics, modifications to his skeleton and muscles, and a microfusion reactor for energy. It could give him two or three times the strength and speed of an unaugmented human. Given how quickly he had responded, he obviously carried a top-quality system.

Mine was better.

"My apologies." The pilot lowered his hands. "I didn't mean to startle you."

"No harm done." My thoughts hummed with warnings. Biomech webs cost as much as Jag star fighters and weren't available to civilians. I'd received mine when I served in the Pharaoh's Army. Either this pilot had been a military officer or else he worked for someone with more access to military technology than even some branches of the military. Illegal access. I was beginning to wonder if this job was worth even the huge cut of cream it put in my bank account.

We crossed the roof and entered an onion tower through an elegant archway. Inside, stairs spiraled down, nothing mechanical, no modern touches, just a beautifully designed staircase. Lights came on as we descended, however, golden and warm. Tessellated mosaics inlaid the ceiling in gold, silver, and platinum. The place reeked of wealth.

At the bottom, we reached a gallery of horseshoe arches. Our footsteps echoed as we walked through a forest of columns tiled in precious metals. I saw no sign of tech-mech, but golden light poured around us, and it had to come from somewhere. We left the gallery through another large archway and followed halls wide enough to accommodate ten people side-by-side. Mosaics patterned the walls, blue and purple near the floor, shading up through lighter hues, and blending into a scalloped border at the ceiling far overhead.

The low gravity, sharp air, and exotic decor saturated my mind. As we forged deep into the maze of halls, my spinal node created a map. We walked in silence. I tried to talk with the pilot, but he never responded. Finally we climbed a staircase that swept up to a balcony. At the top, we passed two archways and went through the third. The door swung on ancient hinges that should have creaked but in this unreal place were so well oiled, they didn't even whisper. In the study beyond, bookshelves lined three of the walls. And they held real books. Not holobooks, mesh cards, or VR disks, but tomes with paper pages, the type usually found only in museums. One lay open on a table. Calligraphy in glimmering inks covered its pages, which were edged in gold. I had never seen even one such book, let alone a room packed with them from floor to ceiling.

A dark-haired woman stood across the study gazing out an arched window with her back to us. She turned as we entered, and her presence filled the room. She stood two meters tall and had a military bearing. Dark hair swept back from her forehead with gray dusting the temples, and her chiseled features could have been on a classic statue with her high cheekbones, straight nose, and tilted black eyes. The elegant cut of her dark tunic and trousers showed no hint of flamboyance. She could have been any age from forty to one hundred and forty; I had no doubt she could afford the best treatments available to delay aging.

The woman inclined her head to the pilot. "Thank you, Captain. You may go." She spoke in Skolian Flag, a language adopted by dignitaries who interacted with many different peoples. However, she had an Iotic accent. It almost sounded authentic. Almost. No one spoke Iotic anymore except scholars, noble Houses, and pretenders who wanted to sound cultured.

The pilot bowed and left the study. I wondered if my host expected me to bow. I didn't move.

The woman considered me. "My greetings, Major Bhaajan."

I nodded to her. "I'm afraid you have the advantage of me, Lady." I didn't know if she truly carried that title of nobility, but it was more tactful than *Who the hell are you?*

"Matriarch," she murmured, "not Lady."

I froze. Hell and damnation.

I quit hoping she was a crime boss. Her Iotic accent wasn't "almost" authentic, it was genuine. This was no phony palace. I had come to the real thing.

"Which House?" I asked. Blunt maybe, but finesse had never been one of my strong points.

Her gaze never wavered. "Majda."

I felt the blood drain from my face. Majda. Wrong again. I wasn't facing nobility.

This was royalty. Genuine, bonechilling royalty.

III
Majda

The Matriarch indicated a brocaded couch with gilt-edged legs. Wooden legs. And Raylicon had no trees. "Let us sit," she said in her terrifyingly rich voice.

My knowledge of how to behave with royalty was exactly zilch. However, the Majda Matriarch also served as one of the Joint Commanders in charge of the Skolian military, specifically the General of the Pharaoh's Army. And she had used my military title, though I had been out of the army for years. Military protocol I could handle. So I said, "Thank you, General."

She inclined her head, accepting the title. I sat on the couch and she settled on a wingchair. A table with red and gold mosaics stood between us. Majda crossed her long legs and light glinted on her polished knee-boots.

"Would you care for a drink?" she asked. "I have a bit of Kazar brandy."

Seriously? I'd give a decade of life for genuine Kazar. I said only, "Thank you, yes."

Majda touched the scrolled arm on her chair. A circle the size of her fingertip glowed blue, but nothing else happened.

Then we sat.

I had no idea what to do with the silence. She would set the conversation. So I waited, racking my brain for what I knew about the Majdas. Five millennia ago, the Ruby Dynasty had reigned over an empire led by the Ruby Pharaoh, who was also Matriarch of the House of Skolia. Although the elected Assembly ruled the Imperialate now instead of the dynasty, the Skolias still wielded substantial power. After the Skolias, the Majdas were the most influential House. They no longer ruled Raylicon; in these modern times, their empire was financial. They controlled more wealth than the combined governments of entire planets.

They also controlled a significant portion of the military. During the Ruby Empire, the House of Majda had supplied generals to the Pharaoh's Army. Today, they dominated the two largest branches of Imperial Space Command, the army and the Imperial Fleet. Majda women served as officers. Only the women. Of all the noble Houses, Majda adhered most to the old ways. They kept their princes secluded, never seen by any women outside the family.

A man in dark clothes entered the room carrying a tray with two crystal tumblers. Gold liquid sparkled in them. He set the tray on the table and bowed to Majda.

The general inclined her head. "Thank you."

He left as silently as he had come. I stared after him. No one had human servants anymore. Robots were less expensive, more reliable, and required less upkeep.

Majda indicated the tumblers to me. "Please be my guest."

We both took our glasses. The brandy swirled in my mouth, went down like ambrosia, and detonated when it hit bottom. Saints almighty. I sat up straighter. The nanomeds in my body would keep me sober, but gods, with brandy like this, I was tempted to get drunk.

"That's good," I said, ever the master of understatement.

Majda sipped her drink. "You have an interesting reputation, Major Bhaajan."

"You've a job for me, I take it."

"A discreet job."

Discretion was my specialty. No messes. "Of course."

"I need to find someone." She considered me. "I'm told you are the best there is for such searches and that you know Cries."

"I grew up here." I had no wish to remember my youth. I had lived in the undercity, deep below the gleaming City of Cries, a dust rat surviving on my wits, my ability to steal, and my sheer cussed refusal to let poverty kill me. I knew Cries in ways no Majda could understand. Before she could bring up any more about my past, I changed the subject. "I'll need to see all the details you can give me about this person and how she disappeared. Holos, mesh access, traits, everything on her habits and friends."

"You will have the information." Her voice hardened. "Be certain you never misuse it."

That didn't sound good. "Misuse how?"

"He is a member of this family."

He. *He*. Ah, hell.

Majda had lost a prince, one of those hidden and

robed enigmas that fascinated the empire. You could end up in prison just for trying to glimpse one of their men. It wasn't so long ago that the penalty for a woman who touched a Majda prince was execution. My life wouldn't be worth spit if I offended this House, and I couldn't imagine a better way to piss them off than to trespass against one of their men.

"What happened to him?" I asked.

She tapped the arm on her chair and the room dimmed. Curtains closed over the windows. A screen came down in front of the wall across from us and a holo formed, the image of a man. He stood in a room similar to this one, but with wood paneling and tapestries on the walls instead of books. He looked in his early twenties. Luxuriant black hair curled over his forehead and he had the Majda eyes, large and dark, tilted upward. His broad shoulders, leanly muscled torso, and long legs had ideal proportions. He wore a tunic of russet velvet and red brocade, edged in gold, and darker trousers with knee hoots. The word gorgeous didn't begin to describe him. He was, without doubt, the most singularly arresting man I had ever seen.

He wasn't smiling.

"His name is Prince Dayjarind Kazair Majda," the general said. "He is my nephew. No woman outside this family has ever seen him in person." She paused. "Save one."

Had he run off with a lover who had a death wish? I spoke carefully. "Who?"

"Roca Skolia."

That wasn't what I had expected. "You mean the Pharaoh's sister?"

"That is correct."

Well, well. Roca Skolia was heir to the Ruby Throne, first in line to the title of Ruby Pharaoh. She not only held a hereditary seat in the elected Assembly that governed the Imperialate, she had also run for election and won a seat as a delegate. She had risen in the Assembly ranks until she became the Foreign Affairs Councilor, making her one of the most powerful politicians in the Imperialate. If this Majda queen expected me to investigate Roca Skolia, she had a far higher estimation of my skills than even I did myself.

"Your Highness," I said, "I can't force a member of the Ruby Dynasty to return your nephew."

"He is not with Roca. They were betrothed. Almost." A thinly concealed disdain edged her voice. "Two years ago, Roca broke her agreement in order to marry some barbarian king." After a pause, she added, "Reparations were offered. Eventually my House accepted them." Her tone implied acceptance hadn't come easy. "I had thought the matter settled. Then three days ago, Dayj ran away."

"How did he leave?" It wouldn't surprise me if this Prince Dayj had better security guarding him than some heads of state.

"We aren't certain." She set her drink on the table. "I have always viewed my nephew as a pleasant and good-natured young man, but without much depth. I may have underestimated him."

"Do you have any idea where he went?"

"None."

"What do the authorities in Cries say?"

Her voice cooled. "Majda has its own police force."

"But they can't find him?"

A pause. "They haven't exhausted all the possibilities."

Right. That was why they had brought me in, a stranger from another planet. "Could someone have kidnapped your nephew?"

She spoke coolly. "It would be almost impossible to take him from here even with his cooperation. And we've received no ransom demand." Her gaze darkened. "If he left of his own free will, which we believe he did, he knows nothing about survival outside this palace. He can read and write, but beyond that he has no experience in taking care of himself."

Maybe. If he had been able to outwit the Majda security, he was probably more savvy than she believed. "Did he leave a note?"

"On his holopad." Her voice sounded strained, as if she were in pain but trying to cover it. "It said, 'I can't do this any longer. I have to go. I'm sorry. I love you all.'"

Such a simple message with such a world of hurt. Yet she mentioned only a broken agreement with Roca Skolia from two years ago. "So you think he's still upset about the betrothal?"

Majda snorted. "Hardly. He never wanted to marry Roca."

"Then why do you mention it?"

"Because he said the same thing after she broke the betrothal. Except not that sentence about having to go."

"Has he ever talked about leaving?"

Majda waved her hand. "He never says much, just male talk. Inconsequentials."

I could already see plenty of reasons why Dayjarind

Majda might have run off, but I couldn't suggest any of them to the Matriarch. So I said only, "General Majda, if he can be found, I'll do it."

"No measure is too extreme." She leaned forward. "Whatever you need, we will provide."

I spent the morning in a private suite the Majdas gave me in the palace, trying to figure out who might have helped Dayj escape. He was one of nine Majda princes here, including his father and two younger brothers. His Uncle Izam was consort to Vaj Majda, the Matriarch. Izam and Vaj had three daughters, Devon, Corey, and Naaj, and one son, Jazar. The Matriarch's two sisters lived in the palace with their families, but her brothers had married and left Raylicon. The older brother continued to live in seclusion with his wife, the Matriarch of another noble House, but the general's younger brother had pulverized tradition and scandalized his family by attending college. He was now a psychology professor at the Royal University on Parthonia. Good for him.

Dayj had an odd life. His elders paid excruciatingly close attention to ensure he behaved as expected for an unmarried man of his station. I hadn't known people still lived by those rigid codes, over five thousand years old. He could never leave the palace without an escort. On the rare occasion when he had permission to venture beyond the boundaries of his constrained life, he wore a cowled robe that hid him from head to toe. He couldn't communicate with anyone outside the family, which meant he never used the meshes that spanned human-settled space, a web of communications that most people took for granted.

He had no formal schooling. However, he used the Majda libraries extensively. I wondered if Vaj Majda had ever bothered to check, given her comments about his supposed lack of depth. He read voraciously in science and mathematics, art and culture, history and sociology, psychology and mysticism. His education went beyond what many of us learned in a lifetime. I couldn't imagine what it must be like for him, confined here, knowing so much about the freedom beyond his cage.

Still, it was a golden cage. He lived in a manner most people only dreamed about, if they could envision it at all. His family lavished him with jewels worth more than my entire life's earnings; with tapestries sought by collectors throughout the Imperialate; with gourmet delicacies and wines. Anything he wanted, they gave him as long as it didn't break his inviolable seclusion. He was among the greatest assets owned by Majda, an incomparably handsome prince who would bring great allies and fortune to the House through his marriage.

No wonder he had run away.

I wondered how he felt about the betrothal to Roca Skolia. He had almost given Majda a direct line into the Ruby Dynasty. I easily found broadcasts on the subject. They made the perfect couple, and their arranged betrothal had fascinated the public. So what had Roca done? Two years ago, she ran off with a farmer from some remote colony, one of the ancient settlements stranded five thousand years ago after the Ruby Empire fell and only recently rediscovered. The fellow apparently carried the blood of the ancient dynasty; either that, or he and Roca married out of love and the Ruby Dynasty scrambled for a royal connection to justify the union. The convoluted web of politics that tangled around all these people made me inestimably grateful for my simple life.

Watching the holos of Dayj and Roca, I doubted he had suffered much heartbreak when she broke the agreement. His family recorded those strained visits; privacy seemed less valuable to them than ensuring that he and the Councilor maintained the proper behavior. Like Dayj, Roca was too beautiful. It was annoying. She had gold hair, gold eyes, golden skin, and an angel's face. The two of them sat in wingback chairs, drank wine out of jeweled goblets, and conversed stiffly. Despite their perfectly composed sentences, neither seemed to enjoy the visits. Power, beauty, and wealth apparently didn't translate into romantic bliss.

Regardless of how Dayj had felt about his intended, it had to have hurt when she dumped him. His family had molded his life with one goal in mind: he would become the consort of a powerful woman. They achieved the pinnacle. He literally couldn't have done better; the only more powerful woman was the Pharaoh herself, and she had to marry within her family, an arcane law that had managed to survive our legal system for millennia. Dayj had done exactly what he was supposed to do, and it had collapsed on him.

I had landed in one holy mess. To solve this, I had to talk to the Majda princes, who would know aspects of Dayj that he probably never revealed to the women of the household. A million ways existed to trespass on the honor of the Majdas. One misstep could embroil me in more trouble than I'd ever seen. I disliked jobs from crime bosses, but even that would be easier to deal with. All criminals had to worry about was the law, or more accurately, not being caught when they broke it. Majda was a law unto itself. The police would look the other way if the Matriarch decided to take that law into her own hands.

If I botched this, I was, literally, royally screwed.

Prince Paolo had married Colonel Lavinda Majda, the Matriarch's youngest sister. A son of the Rajindia noble House, Paolo had led a relatively normal life prior to his marriage and earned several university degrees. Gods only knew why such a man would agree to live in seclusion, but even I wasn't blind to the benefits of marrying into the House of Majda.

I couldn't see him alone, of course. Four male guards accompanied me into his study, led by Duane Ebersole, a retired major from the Pharaoh's Army, a powerfully built man who projected a sense of self-assured authority. His people were recording this meeting. A female guard remained outside, Captain Krestone, another former officer who headed palace security and missed nothing. One thing I'd say for the Majdas; they chose their staff well. Both Krestone and Ebersole impressed me with their calm authority and a situational awareness that I recognized only because I'd also been taught to keep that same alert attention to all details, large and small.

Paolo was seated behind his large desk. A clutter of data spheres, holosheets, and light styluses lay strewn across its surface, which consisted of a glossy black holoscreen. He leaned back as I sat across from him in a wing chair with smart cushions.

"My greetings, Major," he said.

"My greetings, Your Highness," I answered.

He studied me with dark eyes. Of course he was handsome, even including the streaks of gray in his hair and fine lines around his eyes. All the Majda men I had seen were unusually good-looking, every one of them dark, well-proportioned, and undoubtedly fertile. The Matriarch might consider Dayj shallow, but maybe she ought to look at her own values. Majda women hardly seemed to choose their princes for depth. Then again, maybe there was more to it. Paolo Rajindia Majda was no fool. Before his marriage, he had earned a doctorate at the Architecture Institute associated with Imperial College on the world Metropoli, one of the most elite academic institutions in the Imperialate.

"You've come to ask about Dayj," he said.

"That's right." I had intended to talk with Dayj's parents first, but they were both at the starport with the police, trying to find out if he had gone offworld.

Paolo rested his elbow on the arm of his chair. "Do you think he left Raylicon?"

"I've no idea." I tried a probe. "It depends how much help he had from inside the palace."

Paolo didn't twitch. "What help?"

"To escape, he needed the aid of someone inside."

His voice cooled. "Why? You don't think he could figure it out himself?"

Interesting. Paolo didn't like hearing his nephew's intellect talked down. "I've no doubt about his intelligence," I said. "However, he has no experience outside the limitations of his life here."

He spoke dryly. "If you have no doubt about his intellect, Major, you're in a minority here."

"Maybe he didn't appreciate that."

"Maybe not," Paolo picked up a light stylus and tapped it against his desk. "Dayj could be vain and self-absorbed, but no one ever gave him a chance to be anything else. If anyone took the time to look, they might find a very different young man under his outward veneer."

I wondered who he meant by "anyone." Dayj's parents? The Matriarch? Her siblings? Paolo probably had a different take on Majda princes than family members who grew up at the palace.

"You've an interesting background yourself," I said.

"That was tactful." He spoke wryly. "Shall I answer the question you really wanted to ask?"

"What question is that?"

"Why am I willing to live in seclusion when I had job offers from some good companies?"

According to my research, those "good companies" were all elite architectural firms. I asked. "Did you want a job like that?"

"I have my own small business." He motioned at the holosheets on his desk. "I've designed buildings in a few places, including Cries. Also in your corner of space, Selei City."

Ho! Those were two of the most prestigious markets in the Imperialate. "You have your own firm? How?"

Paolo was watching me closely. "That I can't leave this place, Major, doesn't mean I can't work. I have a staff. They take care of anything that requires interaction with the outside world. It leaves me free to be creative."

"Nice setup," I said. "Except you can never touch your creations." He could walk through virtual simulations of his buildings, but he could never set foot in them.

He shrugged. "We all pay a price for our dreams."

"And Dayj?"

"Ah, well. Dayj." His exhaled. "He has more than the rest of us. And less."

"Meaning?"

"You've seen holos of him?" When I nodded, he said, "Then you know. He's one of the best-looking men in the Imperialate."

What was it with them and this beauty thing? Even as a child, I had resented it when vendors in Cries gave me food because they thought I was pretty but let my friends go hungry.

I crossed my arms. "Life has more to it than appearance."

"Yes, well, no one ever bothered to tell my nephew that." He shook his head. "From a certain point of view, Dayj is perfect. The epitome of the Majda prince."

Even knowing they were recording this interview, I couldn't hide my anger. "A prize, right? The ultimate trophy, bred from birth to marry a Ruby heir."

His voice cooled. "Take care, Major."

Yes, antagonizing the House of Majda was dangerous. But if I was going to find Dayj when none of their own people had managed, I needed to look where they didn't want to go even if my process of getting there offended them.

I said only, "How did he respond when the betrothal fell through?"

Paolo remained silent as he studied my face. Finally he said, "He seemed numb. It wasn't that he mourned her loss. He hardly knew her. But what did he have left? Nothing."

For flaming sakes. "Did you people actually tell him that?"

Paolo spoke with an edge. "Make no mistake, Major. This family loves Dayj and will do anything to bring him back. You may not like what you hear, but that won't change the truth."

"Maybe that's the problem." I met his gaze. "Dayj's truth might be different than what everyone here believes."

His face took on an aristocratic chill. "Whereas you claim to know it?"

"No," I said. "But I mean to find out."

Dayj's parents were Corejida and Ahktar. Corejida was the middle Majda sister, younger than the Matriarch but older than Lavinda. She resembled General Majda, but with a less imposing presence. Her clothes had a softer look, light blue trousers and a tunic that molded to her body. Right now, she was pacing across the circular alcove. The room had polished walls tiled in pale blue and silver mosaics, as if we were inside a jeweled box. Its arched windows stretched from floor to ceiling and showed a lofty view of the mountains outside, peaks with a desolate beauty. General Majda stood by one of the windows facing us, her gaze intent on her sister.

Chief Takkar, the head of the Majda police force, was leaning against the wall with her brawny arms crossed. She had only a cold stare for me. Her black uniform matched the one worn by the pilot who had picked me up in the flycar. Like everyone else here, Takkar was physically fit, with black hair and dark eyes. Hell, I was physically fit, with black hair and dark eyes. Did the Majdas subconsciously choose their employees to resemble themselves? Who knew, maybe it wasn't subconscious.

Four guards stood by the arched exit across the room, making sure that, gods forbid, I didn't sneak deeper into the palace and trespass on the men's quarters. At least Krestone, their captain, didn't show any of Chief Takkar's hostility toward me. Krestone remained by the doorway, alert and focused, the solid sort who spoke rarely and saw a great deal.

"We have to find him," Corejida was saying as she paced through a panel of sunlight that slanted through a window and across the floor. "Gods only know what has happened out there. He could be hurt, lost, starving." She looked as if she hadn't slept for the last three days.

"Has he talked about anything outside the palace?" I asked. "Any place, in any context?"

"We've already been through this," Takkar told me. "He never spoke of other places."

"I'd like to hear Lady Corejida's thoughts." I wasn't sure why Corejida went by the honorific Lady; it seemed rather modest for such a highly placed House. She was hard to read. Although Majda women seemed to prefer military titles to noble address, she had never joined the military. Finance was her specialty. Someone had to run the Majda empire.

"Does Prince Dayjarind have any special interests?" I asked. "Subjects he likes to read about? Hobbies? Favorite pursuits?"

"He's been talking about landscapes lately." Corejida rubbed the back of her neck as she paced, working at the muscles. "He looks at holo-images in the library."

"Did he mention any holo in particular?" I asked.

She paused in front of a window and stood facing me, backlit by the streaming sunlight. "He likes imaginary scenes, impossible images created by mesh systems."

Vaj spoke in her husky voice. "Dayj has always been that way. Dreaming whatever boys dream."

I hardly thought a twenty-three-year-old man qualified as a boy. "Did he want to make landscapes?"

They stared at me blankly. Corejida said, "Make them?"

I thought of Paolo with his architectural firm. "Yes, design them."

His mother squinted at me. "You mean, create his own art?"

"Maybe that was why he enjoyed looking at those scenes," I said. "He wants to be an artist."

"I don't think so," Corejida said.

"Did you check his mesh account?" I asked.

Chief Takkar spoke tightly. "We've checked every account he's ever used." Then she added "Major" as if it were an afterthought, making my title sound like an insult.

I considered the police chief. "I'd like to take a look."

Corejida spoke quickly, before Takkar could respond. "It can be arranged." Lines of strain showed around her eyes. "Anything you need. Just find my son."

Takkar pressed her lips together. If I found a clue that she had missed, it wouldn't reflect well on her. Well, tough. I wasn't sure what to make of her. Territorial, yes, and defensive. That her people had failed to locate the prince put her in a tight spot. Anything

I found that she had missed could make her look bad. As much as she might resent my presence, however, it would benefit her to work with me. The sooner we located Dayj, the better for everyone.

Whether or not Takkar saw it that way remained to be seen.

"I'm not sure what you think I would know," Krestone told me. "I'm assigned to Lavinda Majda's guard, and her husband Prince Paolo. I don't interact much with Prince Dayjarind."

We were in the living room of my palace suite, relaxing on large pillows on the floor. The black lacquered table between us reflected the crystal goblets of wine a servant had poured and the matching decanter he left on the table, half full of a red liquid. It was all gorgeous, but really, how could anyone enjoy a drink packaged like that? You couldn't swig ale from a crystal goblet.

"I'm talking to all the palace guards," I said. Which was true, though that was partly so it didn't look as if I had singled out Krestone. Of all the people I'd dealt with here, she struck me as the one most likely to offer useful information. I doubted the Majdas were deliberately making matters difficult; they wanted me to succeed. But they rarely if ever had strangers prying into their private lives, and they raised barriers without realizing they were hindering my work.

"I wondered when you last saw Prince Dayjarind," I said. "I'm trying to get a sense of his actions before he disappeared."

"Three days ago," Krestone said. "It was a few hours before he disappeared." She picked up her goblet, which startled me. Then again, she was no longer on duty. During her free time, she could drink whatever she pleased. Well, what the hell. Even if it looked too perfect to consume, the wine was still just wine. I picked up my goblet, too.

"I saw him that morning." Krestone took a swallow of her drink, then blinked at the glass. "You know, this is actually good." With a rueful smile, she added, "When it comes to liquor, I'm more of a shoot-'em-first-and-ask-questions-later type."

I couldn't help but laugh. "Yah." I took a swallow of wine. Ho! Good hardly described that blissful moment. I said only, "It's not bad."

Krestone grinned, and we both drank some more. Then she said, "Dayj came by Paolo's office that morning. He wanted to return a book Paolo had lent him."

"Did Dayj seem upset?"

"Maybe a little distant. He's often that way, though." She shook her head. "It's hard to say. I was outside. Only his guards went inside Paolo's office with him."

"Did they talk long?"

"A few minutes."

I nodded, disappointed. Dayj's guards had told me the same. "Had you seen him with anyone unusual recently?"

"Never. Just his family, and of course Captain Ebersole, Hazi, Oxil, or Nazina."

That was quite a list. "Who are Hazi, Oxil, and Nazina?"

"Bodyguards attached to the palace," Krestone said.

Oh. No surprise there. I'd have to check my notes, but I'd already talked to Duane Ebersole, and I was pretty sure Hazi, Oxil, and Nazina were also on my list. No wonder Dayj was going stir crazy, with so many people constraining his life.

"Do you remember anything else?" I asked.

"Nothing, sorry." As the captain put down her drink, the comm on her gauntlet pinged. She tapped the receive panel. "Krestone here."

Takkar's voice rose out of the comm. "Heya, Kres. You busy?"

"I'm off right now," Krestone said. "What do you need?"

"We could use your help. We're doing shift assignments."

"Be right there," Krestone said. "I was just talking with Major Bhaajan."

Takkar's tone cooled markedly. "Well, fuck. She causing you any trouble?"

Krestone glanced at me with a look of apology. Into the comm, she said, "None at all."

I spoke, raising my voice enough so Takkar could hear. "Got a problem with me, Chief?"

A silence followed my question. Then Takkar said, "Krestone, we're at the station. Come when you can. Out here." The comm fell silent.

Krestone gave me a rueful look. "Sorry about that."

"No problem." I shouldn't push Takkar, but you could find out a lot about people from the way they reacted when they were irritated.

Unfortunately, so far I hadn't found out squat.

"Lumos down to five percent," I said.

The lights in my suite dimmed until I could barely see the console that curved around my chair. I leaned back, my hands clasped behind my head, and put my feet on the console. "Jan, show me the landscapes that Prince Dayjarind collected."

"Accessed." Jan's androgynous voice came from the Evolving Intelligence brain, or EI, that ran the console. A holo appeared above the console, a startling scene in three dimensions. Waves rose impossibly high over a sapphire beach and crashed down on the glittering blue sand, spraying phosphorescent foam. The physics made no sense. Unless it was an unusually low-gravity world, those waves went up far too high and came down far too slowly. When they built to their highest point, they looked like tidal waves. The ocean should have receded far back from the beach as each wave pulled up all the water, but it didn't. None of that mattered, though. Artistically, the scene was breathtaking.

"What planet is that on?" I asked.

"It isn't," Jan said.

"Is it pure fiction?" I asked. "Or does it resemble a known place?"

After a pause, Jan said, "The scene has a nine percent correlation to the Urban Sea on the planet Metropoli."

Nine percent didn't say much, but it wasn't negligible. "Show me another one he liked."

Over the next hour, Jan showed me Dayj's collection of oceans, beaches, and mountains, a valley of opal hills, a plain of red reeds under a cobalt sky, a forest of stained-glass trees. At first I didn't see any correlation between them, other than their eerie beauty. Then it hit me.

They were all empty.

"Do any of his landscapes have people in them?" I asked.

Another pause. Then Jan said, "None."

I exhaled, saddened.

Vaj Majda spoke coldly. "Offending my family and staff achieves nothing, Major Bhaajan."

One day at the palace and already I had insulted people. Apparently neither Takkar nor Prince Paolo liked my attitude.

We were standing before a window in the library, bathed in sunlight. "The whole point of bringing me in," I said, "was to get new insights, to see if I can find what others missed."

She considered me, one of the few people I knew who was tall enough to look down at me, not by much, but it was still unsettling.

"And have you found anything?" she asked.

"I ran correlations on Dayj's landscapes with real places."

The general waved her hand in dismissal. "So did Takkar's people."

"True. But I searched for negatives."

"Negative in what sense?"

"I looked for what was missing."

"And?"

"He doesn't like the desert. No images at all."

Majda tilted her head, her face thoughtful. "He lives on the edge of a desert. It might seem harsh or mundane to him."

I'd wondered the same. "He likes the ocean."

She smiled with unexpected grace. "Perhaps he dreams of the age when the Vanished Sea stretched here to the horizon and sent waves crashing into the shore."

Interesting. A bit of a poet lived in the conservative general. I struggled to express an idea that was more intuition than analysis. "You say he's a dreamer. He likes to read stories. He enjoys exotic landscapes that exist only in the mind of an artist. All places. No people."

"I'm not sure I follow your meaning."

"He's lonely."

She frowned. "That is the best you can do? His holos have no people, therefore he is lonely?"

"Doesn't it bother you?"

"I hired you to find him. Not give him therapy."

I spoke carefully. "Your Highness, if I offend, I ask your pardon. But to find him, I have to explore all possibilities. Maybe your nephew dreamed of places rather than people because he saw his life as empty. Without companionship. Actual places are no more real to him than the creations of an artist's imagination. What greater freedom is there than to visit a place that doesn't exist?"

"If it doesn't exist," she asked dryly, "how will you find it?"

"I think he went to the sea." I let loose with one of my intuitive leaps. "He feels he is vanishing. And he lives by the Vanished Sea. So he went to find a sea that exists."

"That strikes me as exceedingly far-fetched." She sounded puzzled, though, rather than dismissive.

"Maybe." I waited.

"Raylicon has no true seas," she said.

"So he's never seen a real ocean."

"We have found no trace that he went offworld."

"Then either he faked his ID or he didn't go offworld."

She raised her eyebrows. "I'm paying you for that analysis?"

Well, all right, it didn't come out sounding brilliant. I tried again. "I think he will try to buy a false identity and passage offworld. He was wearing expensive clothes the day he disappeared. The gems alone on them are worth a fortune. He didn't lack for resources."

The general shook her head. "Takkar and her people checked the black market, not just in Cries, but across the planet. They found no trace of his gems."

"I can do it better."

She gave me one of those appraising Majda stares. "You certainly don't lack for self-confidence."

"With good reason."

"What do you need, then, to find him?"

"Complete freedom." I met her gaze. "I work on my own. No Chief Takkar, no surveillance, no guards, no palace suite, no records of my research, nothing."

"Why? We have immense resources at your disposal." She continued to study me with an unsettling intensity. "What do you have to hide?"

"Nothing." I shook off the odd sense that she was trying to look into my thoughts. "I know this city in ways your police force never will. But I won't get anywhere without privacy, not where I'm going. If people think Majda is looking over my shoulder, they won't talk to me."

Vaj stood there with the sunlight slanting across her tall form. Finally she said, "Very well. We will try it your way." Then she added, "For now."

A visitor showed up as I was preparing to leave my palace suite. The knock came when I was packing my duffel. I opened the door to find Captain Krestone and four male guards outside. A hooded figure stood in their midst.

I froze, flustered. That hidden enigma had to be a Majda man. His dark blue robe had metallic patterns embroidered along the hems, probably thread with real gold spun into the strands. I saw a shadowed face within the cowl, but no details. No clues to his identity.

I wasn't certain if protocol allowed me to address him, so I spoke to Krestone. "My greetings, Captain."

She wasted no time. "Prince Ahktar wishes to speak with you."

Ahktar. Dayj's father. Good. "Yes, certainly."

Krestone handed me a scroll tied with a gold cord. I blinked. The Majda universe had almost no intersection with the one where I lived, where few people even used paper, let alone parchment. I unrolled the scroll. Inked in calligraphy, it granted me permission to speak with Prince Ahktar.

Bewildered, I stepped back so the prince could enter with his retinue. It was only after Krestone closed the door, staying outside, that Ahktar pushed back his cowl. He resembled Dayj, but the arrangement of his features was somehow different, so that he had nothing of his son's spectacular looks. I had also discovered that his family, the House of Jizarian, held the lowest rank among the nobility. Whatever Corejida's reason for marrying him, it wasn't for his appearance or aristocratic status. How refreshing.

"My honor at your presence, Your Highness," I said.

He inclined his head. His strained expression was one I had seen before, an expression that was the same regardless of person's rank or wealth, the anguish of a parent faced with the loss of a child. Whatever else I thought of the Majdas, they genuinely seemed to love Dayj.

Ahktar spoke. "Major, can you find my son?"

"If it's humanly possible," I said.

He extended his arm and his sleeve fell down, revealing the jeweled cuff of his shirt. A carved box lay in his palm, wood with enameled panels. "I don't know if it will help, but Dayj valued this."

I took the box. Tiny mosaics covered its sides. "What's inside?"

"Dirt. I couldn't open it, but I analyzed it with a mesh system." He pushed his hand through his thinning hair. "Dayj has had it for several years. I don't know why he kept the dirt, or if it can help you find him, but anything is worth a try."

I rubbed my thumb over the box's tiled panels, which showed birds in flight, blue, green, and red against an ivory background. I had seen plenty of puzzle boxes, but none like this. "Thank you."

"Just find my son." In a low voice, he added, "Alive."

So. Ahktar had acknowledged what none of us wanted to admit. Dayj's chances of staying alive and unharmed on his own might be as vanishing as the ocean beyond the City of Cries.

IV

The Black Mark

I spent the endless Raylicon evening in the penthouse of a tower. The building belonged to the Majdas. Its sunken living room was larger than my whole apartment in Selei City, and one entire wall consisted of dichromesh glass, which polarized during the day to mute sunlight. Tonight it gave me a panoramic view of the City of Cries to the east, the Vanished Sea stretching everywhere else, and the gloriously crimson sunset that flamed on the horizon where the sea met the sky.

I sat sprawled in a white chair near the window while I fooled with the box that Dayj's father had given me. I could have a mesh node figure it out, but its solution might offer a clue to Dayj. After twenty minutes of my poking and sliding its panels, the top opened with a loud click. Ahktar was right: the box held dirt. Or dust, actually. That was it. Just dust.

Red and blue dust.

I knew where to look for Dayj.

✧ ✧ ✧

No water had flowed for millennia in the aqueducts beneath Cries. The empty conduits networked the subterranean spaces under the Vanished Sea and the ruins of the old city. They were actually more like underground canals, but what few records we had of ancient Cries referred to them as aqueducts. The people who lived here used that name to mean the entire undercity, a world of ancient waterways, yes, but also mazes of tunnels and caves. In past ages, mineral-laden water had trickled through the stone, dripping from the ceilings to form stalactites that hung like stone icicles, or forming stalagmites on the floor, gnarled cones of rock that thrust up from the ground. Those eerie formations filled the caverns like a huge lacework of rock created by some mad giant.

The ancient builders had created stone mosaics on the walls, artwork so well designed it had survived for thousands of years. Totem poles of gargoyles grimaced at corners, and pillars stood like sentinels at the junctions where canals met. Those long-dead architects had been geniuses, using beams, supports, and arches to support an underground network that lasted for millennia. But to what purpose? These canals couldn't have all carried water even when the sea existed, and they had been built after the Vanished Sea did its vanishing act. The canals were too large and on too many levels, stacked at least three, even four levels deep. Such a gargantuan system would transfer incredible amounts of liquid. For what? No one had an answer. Like so much of our history, their reason for existence had vanished in the Dark Ages after the collapse of the Ruby Empire.

Today I walked along an edge of one canal. I wore

black trousers, a black muscle shirt, and black boots, and no jacket hid my shoulder holster or its pulse gun. A laser stylus hung from a cord around my neck. Its actual purpose was to write on holographic displays, but I used it as a lamp. One of my many quirks. The stylus created a sphere of light around me, pushing back the gloom. Nothing, however, could push back the shadows this place had left in my memories. I shook my head, turning away those thoughts. I didn't want to remember.

My route ran along a wall of the canal. The path, what we called a midwalk, was a ledge set about midway from the floor to the canal roof. The dropoff from here to the bottom of the canal was deeper than most, maybe four meters. This was one of the largest aqueducts; the distance to the midwalk on its other side was about eight meters. Dust crusted the path and piled up in the canal below, a distinctive powder unlike anything I had seen anywhere else.

Red and blue dust.

How had Dayj ended up with a box filled with grit from these aqueducts? I couldn't imagine him just walking out of the palace, yet he had apparently done exactly that three days ago without leaving a trace.

I was only two levels down from the surface, close enough that Cries had put in a few lampposts to light this area. One glowed a ways up the path, both here and on the midwalk across the canal. A trio of musicians had gathered on the other side. Two were singing, harmonizing in minor tones, and the third played a bone-reed pipe, its notes drifting through air. Their haunting song echoed in the open spaces like an ancient chant. A fourth youth was working in the canal below them, tagging their territory with a dust sculpture fashioned into a flying lizard, its wings spread wide, dark red but veined by blue streaks.

Up ahead on my side, a dust gang lounged on the midwalk, two girls and two boys in their teens, leanly muscular, dressed in leather and dark muscle shirts, with knives in sheaths on their belts. Two of them gripped broken metal bars. They all had a hieroglyph tooled into their wrist guards, the symbol for "Oey." The taller girl stood at the front of the group. A cyber-rider stood with her, the silvery tracings of conduits on his arm forming the Oey glyph. They watched me with cold stares, ready to repel my intrusion from their world. No strangers allowed.

Without thinking, I jerked my chin. The motion was instinctual, an acknowledgment that this was their territory. I didn't even realize I had done it until I finished. Their reaction was almost invisible, just the barest relaxing of their posture. I didn't touch my gun. I could draw it faster than any of them could move, but I had no desire to shoot anyone. They watched as I walked by them, no one speaking, their gazes cold—but they let me pass.

Like knew like.

I had been born in the ruins beneath a dead sea. We were a sparse population in the undercity. Cyber-riders manipulated tech-mech and the Cries meshes from the shadows. Punkers ran drugs for the cartels, either the Kajadas or Vakaars, the wealthiest undercity bosses. Dust gangs learned to fight, as I had done in my youth. We had trained rigorously to perfect our skills, not only to protect those within our circle of people, but also for fun. Gangs ran in packs of four, usually two girls and two boys. Our fights with other gangs were often a challenge more than a threat. If we were lucky, we grew up. Adults bartered for jobs in the shadowy undercity culture, where the economy worked on trades rather than Imperial credits. They started families, set up ventures to support their circle, or became artisans or tech-mech wizards. Some graduated to hardcore crime.

Almost no one left the aqueducts. The above-city, the City of Cries, considered us a slum. They had no idea of the depth in our culture. We wanted it that way. We didn't bother them and they didn't bother us. Ironically, when I enlisted in the army, the intense training of the dust gangs and our code of loyalty served me well, helping me survive and eventually even thrive in a military culture where at first no one had believed I would last even a season.

What had happened to my parents? My mother died giving me birth and I had never found my father. Too many of the dust rats from my youth were also gone. Murdered. In prison. Dead by disease, illness, accident, poverty, or poisoning from unfiltered water. The memory of their faces haunted me in the gloom and parched air.

A few had survived.

I found the Black Mark at the junction of two hidden tunnels. I was surprised to see it in a place I remembered from so many years ago. Jak constantly shifted the location of his casino and he rarely used the same place twice. He could fold it down, pack it away, and vanish as completely as the sea above had done eons ago, under the desiccated sky of Raylicon.

Gambling was illegal on Raylicon, especially in Cries, a place that defined the bastion of conservative tradition. You couldn't find the Black Mark unless you knew where to look, and you wouldn't know unless Jak invited you. He didn't need a crowd; the expense accounts of his clientele more than made up for their limited numbers. They wanted an exclusive establishment and he was more than happy to oblige. He had the cream of the criminal elite at his fingertips.

Tonight the intersection was dark except for the casino's faint glimmer. It nestled in a crevice of the tunnel wall, no windows showing, nothing except sleek black walls. No one intercepted me as I approached, though security was surely monitoring my approach. The building seemed part of the tunnel, just barely visible due the iridescent sheen of its black walls. No entrance appeared.

"Jak," I said to the empty air. "Open up."

Silence. I waited.

A wall of the casino shimmered. When the light faded, Jak stood framed in a doorway there. He was dressed in black as always, both his trousers and pullover. His black hair spiked on his head and his coal eyes smoldered with energy.

"Major," he drawled. "You're back in Cries, I see."

"Looks like it." Seeing him stirred up memories I wanted to stay hidden.

He lifted his hand. "Come in. Improve the decor."

I walked past him into a dimly lit foyer with a hexagonal shape. "I never did before."

His lips quirked upward. "Good to see you, too, Bhaaj. What brings you to haunt my life?"

Haunt indeed. We were ghosts from each other's

past. I looked around the foyer as the entrance faded into a solid wall. The only light came from several niches at different heights that gave off a dim red glow. Each held a jeweled human skull inset with rubies, emeralds, or diamonds. The skulls gaped with their glittering smiles and bejeweled eye sockets.

"Looks like you already have people to haunt your life," I said.

"Not like you." His voice was dark molasses.

Damn. That voice had always been my undoing. In the dark of the canals, in our youth, he would whisper to me in those dusky tones, calling me a warrior goddess, and I would be done for.

Stop it, I told myself.

"I got haunted by Majda," I said, slipping easily into the terse undercity dialect.

His smile vanished. "I've nothing to do with them."

"Glad to hear." Restless under his gaze, I crossed the foyer and traced a pattern on the wall. Nothing happened. He had changed the combination. I wondered why the Black Mark was here in a place I knew from so long ago. He never used a location for long. Might be coincidence. Might not.

Jak came up beside me. "Been a long time."

I looked at him, really looked. It hurt. I recognized the scar over his left eyebrow, but he had a new one on his neck. I touched it, remembering other scars in places that didn't show right now.

"You've been busy," I said.

He grasped my hand and brought it down to his side. His fingers tightened around mine, clenching. When it began to hurt, I activated my biomech web and extended my fingers, prying his hand open.

He let go of me with a jerk. For a moment I thought he would say painful words. Instead he leaned against the wall by a skull with sapphire eyes and crossed his arms. "What about Majda?"

"They hired me."

"Over their own people?"

"That's right."

"Not bad."

I grimaced. "If it doesn't kill me."

"Majda won't kill you." His voice sounded casual, but it didn't fool me. "Might ruin you, though. Get on their bad side, you got nothing. They make sure you live to know." Dryly he added, "Unless you offend their men. Then you're dead."

That was too close to my thoughts. "Met two princes."

His eyebrows went up. "And you're alive?"

"For now." I shifted my weight. "You got an office?" He would have the best security in the place where he did his work.

"We're in it."

"The entrance to the Black Mark?"

His grin flashed, with a hint of menace. "Only an entrance when you came in. No more. The room moves."

I didn't doubt it. I still didn't believe it was his office, but it would have to do. "Secure here?"

"Yah. Why? Majda got problems?"

"It's private."

"I ken."

I recognized his meaning. He would keep whatever I told him private. So I said, "They lost a prince."

He stared at me. "For ransom?"

"Nahya. He ran off."

Wicked pleasure sparked in his eyes. "Good for him."

"Jak."

"Majda princes live in prison. Not good, Bhaaj. You shouldn't help put him back."

I scowled at him. "They hired me to do a job. I took their money. So I'm doing the job."

He returned my glower. "Why would I help them oppress him?"

"That a no?"

"You didn't ask a question."

"I need to know if he bought passage offworld."

His expression shuttered. "People don't announce they're Majda. Even someone who'd spent his life in seclusion ought to have more sense."

I paced across the hexagonal room to the wall where I had entered. Gods only knew where it would let me out now. "Probably tried to sell his clothes."

Jak laughed in his whiskey voice, deep and inebriating. "You think people'd pay to wear clothes worn by a Majda prince?" His tone became thoughtful. "Actually, they might. Could be lucrative, making that claim."

I turned around to him. "Jak."

"Why would I care about his clothes?"

"They got diamonds. Sapphires, gold, opals. Real, not synthetic."

He gave an incredulous snort. "He went undercity dressed like that?"

"I don't know. You hear anything?"

"Nothing. I'd like to, though."

"I think he went offworld. Couldn't leave as a prince. He needed a new identity."

Jak stalked across the foyer to me. "So you came here, asking me to find out?" His lean muscles rippled under his clothes and he emanated a sense of barely controlled aggression.

"Depends," I said.

He stopped in front of me. "On what?"

"The price."

"You got a Majda expense line?"

"Yeah."

"Then you don't care about price."

I touched the cleft in his chin. "I wasn't talking about that kind of price."

He caught my hand and held it in his tight grip. "What, Bhaaj?"

I was too aware of how close he was standing. "Seven years ago you vanished."

"Someone owed me money. I went to get it."

"They were killers."

"Didn't scare me."

"Yah, well, I thought you were dead." I pulled away my hand. "Selei City has been restful."

"You're bored there, Bhaaj."

"Want to be bored."

"Why did you come here?" he demanded. "For my help or my apology?"

I wasn't sure myself. "Whatever you got to give."

He considered me. Unexpectedly, his mouth quirked up. "I dunno. I help you with Majda, will you try putting me in seclusion?"

What an alarming thought. He'd pulverize me. "Gods, no."

He burst into his intoxicating laugh. "Good." His smile faded. "If I hear anything, I might let you know."

It was more than I had expected. I nodded, sealing our bargain, and then stood there, uncertain what else to say. When the moment became awkward, I said, "Guess I better go."

He touched my lips. "Come back sometime when you don't want anything."

I resisted the urge to kiss his fingers. I had no intention of asking him for anything except information. For some reason, though, when I opened my mouth, what came out was, "Might do that."

"Good," Jak murmured. He tapped a panel by a gold-plated skull. The wall shimmered and vanished, revealing the junction outside where I had entered. I hadn't felt the room turning, but that entrance was across the foyer from where I had entered.

He spoke in a shadowed voice. "See you, Bhaaj."

"Yah." I headed back out into the canals. Oddly, I felt lighter.

Damned if I wasn't glad to see Jak—which could only mean I had flitflies for brains.

I fell asleep on the couch in my new penthouse and woke up about seven hours into the forty-hour night. Through the window-wall across the room, I saw the lights of Cries glittering to the east. I went to the console, settled into its exorbitantly comfortable chair, and activated its EI. General Majda had promised me freedom from surveillance, but I believed that like I believed Jak was a paragon of virtue.

At least I could do something about the EI. It took almost no time to find the spy codes they had installed to monitor me. It took a lot longer to deactivate them; Majda security did good work. After I finished neutralizing, blocking, or distracting the spies, I told the EI to search the Raylicon meshes and any offworld systems it could access. My goal: investigate the three Majda sisters.

They made quite a trio. As General to the Pharaoh's Army, Vaj Majda commanded the oldest branch of Imperial Space Command. The army had served the Ruby Dynasty for six thousand years. After the Imperator who oversaw the entire military, Vaj Majda was arguably the most powerful officer in ISC. I wondered how she felt about answering to a male Imperator. If she was against men serving in the military, she gave no public indication of that belief. She was no fool; to succeed in her career, she had to accept the realities of modern Skolia, where nearly as many men as women served in ISC. It even affected her staff, as evidenced by Major Ebersole's position of authority on her staff, or the man who had brought me to Raylicon on the flyer, probably a retired military pilot.

"EI," I said.

"Attending." It spoke in slightly nasal voice.

"Do you have a name?" I asked.

"Not yet. I was installed this morning."

"What should I call you?"

"I have no preference."

I'd have to think of a name. Anything was better than *Hey, you.* "Can you answer questions about the Majdas?"

"Yes, I have a great deal of data on their House."

We would see about that. "I was wondering how the general reconciles the way her House treats Majda princes with the fact that most Skolian men have equal rights with women."

"Majda princes hold to a higher standard."

"That so?"

"Yes."

"Who appointed the team that programmed you?"

"General Vaj Majda."

That figured. I buckled down and set to work, researching the House. They had more corporations, investments, and financial connections than I could count—and as far as I could tell, it was all legit. I delved into data grottos unknown even to ISC intelligence and found nothing. Majda came by their wealth legally. It added to their invulnerability; they couldn't be blackmailed. If someone wanted to manipulate them, kidnapping one of their princes might be the only way.

They threw me a few surprises with their husbands. Prince Paolo had the rank, heredity, and looks expected of a Majda consort, but he lacked the supposed "moral" background. Granted, if all grooms among the aristocracy truly had to be virgins on their wedding night, the noble Houses would die out for lack of mates. They were discreet, however. Paolo, however, had openly enjoyed love affairs as a bachelor, yet Lavinda married him anyway. It didn't take long to see why. He excelled at business as well as architectural design. He knew how to make money, and I had no doubt he was doing it in buckets for Majda.

Nor was Paolo the only one. The general's consort, Izam, had lived in seclusion his entire life, but that didn't change his genius for finance. His name was associated with the boards of a good fraction of their corporations. Vaj might be rigid in how she expected her consort to live, but she was too savvy to ignore his prodigious business acumen.

"What about Ahktar?" I asked. "Dayj's father. Does he do finance?"

"I see no indication of such," the EI said. "However, I have almost no data on him."

"Can you connect me to the EI at the palace called Jan?"

"Yes, I can create this link."

"Good. Set it up." I made sure my security fixes were in place. I didn't want any Majdas eavesdropping on my talks with Jan, either.

A mellow voice came out of the console, the same EI that I had spoken to about Dayj's holo landscapes. "My greetings, Major Bhaajan. What can I do for you?"

"Hello, Jan." I settled back in my chair. "What do you have on Prince Ahktar's education?"

"He has none."

"He must read."

"He rarely uses the library."

"Does he involve himself with Majda finances?" His wife ran the corporations, after all.

After a moment, Jan said, "I find no indication that he has either an interest or the talent for such an involvement."

I tapped my chin. "Almost no rank, money, or skills. He's not handsome. No business sense. Why did Corejida marry him?"

"You wish me to offer a theory?"

"I wish."

"She loves him."

I blinked. "What?"

"She loves him. This is an acceptable reason to marry."

"Sure, for the rest of us. Majdas live in another reality."

"I have no records of any aptitude tests for him.

Informally, however, I can offer conclusions based on his behavior."

"Go ahead." This was fascinating.

"He nurtures. He probably has a great aptitude for nursing or social work. It also makes him a good parent."

"Oh." Was I that cynical, that I hadn't believed Majdas could feel love?

In my youth, I had feared, envied, even hated the Majdas, who lived in their stratospheric world of privilege. I'd been born in the undercity and left at an orphanage in Cries, what we called the above-city. I'd lived for three years before I ran away with an older girl, a "mature" orphan all of five. She had lived in the aqueducts until the city inflicted one of its periodic sweeps on us, rounded up a handful of undercity kids, and dumped them in an orphanage. We always ran away as soon as we could, back to the aqueducts. Back home.

Unlike most of my people, I had always wanted out, but on my terms, not those of some Cries authority. The day I reached my sixteenth birthday, I enlisted, and after that, I'd worked like a fanatic to qualify for officer training. People said it was impossible for an enlistee with no connections to win a place in that program, but I'd done it, more out of sheer, cussed determination than because I was better qualified than the other applicants. I had resented those cadets with the advantages of a privileged birth that made it so much easier for them to advance. With Dayj's parents now, however, I only saw two desperate people who loved their son. I couldn't forget their haunted expressions as they entreated me to find him.

"Jan," I said, "do you know any reason why one of the Majdas might help Dayj escape?"

"Escape implies he was in prison."

I didn't bother to deny it.

After a pause, Jan said, "I can think of no reason why any member of his family would facilitate his departure."

"Has anyone connected to the Majda family or the palace staff ever shown any indication they might sympathize with Dayj if he wanted to run away?" I thought for a moment. "Have any of them donated to a cause that supports ideals consistent with any wish he might have to break tradition? Made grants to such institution? Invested in a company? Supported either an individual or an organization, legal or otherwise, that might have helped Dayj leave?"

Jan was quiet for a while. Finally she said, "I find no such connection."

"That can't be." With a business empire as vast as the Majda holdings, it would require a deliberate effort to exclude every such person or group.

"Such a link would be offensive to the House," Jan said.

So it was a deliberate exclusion. "Someone must have helped him. He's smarter than they think, a lot smarter, but even given that, he couldn't have done it alone. Security is too tight." I thought about negatives. "Who in your opinion is *least* likely to help him leave?"

"General Majda," Jan said.

"Not his parents?"

"They, also. But if he were truly unhappy, it would affect them more than the general."

"Doesn't she care about his happiness?"

"Yes," Jan said. "Despite her reserve, she shows great affection for her nephew. I would call it love as far as I can determine that emotion."

"What about the other princes?"

"Of the consorts, the one least likely to help Prince Dayj leave is probably Prince Paolo."

That was the last name I expected to hear. "I would have thought the opposite. Paolo knows what freedom is like."

"And he gave it up. Why, then, should Dayj have it?"

"I see your point." I sat up, planting my booted feet on the floor, my hands clasped between my knees. "What about his uncles? One of General Majda's brothers teaches psychology at a university."

"Tam might help. However, he no longer lives on Raylicon."

"Tam?"

"Tamarjind Majda. The psychology professor."

"He wouldn't need to live on Raylicon to help." He could use the Kyle meshes to talk with his family. That web bypassed spacetime, making it possible to communicate via a universe where light speed was irrelevant. It allowed people to converse across interstellar distances.

"I have no record of any communication between Prince Tamarjind and Prince Dayjarind," Jan said.

"Who does Tamarjind talk to when he contacts the palace?" It used to be his home, after all.

"His sisters and nieces. Never his male relatives."

"Why not?"

"General Majda forbade such communications."

I scowled. "Because he's a bad influence?"

"Yes."

"You know, Jan, I'd feel better if you said, 'In the general's opinion' rather than just 'Yes.'"

"That would be inconsistent with my programming."

"Yah, well, that's the problem." Then I added, "But thanks for the information."

After I signed off, I sat in the dark and pondered. I had an idea how to find Dayj.

If I was lucky, it wouldn't kill me.

V

Scorch

I hid in the mountains above the palace and spent the day spying on my employers. The jammer in my backpack shrouded me from sensors, and I had dusted my face with holo-powder. Smart dust. Nanos in the dust and in the cloth of my clothes formed a network I could link to the jammer, which then projected holos around my body of whatever lay behind me. In other words, I became invisible, provided no one looked too closely. The inner surface of the jumpsuit kept me warm and the outer surface matched its air temperature. It confused infrared sensors; if they couldn't register the heat I generated, I became invisible to them. Sonic dampers in the jammer interfered with sound waves. It even created false echoes to fool neutrino sensors, which could penetrate almost anything. If Majda security made a concentrated effort, they could still find me, but I hadn't given them cause for such a search. Not yet, anyway.

I sat on a ledge against a cliff and watched the palace with my spyglass, checking everyone who went in or out of the building. I spent hours up there, protected from the icy wind by my climate-controlled jacket. Although Raylicon had a ninety-three-hour day, atmospheric churning and weather machines kept the climate from becoming too hot or cold for human life. I began my vigil before dawn and kept at it for hours. When boredom set in, I played Bulb Blaster, a game on my gauntlet that consisted of blowing up sky balloons with ludicrously creative guns. Mostly, though, I watched the palace.

No one used the main entrance, a great arched affair fronted by imposing columns. Two other entries were visible from my vantage point, a servants' door around the back and a family entrance on the side facing me. Servants came and went all day, but none of them did much. Mostly they stood around and chatted in a garden just overgrown enough to look artistic. They probably didn't have many duties, given that robots could do most tasks as well as humans.

Eventually I felt drowsy. Most of us on Raylicon slept three times a day, once at noon, once when night started and once toward its end. I fastened a cable from my belt to a ring I drilled into the cliff wall. The cable would judge my safety and reel me in if I rolled too close to the edge of the ledge. Next I set my gauntlet to alert me if anything interesting happened. And then I went to sleep.

When I awoke a few hours later, the sun had barely moved. I resumed my vigil. And finally someone came out of the family entrance: Colonel Lavinda Majda, the youngest sister. She and three people in black clothes walked down a driveway bordered by trees. The woman in front was Captain Krestone, who was also a pilot, and I recognized the man in civilian clothes as one of the colonel's aides. The second man was Duane Ebersole, the ranking officer among Lavinda's guards.

The driveway sloped away from the palace, and a flycar stood on the lawn at the base of the slope. Beyond that landing field, or landing meadow actually, mountains rose into the sky, including the one where I sat hiding.

I spoke into my gauntlet. "Max, get me a tracer on Colonel Majda."

"Done," a male voice said. It came from Max, the Evolving Intelligence in my gauntlet. Most people couldn't afford a gauntlet EI, but in my line of work, he was invaluable. I could even "think" to him; he connected to the threads in my biomech web through sockets in my wrists, and those biothreads linked him to the node in my spine.

"Send the green bot to follow them," I said. I had two beetle-bot tracers, one with green wings and the other with red, both small enough that they fit together in the palm of my hand. I could only afford those two, but they were well worth the investment.

"Dispatching," Max told me.

"Good." I started down the mountain then, headed for Cries.

"A message is waiting for you," the EI at my penthouse announced as I walked in the door.

I stepped down into the sunken living room as the doors closed behind me. "Who's it from?"

"I don't know," the EI said. "I can't ID the message."

I frowned. It should be easy to read the sender's ID—unless they deliberately hid their information. "Did you scan for traps, viruses, or mesh plagues?"

"Yes," the EI said. "The message is clean."

As I crossed the living room, its window-wall polarized to cut down glare from the setting sun. I stood before the window and stared out at the Vanished Sea, a red desert streaked with blue mineral deposits left by the dried-up ocean. Whatever terraforming had made this world habitable before we humans arrived was slowly failing over the millennia. We could still live in this region, but eventually all of Raylicon would become hostile to human life. Someday we either had to heal this planet or leave.

"Shall I play the message?" the EI asked.

"Go ahead," I said.

A familiar voice rose into the air. "Heya, Bhaaj. Got dinner."

I went over and flopped down on the couch. I put my feet up on the glass table in front of the sofa. The table polarized to mute reflections of the sunset.

After a few moments of silence, however, I asked, "Is that all?"

"It appears so," the EI said.

Pah. "Send this reply," I grumbled. "I got work to do."

"Send it where?"

Good question. If the EI couldn't ID the message, it couldn't reply.

"Never mind." I stood up again. It seemed I wouldn't get any rest after all. "I'll do it in person."

The gambling dens at the Black Mark were no less notorious tonight than the last time I had seen them, seven years ago. Jak took me through the main room, no doubt to show off the place. We followed a raised walkway that skirted the central den, and a glimmering rail separated us from the pit. The players at the tables below wore evening dress or stranger couture, spiky-shouldered tunics and skin wraps that left more parts of the body exposed than covered. Waiters served drinks while Jak's patrons spent millions. Other more sensual pursuits would be going on in private rooms. The Black Mark was discreet. Criminal, but circumspect.

I tried not to notice Jak as he walked at my side. He had on black pants and a ragged black tight-shirt with no sleeves. He looked like a thug. One hell of a sexy thug, but I wasn't noticing.

Not noticing. Really.

"You like my new art?" He motioned at the holos that swirled in spirals and twists on the walls. If I looked too long, I felt sick.

"What's it for?" I asked. "To make people give back whatever they ate downstairs?"

He slanted a look at me. "Disgusting, Bhaaj."

"Yah. Well."

He smiled, the barest hint of that killer grin. "It increases their susceptibility to suggestion."

"Makes me dizzy."

"Really?" He seemed intrigued. "I wonder why it doesn't work on you."

I scowled at him. "The army trained me to resist coercion, Jak. Programmed it into my biomech. Your dastardly attempts to lure your customers into spending large sums of money won't work on me."

A wicked gleam came into his eyes. "Shall I lure you elsewhere, Bhaaj, my sweet?"

"Call me 'your sweet' again and I'll flip you over this railing."

He laughed, his voice rumbling. "Might be fun."

No way would I risk answering that one.

We reached a dark hall with galaxies swirling around us, and after a few minutes of those demented stars, we entered a black room with niches in the walls like in the entrance foyer. Instead of skulls, however, these held exotic drinks lit from within by lasers. The glass table in the center of the room was set with black china, goldware, and goblets. A decanter of red wine sparkled next to several covered platters.

"You like?" Jak asked.

"It's different," I said. Eerie décor, but gorgeous in its own dark way. The undercity nurtured its own unique ideas of beauty.

"Same as always," Jak said.

"Doesn't all this black depress you?"

"Never." He nudged me toward the table. "Sit."

So I sat. Jak settled across the table from me and uncovered the platters, revealing steaks in pizo sauce, tart-bubbles, and sweet clams. He had always set a good table.

I poured the wine. "You going to tell me why I'm here?"

He was all innocence. "What, I can't invite an old friend to dinner?"

I gave him a goblet of red wine. "Your motives are always ulterior."

"Just got dinner, that's all." He leaned back in his chair, letting the muscles of his torso ripple under his thug shirt. He knew what it did to me when he moved like that, slow and languorous, danger contained but never controlled.

I drank half my glass of wine in one swallow. Thank gods for nanomeds.

"Should I?" he murmured.

I regarded him coolly and hoped he didn't notice the heat in my face. "Should you what?"

He said exactly squat, just sat there looking at me. If I didn't distract myself, gods only knew what trouble I could get into here.

"So," I said. "You got nothing to tell me?"

"Depends. You want the spit on your runaway prince?"

I sat up straighter. "What'd you hear?"

He swirled his wine. "Rumors."

I regarded him warily. "What'll it cost me?"

"Your company for dinner."

"And?"

"And what?"

I frowned. "Having dinner with you is too easy."

His grin flashed. "That a compliment?"

Damn, that smile ought to be classified as an illegal narcotic. "Jak."

"Yah?" He sat there looking dangerous with those simmering dark eyes. The tight-shirt was unraveling along one shoulder, showing glimpses of roughened skin. I wondered how it would feel to run my hand under the cloth.

Get a grip, I told myself. *And not on him.* I loaded my plate with bubbles, a dish I vaguely remembered originated on the home world of some Ruby Dynasty queen. It all looked very round.

We ate in silence. Jak washed down his food with wine and relaxed in his chair, his goblet in one hand.

After he had watched me for a while, I put down my fork. "What?"

"A good-looking man sold some gems under the city," he said.

I tensed. "Prince Dayjarind?"

"Don't know. But these were genuine, the real biz, flaws and all. Worth a lot more than he got. Still brought him enough to buy a new ID."

"When?"

"Four days ago."

Four days ago, Dayj had left the palace. If he had immediately sold his jewels on the black market, he must have already had a connection with someone. "Know where he went?"

"Rumor says he tried to go offworld."

"Tried?"

"Yeah. Tried." No trace of Jak's smile remained. "Man who looks that good will get himself sold if he isn't careful."

"Hell, Jak." I felt cold. "What happened?"

"Don't know. Just rumors. Some say he went off-world, others say he got heisted."

"You can't 'heist' a royal heir. Anyone in this city who sees this guy or hears his accent will know he's a Majda."

"Maybe. Maybe he's worth the risk." His voice hardened. "Trader Aristos would pay the moon for him."

"Skolians don't sell to Traders."

"Offer anyone enough money and they'll sell out."

"Says who?"

"Don't know." He finished his drink. "Aqueducts are a big place. Especially the Maze. You can get lost in there."

The Maze. I'd been there twice in the past ten years, and that was two times too many. It looked, though, like I'd be going again. I said only, "Thanks, Jak."

He met my gaze. "Didn't say anything."

I speared a bubble with my fork. "Didn't hear anything."

Jak nodded to me. We ate for a few more minutes. Then he said, "You like the dinner?"

I knew he was asking about more than food. If I had any sense, I would say no. For some reason, instead I said, "Yah, I do."

He gave me his should-be-illegal grin. "Thought you would."

"Cocky tonight."

"You like, Bhaaj." When I snorted, he let go with that throaty laugh that had always been my undoing. It hadn't changed, neither the sound nor its effect on me.

"Shouldn't look at me that way," he said.

"What way?"

"Like you want me for dessert."

"In your dreams." Or mine.

"Right, Bhaaj."

I put down my fork. "I need to go. Got an appointment in the Maze."

He spoke softly. "You're scared. Of us."

It flustered me when he was right. "Got to go."

"For now."

I knew what I should tell him: I had a job to do and when I finished, I was leaving Raylicon, assuming I was still breathing. I opened my mouth to tell him that and out came, "Yah. For now."

His gaze smoldered. "Thought so."

Gods. It was a good thing I had business in the Maze, because I didn't trust myself to stay here.

Over the millennia, the aqueducts under Cries had bent under the weight of their age. Our ancestors built well, but five thousand years takes a toll on even the greatest architectural wonder. In one section, all that remained was a maze of half-blocked passages and caverns thick with mineral-encrusted outcroppings.

I followed a crumbling aqueduct toward the Maze, my laser stylus hanging around my neck, providing a glow to light the way. Memories came at me from all sides, like flashes of pain. When I was nine, I had stood on this path while a small child with a dirty face held out her hand, tears on her face because she was cold and had nothing to eat. I'd lifted her into my arms and held her while she cried. She had no name, so I called her Sparks, for the look in her eyes when she saw me. She became part of my circle, which included my dust gang, several adults who helped us, and two single-parent families. She and I lived together while I ran with the gangers, helping to fill our coffers with food, blankets, clothes, toys, and anything useful I could steal from topside.

She fell sick when I was ten. We called it the carnelian rash, an illness that prowled the aqueducts like a specter, turning the skin of its victims red and scaly. No hospital in Cries would take a dust rat. I was the one who nursed her, who used wet clothes to cool her rash, who dribbled filtered water between her swollen lips, who traded raw steak to the drug punkers for the hack that eased her pain—and I was the one who held her in my arms as she died. She went in peace, in her sleep, but I never forgot. Too many memories. Too much hurt.

After I retired from the army, I came back to Raylicon with some nebulous idea that I could find a place to live in the city of my childhood. I wanted to see Cries from the perspective of someone who lived in the above-city. It hadn't worked and in the end, I had left, I thought forever. After all, they say you can never go home again, whoever "they" is. And yet here I was, once more in the undercity.

Today I followed the midwalk of a shallow waterway only about a meter across. Up ahead, its wall had fallen, blocking my way, a mound of rubble nearly as tall as me. It hadn't been here seven years ago. I clambered over the debris and squeezed through the hole it left in the wall, entering an even narrower canal. It didn't surprise me that this entire area seemed deserted; with such a low population in the undercity and such extensive aqueducts, you could walk for a long time without seeing anyone.

Of course that didn't mean no one was here. These canals were networked with crannies, and crevices, and anyone could be watching from a hiding place. Although my holstered pulse gun was visible, I doubted that was why no one bothered me. For all that I lived and worked in the above-city now, I fooled no one here with my veneer of civilization. They knew their own. However, they hadn't accepted me, either. They were waiting to see what I would do.

I carried the jammer in my backpack, shrouding myself. No doubt Chief Takkar was trying to track me through the biomech web in my body. That was illegal of course, except for the topmost military brass. Like the General of the Pharaoh's Army, eh? Although the signals my web produced were encrypted and invisible to most sensors, Takkar would know how to track them. I knew even better how to hide them. The image-dust on my skin also shielded me against the bee-bots in the

Majda security arsenal. Blasted bees. They searched out the DNA of a specific person and reported in when they found a match. Several had buzzed around me earlier today, but when I activated my shroud, they became confused and wandered away. Although the "bees" were almost too small to see, I had sensors in my gauntlets that could detect their signatures, devices I'd bought on the black market, one of my savvier investments.

Takkar would be thoroughly pissed when she couldn't find me. Tough. The people I needed to talk with didn't react kindly to intruders who came with Majda listening. The cyber-riders salvaged or filched tech-mech from Cries and its garbage dens, and what they did with that "junk" surpassed the best tech-mech Cries had to offer. The undercity would know if I had Majda in my pocket.

I followed the canal to a clogged area with more debris than open areas. Seven years ago, the wall here had a door into the Maze, but now I saw only dust piled everywhere. I nudged off the safety on my pulse gun, then knelt and swept away armfuls of grit. Red powder swirled into the air, saturating my senses with the smell of age and lost dreams.

Eventually I cleared the door. It was hard to see, just a faint seam in the rock that gave away nothing if you didn't know what to look for. It came up to my shoulders. When I stood up and pushed the door with my booted foot, it didn't budge. So I kicked it with the enhanced strength provided by the biohydraulics that augmented my muscles and skeleton. Still no good. I tried again, and again—and the door scraped inward, stone grinding on stone. Drawing my gun, I ducked into the tunnel beyond, keeping its wall to my back. Inside, I had room to straighten up. I pulled the door closed and headed down the tunnel, my footfalls muted, the walls and ceiling close. Good thing I wasn't claustrophobic.

Whoever built the aqueducts had probably drilled these tunnels for access to machinery that had long ago disintegrated. After a while, I came to a junction where three tunnels met. I took the left branch. When I noticed a light ahead, I clicked off my stylus and continued in semidarkness.

Even knowing what to expect, I wasn't ready for the eerily beautiful sight at the end of the tunnel. A cavern stretched before me. Stalactites hung from its roof and stalagmites grew up from the floor, all sparkling in the radiance of an electro-optic torch someone had left jammed into a nearby outcropping. The light glittered off the white, red, blue, purple crystals that encrusted the stone like a gigantic geode turned inside out.

My footsteps echoed as I entered the cavern. That announced my presence just as well as if I had shouted, "Hey, I'm here."

A scrape came from my right. I stopped and waited.

A woman walked out from behind two stalagmites. "Bhaaj."

"Scorch." I kept my arms by my sides and my gun pointed at the ground.

Scorch had led one of the dust gangs here when we were kids, but by the time I enlisted, she had graduated to bigger game. Well-toned muscles creased her dark jumpsuit. I knew her biomech equaled to my own, except that I came by mine legally. Her chin jutted, and her nose dominated her face like on the giant statues in the ruins of ancient Cries. She wore her hair short with a black spike sticking up behind one ear. The torchlight glittered in the mirrored surfaces of her laser carbine and its bulging power pack.

"Long time," she said.

"I went offworld," I answered. "Selei City."

"I heard." She shifted her gun, not quite pointing it at me. "Why come back?"

"Job."

She snorted. "Worth leaving Selei City? Can't see it."

"Majda," I said.

Her expression shuttered. "We don't bother Majda, they don't bother us."

I had no doubt the authorities in Cries knew about the smuggling operation Scorch ran through here, everything from proscribed liqueurs to hallucinogenic silks. Still, I'd never known her to traffic in people. The Traders based their economy on slavery, which was why we were at war with them. They saw us as fodder for their markets. Would Scorch sell to the enemy? I didn't want to believe it, but a Majda prince like Dayj could bring her more than all her other product combined. Even so. It strained credulity to believe anyone would risk that gargantuan offense against the Majdas in their own backyard. Scorch knew damn well that if Vaj Majda decided to clean up this place, she could blast the undercity bare.

"I'm searching for a man," I said. "Good-looking."

She laughed harshly. "So are we all."

"This one had gems to sell."

"Lot of people got gems to sell." Her eyes glinted. "Most don't kick in my back door."

"Used to be front door."

"Used to be guarded." She shifted her gun. "Still is."

I doubted she would shoot me. I'd first met her

here when I was fifteen. I found her lying in her own blood after three of her "clients" left her for dead instead of paying their bill. I'd tended her until she recovered. Saved her life. Scorch might be a psychopath, but she paid her debts. That meant I had a pass here; for the three fools who tried to murder her, it had meant a long, ugly death.

I said only, "Your door let me in."

"For now." She held the gun in what looked like a relaxed grip. I wasn't fooled. She could shoot faster than sin.

Time to bargain. "Got information," I said.

She snorted. "You don't live here anymore. How you got anything for me?"

"Majda. Got access to their mesh." If they caught me offering to sell their private data, they would draw and quarter me. But they didn't have to deal with Scorch. Besides, Vaj said no measure was too extreme. I doubted this was what she had meant, but never mind.

Scorch narrowed her gaze at me. We both knew she wouldn't come by an offer like this again. That she paused for so long could be a bargaining tactic, but it made me uneasy.

"What information?" she said.

"Depends. What do you need?"

"Flight schedules." Her eyes took on a voracious glitter. "For their private ships."

Damn. A smuggler could do a lot of damage with the closely guarded schedule of flights in and out of the private Majda starport.

"Might be possible," I said, maybe lying, maybe not. "Depends what you got."

Her smile turned feral. "I know a lot about good-looking men. What you looking for, Bhaaj, that you can't get legally?"

I crossed my arms. "Dark hair. Dark eyes. Like a nobleman. Good build. Taller than average. Maybe sold jeweled clothes for a fake ID and offworld passage."

Her hand visibly tightened on the carbine. "That one's gone."

"Gone where?"

"Offworld. Don't know."

Maybe she wanted more than the schedules. "Got a lot to sell."

"Not interested."

Ho! That made *no* sense. Scorch would never walk away from the opportunity to steal Majda flight schedules. Now suddenly she didn't want them? Like hell. She was hiding something.

"I hear rumors," I said coldly. "About deals with Traders."

She lifted the carbine and aimed it at me. "Lies."

Sweat ran down my neck. I didn't answer.

Scorch jerked—and fired the carbine.

The burst blinded me. I protected my face with my arm while thunder echoed in the cavern and stones crashed to the ground. Grit and debris rained over me, rough against my skin. When it settled, I cautiously lowered my arm and opened my eyes. The slagged remains of a stalactite lay broken on the ground only a few steps away. If Scorch had fired any closer, I'd be dead.

"Get out," she said.

I beat a fast retreat out of her territory.

✧ ✧ ✧

I didn't turn off the jammer until I was above ground. Within moments my gauntlet comm squawked. I tapped the receive panel.

Takkar's voice snapped out. "Bhaajan, where the hell are you?"

"Greetings to you, too," I said.

"Get back to the palace."

Charming. "You aren't my CO, Takkar."

"Get your ass back here or I'll throw it in jail."

My night was growing progressively worse. "For what?"

"Murder," she said.

VI

The Pin

The Majda police station had no books, tapestries, brocaded divans, or anything else that remotely resembled the aristocratic gentility of the palace. Sleek and sharp, it was all polarized glass and white Luminex, and it looked as efficient as hell. Takkar met me in an interrogation room.

The chief and I faced each other across a table, both of us standing up. Takkar looked ready to blow holes in the sky, preferably with me as the ammo that got pulverized by the strike. People filled the overly bright room. Major Ebersole stood by the wall on my right, his handsome face schooled to neutrality. He would blend well into a crowd, making him even more effective in his job.

The Majda sisters were all here, tall, formidable, and pissed off. Corejida Majda paced like a caged desert-lion on my left, back and forth in front of her sister, Colonel Lavinda Majda. The colonel stood by the door, looking stunned. It didn't surprise me. She had just discovered the dead body of one of her best people. Vaj Majda stood across the table with Takkar, a silent figure who watched us all, her appraising gaze like ice. I had no doubt she missed nothing.

Max, I thought. *Record everything that happens here and store it in file "Interrogation."*

Recording, he thought.

The wall to my right doubled as a holoscreen. At the moment, it was playing the recording made by a Majda bee-bot that had followed Lavinda around today. The playback showed the flycar that had taken the colonel, her aide, her bodyguard, and Captain Krestone away from the palace.

The playback showed Lavinda's flycar as it settled on the roof of an office tower in Cries. Krestone was piloting and Ebersole sat in the front passenger's seat. The colonel and her aide were in the back of the car, working with screens they had rolled out into thin films on their laps. Holos danced in the air above the screens showing graphs, images, and glyphs.

Lavinda was professional with her male aide. It fit my research; the Majdas were scrupulous in their relationships. They treated everyone with the same distant professionalism. If they ever strayed in their personal lives, they had left no trace of their indiscretions. In their circles, heredity determined everything. During the Ruby Empire, the penalty for adultery among the nobility had been execution, and to this day that law remained in force. I had never heard of a noble House executing anyone for fooling around, and I seriously doubted they were all paragons of virtue, but they kept it discreet. As far as I could tell, however, the Majdas actually followed the law. They were annoyingly well behaved, another reason blackmail would never work with them.

In the recording, the colonel disembarked with her aide and Ebersole, and the three of them walked across the landing pad. A bland bodyguard I vaguely recognized from the palace staff met them at the lift shaft, which jutted up from the roof like a spire of modern art. The bee-bot flew with them. The airlift inside was little more than a disk in a chute, but it lowered them so smoothly, it didn't ruffle a lock of anyone's hair. It stopped at upper level of the building, and the four of them walked into a huge place, a confusing expanse of gleaming silver and white Luminex. Then my mind reoriented and I made sense out of the scene. The room spanned the entire floor of the tower. Partial walls of white Luminex stood here and there, but it was mostly open. Abstract sculptures of blue and silver chrome stood in a few areas. It was artistic in a weird sort of way.

The colonel went to a glass-enclosed office with her aide and the bland bodyguard. She left a box of data spheres on the desk and checked the console there. Major Ebersole stood by the door and kept watch on the huge room, which was empty except for the three of them. He grinned suddenly and swatted directly at us, as if to strike our faces. Of course he didn't. However, our view did swerve, showing the other offices as if the camera had swung around. Then it came back to Ebersole and the colonel. Hah! Ebersole had done the supposedly impossible, which was see a bee-bot spying on him, and by swatting it, he made it check the rest of the room. Smart fellow. So far all four of them were quite alive, and with Ebersole there, they seemed likely to stay that way. So when had Lavinda's aide died?

At the moment, the aide was standing at Lavinda's side in the office, checking his mesh glove whenever she asked him a question. The bodyguard stood behind him, looking bored. After about fifteen minutes, the three of them rejoined Ebersole and they all returned to the airlift. The entire visit seemed perfunctory, a company owner putting in an appearance. They rode back to the roof and walked to the flycar.

Krestone had fallen asleep, slouched over the controls. It was the first oddity; she was scrupulous about her duties, and I could never imagine her sleeping at work. Judged from Lavinda's frown, she had the same thought. When her group reached the flycar, the bodyguard opened the door and pulled Krestone back.

The captain's body flopped lifelessly to the side.

Hell and damnation. I had assumed Lavinda's aide was the one who died because he wasn't here, but they must have already debriefed him.

"My people arrived three minutes after Colonel Lavinda commed us," Chief Takkar said. "At that time, Captain Krestone had been dead for eleven minutes."

I wanted to hit someone. I liked Krestone. I couldn't believe she was gone. I also had no clue where the blazes Takkar had come up with me as a murder suspect. I'd been having dinner with Jak when Krestone died. Unfortunately I couldn't prove it; I'd been shrouded, hiding from Majda. Even if I had thought Jak could give me an alibi, I would never ask. No way could I risk drawing Majda attention to the Black Mark.

"What was the cause of death?" I asked.

"She was shot with a tangler." Takkar's voice hardened. "Your area of expertise, Major."

Well, shit. That wasn't evidence. I spoke coldly. "I trained with contraband weapons in the army, if that's what you mean."

All three sisters watched me with their dark eyes. Assessing.

General Majda spoke. "You can use a neural tangler?"

"Yes." I met her gaze. "However, I haven't fired one in years."

"Where were you this evening?" Takkar asked, her voice even more brusque than normal. "For some odd reason, we have no record of your whereabouts."

"I was having dinner with an old friend."

Takkar's snort left little doubt what she thought about my alibi. "His name?"

I crossed my arms. "Captain, are you accusing me of something?"

General Majda answered. "No one has accused anyone." She glanced at Takkar. "Do you have evidence as to who fired the tangler?"

"We will," Takkar said, which I translated to mean, *We haven't a clue.* Tangler bursts were notoriously difficult to trace. They left no residue; they just disrupted neural activity in the brain. No matter. Whoever had done this to the captain would pay. I would see to that.

Vaj Majda was studying me. Her controlled expression and posture gave away nothing. I tried to remain cool, but being scrutinized by the General of the Pharaoh's Army was an unsettling proposition. She spoke coldly. "You may return to your apartment. However, do not leave the city. And don't use any more shrouds."

That was no good. "I can't do my job unless I can assure my sources of secrecy."

"What sources?" Takkar demanded.

I just looked at her. She knew perfectly well I wouldn't reveal mine any more than she would reveal hers.

Vaj spoke in her dusky voice. "Very well, Major. Use your judgment." She left unspoken the obvious warning; if they had no record of my whereabouts, I had no alibi if anything else happened.

Corejida came over to me, her posture so tense she seemed ready to snap. "Have you news about Dayj?"

Normally I wouldn't talk about a case with so many ends dangling. I didn't want to give her false hope. Right now, though, it seemed a good idea to give them something before they decided to toss me in jail.

"It looks like he sold some jewels," I said. "I think he bought a new identity and passage off Raylicon."

"No!" Corejida stared at me. "That can't be. Dayj has no idea how to do that."

Takkar snorted. "It's an absurd suggestion that he could manage that on his own."

"It's no less absurd," I said, "than suggesting I shot Captain Krestone."

"I didn't hear any such suggestion," Lavinda said coldly. "Just an inquiry establishing that you had the requisite experience."

"Stop it!" Corejida told her younger sister.

Lavinda's reaction didn't bother me. She had just witnessed the death of a vital member of her staff, probably someone she liked, given Krestone's personable nature. Vaj Majda unsettled me far more. She stood back, quieter than the others. It didn't fool me. Of the three sisters, she was by far the most dangerous.

"Did Dayj actually go offworld?" Corejida asked me. "Where to?"

"I'm sorry," I said as gently as I could manage. "I don't know yet. I wish I had more news to give you." I meant it. I could see their heartbreak coming from a kilometer away. At best, Dayj had left Raylicon of his own free will and would be difficult if not impossible to trace. Or he could be a Trader pleasure slave, forever beyond our help. If he was still here, he was probably a prisoner.

Or dead.

With the night more than half over, Cries had settled into its second sleep cycle. I went to an empty park and sat in a gazebo built from lacework designed from some shimmery gold stuff. Then I activated my gauntlets. They were plugged into sockets in my wrists, which linked to biothreads in my body. Max sent his signals to the threads, they carried the data to my spinal node, and it fired bioelectrodes in my neurons according to signals it received. I perceived the end result as thoughts from Max. I could reverse the process; if I thought with sufficient force, the electrodes fired and the node picked up my response. Tech-created telepathy. It offered far more security than any shroud.

Wake up, Max, I thought.

I don't sleep, Max answered.

Did you get a full record of the session at the police station?

Unfortunately, yes. Max did such a good job of simulating distaste, I wondered if he actually felt the emotion. **Quite a scene between you and Chief Takkar.**

Friendly, isn't she?

She'd like to knock you into the wall.

Yah, probably, I thought. *You know the beetle I sent to follow Colonel Majda? It should also have a record of the trip that ended with Krestone dead.*

Yes. Would you like a neural dump?

Anything you've got on the murder.

Checking. Max paused, then thought, **The beetle followed Colonel Majda as far as the entrance to the office tower. It calculated that if it entered a space as confined as the lift, Major Ebersole might notice its presence. So it flew down the side of the tower and spied through the window-walls. It came back up when they returned to the flycar.**

Damn. The beetle had made the logical choice, following Lavinda Majda rather than staying with the car, but that didn't help my investigation. *So it didn't see the murder.*

No. But it did record the scene as the colonel and her party returned to the flycar.

Play it for me.

The scene formed like a translucent wash over my view of the park. I closed my eyes and the images intensified. This time I was watching the flycar from a different angle, one in front of the windshield. Again the bodyguard pulled Krestone back. Unlike Takkar's playback, however, this one showed Krestone from the front, enough to reveal what the bee-bot had missed; as the bodyguard moved Krestone, she took a pin off the dead captain's uniform.

My pulse leapt. *Replay that, Max.*

The scene reran. Yes, there! The bodyguard pulled some sort of needle off Krestone's shoulder. In the record made by the Majda's bee-bot, Krestone's body had hidden that action.

Who is that guard? I asked.

Her name is Oxil. She's on staff at both the palace and the Majda Tower in Cries.

She expected Krestone to be dead. I needed more information about this bland bodyguard. *Go back and play whatever you have from the last time Krestone was alive.*

The scene reset to an earlier time and showed the flycar landing on the roof. Lavinda disembarked with her aide and Duane Ebersole. Krestone remained in the driver's seat, visible through the windshield. The captain raised her hand to the others, either in a salute or waving farewell. Lavinda nodded to her and then walked with Ebersole and her aide toward the lift shaft.

When the bodyguard met them at the lift, Lavinda said, "Oxil, inform security we're on our way down."

"Right away, ma'am." Oxil thumbed her gauntlet and spoke into the comm.

Interesting. Takkar's recording had focused on Lavinda. My beetle watched everyone, which gave me a better view of the bodyguard. *Max, replay that bit where Oxil talks to security.*

The recording backed up and showed Oxil telling security that Colonel Majda was coming down. Oxil started to sign off, then stopped as someone apparently asked her a question.

"Krestone is staying in the flycar," Oxil said. "She has everything worked out up here."

Replay that, Max, and magnify it as much as you can.

Max zoomed in on Oxil's hand. The playback blurred, losing resolution, but it was clear enough. When Oxil started to sign off, she discreetly tapped the comm mesh.

Freeze that! I thought. *She switched channels! She wasn't talking to security anymore.*

Apparently not, Max said.

I studied the image. *She said Krestone had "everything worked out up here." It was a warning that Krestone figured out something.* I gritted my teeth. *Oxil told someone to kill her.*

You have no evidence to support that.

Yet. I couldn't prove it, but I had no doubt Oxil had set up Krestone's murder. *Can you identify that pin Oxil took off Krestone's body?*

I'd say it's a data storage device.

It looks familiar. I couldn't recall why, though.

Max asked, **Shall I forward this recording to Chief Takkar?**

Hell, no. Oxil works for her.

You can't withhold evidence.

I'll send it to General Majda.

Shall I do that now?

No.

Why wait?

I have my reasons. Before Max could push anymore, I thought, *I wish I could remember where I've seen a pin like that before.*

I have a suggestion.

Yes?

Your vital signs indicate extreme fatigue. Go home and sleep.

I smiled wanly. *A good idea.*

I headed to the penthouse.

"Major, wake up."

I grunted and turned over in my airbed.

"Major Bhaajan, you must wake up."

"Go away," I muttered.

"You have a visitor," my tormentor said.

I flopped onto my back. The voice belonged to the EI that ran the penthouse. Too bad I hadn't named it yet, because at the moment I would have liked to take that name in vain.

"I'm asleep," I said. "I don't want visitors." Only the Majdas knew I lived here, and right now I had no desire to see anyone connected with the palace or their charming police force.

"He is rather aggressive," the EI persisted. "He says he will stand outside until you, as he put it, 'goddamn deign to acknowledge my existence.'"

That wasn't Majda. I sat up in the dark, the covers falling around my hips. Then I remembered I didn't have on any clothes. I lay back down and pulled up the blanket. "Fine. Let him in. But I'm not getting up." Closing my eyes, I endeavored to sleep.

"Let him in?" The EI sounded confused.

"That's right." I had no intention of explaining myself to a machine.

I had started to drift off when someone walked into the room. I'd have recognized that booted tread anywhere. "I'm asleep," I muttered. "Go away."

The bed shifted as he sat down. "Bhaaj, come on." Jak pulled the pillow off my head. "You know you're glad to see me."

"Like hell." I turned onto my back under the covers. Light trickled in from the living room and cast his face in planes of light and shadow. "How did you know where to find me?"

"I have sources."

I glowered at him. "Did your sources tell you I'm dangerous when bat-brains wake me up?"

His wicked grin flashed. "Sounds interesting."

"You make me crazy, Jak."

His smile faded. "I also heard the Majda police chief tried clinching you on a murder rap."

"She doesn't have any evidence against me."

"That's right. I just got back from the station."

"What?" I sat up so fast, I forgot I wasn't wearing any clothes. Then I grabbed the metallic blanket and smacked my fist against my chest, covering myself. "Why did they bring you in?"

"They didn't." He was watching my gyrations in the blanket with a great deal of interest. "I went in on my own."

"What for?"

"To tell them you had dinner with me."

I gaped at him. "You gave me an alibi?"

"Yah."

"If they start sniffing around the Black Mark—"

"They won't find shit. I moved it."

"Even so."

"Even so." His gaze was dark.

I had never known Jak to put anything ahead of the Black Mark. To risk Majda attention so he could give me an alibi was so far off from what I expected, I just stared at him.

"Major Bhaajan, stunned into silence?" He smiled. "That's one for history."

I scowled at him. "Ha, ha."

"That sounds more like the Bhaaj I know."

"Jak." I spoke awkwardly. "Thanks."

He stabbed his finger at me. "Just be careful."

"All right." I tapped his chin. "You still got that cute dimple."

He folded his hand around my fingers. "You're going to ruin my reputation, you go telling people Mean Jak has a cute dimple."

"I hear Mean Jak has other attributes, too." I let go of the blanket, and it fell onto the bed, around my hips.

His gaze turned dusky as he stared at me, good and long. Then he pulled me into his arms. "You're looking good, Major."

"So are you," I murmured as I slid my arms around him. He moved his palm up my back, making my skin prickle. Then we lay together on the air mattress. I rolled with him onto my side while we tangled our legs in the sheets. He felt good in my arms, his body lean and familiar. His kiss was hungry, seven years hungry, but I remembered it as if it had been yesterday.

They say night lasts forever on Raylicon. This time, I was glad for the endless hours. Jak and I had plenty of time. Maybe I wasn't thinking clearly, but tough. When the sun came out we could deal with the reasons we shouldn't be doing this.

For tonight, we would forget.

I sat up with a jerk. "Scorch!"

"Ungh," Jak mumbled. He pulled a pillow over his head against the sunlight streaming through the windows.

"Max," I said. "Can you hear me?"

"Yes." His voice came from my gauntlets, which I had dropped on the floor last night.

"Check the EI for this place. Is its spyware still blocked?"

"Yes."

"Good. I remember where I saw the pin that bodyguard took off Krestone. Scorch smuggles them. It's a recording device."

"You think Scorch was spying on Lavinda Majda?" Max asked.

I swung my legs off the bed. "Could be."

"Scorch wouldn't be that stupid," Jak mumbled under the pillow. "She gets busted for spying on Majda, she's sorry she's alive."

"She's a risk-taker." I padded across the room and into the bathing chamber. The tiled pool was bigger than my living room in Selei City. As I slid into the water, soap-bots swam around me, glittering like silver and blue fish. They even matched the color scheme of the tiles. Welcome to the Majda universe.

Jak appeared in the doorway, framed in its horseshoe arch, holding the sheet around his hips. His lean chest with its chiseled muscles and dark hair showed above the wrinkled blue cloth. Nice.

"There's risks and there's insanity," he said. "Scorch has a lucrative operation. She wouldn't risk it by rizzing-off the General of the Pharaoh's Army."

I slid into the pool until only my shoulders were above water. "That depends on the stakes."

Jak leaned against the doorframe. "The undercity survives in the shadow of Majda. We don't bother them, they don't notice us. Why would Scorch upset that balance?"

"Maybe she's selling to Traders."

"I hope you didn't say that to her."

I squinted at him. "I might have, uh, implied it."

He stared at me. "And you're still alive?"

"She fired a damn laser carbine at me."

"I take it she missed." He grinned suddenly. "Or maybe she didn't. You've a harder head than anyone else I know."

"Ha, ha. Funny."

"Scorch wouldn't sell a Majda prince."

"I don't know, Jak. A Majda guard pulled Scorch's recorder off Krestone's body."

"You think this Oxil guard works for Scorch?"

Good question. "Could be."

"Why kill Krestone?"

"I'll bet the captain was figuring out some of this."

"Still makes no sense." He shook his head. "Scorch hates the Traders. Why endanger her operation in a way guaranteed to bring down Majda's wrath? It's crazy."

I thought about that. "Not if Scorch disappears off-planet. If she's sold Dayj, she can afford to go anywhere."

"I'm surprised she didn't fry your ass."

I smirked to cover my unease. "She likes me."

"Yah, the same way Chief Takkar likes you."

"Oxil works for our dear captain."

Jak made an incredulous noise. "You think the Majda police chief is involved in a conspiracy to sell Majda princes to slave traders? What mental asylum did you escape from?" He came over, sheet and all, and crouched by the pool. "Scorch is going to kill you."

"No she won't. I saved her life once." Of course, in her view that debt was now repaid. "Besides, if I disappear, people will look for me. It will draw too much attention to her."

He pulled off the sheet and slid into the water. "Maybe."

I swam over to him. "Hey, it's fine." So was he.

As we drifted together, though, I wondered who I was trying to convince, him or myself.

Jak took off after our bath, but not before extracting a promise that I would have third-meal with him, which most people ate before they slept at noon. Interesting timing. He wanted to come to the penthouse, too, which meant either he liked the place more than he would admit or else he didn't want me knowing where he had moved the Black Mark.

Out on the balcony, I released my beetle-bots, the red one to look for Oxil and the green to find Scorch. Then I went inside, sat at the console, and data-mined the meshes for info on Scorch. I found zilch: she hid better than a special ops agent. After an hour of work, I finally located a news holo with her in the background. The colorful image floated above my console showing a crowd of people gathered in a Cries plaza. They were watching a broadcast playing above a public holo-pedestal, a story about some government event in Selei City on the world Parthonia. That was why I had set up my business in Selei City; it served as the seat of an interstellar government, offering plenty of opportunities for a discreet investigator.

Scorch watched the broadcast with an odd look, a mixture of fascination and loathing. I didn't see why; the story looked boring, just images of people filing into a building. The reporters went on and on about the excitement of the event. It must have been a slow news day. Given that the Assembly met four times a year, every year, and that half the delegates only attended as VR simulacrums, the broadcasters were really pushing it with all this supposed excitement.

After the holo finished, I sat rubbing my chin. Why would Scorch care about who went to a routine Assembly session?

A light flickered on my gauntlet and Max's voice rose into the air. "Want to chat?"

I recognized the code phrase. "Go ahead. We're secure."

"I have a trace on Oxil," he said. "The red beetle picked her up by a lake at the palace."

"Good work. Link me in."

Max connected me to the beetle through his comm network. As I closed my eyes, a scene formed; I was on the shore of the Lake of Whispers, one of the few fresh water bodies on Raylicon. I wasn't actually seeing the feed real-time. The beetle recorded the scene, digitized the data, and sent it to Max, who relayed it to my spinal node, which converted the data into signals that my brain could process as optical input. So I "saw" the scene. With all that going on, a delay existed between what was happening and when I saw it, probably a few minutes in this case, when I wasn't that far away from the scene I was watching.

The lake spread out before me like a green mirror rippled with breezes, reflecting the pale sky and surrounding foliage. Imported trees grew around the edge of the lake and dropped silky green streamers into the water. Huge, flat flowers floated on its surface like red and blue disks. It was beautifully alien, all the more so because that profusion of plants didn't naturally occur in Cries. Raylicon hadn't dried out completely; we had fresh water underground if you went deep enough, but it wasn't easy to find.

Oxil stood gazing at the lake. She wasn't doing much

except enjoying the view. Breezes ruffled her spiky black hair. Probably she was on a break from work.

After five minutes, I said, "Max, this is boring."

"Sorry."

"Bring me out." I opened my eyes as the scene faded. "Let me know if anything happens."

"Will do. I have a report now from the other beetle."

I sat up straighter. "It found Scorch?"

"Partially."

"How partially?"

"She is well shrouded. The bot can't record her voice or actions. However, it did locate her in the Vanished Sea."

"Why is she out there?" Few people braved that barren desert.

"I don't know."

I stood up. "Think I'll go for a visit."

I jogged across the sea basin, doing my best to keep to the shadows cast by ridges that rose from the parched ocean floor like giant wrinkles. My feet pounded the ground, my smart clothes cooled my skin, and the jammer in my pack shrouded my progress. Max registered my speed as seventy kilometers per hour. Going on foot afforded better security than a flycar; it was easier to hide a person than a vehicle. I would have to walk at least part of the way back, though. At these speeds, my body built up damage faster than my nanomeds could do repairs. Even with high-pressure hydraulics to support my augmented skeleton and a microfusion reactor to provide energy, my body couldn't handle the stress of such speeds for long before it began to break down.

It took me twelve minutes to cover fourteen kilometers. As I neared my destination, Max thought, **Best to hide now.**

I focused my vision on a bluff ahead. *How about there?*

Yes, that would work. Scorch is on the other side.

I climbed the jagged rock formation to a cleft at the top. By wiggling through the opening on my stomach, I reached a point where I could train my spyglass on the other side of the bluff. Scorch was down there with a woman I didn't recognize, the two of them partially hidden under an overhang mottled with blue and green mineral deposits. A flycar also waited in its shadow. Both Scorch and her companion wore clothes patterned in colors like the desert, offering yet more visual camouflage. I couldn't hear them, either. My beetle was circling the bluff, but even this close it only managed to send me a few random words of their conversation.

Easing down the bluff, I crept nearer, silent and shrouded. When I crouched in the shadow of a rock spike near the ground, I finally picked up their conversation.

"...on the ship," Scorch was saying. Her spike of hair stood up behind her ear and glistened with oil. She still had the laser carbine, which she held down at her side.

"The ship is gone," the other woman said. She looked like a drifter from the port, with her ragged jumpsuit and scuffed boots. However, she wore a top-notch shoulder holster that held a tangler snug against her body.

"What about the passenger manifest?" Scorch asked.

"I took care of it," her companion said. "The manifest has his fake name. Caul Wayer."

Scorch frowned. "The name on that ID I sold him was Caul Waver. Not Wayer."

The other woman shrugged. "Waver, Wayer, the port made a mistake. Happens all the time. You're set."

"Good." Scorch indicated the woman's tangler. "I'll take that back."

Her companion pulled out the gun and tossed it to her. Scorch grabbed it out of the air, flipped it around—

And shot the drifter.

VII
The Caverns

Once before, I'd seen someone die by tangler fire. It wasn't any easier to take this time than the first. The drifter fell to the ground in a violent seizure as the shot scrambled her brain. She convulsed so hard that her body arched high off the ground. It took several minutes for her life to end, and it seemed like eternity. I didn't realize that I'd lunged forward until my foot hit a rock and I sprawled on my stomach. The thudding of the drifter's convulsions covered my fall; otherwise my futile attempt to stop the murder could have ended with Scorch shooting me, too.

Scorch wasn't done yet. She used the laser carbine to incinerate the drifter's body, leaving nothing but a few ashes. Even as I watched, the breezes stirred them into the air. It wouldn't be long before they dispersed altogether.

Without a backward look, Scorch boarded the flycar. Seconds later it soared away over the desert.

I didn't move at first. When Scorch's flyer was no longer visible in the parched sky, I walked to where the drifter had died. Most of the ashes were already gone. I clicked a hollow disk off my gauntlet and scraped a bit of the remaining powder into the container.

I headed back to Cries.

"Message incoming," Max said.

I jerked, surfacing from the trance I had fallen into during my fourteen-kilometer hike across the Vanished Sea. I had just reached the outskirts of Cries, exhausted and numb.

"Message?" I asked.

"From Jak," Max said. "Do you want to receive?"

"Go ahead."

Jak's voice growled on my gauntlet comm. "Got dinner, Bhaaj. Alone."

Damn. I had forgotten to meet him at the penthouse. "Sorry."

"Where are you?"

"Muttering Lane. Near the seashore."

"Be there in—" He paused. "Three minutes."

"Thanks."

I kept walking, headed into a deserted industrial district. After a while, a sleek black hover car edged around a warehouse and settled on the cobblestones up ahead. I activated the dart thrower in my left gauntlet and kept walking. You could get a license to carry darts, which only stunned, or even a pulse gun, but not a tangler. Never a tangler. You couldn't trace tangler shots and they made death into a slow torture. Police hated them. I hated them. Right now I didn't like myself, either. How many people had died by Scorch's hand because I saved her life all those years ago? And for what? So I could call in the favor decades later and figure out that she had sold or killed a Majda prince. If I had let her die, maybe Dayj would be all right.

Right, I thought bitterly. If Scorch had died, someone else would have risen to fill the vacuum she left in the ugly side of the aqueducts, and I was a fool if I thought otherwise. This was what I had hated about the undercity, one of the reasons I had never wanted to come back.

When Jak jumped down from the hover car, I deactivated the dart thrower. I walked up to him and put my arms around his waist. He held me, my head against his shoulder.

"Want to tell me about it?" he asked.

"Not now." I let him go. "Take me home?"

"Yah."

I slid into the passenger seat and he took the driver's side. Not that it mattered where we sat; neither of us drove. He entered our destination and the car headed back to my place. Its sleek black upholstery shifted under me, trying futilely to ease the tension in my muscles.

"Not hungry for dinner," I said.

Jak was watching me. "What happened, Bhaaj?"

I took a breath. Then I told him.

When I finished, Jak said, "You could be next."

I stared out the window at the outskirts of Cries passing below us, long stretches of stone terraces that went on and on, aesthetic and empty. I said only, "I know."

"That name, Caul Waver, it sounds like an alias."

"Apparently." I shook myself mentally and said, "Max, any luck in finding either the name Caul Wayer or Caul Waver on the passenger manifest of any ship?"

"Sorry, nothing." His voice came out of my gauntlet comm. "The port mesh system is well-protected."

"I can have Royal check," Jak said.

I squinted at him. "Who?"

"Royal Flush."

"Oh. Yah." I'd forgotten. He had named his gauntlet EI after the legendary poker hand that earned Jak the money to start the Black Mark. He'd been training that EI for decades. It was famous. Or maybe infamous was a better word. Jak never offered its services for free. "What price?" I asked.

His gaze darkened. "That you don't get yourself killed."

I managed a smile. "Deal."

While he spoke into his comm, telling Royal what we wanted, I watched, intrigued. Jak had one of the best networks in the undercity. Rumor claimed his system was even more extensive—and more shadowy—than the Cries military network. I didn't try to see what pass codes he entered. Honor among thieves and all. I no longer stole from anyone, and I hadn't since I entered the army, but I never forgot the code.

Jak glanced at me. "Can you give me the ashes of the woman Scorch killed? If Royal can ID them, it might help his search."

I handed over the disk. "Max got a partial analysis. The DNA doesn't correspond to anyone he recognized."

Jak clicked the disk into his gauntlet. "You believe this Caul Waver is Prince Dayjarind?"

"Possibly." I thought back to Scorch's meeting with the drifter. "They said the name was on some manifest. It could be a ruse. Scorch killed that drifter so she wouldn't talk. I'll bet the drifter killed Krestone." Thinking about the case helped me regain my equilibrium. "I want to know what that pin on Krestone's body recorded."

"Whatever Lavinda Majda talked about in the car." Jak frowned at me. "You think Colonel Majda helped Dayj escape?"

"I suppose anything is possible." It seemed about as likely, though, as me sprouting a new head. I thought about the other people in the flycar. "If I had to guess, I'd bet Scorch was spying on Krestone rather than Lavinda Majda. I can't imagine one of the sisters betraying the family."

Jak snorted. "Freeing a demoralized young man is hardly a betrayal."

"I know. But they don't see it that way." I pushed back my dusty hair. "They have a point, Jak, however much we don't like it. No way could Dayj deal in the undercity. Scorch would make byte fodder out of him."

"You think she sold him?"

"I'm hoping I'm wrong."

Max suddenly spoke. "I have new data on Oxil. Incoming."

"Oxil?" Jak peered at me. "What is that?"

"Not what. Who. Just a second." I closed my eyes as my node translated Max's feed into images I could see. A forest of drooping trees and wild flowers formed. Oxil was walking a few paces ahead as she spoke into her gauntlet comm. The beetle-bot hummed in closer so I could hear.

". . . nothing more," Oxil said. "Her dinner date gave her a damn alibi." A pause. "They may arrest her anyway. The source of her alibi isn't at all reliable."

I smiled, my eyes closed. "Majda police don't like you, Jak."

"Feeling is mutual," he muttered.

Oxil leaned against the mossy trunk of a tree. I missed her next words, but then the beetle hummed in closer.

"—best if I don't talk with you from here," Oxil was saying. "The risk of detection is too high." She paused. "All right. The cavern. One hour." She lowered her arm, and the view receded as my bot flew away before Oxil noticed it hovering about.

I was about to withdraw when the beetle sighted two people through the trees. *Follow*, I thought to it.

We moved past the branches and came out at the Lake of Whispers. Corejida and Ahktar were standing on the shore together, their hands clasped as they gazed at the water.

Corejida was crying.

She made no sound, but tears ran down her cheeks. Ahktar slid his arm around her waist and she put hers around his. They held each other, their heads leaning together.

"They'll find him," Ahktar said. His voice caught.

"Yes," Corejida whispered. "Surely they will."

I felt small. Their son's disappearance was killing them and I hadn't done a damn thing to help. Not knowing if he was alive or dead had to make it even worse for them.

The scene faded and I opened my eyes to see Jak watching me.

"Oxil works for Scorch," I said. "She must have been Dayj's inside contact at the palace."

Jak lapsed into dialect. "Scorch got him ID. Scared shitless Majda will find out."

"Then should have killed me," I said.

"Knew people'd look for you. And she owed you." His gaze darkened. "Won't stop her a second time. Paid her debt."

He had a point. "If I don't find Dayj, Majda fires me. Then Scorch kills me."

"Yah."

I wished he had a reason to argue the point.

Jak's gauntlet hummed. He tapped the comm. "What?"

Royal Flush answered in that sleek, sensuous voice of his, the one that women fell in love with before they realized he was an EI. "I have data on Caul Waver."

"That was fast," I said.

"Of course." Royal sounded smug. Given his programmer, that figured.

"What do you have?" Jak asked.

"I found the identity of the drifter that Scorch killed," Royal said. "She worked at the port. I checked the meshes where she had access and found the passenger manifest we need. It says Caul Waver left Raylicon seven days ago, bound for Metropoli."

Damn. "Eleven billion people live on Metropoli," I said.

Jak grimaced. "It won't be easy to find him."

"If he actually went there." It made sense, though. Metropoli was one of the most populous Skolian worlds. Its copious seas teemed with life, which I suspected Dayj would like.

Jak met my gaze. "Time to tell Majda."

"If I tell Majda," I said, "they'll focus on Metropoli." It would take immense resources to search such a heavily populated world, pulling their attention away from Cries, which was probably exactly what Scorch wanted. Maybe she had let me live so I would follow Dayj's supposed trail to Metropoli and lose him forever.

"If I go to Majda now," I said, "I'll miss Oxil's meeting in the cavern."

"What cavern?"

"Not sure. Oxil is meeting someone in a cavern. My guess? It's in the Maze."

"You go to the Maze," Jak said, "you're going to die."

"No, I'm not."

"That's right. Because I'm coming with you."

"No." I didn't want Jak risking his life for my job. "I was hired to do this. You weren't."

"You remember how rizzed you got when I disappeared seven years ago to collect my money? You thought I had died."

"Yah." I would never forget. When he had showed up at the Black Mark after three tendays, grinning and rich as sin, I'd been ready to throttle him.

His gaze darkened. "I won't go through that with you."

We would see.

Jak and I strolled with the evening crowds, tourists or Cries locals out on the town. Or more accurately, under the town, though just barely. We were on the Concourse, the only undercity locale with businesses the above-city considered legitimate. Cries looked after the Concourse, kept up the lights, did repairs, and even sent bots down here to clean up. The city council had ideas to convert this area into a park. So far they had done nothing more than talk; the undercity bosses had enough influence above-city to push the idea far back in the urban planning queue. The

Concourse was supposed to be part of the undercity, but if any of our actual population came up here, the police chased them back to the aqueducts or threw them in jail for the night.

My beetle had followed Scorch here, but it lost her after she entered the Maze below in the aqueducts. I didn't intend to enter the Maze the same way I had before. Last time I wanted her to know I was coming. This was different.

Nowhere in the crowds on the Concourse did I see anyone from the aqueducts except Jak and me, and we knew how to blend in with above-city types. Every now and then, someone from the undercity did find employment on the Concourse. They usually spent their earnings here, for supplies or food. We didn't use money in the aqueducts; the economy worked on barter. Some people spent their above-city chits at Jak's casino, mixing with the glamour-riz crowds from Cries.

"No dust rats here," I said.

Jak's voice took on an edge. "Little Jaks and Bhaajs still aren't welcome."

So it hadn't changed. When we had come here as kids, it had usually ended in trouble. A few vendors just shooed us away, and a cloth merchant had once given me a clean shirt, but such kindness was rare. Most shop owners called the police or used us for target practice, intent on cleaning up the scourge of dust rats.

We were no angels, either, though. I had done stupid things in my youth, letting hunger cloud my judgment. One time, a cop caught me filching jabo fruit from a café. I told him the truth, that I hadn't eaten all day, but he didn't believe me. He said I was too pretty to shoot, that maybe we could work out a deal. When he put his hands where I didn't want him touching me, I threw him over my hip and ran like hell. I managed to escape back into the aqueducts, which was why I didn't have a record, but it had been close.

My strongest memory of the Concourse, however, came from another day. We hadn't done anything wrong that time. A vendor saw me and Jak running by his stall, two undercity adolescents. We hadn't stolen anything; we were just two kids out for a lark, enjoying the sunshine streaming through the skylights, a sight so rare for those of us who lived underground. The shop owner fired iron balls at us, pelting our bodies, leaving us bruised, bloodied, and beaten, Jak with two broken ribs and me with a cracked femur, our joy in the sunlight ruined.

"Do the gangs still fight back?" I asked.

"Always," Jak said. "In the shadows."

I nodded, remembering how our gang had prowled up here at night, protecting ourselves with numbers. We learned to fight as a form of gang identification, and we were damn good at the rough and tumble. It wasn't like we had much else to do. None of us had been in school or had jobs.

"Who trained us?" I said.

He gave me a quizzical glance. "What?"

"Our gang. We had incredible discipline." I couldn't remember anyone actually teaching us how to fight. "Military almost."

He shrugged. "We trained ourselves. What works for military works for rats."

I continued to think as we walked. "One reason I succeeded in the army was because I already knew discipline. Hell, it was easy. They yelled at us a lot, sure, but they didn't kill us for screwing up and we had plenty to eat."

His voice hardened. "What, are you saying dust rats should join the army?" He looked as if he wanted to punch the wall. "Give our lives for the people who let us starve? What a way to swell the enlisted ranks, eh? Draft all the rats. Let us die on the front lines. After all, we aren't valuable."

"For flaming sake, Jak. You know I didn't mean that."

He looked like he still wanted to be angry. "So what the hell do you mean?"

I spoke slowly, thinking it through. "A way to improve the lives of our young people. They need a structure that supports them, one that comes from the undercity itself. The gangs are a start, but they aren't enough."

"We have our own ways," Jak said. "No interference from above."

He was right, mostly. Sure the undercity was rough, but we also had rich, ancient culture. And *freedom.* We lived unencumbered by above-city strictures. As a child, I would rather have died than give up that freedom. Hell, I almost had more than once, from sickness or violence. That attitude had made sense to me then, but it was a hard way to live. The authorities in Cries didn't care. They ignored us as long as we didn't bother them. If we upset the balance, they rounded up a few of us, threw the adults in jail and dumped the kids in orphanages regardless of whether or not they were orphans. A better way had to exist, one that preserved our community and culture without crushing us in poverty or the animosity of Cries.

A large, bulky man came up alongside Jak. He looked like a tourist out for a jaunt judged by his clothes. I wasn't fooled. I knew him too well. Under that amiable exterior, he could be as mean as sin.

"Heya, Gourd," Jak said.

Gourd nodded. Then he looked across Jak at me. "Good to see you, Bhaaj."

"Yah," I said. "Good seeing."

He spoke to Jak. "Got time?"

"Enough," Jak said.

I could tell Gourd wanted privacy. "Got to go," I said.

"No you don't." Jak glanced at Gourd. "What's up?"

"Commander Braze lost a hundred thousand on holo-roulette."

Jak gave a satisfied smile. "Good."

"Not good. She's ready to drill someone." Gourd scowled at him. "Says you got contraband holos in the casino that make people gamble too much."

"She can't do rizz," Jak said. "Get herself court-martialed for gambling."

"She's got ties," Gourd said.

Jak frowned. "What ties?"

Gourd told him. It seemed Commander Braze had relatives with less than sterling backgrounds and enough connections undercity to add a lot of grief to Jak's life.

"She wants her credit back," Gourd said.

"Yah, right." Sarcasm could have dripped off Jak's voice.

"Could make it hot for you," Gourd said.

"I give in to Braze, every rizzpunk in Cries will think they can take me."

Gourd didn't look surprised. He nodded to us both and took off, headed back to wherever they had moved the Black Mark.

"You got trouble?" I asked.

Jak shrugged. "I'll manage."

I hoped so. It sounded like Braze's people could buy him a lot of misery. I doubted Braze cared as much about getting back her credits as she did about saving face over this business with Jak and his blasted holos.

"Could be a mess," I said.

"No worry." Jak glanced around with that honed awareness of his that could be so unnerving. "How will you find Scorch?"

"I need another entrance into the Maze. Know any?"

He shook his head. "Scorch changes doors like I move the Black Mark."

"So maybe we make our own door," I muttered.

Jak frowned at me. "What are you up to?"

I tapped the pack slung over my shoulder. "I need a better shroud. Got anything?"

"Plenty." Then he said, "At the Black Mark."

I didn't expect him to tell me its location. The less I knew about his operations right now, the better. We couldn't tell how this would play out, whether I would end up working with the police or in their custody.

I motioned at a café with canopies over its outdoor tables. "I can wait there. I'll have a kava."

He grinned. "Bhaaj acting like a tourist."

"Like hell," I grumbled. "Go on. Get out of here."

Laughing, he said, "Be back."

He set off at a brisk walk down the Concourse

while I headed toward a bridge that arched over the wide boulevard. Ancient architects had built that span from red-streaked blue stone, and the Cries Parks and Recreation people saw to its upkeep. I had just reached its high point when Jak turned a corner on the throughway below. As soon as he was out of sight, I double-checked my jammer to make sure I was shrouded. Then I jogged back to the Concourse.

I set out for Scorch's cavern. Alone.

Seven years ago, after Jak disappeared, I had mapped the cavities above Scorch's Maze while I searched for him. I knew she had a part in that scheme to cheat him out of millions even if I had no evidence. Given that it involved Jak's illegal casino, I could hardly take my suspicions to the police. But I had never forgiven Scorch.

I crawled through cavities barely big enough for my body, with ragged holes everywhere. Spiky mineral buildups encrusted the openings. I wriggled on my stomach with the jammer in the pack on my back. Although it hadn't shrouded me from Scorch's security at the old entrance, I wagered it was more difficult to monitor this convoluted network of natural passageways. I was betting my life on winning that wager.

The infrared enhancements in my eyes bathed the world in a lurid red glow. The hotter an object, the more it glowed red to my IR sensors. Although the stone didn't generate enough heat to make small details clear, I could see where I was going. I wished I could double-check my location relative to the Maze. My shroud interfered with the weaker signals I could use to explore the caverns, and I couldn't risk stronger probes because Scorch's security might pick them up.

I stopped at a hole deep enough for half the length of my body. If my map was accurate, I'd reached the edge of Scorch's operation in the Maze. A quick check of my ammo verified I had three full cartridges. I deactivated the EM pulse the bullets released on impact. It could disable electro-optical systems within a small range, but it was of no use here, where the pulse had nothing to act on but stone. If it did manage to affect equipment somewhere, that would ruin my element of surprise. I was also close enough to the target that the pulse might affect my own equipment. I did make sure, however, that the sonic damper on the jammer was operating. And then I fired at the floor of the hole in front of me.

The serrated projectiles from my gun tore into the bottom of the well, boring it deeper. Although the damping field muffled the noise, my shots still weren't silent. Damn. I fired again, drilling even deeper. Debris crumbled from its sides. Gripping my gun in one hand, I eased into the chute I had enlarged. The sides felt warm. When my feet touched the bottom, my head was a handspan below the top. I held still and listened.

Nothing. No voices or machinery. If I had chosen well, the silence meant I was above an empty cave; if I was wrong, I could drill for hours and never break through.

With my back against one wall and my boots braced against the other, I scooted partway up the chute and fired at the bottom again. I gritted my teeth as debris pelted my body. Then I hammered the hard, blocky heel of my boot into the bottom of the hole with enhanced strength and speed, over and over. Still nothing. I fired, deepening the chute, then hammered the ground again. I might as well be trying to drill through the blasted planet—

My heel cracked the bottom.

Ho! I probed with my foot and pebbles fell away from the crack. They dropped for about as long as I would expect in a cavern before they clattered on the ground. No light came from below, which could mean I had found an empty area. I hoped. I needed extra care here. That scatter of debris wasn't likely to draw attention; it happened often in these caves. But anything as heavy as me dropping from this height could set off alarms. I worked as quietly as possible, and I managed to widen the opening without more rocks falling. Finally I eased my body down and out, clenching the edges of the opening. So there I was, hanging from the ceiling.

I had hoped to come out near a rock formation, but the closest was a full body length away, a ridged pyramid standing in a cluster of smaller spikes. My handhold crumbled in my grip, dropping more pebbles to the floor. Blast! I would fall in seconds. With a grunt, I swung toward the pyramid. That effort destroyed what little remained of my grip, and I lost my hold as I moved through the air. I rammed into the pyramid and threw my arms and legs around it while I slid to the ground. I managed to slow my fall enough so that when my boots hit the floor, they made almost no sound. I crouched down and waited.

Silence.

After several moments, I reached back into my pack and switched off the damper. Although I wanted its silencing effect, I couldn't hear enough through its field. Still silence. That didn't mean I was home free. The last time I had come down, Scorch had known as soon as I entered her empire.

The hole I had made in the ceiling hid itself by looking like all the other ragged crevices up there. Good. I looked around the cave as I stood up. Crates with military markings were stacked all around me. Scorch was selling illegal arms, tanglers and laser carbines it looked like. The only other exit from this smuggler's den was a narrow space between two columns of rock on the other side of the cave. A length of canvas hung there like a door. I didn't see any other escape route, and none of the crates were close enough to my hole in the roof to help me to climb out. I could move them, but it would be noisy and take too long. If Scorch caught me here again, she'd go for a kill.

I turned the damper back on and tried opening several crates. Nothing worked, including shooting them with my muted gun. Smashing them would make too much noise even with the damper. A fortune in weapons, and I couldn't steal a single one. Of course, I had my pulse gun. I'd take that over a tangler. If Scorch was selling these to the Traders, I hoped she died a miserable death. Better yet, I hoped they double-crossed her and sold her into slavery. It was probably too late for Prince Dayjarind, but if Scorch had smuggled him to the Trader Aristos, she deserved the worst.

I loaded my gun with the second cartridge. Then I went to the exit and pushed aside the canvas, my weapon up and ready while I checked the area. A pathway curved by outside. Columns lined the pathway, created in some past age when the tips of the stalactites from the ceiling had met the cones of stalagmites jutting up from the ground. To my left, ripples curved along a wall as if it were a curtain. The barrier looked filmy but it registered on my internal sensors as solid rock.

Max, I thought. *How are my vital signs?*

Fine, he answered. **Why do you ask?**

I was wondering if you could monitor other people the way you monitor me.

Not like you. I get your medical data from the nanomeds in your body.

They might have nanos, too. Most people who could afford health meds carried them. Scorch's illegal biomech would certainly include meds.

I know the protocols for the chips in yours. I don't for theirs.

Can you hack them?

I will try, Max thought.

Good. Let me know if you find anyone.

I set off along the path. In my IR vision, crystals glinted on the rocks like rubies. A drop of water fell from above and splashed on my nose. I had grown up on Raylicon and my biomech was programmed to respond to different worlds, so until now I hadn't noticed the lighter gravity here compared to Parthonia. But I was walking down a steep grade, enough to give me trouble in timing my steps. It slowed me down.

I have a signal, Max said.

Who?

I don't know. I can't crack their network. They're up ahead. Max was quite effectively simulating concern. **I advise caution.**

I eased along the curtain of stone, my back to its

rippled surface. Ahead on the path, an oval glowed brighter red than the surrounding rock. As I edged closer, I realized it was a canvas door hanging in the entrance of another cave, hiding whatever waited beyond.

Max, can you tell what's behind that canvas?

Someone is either sitting or standing several paces back from the entrance, he thought. **To the left.**

Got it. I swept aside the canvas, jerked up my gun—

And nearly blasted His Highness, Prince Dayjarind Kazair Majda, into oblivion.

VIII

Dayj

He was sitting on a rough pallet by the wall of the cave, staring into what had to be total darkness for him. Although he surely had health meds in his body, I doubted they included military bioware like the IR sensors in my eyes. I could see him, however, and it didn't take a genius to tell he was frightened. Manacles circled his left wrist and ankle, with heavy chains that stretched to a ring embedded in the wall. A blanket lay bunched up at one end of the pallet and a jug stood nearby. His clothes were simple but clean, dark trousers and shirt, nothing like the expensive garments he had worn in the Majda holos.

He spoke in a pure Iotic accent. "Who is it? Who is there?"

Gods. That deep, sensual voice alone could have women at his feet.

Lowering my gun, I fumbled for the stylus around my neck. I came to my senses before I turned it on. Scorch would monitor this cell even better than her storerooms. I hadn't expected she would keep Dayj for herself. It truly was insanity. She had to leave Raylicon; she could never pull this off here without the news leaking. But she couldn't escape with Dayj now, not with every port under surveillance.

I went over and crouched next to him, speaking in a low voice. "I'm here to help."

He snapped up his clenched fist while he protected his face with his other arm. I caught his wrist before he struck me, but his action told me a great deal about how Scorch treated him.

"I won't hurt you," I said. Up close, I could see him better. I should have been ready, but no holo could prepare anyone for the full impact of Dayjarind Majda. Even with his face ragged from exhaustion and fear, he was so beautiful, it was hard to believe he was real.

His voice rasped. "What do you want?"

"Your family sent me." My mind spun with plans. His cell was small, little more than a large hole created when mineral-laden water had dissolved the softer rock and left a shell of harder stone. As I scanned the area, my sensors located two holo-cams monitoring the cave.

One was pointed at me.

I spoke fast. "Your Highness, it won't be long before I'm discovered, if I haven't been already. We have to go. I'm going to shoot off your chains with my gun."

He was looking at me in the dark, though he probably couldn't see squat. "How do I know you won't shoot me?"

"You have to trust me." I wondered if his voice rasped so badly because he had been shouting for help. No one would hear him down here except

Scorch and the few people she let enter her empire. Or maybe he had been screaming for other reasons.

Gritting my teeth, I aimed at a point on the chain between his wrist and the wall. Sweat gathered on my forehead. I didn't want to risk hitting him, but if he had to haul around too much of that chain, it would slow us down.

"I'm firing," I said. "Don't move." I held down the stud long enough to shoot two projectiles, their explosive power muffled by the damper. The first damaged the chain and the second cracked it in two. It took two more shots to break the second chain. Having a stranger fire so near him in the dark had to be disturbing, but Dayj didn't flinch, not once. I had seen ISC officers with less composure than this terrified young man. I wondered if his family knew him at all.

"All right," I said. "You're free."

The chains scraped as he moved his leg, dragging the links across the ground. "Thank you."

I grimaced. "Don't thank me yet. I don't know if I can get us out of here alive."

He felt around the wall next to him until he found a handhold. As he pulled himself up, his leg buckled and he fell against the stone.

I jumped to my feet and reached for him. "What happened to your leg?"

Dayj jerked away when my palm brushed his arm. "Nothing."

"That wasn't nothing."

"It's all right." He took a shaky breath. "After one of the beatings, I couldn't walk for a few days. But I don't think it's broken."

Gods al-flaming-mighty. "Who beat you?"

"She calls herself Scorch." His voice cracked. "She didn't like it when I refused her."

I wondered how Scorch's nose would feel, breaking under my fist, smashed into a million little bone shards. "Can you walk?"

"I think so." He took a lurching step, but he didn't fall. "Not fast, I am afraid."

"Here." I touched his arm, offering support. He tensed, but this time he didn't jerk away. So I slid my arm around his waist. He draped an arm over my shoulder and leaned on me while I helped him limp toward the doorway. Well, damn. The Majdas had better not kill me for touching him.

"Did Oxil bring you down here?" I asked as we pushed our way past the canvas.

"Yes." He spoke bitterly. "I was so grateful to her for sneaking me out of the palace. Gods, I was a fool."

"You aren't a fool." Lonely, yes, but if that made a person a fool, then half the human race was with him. I tried not to think of the past seven years since I had left Jak. "It isn't your fault Oxil is scum."

"I'm afraid I am a rather poor judge of people." Dryly he said, "For all I know, Scorch could have sent you."

I swore colorfully at the suggestion, then remembered who I was with and shut up. "Sorry."

He actually laughed. It was soft and hoarse, but still a laugh. "I have heard much worse in the past few days."

Having heard Scorch's vivid vocabulary, I could imagine. It amazed me that he could retain a sense of humor in all this.

We made our way uphill toward the storeroom,

slowed down by my gravity problems and his injured leg. I thought of the dust in his gift box. His father said he had kept it for years. "When did Oxil first bring you here?"

He glanced at me. "Four years ago."

"Did you meet Scorch then?"

"No. Not until I wanted to go offworld." He continued doggedly with his labored steps. "Apparently she saw me, though, the first time I came down here."

Four years. That fit the date on the news broadcast about the Assembly that Scorch had watched. No wonder she had worn such an odd expression, an intensity that bordered on hatred. The delegates in that Assembly procession had included Roca Skolia, Dayj's intended. Scorch must have loathed the woman who could claim Dayj. I thought of his words: *She didn't like it when I refused her.* Assault took many forms, and ways existed for Scorch to make him do what she wanted regardless of how he felt.

"I'm sorry," I said. "About everything."

He spoke in a low voice. "I just wanted to see the ocean. A real ocean."

"You will someday."

"Perhaps." He didn't sound like he believed it any more than I did.

The canvas door of a storeroom came into view, but it didn't look like the right one. *Max,* I thought. *Have you mapped out this area?*

Yes. The doorway you want is ten meters up the path.

Thanks. We kept going, and I recognized the next canvas as the "door" of the room with the gun crates. We drew alongside the entrance—

A light appeared ahead.

Blast it! I pushed Dayj behind a stalagmite and nudged him at the canvas. Going into the storeroom wouldn't free him; even if he could have climbed to the hole in the ceiling, he didn't know how to navigate the maze up there. But with all the bizarre rock formations and crates in the cave, he had plenty of places to hide.

Dayj slipped past the canvas. When he was gone, I switched off the damper.

A voice became audible. "—don't see anyone here. They may have moved on."

I edged forward in a crouch behind the stalagmites that lined the path. Peering between two of the rock formations, I saw one of Scorch's rizz-punks on the path ahead, talking into her comm. She reminded me of the drifter Scorch had killed in the desert. Scorch probably intended to murder everyone who knew she had kidnapped a Majda prince. These people were fools if they believed otherwise. It could explain why she had so few human guards here; the fewer people who knew, the better. For the same reason, she'd have to erase any records her security systems kept of Dayj.

I considered the rizz-punk. My gauntlet darts shot a powerful sedative, but they weren't as accurate at long distances as the pulse gun.

Max, I thought. *If I fire a dart from here, what is the probability I'll knock out that punker?*

I'd say about thirty percent, he answered. **If you move closer, the odds improve, but you won't have any cover.**

I grimaced. I had reached the last stalagmite where I could hide. Any further, and I'd be in the open where she could see me. She'd blast me to smithereens. If I shot from here and didn't knock her out, she'd know my location. Then I was dead.

Thirty percent. I had a one in three chance of hitting her. The odds were too damn small.

Sometimes I hated this job.

I fired my pulse gun.

She never knew. The shots ripped through her torso, tearing her apart as they sent shock waves through her body. She collapsed, twisting as she fell, and smashed her light when the remains of her body hit the ground. The tunnel went dark—

A laser flared from behind me, its brilliant light stabbing the darkness. The shot pulverized a stalagmite only centimeters from where I crouched. I dropped and rolled as a second shot exploded a stalactite above me. I barely escaped the spear of rock that crashed to the ground. Shards flew everywhere and one stabbed my arm.

Whoever fired at me was to my left, where Dayj and I had been walking only moments ago. The storeroom where Dayj was hiding was also to my left, its entrance between me and the shooter. Darkness shrouded the path, which would hide me if the shooter didn't have IR vision.

A familiar voice grated. "Know you're here, Bhaaj."

Scorch. Shit! She had every possible augmentation: sight, hearing, muscles, skeleton, nodes.

Max, can you locate her? I asked. Blood was dripping down my arm.

I can give you an estimate, he thought. **Ten meters down the path.**

Too close. If I moved, the noise would give away my location. I peered through the rocks, but I couldn't see anyone. Nor could I hear breathing. She was shrouded. If she stood in front of a stalagmite, her holosuit would project images of a stalagmite; if she was by a wall, her suit would show a wall. Conduits in the material would also cool the suit, masking the heat of her body.

Moving with care, I pulled off the stylus hanging around my neck. *Max, can you link to the chip that operates this light?*

Yes.

When I tell you, turn it on. I sighted on the guard I had shot—and hurled the stylus. *GO!*

Light flared as the stylus flew through the air. A laser shot hit the stylus dead on, and I fired toward the source of the beam, spraying the area with the last of my second ammo cartridge. The cavern echoed as the projectiles shattered stalactites.

Darkness and silence descended.

Did I get her?

You hit a lot of rocks, Max thought.

I know that. Did I get Scorch?

I estimate the probability is between eleven and seventy-three percent.

Well that's definitive.

Sorry. It is the best I can do.

I stayed crouched behind an outcropping. That Scorch hadn't returned fire could mean many things: I had hit her, she couldn't find me, she had a strategy I hadn't guessed, or she was recharging the carbine. The longer this went on, the better for her, because I needed ammunition. I didn't think she had fired enough to exhaust the carbine's power, but that assumed she started with a full charge.

Footsteps came from my right, on the path where I had shot the guard. Not good. I looked to see Oxil edge around the curtain of rock, a pulse rifle gripped in her hands. With Scorch in the opposite direction, I was penned now on both sides.

Max, I thought. *This is not good.*

Throw your gun. It will draw their fire. It is of no use to you without ammunition.

I have another cartridge. But they'll hear me when I reload. If I moved fast enough, I might get Oxil before she killed me, but it would leave me an easy target for Scorch, if she was still alive.

You need a diversion, Max thought. **Throw your boot.**

They'll hear me take it off. I paused, thinking. *I can get my gauntlet off faster with less noise.*

Without your gauntlets, you lose your connection to me.

I have two of them. I slid my right hand over my left gauntlet. *Retract the biothreads from my left socket.*

Retracted. Max's thought took on a tinny quality.

I thumbed the release and my gauntlet split open. No sound had yet betrayed me. Steeling myself, I ripped off the gauntlet and hurled it at Oxil while I scrambled to the left.

She fired, hammering the rocks with bullets. In the same instant, a laser shot bored into the cranny I had just vacated. Hell and damnation! Scorch was alive and on to my tricks. I got rid of my spent cartridge, all the time scuttling behind the stalagmites. As soon as I reloaded, I fired at Oxil, but she had dodged out of sight and my shot just cracked the rocky cones that blocked her former hiding place.

Laser fire flared from Scorch's direction and melted a stalagmite only a meter away. I edged back, hoping to throw off Scorch's estimate of my position, and stopped, my pulse racing.

Nothing.

I peered through two rock columns. *Where did Oxil go?* I asked Max.

I believe she has hidden behind the rock formations directly across the path.

A ragged fence of rocky pyramids bordered the other side of the walkway. Oxil could be anywhere back there. *Are you linked to the beetle I sent after Scorch earlier today?*

I lost contact when it reached the caverns.

We're here now, too. See if you can find it.

Searching.

Well?

I can't find it.

It might be in—

Found it.

Good. Bring it here.

Max paused for what felt like forever, though it was only seconds. **I'm having trouble connecting to its controls. It needs to be closer. When it is, I can link your optics to its cameras so that you can see with its eyes.**

Good idea. That would let me see real-time through the bot's eyes, rather than having the view digitized and sent to my spinal node, with the associated delays.

Do it, I thought. *But be careful. If it gets too close to Scorch or Oxil, they'll detect it.*

Another pause. **The bot is here. I'm linking your vision.**

My view of the cavern blurred. The scene refocused, still dim and red, but seen from higher up. I was a beetle flying near the jagged ceiling. Across the path from my hiding place below, a brighter patch of red glowed behind two stalagmites.

Take me lower, I thought.

That will increase the chance that Oxil will detect you.

I'll risk it. Circle back over those last few meters.

The beetle drifted down in a spiral, and the splotch of red resolved into Oxil crouched behind the pyramids of stone.

Hah! Got her.

Got how? You can't shoot her through those stalagmites.

Yeah, but I know her location. I hoped Scorch wasn't trying to spy on me with her own bots, if she had any. *Take the beetle up the path.*

Moving.

I floated under the ceiling through an inverted landscape of small stone icicles. Scorch had shrouded herself well; nothing showed below except for the eerie rock formations.

A splintering crash came from the storeroom.

I snapped open my real eyes and whipped up my gun.

Bhaaj, don't shoot! Max thought. **Dayj is in there.**

Oxil jumped to her feet and fired her pulse rifle at the storeroom. In that same instant, a laser shot came from Scorch's direction and seared the canvas door, setting it aflame. I was already firing at Oxil, knowing exactly where to aim. With the canvas in flames, light filled the cavern. Oxil stared at me as my shots tore through her body, her face lit by the crackling fire. Then she collapsed behind the stalagmites.

"Bhaaj!" a man shouted. "JUMP!"

What the bloody hell? I threw myself backward and slammed into a column. In that instant, a laser shot stabbed across my hiding place, barely missing me. Even as I returned Scorch's fire, I looked the other way, up the path, where the yell had come from. I knew that voice. Jak had arrived.

He was shrouded, but in the lurid firelight from the burning canvas, the outline of his body showed. He had a weapon, either a pulse rifle or a laser carbine. I spun to look in the other direction and finally located Scorch, a human-shaped ripple against the stalagmites.

Jak had his gun pointed straight at Scorch and—

Scorch had her carbine pointed straight at me.

"You shoot me, Jak," Scorch called, "and I shoot her."

"You'll be dead before you fire," Jak said.

"I'm faster," she told him. "You got no biomech."

"I got biomech," Jak told her.

"Lying," Scorch said.

I knew Scorch well enough to recognize that she wasn't sure. If she thought she could move faster than Jak, I'd already be dead. Both Scorch and I had augmented speed, but she had her gun aimed and mine was down at my side. She only had to press the firing stud. I'd be dead before I got off a shot. Unfortunately I knew another truth. Jak was bluffing. He hated the thought of tech-mech inside his body. He had no biomech.

The burning canvas fell to the ground, its flames dying, the light dimming. It left the entrance to the cave open, but at first I wasn't sure if what I saw there was real or a shadow. Then the shadow solidified into a man.

Dayj.

He stood framed in the entrance between two stalagmites with the canvas burning into ashes at his feet. Gods almighty, he had a neural tangler clenched in his hand. The splintering we heard must have been him cracking open one of the crates. I had come closer to breaking them than I realized.

"Dayj." Scorch stood a few steps away from him, her outline fading as the fire died. "You can't shoot. You don't know how to use a tangler." She had an odd tone, as if she were talking to a child.

I hated her tone, but she was right. A tangler targeted the neural system. It took experience to prime the gun, determine the dose, and decide where to shoot.

"You don't think I know how?" Dayj rasped, his Iotic accent a jarring contrast to the lurid scene, with dying flames and glittering rocks. "I watched, Scorch. I listened to you tell that drifter how to kill Captain Krestone, and I watched you get ready to kill your hired assassin."

Shit. Did Dayj realize he had just signed his death warrant? He had told her, in front of witnesses, that he could testify against her. She had to kill him. Letting him live would go against every tenet she lived by—but from what I had seen, she had lost all rationality over the prince.

"Can't learn a tangler that way." Scorch's brusque voice gave me chills. "Even if you knew, you could never shoot. Not you. Drop the gun, Dayj."

I held my breath. If Scorch wavered even a moment, it would give me the opening I needed.

Dayj stared at Scorch, his gun aimed at her. The blaze of the canvas had died to embers and she was almost invisible. She was seconds away from winning. As soon as we could no longer see her, Jak's advantage disappeared. I glanced at Jak, moving only my eyes, not my head. His outline was also fading, which meant Scorch was losing one of her advantages, too, but it also acted as a flag, letting her know how little we could see her.

Dayj stood frozen, gripping the stalagmite next to him, the chain hanging from the manacle on his wrist. He held the tangler in his other hand. Watching him, I knew she was right. He couldn't commit murder. It wasn't in him.

Dayj fired.

Everything happened at once. I threw myself to the ground, blasting Scorch's location with bullets even while her laser exploded a stalactite above my head. Melted debris showered me. Jak fired a fraction of a second later, but Scorch had already ducked to the side. Dayj's shot hadn't hit her. And now Scorch knew; Jak had bluffed about his speed.

Dayj lunged away from the storeroom. I could no longer see Scorch, but he had to be next to her. I couldn't believe it. He was gambling that one of the most hardened undercity killers on the planet wouldn't immediately end his life. And he was right. She hesitated only an instant, but it was long enough for him to yank the pack off her back, smashing it against a stalagmite. Although her shroud didn't fail completely, her disguise faded enough to let me see her blurred outline.

I was already jumping to my feet. Although I moved much faster than normal, everything seemed to slow down. In the instant it took Scorch to recover, I fired. My bullets ripped through her, hammering into her body, riveting her to the rock wall like a drill.

The roar from my gun abruptly stopped. The remains of Scorch's body slid down the wall and crumpled on the ground, leaving a smear of red.

"Ah, gods." Dayj stumbled back and dropped to his knees. Leaning forward with his arms around his stomach, he vomited on the ground.

I stood with both hands clenched in a death grip on my gun, my arms extended out from my body, my thumb pressing the firing stud of my empty pulse gun.

"Bhaaj." Jak's calm voice came at my side. "It's done."

I turned slowly, my gun still up and aimed, now at him. He put his hand on the barrel and carefully pushed the gun aside. "Stand down, Major," he said softly.

I stared at the empty gun. Taking a deep breath, I nodded to him and lowered my weapon.

We went to Dayj then. He had his arms around his stomach and his head down. The remains of Scorch's body lay crumpled only paces away, but I couldn't look. Later, I'd have to face what I'd done here today. Right now, Dayj needed us more.

I knelt next to him. "Are you all right?"

He lifted his head. "Who are you?"

Even in the waning light of the embers from the fire, I could see the haggard lines of his face. "My name is Bhaajan," I said. "I used to be an army officer. Now I'm a PI."

Dayj was still gripping the tangler. I pried open his clenched fingers and took the gun. A quick check and the blood drained from my face.

"These darts are loaded with water," I said. *Water.* That was it. Plain, ordinary H_2O.

"I have no idea how to use this weapon," he said hoarsely. "I don't even know what it is."

"It's a tangler," I said. "Properly loaded, it's the deadliest neural disruptor ever made."

He met my gaze. "I couldn't think of anything else to do that would give you a chance."

I set the gun on the ground. "You have guts." What an incredible understatement. He had just bluffed one of the most brutal criminals on the entire planet with a water pistol.

"Gods," Jak muttered. "Remind me never to let you into the Black Mark." He glanced around. "We should get moving. I'm surprised no automated system has shot at us."

"It is probably because you are with me," Dayj said. "Her systems won't harm me. She reprogrammed them after a laser nearly killed me when I tried to escape."

"We're also shrouded," I said. "From most sensors."

"I can see you," Dayj said. "Your skin shimmers."

"It's holographic powder. The effect breaks down up close." I rose to my feet and offered him a hand.

Dayj stood up and tried to take a step. As his leg gave out, both Jak and I grabbed him. We each slid an arm around his waist, and he put his arms over our shoulders. We headed up the path where Jak had come down, Dayj limping between us.

"We can go out a back door I know," I said.

"Got a closer one," Jak said. "I've a jeeper waiting there."

"A closer one?" I demanded. "You knew about another entrance?"

Jak cleared his throat. "Uh. Well. Yah."

"You, who supposedly didn't know a way in here?" Now that I thought about it, he hadn't had time to get a shroud, go back to the café, and then come here. He must have gone straight to the cavern after we split up.

"Bhaaj—"

"You bastard," I said. "You ditched me."

Jak stared at me across Dayj, his gaze dark. "Of course *you* would never ditch *me*. And never mind that I just helped save your stubborn ass."

"My stubborn ass was fine," I growled.

"Excuse me," Dayj said, "but if the two of you continue this, you will break my spine."

Ho! I hadn't realized I was gripping him so hard. As I spluttered an embarrassed, "My apologies, Your Highness," Jak turned red and said, "Sorry about that." We both loosened our hold.

We soon reached an exit that let us out into a decrepit canal. A jeeper waited, stocky and squat by the rubble of a fallen wall. Holo-paint sheened the armored surfaces of the vehicle, creating a mottled rust and blue exterior that matched the surroundings.

As I helped Dayj into the jeeper, Jak surveyed the area. "No one has come after us yet."

Dayj paused in the doorway. "Scorch didn't want people to know she had me prisoner." In a dull voice, he added, "Anyone who knew, she killed."

I spoke in a low voice. "It's not your fault."

Jak swung up into the driver's seat. "Her behavior makes no sense."

I helped Dayj into the back, where he could lie down if he needed, then closed the door and slid into the front passenger seat. "Why not?"

Jak powered up the jeeper. After it rose into the air and headed down the canal, he looked back at Dayj. "She threw her reason to the wind over you."

It made sense to me. I'd thrown my reason to the wind over Jak more than once.

"Who are you?" Dayj asked him.

"Jak."

"I thank you for your help."

Jak nodded awkwardly. "I set a course for the palace."

"No," I said. "Wait." I turned to Dayj. "Is that what you want?"

He went very still. "I have a choice?"

I took a breath and plunged over the proverbial cliff. "I told your family you went offworld. The port lists a ticket bought by someone with the ID Scorch sold you. It says you went to Metropoli. This jeeper and the caverns are protected from surveillance." I felt as if the world were spinning. If the Majdas ever found out what I was doing, my life would be worth less than spit. "You can't leave Raylicon now, but if the search moves to Metropoli, it will ease up here. Eventually you can go wherever you want."

Jak stared at me in disbelief. "I am not hearing this."

"Why?" Dayj asked me. "Why would you do this for me? Do you realize what my family would do to you if they found out? Or the reward they will give you for bringing me back?"

"This isn't about a reward," I said. "Or their revenge. Some things are more important. Like freedom. You shouldn't have to live that way."

"What way?" He sounded tired. "As one of the richest people in an interstellar empire? There is a real hardship."

"You're a prisoner in your own home."

"The Houses have a rationale that goes back millennia." He rubbed his eyes, then dropped his arm. "It is a rich tradition, Major, not one to discard lightly."

"Then why did you run away?" I asked.

Softly he said, "Because I was starving."

I gentled my voice the best I knew how. "Skolians have settled hundreds of worlds. If you want a well-populated place with many seas, it doesn't have to be Metropoli. You can go somewhere no one would ever know."

His look said it all, the longing, the loneliness, the frustrated dreams. It was there in his dark eyes. He spoke with difficulty. "When I was lying in my cell in the caverns, I remembered a gift my parents had given me when I was little, a globe of Raylicon with deserts in gold, the dead seas in crystal, the clouds in diamond. I thought it was the most beautiful thing I'd ever seen. But they wouldn't let me play with it. I might have broken the globe, you see." In a low voice be said, "That is my life, Major. I can only look at it, never touch it."

"I'm sorry," I said softly.

"But you see, while I lay in the dark, I remembered why my parents gave me such a gift. I remembered their love." He spoke with difficulty. "I want to leave. But I cannot."

I thought of Corejida and Ahktar at the Lake of Whispers, both crying. It gave me a strange feeling. Envy? Grief? No one had ever stood on a shore or anywhere else and wept for me.

"You're sure?" I asked.

He nodded. "I'm sure. I will go home."

Jak spoke. "Maybe after all this, you can convince them to give you more freedom."

Dayj tried to smile. "Perhaps."

None of us said the truth we all knew, that it could never happen.

IX
Homecoming

It was still night when the jeeper reached Majda territory. The comm crackled with a woman's voice. "You have entered restricted airspace. Identify yourself and await instructions."

I spoke into the comm. "This is Major Bhaajan. Notify General Majda that I'm coming in."

"Please hold, Major," the woman said.

"Understood." Apparently the jeeper's shroud didn't work all that well given how fast they had detected us. But it probably still hid the people inside. I reached forward to deactivate the shroud. Once they knew we carried Dayj, we shouldn't have any trouble.

"Wait," Dayj said. "Not yet."

Jak glanced at him. "It's too late to turn back."

"I know," Dayj said. "I just—I want a few more minutes of freedom. Even knowing it's about to end."

A new voice snapped out of the comm, hard and clipped. "Major, this is Chief Takkar. Where the hell have you been?"

Takkar. Oh, great. "Around," I said.

"Don't rizz with me, Bhaajan. You've hidden *continuously* since we told you to stop with the shroud. You're going to need a damn good explanation, and this one had better not involve some disreputable undercity kingpin."

Jak's eyes gleamed. "Don't you like me, Captain?"

Takkar swore like she never would have done if she'd known a Majda prince was listening. I glanced at Dayj. He smiled slightly and shrugged.

I had other issues with the captain. "Tell me something, Takkar," I said. "Where is Oxil?"

"She's off-duty," Takkar said. "Why?"

"You don't wonder where she is?"

"No. Why do you?"

"I have my reasons."

"What reasons?"

"I'll explain when we land."

"Damn right you will," Takkar said. "The police are escorting you to the south park."

"Understood," I answered. Takkar sounded angry but not defensive. It was hard to tell from a voice over the comm, but my intuition said she didn't know about Oxil.

"Captain," I said. "Can you have the Majda sisters meet us when we land?"

"Why?" Takkar asked.

"I have news for them."

Tension snapped in her voice. "What did you find out?"

"I'll tell them."

Takkar just grunted.

I toggled off the comm and turned to Dayj. "How well do you know Chief Takkar?"

"She's been with our police force for decades." He smiled, his teeth a flash of white. "I've always liked her."

It was the first time I had seen his full smile, and I barely heard a word after that. That grin could fry the brains of any woman within a ten-kilometer radius. No wonder Scorch had fallen so hard. She must have seen that dazzling smile when she spied on his visits with Oxil to the aqueducts. Scorch had tried to attain the unattainable and paid for it with her life.

"Do you think Takkar knows about Oxil?" I asked Dayj.

He shook his head. "Chief Takkar is loyal to my family."

Although I disliked Takkar enough to wish he was wrong, his opinion fit my impression of the chief. "They'll give her a lie detector test."

"She'll pass." He pushed back his tousled hair. "Or maybe I am just a bad judge of people. I thought Oxil was a good person. The first time she snuck me out to the canals, I expected she would want something in return. She never asked for anything."

"She wanted you to trust her."

He looked out the window at the landscape below, the lush hills of the Majda forest, such a contrast to the rest of Raylicon. "I did trust her. I was stupid."

"Dayj, no. They were scum. And Oxil was the fool. Scorch would have killed her."

He glanced at me with his dark gaze. "Except you did it for her."

I had no answer. He had seen me shoot Scorch, probably Oxil and the guard as well. Scorch's security system might also have a record of what happened. Any lie detector would verify I believed my actions were necessary to protect Dayj, but no matter how you spun it, I killed three people. Even if the police cleared me of murder, I knew the truth; I was no better than the criminals I tracked.

"Bhaaj, stop," Jak said.

I looked at him and decided to smirk. It was a good way to hide my real thoughts. "It's not every day I get to ride with a disreputable undercity kingpin."

"Your lucky night." He smiled, but it didn't reach his eyes. He knew what I was thinking. He had held me in the past when darkness haunted my memories. This time I wouldn't even have him for long, for he would stay in Cries, which I could never do.

Majda police fliers escorted us to the palace. Jak landed the jeeper on a long, sloping lawn behind the building. As soon as the engines powered down, I opened the door and jumped out. Four police officers waited, along with Takkar and Major Ebersole. The Majda sisters were also there. From Takkar's thunderous expression, I suspected she wanted to slap me in the modern-day equivalent of irons. However impatient she and the others might be, they stayed back while General Majda approached me.

I'd always prided myself on my unflappable calm, but even my confidence wavered when I faced Vaj Majda. I tended to forget how tall she was, a towering two meters. Her dark eyes missed nothing, and right now they were intent on me.

We met a few paces from the jeeper. I bowed from the waist. "My greetings, General."

She spoke in her husky voice. "You've been difficult to find, Major."

"I had good reason."

"And that is?"

I looked back at the jeeper. Jak stepped into the doorway and jumped down to the ground.

"Major Bhaajan." The general's voice tightened. "How you spend your personal time is your affair. I assume you have reason to bring your—companion here."

"He helped." I started to say more, but then I stopped.

Dayj appeared in the doorway of the jeeper.

A cry came from behind us. I turned to see Corejida staring at Dayj, her mouth open. She strode past us, ignoring even Vaj, seeing only her son.

Dayj eased down to the ground, using his good leg for support, and within moments he and his mother were embracing. Corejida kept saying, "I can't believe it." The chain attached to Dayj's wrist hung down her back as he hugged her, but I didn't think she noticed. The other chain, the one on his ankle, lay across the grass. Tears ran down her face and she made no attempt to hide them, pulverizing the reputation of the noble Houses for their legendary emotional restraint.

"Gods," Vaj said in a low voice. "Thank you, Major." It was the first time I had seen her control slip.

I nodded, though inside I grieved for the freedom Dayj would never know. "He's going to need a doctor." I hesitated, uncertain about how much to say. "A therapist, too, I think."

Majda inclined her head. "We will see to his health, both physical and emotional."

"And intellectual?" I knew I should keep my mouth shut, but the words came out anyway.

She considered me. "Dayj has his books."

"It isn't enough." I plunged ahead. "General, I ask your forgiveness if I offend. But please listen." I motioned toward Dayj. "He's a lot smarter than you think. A lot more talented. He needs independence. He's suffocating here."

Anger flashed in her gaze. "I forgive your offense, Major, because you brought him home. But do not overstep yourself."

"He ran away." I had to speak even if it meant I lost the goodwill I had earned by finding him. "Doesn't that tell you anything? Gods know, I can see you all love him. He's a fortunate man." More quietly I added, "If you love him, let him have his dreams."

I thought she would have me thrown off the grounds then. If a gaze could truly have pierced, she would have sliced me to ribbons. "If he ran away of his own free will," she asked coldly, "why is he coming home in chains?"

"Because he trusted too easily. He's never learned to survive on his own."

"All the more reason he should remain here."

"He came home because he loves you all. But he wanted to weep and they weren't tears of joy." I was digging myself a deeper hole, but I owed Dayj. He had saved my life by bluffing Scorch with a water gun.

Majda clasped her hands behind her back. "You take liberties I have not granted."

"You don't strike me as someone who prefers pretty words to the truth." Behind her in the distance, I saw people running down the lawn from the palace, including Ahktar, Dayj's father. He must have tossed on his robe over his clothes without even bothering to fasten the ties. It billowed out behind him, flying in the wind like a cape.

Vaj turned to watch them. "Everyone has their version of the truth, Major."

When Ahktar reached Dayj and Corejida, he threw his arms around them. Other people gathered around, two of them doctors judging by the scanners they turned on Dayj. A police officer knelt by Dayj's ankle and began working on the manacle.

"I do know this," Vaj told me. "I will be forever grateful that you brought him back to us."

I couldn't say more. I should have realized a few words from an outsider wouldn't change anything.

The general went to Dayj then and greeted him. Although far more restrained than her sister and brother-in-law, she left no doubt of how much she meant her last words.

Jak came over to me. "I don't know if he's incredibly lucky or one of the most unfortunate people I've ever met."

I exhaled softly. "Both, I think."

X

New Leaves

Jak tossed my jacket onto the bed. "You want to carry this or pack it?"

I stuffed the jacket into my duffle. "Both."

He wouldn't meet my gaze. We had already gone through the penthouse twice to make sure I wasn't leaving anything behind. Now we were stalling. I had nothing to keep me here. Dayj had told the police I acted to defend him, and Majda accepted it, which meant the city authorities did as well. They wouldn't bring charges against me. Barred the opportunity to toss me in jail, Takkar was more than happy to kick me off the planet. I was free to go.

Except.

I stood by the bed while Jak paced around the room, checking for lost items. I tried to make a joke. "You'll wear a path in this expensive carpet." Ha, ha.

He turned without a smile. In his black trousers and torn muscle shirt, he made a stark contrast to the white walls and tasteful holo landscapes. The holster strapped around his torso held a pulse gun snug against his ribs. Since the business with Scorch, we both went everywhere armed.

I shifted my weight. The obvious thing was to ask for a ride to the starport. I opened my mouth, but somehow what came out was, "Leave with me."

Well, shit. What was wrong with me?

Of course he wouldn't come. He had everything here, money, power, influence. Granted, it was illegal, but Jak had never let that stop him. It did matter to me. He couldn't live my life any more than I could live his.

"You stay," he said, his accent pure undercity dialect.

"Took me a long time to get out."

He crossed his arms and his biceps bulged. "This is your home."

I wished he would stop looking so good. "Can't ever come home."

"It's my home."

"Make a new one."

"You make an old one."

To hell with the undercity terse inability to express anything. "I can't, Jak. I tried to come home once before and it didn't work. I've made a new life in Selei City. I want that life, not a past with so many ghosts and so much grief."

His jaw twitched. "I'm a ghost you want to forget?"

"No!" I spread my hands out from my body. "You come with me."

"You stay."

We stood looking at each other, nothing left to say.

"I have an incoming message," the penthouse EI announced.

"For flaming sakes," I muttered. "Your timing honks."

"Do you wish me to play it later?" the EI asked. "It finished and I now have it in memory."

"Who is it from?"

"It has no readable ID."

"Oh, that's great." I glared at no one in particular, because I didn't have the words to tell Jak how I felt. He just stood there, and I knew he would never say how much this hurt, either. We made quite a pair, him and me, both equally inarticulate.

"Major Bhaajan?" the EI prodded.

"Project the message on the wall," I growled.

"It isn't visual,"

This just got better and better. People masked themselves only if they had something to hide. "One of Scorch's people sending us death threats?"

"I don't know," the EI said.

"Just play it." I was in no mood for breathy threats but we might as well get it over with.

The voice that rose into the air was anything but breathy. Rich and deep, it made the hairs on my neck stand up.

"My greetings, Major Bhaajan," Prince Dayjarind said.

Jar stared at me. "Gods almighty."

I couldn't believe it, either. "He has no access to any mesh outside the palace. No way could he send me a letter."

"Major," the EI said. "Do you wish me to play the recording or would you prefer to continue arguing with your visitor?"

"You know," Jak said, "that EI can be annoying."

"No kidding." To the EI, I said, "Keep playing it."

"I would like to thank you, Major," Dayj continued.

"I am unfamiliar with public meshes, so please excuse my clumsiness if I break protocols. This is the first message I've ever sent."

"He sounds a lot better," Jak said.

"He does." Dayj's voice had lost its hoarse desperation.

"I have had many talks with my family," Dayj went on. "As a result, next year I will attend school, probably Imperial University on Parthonia if I pass the entrance exams. My uncle is a psychology professor there, so I can live with him and his family."

Holy freaking blazes. I gaped at Jak. "He's going to college?" I wished I could have been a beetle-bot in the room during *that* negotiation with his family. "That's incredible."

"Maybe they finally woke up," Jak said.

"Aunt Vaj isn't happy with the decision," Dayj was saying. "But she has given me the blessing of Majda. Her decision to accept it apparently has something to do with a conversation she had with you. Whatever you said, thank you."

Jak cocked an eyebrow at me. "You talking tough with Majda?"

"I said a few things."

"You got a suicide wish, Bhaaj."

I winced. "Just ornery."

"I must go." Dayj's voice lightened. "I look forward to the future. Please also give my thanks to your friend, the man with the jeeper. May you be well, Major Bhaajan. I wish you the best."

Then the room was silent.

"This is a good thing," Jak said.

I smiled. "Who would've thought?"

He scowled. "It shouldn't have taken almost losing him forever to make them wake up and realize he had to go."

"Sometimes you have to take risks." I went over and clasped his hands, a gesture of affection unusual for me, to say the least. He looked flustered. I said, "Come with me. You don't have to stay here, running your damn casino. You could do so much more."

"I like running my damn casino." He didn't drop my hands, though.

"Haven't you ever wanted to see new places? Travel? Go to the stars?" I knew from the spark of interest in his eyes that he hadn't lost that desire. Wanderlust.

"A whole universe is out there for you to conquer," I said.

His wicked grin flashed. "I would, you know."

Gods he was sexy when he smiled. "Worth a try," I said.

"Got no job offworld."

"Find one."

He laughed. "What, no offer to make me a kept man, Bhaaj? Damn, woman, you can afford it. Majda made you sinful rich."

I flushed. It was true, this morning a sum of credit even greater than I expected had appeared in my bank account. I just said, "Figured you wouldn't want that."

"I don't." In a gruffer voice than usual, he added, "Makes a difference that you knew."

"Enough to come with me?"

"You know the answer." After a moment, he said, "Might visit, though."

He had never made that offer before. "I'd like that."

He spoke dryly, "Got Braze's people after me. It's

a good time to fold up the Black Mark for a while." His eyes gleamed. "Maybe open it somewhere else."

"Jak," I warned. He had better not try that in Selei City.

He laughed, deep and full. "I swear, those glares of yours could incinerate a man." His smile became something gentler, much more frightening than his grin, something that almost looked like love. "Just a visit, while things cool down here. Later—we'll see."

"Major, I have another message incoming," the EI interrupted.

Saints almighty. "Who is it?" I growled.

"Chief Takkar."

"Tell her I'm not here."

"The chief is aware that you are here," the EI said. "Also, the message is top priority."

Tough. I didn't work for the Majdas anymore. I didn't have to answer their police chief. Then again, this was Majda. Best not to piss them off.

"Put her on comm," I said. "Audio only." Let her chomp on that.

Takkar's curt voice snapped into the air. "Major, you can't leave the city."

"I've a flight out later tonight," I said. "I plan on being on it."

"If it were up to me," Takkar said, "I'd put you on that flight myself. But this comes from the Matriarch in her capacity as General of the Pharaoh's Army. In other words, it's an ISC order."

I stiffened. "Why? What's going on?"

Takkar spoke grimly. "Those weapons you found were slated for a Trader spy, part of an interstellar ring of weapons dealers. Which means this has gone from a personal matter to one of ISC security." She sounded like she had bitten into a sour fruit. "In the time between when you found the cache and our people arrived, the crates disappeared. General Majda is putting together a team to find out what the hell is going on down there." With a disgust almost as great as when she talked about Trader spies, she added, "And you're on the team."

BOOK II

Beneath the Vanished Sea

XI

The Grotto

I had liked being in the army. It suited me, especially after I made the supposedly impossible jump from the enlisted to officer ranks. I liked being out of the army even better; I preferred to be my own boss. But my years in ISC had given me an education, a resume, and skills I'd never have learned as a dust rat. A life.

I could have said no to General Majda. I was a civilian now. My reasons for considering the job weren't only because angering Majda was a lousy idea; it also had to do with honor and yes, gratitude. Down undercity, you didn't talk about emotions. Admitting them was weakness, and weaknesses got you killed. I couldn't say how I felt about what the army had done for my life, but I could show it. Besides, someone had to provide a link between ISC and the undercity, and far better me than Takkar. So I went to General Majda's meeting about the smuggled weapons.

We convened in the Selei Building, a skyscraper in downtown Cries with a spacious lobby partitioned by glass panels. The tower served as a conference center, purportedly for any group that wished to reserve the space. Given that the only symbols in the lobby came from branches of the military, and that the tower was named after Lahaylia Selei, the Pharaoh of the Skolian Imperialate, I had a good guess as to what "any group" meant. The seal of the Pharaoh's Army dominated the back wall, a striking ruby pyramid.

The walls had smaller emblems of the other branches of ISC: the ancient sailing ship of the Imperial Fleet; a Jag starfighter from the J-Force, the elite fighter pilots of ISC; and the two crossed stalks of grain of the Advance Services Corps. My branch of ISC, the Pharaoh's Army, had the longest history, six millennia of service to the empires birthed by Raylicon. As an enlisted woman, I had served in the troops fighting Trader forces, and as an officer I had led those troops.

A receptionist sat at the gleaming counter in the lobby, a man rather than a robot, and he had my security badge ready. I rode a titanium lift to the forty-second floor. The conference center had glass walls, letting me see inside as I stepped out of the lift. Men and women filled the room, talking or drinking kava, most in green army uniforms, but some in Fleet blue, the russet of ASC, or the black leathers of fighter pilots. It didn't surprise me that General Majda wasn't there; she had probably gone offworld to ISC headquarters. I did see Lavinda, with the gold colonel's bars glinting on her shoulders.

Max, I thought as I walked into the conference room. *How many people are here?*

Fifteen, he answered. **Counting you.**

With so many officers involved, the smuggling ring had to be a lot bigger than just Scorch's operation. I didn't know anyone in the room except Lavinda. She glanced at me and inclined her head. I appreciated that; subtle, no overt attention, but an acknowledgement that I had shown up.

She rapped a laser gavel on the oval table that filled much of the room. "If you'd all take your seats, we can get started."

The higher brass sat at the table and the rest of us took chairs against the wall. A woman in Fleet blue sat on my right, and a fellow in an unmarked shirt and trousers settled on my left. He glanced at me with a slight smile and I nodded, relieved I wasn't the only civilian. Given the way he held himself, though, with the telltale upright posture, he had almost surely once been an officer. Majda made no bones about who they wanted to work for them.

Unfortunately, these were also the people least likely to find anything in the undercity. Yes, they could walk the arid canals and map the caverns. But the dust gangs, cyber-riders, drug punkers, and everyone else in our complicated, convoluted population would remain ciphers, hiding, watching, avoiding, or mugging the intruders in their domain.

Lavinda began with a description of what I already knew and added what they had found since yesterday. "Apparently this woman Scorch intended to sell those stolen arms to ESComm," she said. "We don't believe the Traders yet have the technology used by our latest generation of carbines or tanglers, so the smugglers were selling military secrets as well as weapons."

An angry murmur went through the room. I agreed. "ESComm" meant Eubian Space Command. In other words, the Trader military. Scorch had committed treason, and the moment she betrayed the Imperialate, I stopped seeing her as a civilian. She became an enemy combatant.

I had seen the torture rooms kept by Trader Aristos, the pavilions where they took pleasure in making their slaves scream. Every person in their empire was property, everyone on hundreds of worlds and habitats, all except roughly two thousand Aristos. Those Aristos owned everything: people, government, industry, military. A few thousand of them couldn't control trillions of people with only brutality, and many slaves lived relatively normal lives. But none had freedom. If any group did revolt, the Aristos wiped out the entire population. Better to commit genocide than risk an uprising. ISC had sent me to stop the slaughter on one such world, but we arrived too late. Heat-bar sterilization. Nothing remained of the colony. No people. No plants. No animals. Nothing. Two billion people had once lived there, and the Traders had slaughtered them all.

I hoped Scorch was rotting in hell.

Lavinda continued, setting up the Raylicon arm of the task force investigating what was apparently an interstellar smuggling ring. Eventually she turned to me. "Major Bhaajan."

I straightened up. "Yes, ma'am?"

"Your assignment," she said, "is to find out what you can from the undercity."

The cavern was empty.

The last time I had been here, crates had filled the cave. Someone had heisted them between the time when Jak and I helped Prince Dayj out of the Maze and when the Majda police arrived. Whoever moved the crates couldn't have been far away during my shootout with Scorch, because they had grabbed the crates so fast. They must have witnessed the fight, yet for some reason they let me and Jak leave with Dayj.

I studied the scrape marks on the ground where crates had stood the last time I came here. *Max, can you analyze the erosion of these tracks? I'd like to know how long ago they were made.*

I need more light. IR wavelengths are too long for a good analysis.

I turned on my stylus and the darkness receded. *Better?*

Yes. After a pause, he said, **Based on the sharpness of their edges, I'd say they were made within minutes after you left here with Prince Dayjarind yesterday.**

I rubbed my chin. These were the only tracks, which implied no one else used this cave besides Scorch. So why did I feel otherwise right now? I was sure I wasn't alone.

Crank up my hearing, I thought. It was quiet enough that the magnification wouldn't hurt my ears. I stood listening . . . yes, there it was again, a rustle at the far wall of the cavern. Half-broken cones of rock jutted up there, some taller than me, others no higher than my knee. Plenty of cover.

Someone is hiding in the back of the cave, I thought.

I might be detecting breathing, Max thought.

Might?

It's hard to tell with the irregular terrain. The texture is chaotic, almost like a fractal in rock. It reflects sound.

Interesting comparison with the fractals. Max's evolution constantly surprised me. *It's someone small,* I thought.

A child perhaps.

A child. I sat on the flat top of a cone, facing sideways so I wasn't staring at the chaotic back wall. I could still see it in my side vision. I shrugged off my pack and took out my lunch, two meat sandwiches rolled up in pancakes and soaked with pizo sauce. My kept my holstered gun on the side of my body away from the back of the cave.

"Got food," I said, lapsing into dialect. I set one of my meat rolls on a nearby rock stump and went about eating the other roll.

A small figure crept out of shadows. I couldn't see her clearly in my side vision, but it looked like she had tousled black hair and wore clothes that had turned gray. She could have been me at eight or nine. She inched forward, grabbed the meat roll, and scuttled back into the shadows.

I kept eating.

After a moment, I said, "Got water." I took two snap-bottles out of my pack, broke the seal on one, and put the other on the stump. Then I took a long swig of the cool water in my bottle.

The girl came out again, a little bolder this time. She walked over, put her hand on the snap-bottle, and stood looking at me, defiant.

I regarded her. "Clean water," I added. It was a valuable commodity here.

She glanced at my holster. "Got gun."

Now that I could see her better, I realized she was older than I'd first thought, eleven maybe. Her clothes were clean, and someone had repaired the worst tears. Wild hair tumbled over her shoulders, ragged but well-washed and brushed. Her dark eyes seemed too large for her face.

"Not shoot you," I said.

"Killed Scorch." She was clenching the neck of the snap-bottle.

"Scorch screwed up," I said. To put it mildly.

"You screwed up." She swept up the bottle and ran back into the shadows like wind whistling past the outcroppings. The sound of her retreat faded within seconds.

That went well, Max thought dryly.

At least she showed herself.

Did you come here to find dust rats?

I shook my head, on odd response given that I was conversing with an EI via a node in my spine. His question bothered me. It didn't seem right for an EI to call our children rats.

Not really, I thought. *But duster kids go everywhere here. They could probably tell me a lot.*

Good luck with that, Max thought. **You'll need it.**

Yeah, I know. I wouldn't have told me squat either, when I had lived here.

In any case, right now, I had someone else to find.

Gourd took his name from the gourdex vines that grew in the Vanished Sea, one of the few plants that thrived in that wasteland. They were muscular reeds, big and low the ground. Their gourds held moisture, and their tendrils dug deep into the desert, mining fresh water. The human Gourd filtered water. In our youth, he had been part of my dust gang, along with

Jak and Dig, the girl who freed me from the orphanage. The four of us grew up together, inseparable, as tight as a fist holding gold swag. But now? I had no idea if Gourd would even talk to me.

The Grotto wasn't the only body of water in the aqueducts, but it ranked as the largest, a lake fifty meters across, far underground. The brackish water was undrinkable, poisonous to those foolish or desperate enough to swallow too much. Gourd built equipment to make the water drinkable. He bartered for parts with the cyber-riders who mined the garbage lines under Cries or stole tech-mech from shops on the Concourse. Every generation here produced wizards who drew miracles out of dilapidated, mismatched tech-mech. Gourd put together low-pressure distillation machines, reverse-osmosis devices, or super-filters. He had a knack. That was what we had said. *Gourd has a knack.* I knew now it was far more than "a knack." He was a brilliant engineer, better than even most professional technologists in Cries.

The Grotto lay deep, four levels below the city, in complete darkness. I wore my stylus around my neck, creating a sphere of light. Crusted minerals on the nearby rocks glittered like a million spark-flies, red and blue, with accents in white, green, and purple. Lacy rock formations surrounded the water, stone columns riddled with holes, small and large. Max was right, they did resemble fractals repeating their patterns at ever finer detail.

I sat on a rock stump by the lake and fooled with my stylus, shining it across the dark water. The grotto was eerily silent, just my breathing and the drip of water somewhere. Memories poured through me.

One of my closest friends had drunk from this lake when we were both six. She nearly died. Back then, our circle had included a dust gang in their twenties, and they took care of her. She recovered, but I never forgot the terror of seeing her lying in the dark, shaking with illness.

Another memory came, this from the only time the Cries police had actually ventured all the way down here on one of their raids. They scooped up duster kids and hauled them off to Cries. The children trickled back to the aqueducts over the next year, bringing tales of holding cells and work farms. We celebrated their return to freedom. The irony didn't escape me, that we rejoiced in having a tougher life here than what they had left behind. The farms were hard labor, yes, cheaper to use children rather the bots to bring in water mined from the beneath the desert. Even so. They fed you regularly and didn't ask for more than a person could give. I had probably worked harder in my army training than I would have on a farm. But who cared? It wasn't freedom, and that lack destroyed us, parching our spirit like the dry air of the desert.

In the undercity, we came of age with our bitterly won freedom and the emotional scars it bequeathed us. Yes, we lived in caves and the ancient ruins of a dead civilization, and we used canals as throughways instead of roads, but it was a community, *our* community, not a slum, as they called us in Cries. The undercity was unique. In all my travels, I had never seen another culture like this one. Our world had its own beauty, one as haunting as the reed music that often drifted through the canals, those ancient melodies played by some unseen piper.

Rattles came from my right. A pair of eyes gleamed in the light over there, behind a pillar of stone. As soon as I looked at them, they disappeared with a scraping noise.

I set one of my snap-bottles on a nearby shelf of rock crusted with minerals salts. "Got water," I said. "Three bottles."

My voice echoed in the dark spaces of the Grotto. I pulled the half-empty bottle out of my pack and took a swig of water. Then I sat holding it, my boots braced against a cavern floor thick with minerals. The snap-bottle I had left on the ledge caught glints from my stylus and gleamed in the darkness.

"Got trade," I said to the empty air. "Water. Gourd."

Silence.

After a while, Max thought, **This is getting you nowhere.**

Be patient, I thought.

It's been twenty minutes.

This can't be rushed.

Someone is going to attack you for those bottles.

They're kids, Max.

That makes no difference.

I can defend myself. But they won't attack.

Why not?

It's not how these things work. I hoped I was still right about that.

Rustles came from the rocks all around me. I continued to sit.

A deep voice abruptly spoke behind me. "You got light."

I glanced around. "Heya, Gourd."

He walked into the light, a huge, muscular man

with graying temples, and leaned his bulk against a nearby column with his brawny arms crossed. He wasn't dressed as a "tourist" anymore, but in his natural clothes, a black muscle shirt and heavy trousers with a knife sheathed on his belt.

A boy ran forward and grabbed the bottle I had left on the ledge, then retreated back into the shadows. I took out two more snap-bottles and set them on the ledge. I had promised them three.

Gourd watched me. "Good snap," he said.

I nodded. Two girls ran out and grabbed the bottles. They glanced at me, then darted away.

I smiled slightly at Gourd. "You got fast dusters."

"They don't trust gifts."

"Not gifts. Bargain. Water for you."

"So you got me."

I indicated a nearby ledge. "Come sit."

He considered me, his dark gaze impossible to read. Then he pushed away from the column and went to sit on the ledge.

"So," he said. "You want to talk?"

"About Majda."

His expression became even more shuttered, if that was possible. "Majda got nothing here."

"They got trouble," I said. "Scorch committed treason."

He gave a sharp wave of his hand. "We're not the military, Bhaaj. Not our concern."

I heard the suppressed anger in his voice. He had always thought I betrayed the dust gang when I enlisted. I didn't know if he would ever forgive me.

"It is our concern," I said. "Scorch has no honor."

"Scorch has no life. You killed her."

That sounded like Gourd, as blunt as always. His face showed no emotion, but I could still read him even after all these years. He didn't regret Scorch's death. She had been bad enough in our youth, and time had only deepened her psychotic view of the universe.

"She was selling weapons to slavers," I said.

He stiffened. "To the Traders?"

"Traders, yah. Maybe sell people, too." She had broken our unspoken code to protect one another, and she upset our uneasy balance with Cries, drawing their attention to the undercity.

Gourd's voice darkened. "So Majda is coming here."

"Not yet," I said. "They sent me."

"You got to warn Jak."

"He already knows."

"What did he say?"

"Close up the Black Mark for a while."

Gourd pushed his hand through his shaggy hair. "Why are you telling me?"

"You know the dusters." He kept the children supplied with water.

He frowned at me. "Dust rats won't help Majda."

A sudden anger surged in me. "Not *rats,*" I said. "Rats are vermin. Dust gangs are children. Human children."

He spoke quietly. "Yah."

I was a dust rat. That identity would be forever ingrained in my psyche, my heart, my soul. Nothing would heal the scars, no matter how many high-end clients I served, no matter how many credits I accumulated.

Except I did have money now. "We got to do something for the kids."

He regarded me warily. "Do what?"

"Make their lives better."

Anger crackled in his voice. "Don't want charity."

"Oh, fuck that." I was tired of putting pride before sanity. "We'll find a way."

For a long time he was silent, and I was sure I had pushed too far.

Then he said, "What way?"

Good question. The Cries authorities would say we needed schools for our children and jobs for the adults. They refused to see we already had both. We learned from doing, from knowledge passed down generation to generation. The cyber-riders were engineers and neural-mech surgeons who passed their knowledge orally and in their circuits. Older gangs taught younger ones how to fight. We learned architecture, history, and anthropology from living in these ruins and manipulating them to fit our lives, and biochemistry so we could grow edible plants in dust and mineral-heavy water. The list of subjects went on an on. I had never realized how much natural knowledge I had accumulated until I left the undercity.

Adults found the work they chose, not what Cries told us that we should want, cyber-riders with their tech-mech, dust farmers growing food, crafters designing goods, caregivers looking after children, and yeah, even Jak with his casino, which employed a substantial number of people. We traded services and goods rather than buying or selling. Even if my people wanted above-city jobs, no one in Cries would hire a "slum rat," and trying to remake us into the above-city's idea of proper citizens would destroy the heart of this place. Life here could be harsh, but our heart beat like drum, strong and firm.

So what would improve life here? What worked for me wasn't for everyone, indeed probably not for many. I had succeeded in the army because I wanted it so much, the desire to do well burned within me. I doubted most of my people would share my passion for a job that imposed so many constraints on their lives, and without that fire, they weren't likely to survive in ISC.

Maybe the best idea was to start simple. So I said, "Water."

Gourd motioned at the lake. "We got water."

I snorted. "We got lethal shit."

He shrugged. "I fix it."

An idea was forming in my mind. "You need good equipment. Good tech."

He met my words with silence, but at least he didn't refute them.

"Dunno," I said. "Scorch had a big operation. Maybe she left some tech behind." In truth, whoever stole Scorch's crates had taken everything. But if some high-end desalination equipment happened to appear in one of her caverns, top-notch machinery that wouldn't easily degrade, fail, or corrode, who was to say where it came from?

Gourd considered me. "Might send some rats to look." He stopped, then said, "Might send some *gangers* to look."

I nodded. "Gangers" at least acknowledged the children's humanity. "Tomorrow," I said. I needed time to find good desalination equipment.

He stood up. "Maybe."

I rose to my feet. Maybe. That meant we had no bargain unless he later decided to accept the equipment. I had hoped he would tell me more about Scorch's operation, but he left no openings for me to ask. I wanted to say so much to him. *Don't be angry, Gourd. I miss you all.* Of course I couldn't speak those words. It was weakness.

"Gourd—" I hesitated.

He watched me warily. "Yah?"

"What do you hear from Dig?"

"She has her own circle now."

"Alive, then?"

He nodded. "Alive."

The tension in my shoulders eased. Alive. All four of us had survived, which wasn't always the case with dust gangs. When all this was over, maybe I could find her.

Gourd took off, but just before he disappeared into the inky shadows, he turned around.

"Bhaaj," he said.

I tried to make out his face in the darkness. "Yah?"

"Scorch also used the Alcove. I don't know why." He paused. Information was never truly free. After a moment, he added, "Maybe my gangers will find some tech-mech there tomorrow, heh? A good bargain."

With that, he was gone.

XII
Lavinda

Colonel Lavinda Majda resembled a younger version of her sister the Matriarch, but with a different quality that was hard to define. She wasn't more willowy than Vaj and not quite as tall, but still with that familiar upright carriage. She exuded the confidence of someone who didn't even realize she was self-assured. I knew I was in the presence of a damn good officer when I spoke with her, but she lacked some indefinable edge that Vaj possessed. Lavinda seemed more human.

We stood in a sun-drenched chamber on an upper floor of the palace. Light poured through the many arched windows and pooled on a floor of interlocking tiles designed from blue stone that people mined out of the dead seas. I had grown up breathing the dust of those rocks, but no trace of grit showed in these polished tiles that paved the floor in graceful mosaics.

Lavinda was doing the Majda thing, standing at the window, looking out at the view with her hands clasped behind her back. I wondered if she realized what a luxury she owned, that she could stay here as long as she pleased, flooded with sunlight, staring at the mountains.

I spoke. "Colonel Majda, my greeting."

Lavinda turned to me. "Ah. Major." She inclined her head. "Thank you for coming."

I hadn't thought I had a choice. A summons from Majda, no matter how politely phrased, was still a summons. "Did you want an update on my investigation?"

"If you have anything to report."

It had only been two days, but it seemed a good idea to give her something. "Scorch may have had another base of operations in the aqueducts, one we didn't know about."

"May?" She came over with her easy, long-legged stride. "You haven't checked?"

"That's where I was headed." I would already be there if she hadn't called me to the palace.

She considered me. "Chief Takkar says you continue to shroud your movements."

"That's right."

The colonel waited. I had nothing more to say.

After an awkward silence, Lavinda said, "Major, I understand why you feel the need." Dryly she added, "I would be an idiot if I didn't."

"Idiot" was the last word I expected to hear from a Majda in a sentence about herself. Lavinda was definitely different from Vaj. I said only, "I'm better able to do my job that way."

"I know." With a tired exhale, she pushed her hand through her hair, leaving the short locks tousled. "I cannot, however, speak for the task force commanders at HQ."

Undoubtedly she meant her sister, who was offworld,

heading up the main investigation at ISC headquarters. "Is there a problem?"

Lavinda began pacing. "From what we've learned, Scorch's operation was a minor part of a much more substantial smuggling operation centered elsewhere than Raylicon. It looks like she simply offered a way station they could use to pass through with their goods."

On the surface, that made sense. Something felt wrong, but I didn't see what, not yet. "I'll let you know if I discover anything."

Lavinda nodded, preoccupied. She stopped at the window and resumed her Majda stare at the mountains. This was getting us exactly nowhere. I went over and joined her at the window. "It sounds like the major work of the investigation is taking place offworld."

"Most."

I waited with her, all agaze at the mountains. Sure, they were nice to look at, those majestic peaks of blue and red stone. But still. Why stare at them so much?

"It's meditative," Lavinda said. "It calms my mind so I can think more clearly."

Ho! I stepped back, staring at her. "Why did you say that?"

She turned to me. "You wondered why I liked to look at the mountains."

My pulse stuttered. "How could you know that?"

"You practically shouted it."

No, I had not practically shouted it. I had not practically whispered it. I had not spoken one freaking word.

"I can't usually get thoughts," Lavinda said. "Most of the time, I only sense moods."

Sweat beaded on my forehead. "You're a psion."

"An empath," she said. "I'm a bit of a telepath, but I can only pick up unusually strong thoughts, and even then, only if a person is close by." She was watching me closely. "You shield your mind well. Usually I can't read you at all. You relaxed here for a few moments."

Well, shit. No, I couldn't think that. She might pick it up. But she said I had shields. Damn right. I was no expert on psions, but even I knew that most people raised natural barriers to protect their minds without even realizing it. In the army, we had learned methods to strengthen and control those barriers. I imagined an iron wall ten feet thick clanging down to protect my mind.

Lavinda winced. "That much force isn't necessary."

I spoke carefully. "I'd heard that some royals were psions." I hadn't ever really believed it, though. The words *empathy* and *Majda* seemed incongruous.

"It varies," Lavinda said. "I'm the only full psion in our family. Both of my sisters show traces, as did our parents and most of our children. Dayj and his father are full empaths."

That was one little fact the EI at my penthouse had neglected to mention when I asked about the Majda husbands. No wonder Dayj's mother had married Ahktar. Empaths were rare, less than one in a million. Someone with Lavinda's ability was probably one in a ten billion. How very nice for the Majdas, that life bestowed them with yet another advantage over the rest of the universe. Like they needed more.

Don't, I told myself. Resenting the Majdas served no useful purpose.

Don't what? Max asked.

Nothing. I needed to be more careful. It was odd Lavinda said I had dropped my defenses. It was true, though, I did feel a bit more relaxed with her than I did with her sisters or Chief Takkar.

After several moments of me pondering, Lavinda gave a wry smile. "You're an unusual one."

I blinked. "I am?"

"Very few people can stand in silence with me. Most get nervous and talk to fill the empty space. You don't."

"You like that?" She had smiled. Sort of.

The colonel spoke dryly. "I don't need people to tell me what they think I want to hear. They fill up my hours with useless words."

Even after I had learned to converse in the above-city style rather than the abbreviated dialect of the aqueducts, I'd never been one for much talk. However, I did need answers, especially after her cryptic comment about offworld task force commanders. "We should talk more," I said. "Why did you say we have a problem with the taskforce?"

"They want me to send troops into the aqueducts," Lavinda said. "The exact wording on the communiqué I received was 'Clean up the blasted place.'"

Damn. "Colonel, if you send down soldiers, my people will hide, not only themselves but anything useful we could hope to find." They were experts at disappearing. Like Jak. He could close up his casino in less than an hour, and even I couldn't find him. "They'll scatter into the dark. You'll never find what you're looking for."

Her voice cooled. "I have full ISC resources, Major. We can rout out anyone or anything."

I doubted she had any idea how much stolen tech-mech was floating around the undercity, including from the military. I couldn't say that, so I gave her another truth. "If you do track people down, what will that achieve? No one will talk to the military. You'd have to interrogate citizens who've done nothing wrong, and they couldn't give you a good picture even if you did. I doubt my people even know how much they know. You need someone who can convince them to trust her with enough pieces of the puzzle that she can assemble it into a coherent whole."

"That person being you, I assume?"

"That's right."

She watched me with one of those appraising Majda stares. "Very well, Major. I will give you three more days. Beyond that, I need results or we do it my way."

Three days to stop a disaster. ISC wouldn't see their attempts to "clean up the slums" as a threat, but they didn't know my people. Families would hide. Children would flee. Gangs would stalk the shadows, ready to explode. The drug punkers would arm themselves. If ISC went into the undercity with force, my people would fight back. It could only end in violence and death.

"Major?" Lavinda was watching me with that unsettling scrutiny, except now I understood. She was trying to read my mood. I imagined the barrier still protecting my mind.

"Three days," I said. "I can work with that." It wasn't enough, but it was better than nothing.

We took our leave of each other then, but just as I reached the arched exit of the room, Lavinda said, "Major, wait."

Puzzled, I turned around. "Yes?"

She was standing by the window, facing me in the

streaming sunlight. "Your army records say that you lived as a 'feral child' before you enlisted. What does that mean?"

My shoulders tensed. "Probably that children run in packs in the undercity."

Lavinda frowned. "And their parents let them do this? Why aren't they in school?"

Gods. She had no clue. "We learn, just differently." My voice cooled. "Even if children in the aqueducts wanted a formal education, no Cries school would take them." I'd heisted my education, sneaking access to the most elite virtual schools by shadowy pathways few people knew existed. I learned enough to get me into the army, and once there I enrolled in every class they had available to recruits. I'd studied in a fury, making up for all those years of eking out an education from a system denied to us.

Lavinda blinked. "None of our schools will take undercity students?"

"None," I said flatly. I had tried every blasted one.

She said, "I understand you were part of a gang."

"That's right." Was that supposed to justify denying me an education?

"Where were your parents?"

"I don't know."

She frowned. "Some records must exist. Where were you born?"

"The Down-deep." I was lapsing into dialect, even knowing I should use above-city speech with a Majda. It was instinctual defense against her questions.

"The what deep?" she asked.

"Down."

"What did you say?"

"Born under the aqueducts."

"Then how did you end up in the orphanage?"

"Someone left me there." I did not want this conversation with a Majda. Not now. Not ever.

"The orphanage must have records of your family."

"Nahya."

Her forehead furrowed. "What?"

Above-city, I told myself. *Talk like her.* "No," I said. "They have no records of my parents."

"How long were you there?"

"Three years."

She looked frustrated. "Did someone adopt you?"

"No. I ran away."

"At *three* years old?"

"Yes. With an older girl." I clenched my fist, then realized what I was doing and forced my hand to relax. "This is all in my army files."

"I'd like to hear what you have to say."

"Nothing to say."

"How did you and the other girl live on your own?"

"With other rats." Damn! I'd sworn never use that word again.

Her forehead furrowed. "Other what?"

"Other children."

She spoke carefully. "My understanding is that very few children live in the slums. The authorities in Cries collect the younger ones and find them better homes. They've had less success with the gang down there."

"Gangs."

"There's more than one?"

Gods, she had no clue. "Kids form groups. It's a support system, especially for those without enough to eat."

"I hadn't realized." She hesitated. "Maybe we could help."

You bloody think so? I held back the angry words.

Think what? Max asked.

Nothing. Gods. Now both Max and Majda wanted access to my brain.

I believe she genuinely wants to understand, Max thought.

I didn't know what to make of Lavinda's interest. If I said nothing, I might lose the chance to help my people deal with their unrelenting poverty. If I screwed this up, though, ISC would send in troops or take away our children.

I spoke with care. "Colonel, the undercity is a valued community to its people. They don't want it torn apart." She would understand community, being part of two that were close-knit, the military and aristocracy. "But they could use help. For one thing, the children need better food."

She rubbed her chin. "I thought someone ran a soup kitchen down on the Concourse."

That was news to me. "Who?"

"I'm not sure. It's been there several years, I think."

A soup kitchen. It was a generous idea, but my people would never go. They hated anything with a whiff of charity, besides which, they'd believe the kitchen was a place to trap kids so the Cries authorities could haul them off to the orphanage. Which for all I knew might be true. Nor were they likely to visit the Concourse openly, with all its lights and crowds, especially given that vendors or the police might shoot at them.

"I'm sure it's a nice place," I said.

Lavinda was studying me again. "Major, I'm not your enemy."

Of course she wasn't my enemy. We both were loyal to ISC and the Imperialate. Except I knew that wasn't what she meant. The idea that an aristocrat might actually care what happened under the city was so hard to process, my brain wanted to shut down.

Careful, Max thought. **You might not like her solutions to the problems you both see. But, Bhaaj, she could help. You have to figure out what you want and convince her to do it your way instead of sending in troops.**

I don't know what I want. Not yet. I spoke with difficulty. "Colonel, it's hard for me to talk about my youth. But I appreciate your interest in helping. Give me some time to think about answers to your questions and let's talk again."

"I understand." She inclined her head. "Take all the time you need."

After that I really did take my leave, and I was glad to escape the palace. I didn't yet know how to absorb this latest development. A Majda had taken a personal interest in the undercity.

What would that mean?

XIII
Memory

The Alcove was in the Down-deep, several levels below the Maze where Scorch had locked up Dayj. No passages led there; you had to ease your way past stone walls and outcroppings. You wouldn't find the Alcove without previous knowledge, luck, or just plain cussed determination. I'd found it when I was ten. I had decided to memorize the Maze, and I stayed with the project until I could go places few people knew existed. Over the years, though, the pathway had changed. I wasn't sure today if it become more encrusted with minerals or I was just bigger, but I had a hard time squeezing between the walls and rocky cones, especially with my backpack stuffed by the jammer and filtration equipment.

The Alcove, however, didn't look much different than I remembered. Smaller, maybe. It was a few meters across with no real open space, just rock formations sticking up or hanging from the ceiling. I set up my desalination equipment next to the only section with a solid wall rather than a lacework of rock. I had bought the best apparatus available for personal use in homes. The heavy-duty get-ups used by the city would have been better, but I'd need a license to purchase anything that big, and those permits weren't easy to come by. Regardless, Gourd could perform magic with this little gem.

While I worked, I brooded on my talk with Lavinda. I'd always be on guard with her now, knowing she could feel my moods if I slipped up. And yet it was true, I was more comfortable with her than with the other Majdas. That empaths felt other people's moods wasn't the same as saying they empathized with people, but the two traits often seemed to go together.

I knew about psions from the army; ISC tested every soldier for the traits. Telepaths could access the Kyle, a universe where physics as we knew it had no meaning. The constraints imposed by the speed of light didn't apply there. Your thoughts determined your "distance" from someone else; think a similar thought and you were next to each other regardless of your location in real space. Telepaths didn't enter the Kyle, they accessed it with their minds. Once there, they could communicate across interstellar distances with no delay.

At least, we of the Skolian Imperialate communicated that way. The Traders and the Allied Worlds of Earth couldn't use the Kyle webs unless we gave them access. The Traders had a bigger military, one better armed than ISC, but we had better communications. We were faster. With that advantage, we just barely held our own against them. That advantage came from the Ruby Dynasty, the strongest psions known. Only Ruby psions could power the Kyle web; it would kill anyone without their mental strength. Four of them existed, five if you counted Roca Skolia's new husband, who supposedly descended from the ancient Ruby dynasty even though he was a simple farmer. If he was a full Ruby psion, that explained the marriage. Nothing else mattered. The dynasty no longer ruled, but they were irreplaceable. They were the only reason we could use the Kyle.

Although only Ruby psions could build or maintain the Kyle web, any telepath with training could use the network. In fact, it took more of them than existed to keep the communications of an interstellar empire flowing. They were notoriously difficult to clone, impossible in the case of the Rubies. It made psions among the rarest, most valued resources of an empire. Without them, the Kyle web would disintegrate, and without it, we would fall to the relentless war machine of the Trader slave empire.

I didn't envy the Ruby Dynasty. They paid for their privileged lives with an inhumanely high price; they could never let up, not for a season, not for day, not for an hour. If they died, so did the Imperialate. Seen in that light, I didn't resent the Majdas, either. They had the responsibility to see that the Ruby Dynasty survived.

I couldn't solve the problems of an empire, but at least I could help people get clean water. I sat back, regarding my work on the filtering equipment. I'd set out the parts and ensured they worked according to spec, especially the osmosis membranes, which were the most sensitive. I didn't finish putting the equipment together, though. Gourd would decide what he wanted to do with the pieces, incorporating them into his wizard's creations.

I stood up, rubbing the small of my back. It seemed unlikely Gourd would send me here without a reason, but I saw nothing Scorch might have left in this place. I walked around the cave, stepping between the outcroppings. Nothing unusual showed, not on the floor, columns, or rippled stone curtains that formed partial walls. What had I missed?

Of course. The ceiling. Looking up, I saw a chaotic landscape of silicate icicles crusted with salts that glittered in the light of my stylus. Shadows filled in the crevices above me, sparkling here and there—but wait, that gleam looked different. I pulled off the stylus and reached my arm straight up, pointing the light at the silvery glint. It revealed a curve of metal, some round thing embedded in the rock up there.

"Huh." I hung the stylus back around my neck, then clambered up a rock formation and stood on its flat top. That brought me close enough to the ceiling that I could reach into the crevice. As I brushed away the crusted dirt and mineral salts on the silver curve, grit rained down on me.

Max, are you getting this? I thought.

Yes. Just keep the lenses in your eyes clear of the dirt.

I'd hope so. The silver curve looked like a fat pipe sticking out of the rock, its surface pitted with age. It wasn't metal, but a composite. I had seen that material in a few other places around the aqueducts, part of the ancient ruins. Although that was interesting, it told me nothing about what Scorch had wanted with a place as inconvenient as the Alcove.

How old is that pipe? I asked Max.

My spectral analysis suggests thousands of years.

It looks like part of the original City of Cries.

Probably. This cave is beneath those ruins.

I scanned my light over the symbols etched into the pipe. *Translate those glyphs.*

I can record them, Max thought. **However, I doubt my translation attempts would be useful. Neither anthropology nor ancient languages are among my specialties.**

He had a point. I had acquired Max to help me investigate crimes, not ancient civilizations. *Do what you can.* I should tell someone at the university about this pipe. Maybe Doctor Orin was still there, the anthropologist who had studied these ruins when I was a kid. He bribed me back then with cocoa bars to show him artifacts. Gods, I had loved those treats. Never mind that he should have given me healthy food instead.

I needed to wait, though, before I looked up Orin. He would come here to study the artifact, and right now I couldn't risk disturbing any evidence this place might reveal about Scorch.

After I returned to the aqueducts, I walked alone along a deep, narrow canal. Its walls had collapsed in several places, leaving ragged holes, as if the canal had frayed like an old shirt worn for too many years. I stopped, straining to hear a sound that barely registered on my senses, the distant rattle of pebbles.

Someone is following us, I thought.

It is hard to judge, given the echoes, Max answered. **But I believe they are on the other side of the wall and about fifty meters behind you.**

Send the green bot to spy on them.

A rustle came from my backpack as its flap lifted by my ear. The bot whisked out and darted into a crack in the wall.

I kept walking. After a moment, I caught a faint scraping from the other side of the wall.

Three women are stalking you, Max thought. **Two are carrying knives and the third has a laser carbine. They are wearing the insignia of a dragon-hawk. I believe that refers to the Kajada drug cartel.**

Well, shit.

Do you want me to do anything?

Keep the beetle spying on them. A thought came to me. *How'd you know about the cartel?*

It's in your memory files.

Those files are old. Like from my childhood.

The insignia is unchanged.

It didn't surprise me that the Kajada cartel had survived. Running drugs was as lucrative here as anywhere else, maybe even more so given the concentration of wealth in Cries. It was Raylicon's only modern city. The Abaj Tacalique, the traditional bodyguards of the Ruby Dynasty, lived in ruins far out in the desert, following a strict life of asceticism and military training, but they were the only other substantial community on the planet, and like Raylicon itself, they were dying out.

I continued along the midwalk, my ears so hypersensitized that they picked up a trickle of water far in the distance. Another scrape came from the other side of the wall.

They're getting closer, I thought.

Yes, Max said. **They are about four meters back now.**

My augmented hearing went into overdrive and

the noise became a rumble. One of the women was moving ahead, probably to come out in front of me. I knew the ploy; distract the target from the front while the others came in behind. Crafty thieves, eh? My pulse gun and jammer would be a goldmine for them, even worth killing for. My other supplies had value, too, especially the water, food, and tech. My climate-controlled leather jacket would be a real highlight. And gosh, here I was, all alone and unsuspecting. Idiots.

Hadn't they listened to the whisper mill that spread news in the aqueducts? Maybe they just felt like fighting. Cyber-riders depended on their brains and gangs mixed force and smarts. Neither group had bothered me. I wouldn't have messed with me either. Drug punkers, however, liked overt force. These punkers were too cocky, but that didn't mean they weren't also dangerous.

Up ahead on the midwalk, a woman stepped out from a crevice in the wall, dominating the pathway. She was nearly two meters tall and gods only knew how many kilos she packed of solid muscle. Beyond her, an old rock fall blocked the midwalk and spilled down into the canal.

She held a laser carbine aimed at me.

Combat mode on, Max thought.

The woman grinned at me like a dust wolf. "You're fucked, babe."

Yeah, right.

I jumped into the canal with enhanced speed, down a few meters. My node figured out how I needed to bend my legs to minimize the impact, and my augmented knees cushioned the landing. I ended up in a crouch, facing the midwalk with my pulse gun drawn and ready.

The other two drug runners were on the midwalk a few meters behind where I had been a moment ago. One of them yelled, her voice eerily distorted to my ears. All three punkers were turning in my direction. The girl with the carbine snarled and slowly brought her carbine to bear on me. Except she wasn't actually slow, she was whirling around with exceptionally fast reflexes.

I was faster.

I fired my gun, aiming to disable rather than kill. Under the force of my shot, the carbine flew out her hand and shattered against the wall. The EM pulse from my bullets didn't have enough range to affect me, but it ought to fry her electronics.

The other two punkers stood there gaping, obviously trying to figure out how I was suddenly on the floor of the canal. For freaking sake. They should at least throw their knives. They wouldn't hit me; my node was calculating trajectories based on their movements and fine-tuning my reflexes to avoid any projectiles they might heft my way. But still. Their reaction time sucked dust.

All those thoughts went through my head as I sprinted to the rockfall behind the punker whose gun I had pulverized. She turned, trying to follow my progress as I ran up the rock fall. The debris shifted under me, starting a miniature avalanche into the canal, but I was going fast enough to outrun its fall. By the time she finished turning, I was on the midwalk again, on the other side from where I had started, with the sliding mound of debris at my back and my gun gripped in both hands, aimed at her head.

The punker stared at me with her mouth open. Her hardened features made her look older, but I doubted she was more than eighteen, seven years shy of her majority according to Skolian law. Yeah, right, a kid. Down here she was a full adult. Her shirt left the lower half of her muscled torso bare, revealing silvery-black conduits in a star pattern on her hard-as-rock abdomen, and one of her arms looked like tech-mech. It wouldn't surprise me if she had been born without the arm and had stolen the parts to make the limb. Many of my people used implants to compensate for such problems. I hadn't realized until I took genetics classes in the army that the rate of birth defects was unusually high in the undercity. It was no wonder, given our inbred population. Hopefully my pulse gun had disabled whatever tech-mech she carried in her body. Beyond her, the other two girls stood staring at me.

I scowled at them. "You stupid shits."

They looked like cornered warriors poised to jump, but none of them moved a hair's breadth. One of the two girls farther back seemed familiar, though I couldn't figure out why. They hadn't been born when I left the aqueducts the first time, and they would have only been ten or eleven the last time I was here.

I called to the girls farther back on the walk. "You two. Get over here."

They came forward, wary and careful. The girl in front of me, the leader probably, tensed up, her fingers twitching.

I glanced at the knife on her belt. "Don't bother," I told her. "I can fire before you reach it."

She glared at me, but she relaxed her hand.

The other two joined her, and they stood like a trio

of surly war goddesses with a feral beauty, their hard abs showing though tears in their muscle shirts, the oil on their biceps gleaming in the light of my stylus.

The leader spoke. "You kill?"

"It's not worth the bother." I had no intention of killing anyone. They needed to learn better judgment, though. "Unless I get pissed again."

None of them had anything to say to that.

"You all punk for Kajada?" I asked.

"Maybe," the leader said.

"Jadix Kajada?" I asked. She had ruled the cartel with an iron hand during my day.

The leader spat to the side, her response a commentary on my question rather than the drug queen. "Jadix is dead. Long time."

"What Kajada then?" I asked. "Dig?" She had been Jadix's daughter, but she had run with our gang rather than with the punkers.

"Maybe." The leader frowned, obviously trying to figure out how I fit into her universe. And she did know Dig. I could read her tells. Not only hers; the other girls also knew who I meant. Damn. I had hoped Dig would find a better life than running a drug cartel. I doubted she knew what her punkers had just tried to pull. The code that bound Dig and me together was stronger than cartel ties, as strong as blood kin.

"You tell Dig," I said. "Tell her that Bhaaj said to cut the shit." I motioned with my gun. "Now go on. Get out of here."

They took off, sprinting back the way they had come. Within moments, they dodged into a crevice in the wall, knocking broken stone from its edges. Then I was alone again on the midwalk.

Combat mode off, I thought.

Toggled, Max said.

I set off again, thinking. So Dig had ended up in the family business after all. It hadn't been a given when we were young, and I had hoped she would find a different life. She had never much liked her mother, a drug queen who hadn't even shown up at the orphanage after the police caught Dig in one of their roundups. Instead of telling the authorities she was Dig's mother, Jadix had sent one of her punkers to smuggle supplies to her daughter. Why? So Dig would organize an escape at the mature age of five-freaking-years-old. Dig succeeded and took me with her, but she never forgave Jadix. It was why she had run with our dust gang instead of the punkers.

"Damn fool kids," I muttered. I wasn't sure if I meant us or drug punkers from today.

They aren't "kids," Max thought. **They are hardened criminals. That one with the rifle would have killed you for the gear you're carrying.**

It's all wrong, Max, I thought. *In another life their only worries would be what university they're going to attend.*

I doubt they have any interest in attending a university.

That's not the point.

Bhaaj, Max thought abruptly. **You have another stalker.**

I tilted my head, listening. Someone was breathing nearby. I concentrated, turning in a circle. Yes, it was there, inside another rockslide that blocked the path, where the rubble piled against the wall. A dark cavity showed near the ground, half-hidden. It didn't look big enough to hide a person, but when I pointed my stylus at it, the light drew a gleam from within. Crouching down, I peered into the hole. A small child stared at me with a frightened gaze.

I used a much gentler voice than when I spoke to the punkers. "Come out?"

He continued to stare at me.

"I won't hurt you," I said.

No answer.

Shrugging out of my pack, I sat down and took out my half-finished bottle of water. Setting it on the ground in front of the hole, I said, "Done with this. No room to carry it anymore."

A scrambling came from inside the hole, and a small boy crawled out, a fellow of about five. He sat on his haunches and picked up the bottle, peering at it with a furrowed brow. Then he looked at me. "Water?"

"Yah," I said. "Fresh water. You take."

He put the closed top of the bottle into his mouth and bit down hard. When the top cracked off, he spit it onto the path. Then he gulped down the liquid with barely a pause. After he finished, he put the bottle in the exact same place where I had set it down. He crouched there, all dirt smudges and ragged clothes, and waited.

I tapped my chest. "Bhaaj." We never freely gave out our names, but if he knew mine, he might give me his, especially at his young age.

He patted his chest. "Pack rat."

I titled my head at the rock fall that blocked the path. "Play in rocks?"

"Got no play." His dark eyes looked too big for his gaunt face.

"Who do you run with?"

"Got no run."

I wasn't sure what he meant. That he had no circle? Although he looked thin, he was alive, which at his age implied someone was taking care of him.

"Got gang?" I asked.

"Nahya."

"Got who?"

"None." He mouth worked as if he were struggling not to cry.

Damn. "What happened?"

"New yell make old yell go away."

"Who yell?"

"Old yell, gone. New yell make old yell go away."

It sounded like a turf fight. Someone must have run off his guardian, who for some reason had left this boy behind.

"Come with?" His chin quivered.

He looked so scared. "Yah," I said. "I go with." As I stood up, he scrambled to his feet. Gods, he didn't even come up to my waist.

I pointed to the snap-bottle and its broken top. "Take." We kept our spaces clean. No one else would take away the litter if we didn't ourselves, and contrary to what the above-city believed, the undercity was neither dirty nor a slum.

He gathered the litter. After a hesitation, he offered it to me.

I nodded as if he were grown up, adult to adult. Then I stuffed the junk into my backpack and shrugged back into the straps, settling the pack on my back.

We set off, headed deeper into the aqueducts.

✧ ✧ ✧

I heard the crying before we reached Pack Rat's home. We were two more levels down from where I had fought the punkers, walking along a narrow tunnel. The darkness was complete, pitch black except for the light from my stylus. The crying drifted through the tunnel, reedy and forlorn.

I looked at the boy at my side. "Who cries?"

He looked up at me with his frightened gaze. "New yell."

An unwelcome chill ran up my spine. I had thought I was walking into the middle of a turf war, but this sounded even worse. I suddenly wanted to leave, *needed* to leave. But I forced myself to keep going.

"Here." Pack Rat came to a halt.

I stopped, peering into the dark. The rough tunnel looked no different here than anywhere else. The crying was a little louder, but still faint with distance. Wait—yes, to the left, an opening showed in the wall, a crevice about two-thirds my height. The boy slipped through it. I squeezed after him, crouching down, and my pack caught on the upper edge. Pulling it free, I pushed through to the other side. The crying was louder now, not distant, I realized, but close by and weak.

As I straightened up, my head scraped the ceiling. I scanned my light across the small cave, and it played over wall hangings and carpets, all gracefully woven in gray, blue, black, and white threads. Someone had created them with loving attention. A filtration machine caught water dripping from in a niche in the wall and let filtered liquid trickle out of spouts on its other side. One stream ran into a planter filled with pizo stalks growing in modified dust. Piles of wrapped food were neatly stacked against a one wall. My light played over several balls on the floor, a stick doll, two music reeds, candles and a flint, blankets bunched up near the back—

Ah, gods, no.

The blankets half covered a young woman. I couldn't move. I stood there, my heart slamming in my chest, and for one moment I could think only of whirling around and running from this place, running and running until I couldn't think any longer.

I drew in a rasping breath. Then I went over and knelt by the woman. She looked as if she were sleeping, her gaunt face at peace. Her skirt covered her knees and legs. Blood soaked it and had dried into dark splotches. She had probably been dead less than a day.

A baby lay cradled in her arms, crying weakly.

Someone was whispering in a ravaged voice, the same words over and over, *Gods, oh gods, oh gods.* My voice, my whispers. I picked up the dying baby and she whimpered. My arms were shaking so hard, the child quieted as if I were rocking her. I wanted to scream, but I could only kneel there, my voice frozen in my throat.

Pack Rat came to my side and put his hand on the baby. "New yell." He looked at the woman and tears ran down his face. "Old yell. Much yell. Then no more."

Yelling. Birth. No child should go through what this boy must have witnessed, his mother's death while she brought his sister into the world. How could this have happened? Where the bloody hell were this woman's people, her circle? How could she have been alone here, dying in the dark?

Somehow I moved. I had no idea what I was doing. I slid down against the back wall holding the woman and her baby in my arms, and the boy against my side. Tears rolled down my face, tearing out of me, tearing me apart, Major Bhaajan, the ganger who never wept. I sat there rocking the mother and her children, crying for them—and for another baby who had been born in these tunnels decades ago, deep down in the dark.

I wept for my own mother, who had died in this same way, giving me birth.

XIV
Dig

Streamer-leaves hung from trees in the park and rustled as breezes stirred them under a sky rich with stars. I sat in a gazebo designed from an iridescent white lattice. Although the night had passed well into the first sleep period, the park sparkled with lights. Somewhere in the distance, a man laughed and a woman spoke in a lighthearted voice.

I couldn't move. I couldn't think. I couldn't even hate all these beautiful people living in their perfect city, unknowing that a woman had died in the Down-deep below Cries. I wanted to rage at them all, to rage at a universe that could let mothers die in the dark, but I had gone numb.

"Bhaaj." The deep voice spoke from shadows beyond the gazebo.

I didn't move.

A man stepped into the gazebo and walked over. He sat next to me, but I kept staring ahead.

"We found a family to take care of the baby and the boy," Jak said. "A bartender in the Black Mark and her husband." He used above-city speech, and somehow it helped, creating distance from what had happened, like a veil over my memories.

I glanced at him. "Is the baby still alive?"

"Yes, they say she'll make it."

I couldn't speak. I opened my mouth, but no words came out, so I shut it again.

"Bhaaj." He was watching me with his too-perceptive gaze. "You did a good thing."

"I didn't do shit." My voice cracked. "Who left her alone down there?"

"She was a cyber-rider."

"So what?" I was starting to feel, and no matter how hard I tried, I couldn't stop it. I wanted to rip something apart, anything, or to hit a wall over and over until I couldn't feel any more pain. "I don't care how much riders like to work alone, they still have support circles. They wouldn't let one of their own give birth alone. Where is the father?"

He lifted his hands, then let them drop. "No one knows him. No one knows her. She stayed away from everyone, even created her own mesh networks so she didn't have to interact with people."

"Everyone is supposed to have a circle. People should have checked on her."

"Yah," he said softly. "The system broke down."

"The system is fucked."

"Bhaaj—"

"Stop." I was shaking with an anger so big, I had nowhere to put it. "I can't. Not now."

He didn't push. We fell silent, gazing at the park. Across several lawns, a pavilion stood with glowing lanterns strung along its roof. Why I had come here, I didn't know. Down below, I had sent my green beetle to find Jak, and by the time he arrived at the cave with the dead mother and her orphaned children, I had stopped crying. But those tears left a hole inside me. Or maybe they forced me to see the emptiness that already existed. How long had my mother lain dead in a cave after my birth? Had my father left me at the orphanage, a squalling baby protesting the indignity of life? That wasn't the way of the undercity, to seek help from above. I had tried to find him, but no one knew anything. Whoever he had been, wherever he came from, I would never know.

"Enough," I said.

Jak glanced at me. "Of what?"

Unbidden and unwanted, words tore out from deep within me, jagged like shards of broken glass. "The criminals aren't the dust rats or the riders or the punkers. It's everyone up here living their magical lives, oblivious to the children dying in the dark."

It was a long time before Jak answered. Finally he said, "Maybe."

"Maybe?" I wanted to shake him. "How can you say 'maybe'?"

"We let the system break," he said. "Us. The undercity. We don't need the above-city to fix us. It's our world to make better, not theirs."

"Asking for help isn't a crime."

"They 'help' by stealing our children. What do you think they would do if we kidnapped theirs?" Anger edged his voice. "Our children always come back. You did. You came home."

I didn't want to hear him. "It's home because we don't goddamned know any better."

"Maybe."

"Stop it."

"Why, because you think you know better?" He spoke in perfect above-city speech, contrary to the prejudice in Cries that our language was the result of stupidity and poor education rather than the evolution of an ancient dialect. "The aqueducts won't stop being home because you say they should. Why do you want the above-city? People here, in those rare times they deign to notice us, claim they *know* us. They don't know shit. They discount our lives, our histories, what we feel, they even tell us, when we recount our experiences, that those experiences aren't valid. No matter what they say, that won't stop the undercity from being our home."

"And it's such a great home." I rounded on him, shaking with that terrifying anger I had always channeled into anything else so I wouldn't feel it crushing me. "Dying in secret. For what? The only way I could ask for your help tonight was to send out a spy beetle, which found a dust ganger who helps Gourd, who found Gourd, who had to search you out because you're so damn secretive, lately even I can't find you. What the bloody hell are we all hiding from?"

"It's not hiding," Jak said. "It's a way of life." His voice was unrelenting. "Yours, too. You can leave the physical aqueducts, Bhaaj, but you can never take them out of your heart."

"I never wanted to come back."

He looked away, his expression shuttered.

I exhaled. I had left him, too, that day I walked out of the aqueducts. We were talking in above-city speech because it was too difficult to say these things in the undercity dialect. But for this moment, I needed the language of our youth. In its lack of words, it would speak volumes.

"Got one reason to come back," I told him. "One damn good reason."

He looked at me, the hint of a smile curving his lips. "Yah, Bhaajo."

That nickname brought a flood of memories. He had called me Bhaajo the first time we made love, the two of us twelve years old. I had loved Jak, and denied that love, for my entire life.

We sat together, staring across the park at the glowing lanterns that bobbed in the breezes.

After a while, Jak said, "You find anything about Scorch in the Alcove?"

I shook my head. "Just some artifact. Plumbing."

"Yah." He didn't sound surprised.

"Seen the pipes?" I asked.

"Heard about. Never cared to look." He shrugged. "Ruins are all over Cries. Dying cities, dying world."

And dying mothers. I felt so tired. "Got to go home," I said in a low voice. The penthouse wasn't truly home, and it never would be, but I couldn't go back to the aqueducts. I needed this night to push away the shadows, and I knew only one way to defeat them. I spoke softly. "Come with?"

Jak smiled then, that terrifying smile, the one he never showed anyone else. It wasn't cocky or smug or any other part of the Black Mark's owner. This smile was gentle.

"Yah," he murmured. "I come with."

The dawn lined the horizon for what seemed like forever. It had been there when Jak left this morning, after our many warm hours together, and it was still here an hour later. Raylicon turned too slowly for the sun to rise in any sensible manner.

I sat sprawled on the couch with a virtual terminal floating above the table in front of me. "EI," I said.

The penthouse EI answered. "Yes?"

"I have a name for you."

"What is it?"

"Interface."

"Is that a command or the name?"

"The name." It still didn't feel right, but it was the best I had come up with.

"Why do you want to call me Interface?" it asked.

"It's what you are," I said. "My interface with the above-city world. With Cries."

"I don't think it fits."

I blinked. "What did you say?"

"I don't believe it is an appropriate name."

For flaming sake. The EI was arguing with me. "Why not?"

"It refers to a single technical aspect of my functions."

I supposed it had a point. "All right. I'll think some more."

"What can I do for you this morning?"

Good question. "Yesterday Max sent you a recording of an artifact in the ruins."

"Yes, I have it. I did a preliminary analysis on the symbols etched onto its surface."

Although I had thought of asking it for an analysis, I hadn't yet. This EI wasn't designed for that sort of investigation. "Why did you do that?"

"In case you weren't logical enough to ask me to do it."

Maybe I should name it *Annoying*. "What did you find?"

"The hieroglyphics are ancient Iotic, the labels for a plumbing system."

"Well, that's exciting."

"My voice analysis suggests you are speaking with irony."

I smiled. "You think?"

"Not literally. I simulate thought."

I sighed. I didn't believe General Vaj Majda had programmed this EI. She had far more subtlety. "Tell me something. Who designed you? I don't mean who specified the parameters, but who actually set up your programming?"

"Captain Takkar and her techs."

That made sense. However, it also made me wonder. The EI could be irksome, sure, but it wasn't unreasonable. It tried to help. If Takkar had wanted to bedevil me, she could have done a lot worse. My view of the chief shifted like an optical illusion where stairs going in one direction suddenly appeared as if they were going the other way. Maybe Dayj was right that Takkar had no link to Scorch's operation. I wasn't ready to give her a pass yet, but it made me think.

"What I don't get," I said, "is why anyone thought I'd find something useful in the Alcove."

"Perhaps the evidence was removed before you went there."

My gut said no, and so did Max's analysis of the dirt in the Alcove. "No one has disturbed that cave since before we rescued Dayj."

"Then I don't know the answer to your query," the EI said.

I sat watching the horizon, a red line below the dark sky. "This is what I know. Scorch was funneling weapons through the undercity for some arms dealer whose main operation is offworld. Now Scorch is dead." A strange feeling came over me. Remorse? It couldn't be. She had tried to kill me, she'd tortured and assaulted Dayj, and someday she might have sold him. The Traders would pay an unimaginable price for a Skolian prince, a man whose looks would make him a top pleasure slave and whose Kyle abilities would let them steal access to the Kyle net.

Even so. Something was off. "It doesn't add up," I said. "Scorch's operation was one cog in a much larger ring with no other links in the undercity. My job here is almost done. I just need to find the missing weapons. And that drug punker had a nice, new carbine. So the Kajada cartel probably stole the weapons. That explains why they didn't act against me or Jak. Dig would never shoot us."

"It sounds like it adds up quite well," the EI said.

"I feel like I'm missing something."

"You still have to recover the weapons."

"Yah." But that wasn't what bothered me. "Gourd said something was in the Alcove."

"Gourds do not speak."

I sighed. "It's a name. A man."

"Ah. What did he say was there?"

"He didn't know." I sat pondering. "What's unique about the Alcove? Really old plumbing, but who would care except a scientist?" An unwelcome thought formed in my mind. "EI, bring up the images of that plumbing system."

Holos of the artifact appeared, floating above my

table. They rotated slowly, showing me the silvery curve from various angles.

"You know," I said, "that pipe is intact."

"What we can see," the EI said. "Most of it is hidden in the rock ceiling."

"If the rest of it is like what we see, it probably still works."

"Works?"

"As plumbing. It could bring water to the Alcove."

"Possibly. The artifact appears sound. It's designed from a material known for its durability."

Indeed. "So Scorch could have imprisoned someone in the Alcove and used the pipes to provide water." Tightly I added, "Or to withhold it." That offered a way to control her prisoner.

"Do you think she kept Prince Dayjarind there?"

"No, actually not." It still wasn't adding up. "He was in a cave two levels above the Alcove."

"Then who?"

"I have no clue." Maybe I was just talking into the wind. Or the sunrise. Out across the dead ocean, the sun was finally lifting its golden orb above the horizon.

"I've been wondering something," I said. "Why didn't you tell me that Dayj and his father were full empaths, and that most of the Majdas were psions to some degree or another?"

"It isn't data they wish made known."

"You shouldn't withhold facts. You never know what might turn out to be useful."

"I will file your response with the Majdas."

So it did report back to them. No surprise there. I picked up a tumbler of kava I had poured for Jak and took a swallow. It went through me like a jolt of fire. Ah yes, that was good.

"Tell me about this empath thing," I said. "Do the Majdas breed it into their line?"

"Most native Raylicans carry traces of Kyle DNA. Probably including you."

"Yeah, right." I was as empathic as a rock. "The army tested me. I don't manifest any traits."

"You descend from the original Raylicans. They were all psions."

"Hardly anyone here is now." The occurrence wasn't any higher in the general Raylicon population than anywhere else. "What happened to them all?"

"Genetic drift. Natural selection. Many negative mutations are associated with the Kyle traits." Then it added, "However, two populations here have bred for them over the millennia."

"The Majdas."

"That is correct. Also, the Abaj Tacalique."

"Huh." I had heard the Abaj were psions. That was why they kept to themselves, living out in the desert. I supposed it also made sense about the Majdas. It wasn't only them, but all the noble Houses and the Ruby Dynasty as well. Royalty and the aristocracy could be compulsive about who they married, with reasons that rarely seemed connected to love.

I sent my beetle-bots to scour the Alcove, and I searched the cave where Scorch had stored her cache of stolen guns. I even lay on my stomach at the back and mapped out the warren of cracks, crevices, and rocks there, hoping to find any stray debris left behind. No luck. I couldn't unearth a single clue about who had lifted the weapons or where they took the crates.

Finally I stood up, rubbing an ache in the small of my back. That was when I realized I had company. A dust gang stood a few paces away, two girls and two boys. The taller girl looked familiar. Yes, I remembered. She had spied on me yesterday, then run off with the sandwich and snap-bottle I left her.

"Ho," I said, for want of a better response. At least they weren't trying to shoot me, like the punkers yesterday. I wasn't wearing my jacket, so my holster with its pulse gun was in full view.

"Find any stuff?" the water-bottle girl asked. Blue and red powder dusted her dark hair.

"No stuff," I said. "You know where it went?"

"Gone," one of the boys said.

"Gone where?" I asked.

"Gone," the second girl said.

"Fast," the second boy added.

"Gone fast, yah," I agreed.

"Not the crates," the water-bottle girl said. "Jump fast." She leapt to one side, snapping up her fists, then stood and regarded me as if waiting for an answer.

I squinted at her. "Jump?"

The first boy repeated the sequence, jumping and then waiting. I wasn't sure, but I thought they were mimicking my moves in the canal yesterday when I had fought the punkers.

"Yah, jump," I said. "Fast." This was so odd. Not only weren't they hiding or trying to mug me, they seemed to expect something. They looked at me, and I looked back at them.

Then it hit me. Of course. The way they stood at

attention, like troops ready for training—we had done that in my youth, too, choosing leaders who drilled us in fighting moves.

I thumped my abdomen. "Got biomech. That's why I'm fast."

"Biomech?" the first boy asked.

"Like a Jagernaut," I said.

Their eyes widened. They might not be familiar with the military, but everyone knew about Jagernauts, the elite fighter pilots of ISC.

The second boy nodded with approval. "Good mech."

"Yah," I said. "Good mech." I kicked out my leg to the side in a tykado move, a form of martial arts I had learned as a grunt and studied for years, both in and later out of the army. My leg moved in a blur. The thick heel of my boot slammed into a stalactite and knocked off the stone tip. Even before it clattered to the floor, I had pulled my leg back. I stood there and held back my grin while they gaped at me, at the broken cone of rock, and at me again.

"Eh," the water-bottle girl said. She kicked her leg to the side in a much slower version of what I had just done. It wasn't bad, actually. She wasn't using enough force and her technique needed work, but she had good height and flexibility.

I nodded, acknowledging her effort. Then I spoke to the others. "You do."

They all tried the same kick. The first boy gave it more force but less height, and the second boy moved awkwardly, but with more speed. The second girl lost her balance and fell against the cone of rock. The others laughed and she glared at them.

"Good start," I told them. I glanced at the girl who had stumbled. "All of you."

"Not rough-tumble," she said.

She had a point. The rough-tumble was what we called gang fighting. These four were good at it, judged by their ability to move, but it wasn't the same as formalized martial arts.

"Tykado is harder than the rough-tumble," I said.

"Teach us," the water girl said.

They all stood watching me with expectation.

Well, hell. I supposed I could drill them on a few moves.

"Need more control," I told them. "Got to warm up, too."

So began the tykado lesson.

I had lunch on the Concourse. Tourists strolled along the shops, all thinking they were experiencing the exotic underside of Cries. Yah, right. The Concourse was a glossy cheat. It ran one level below ground, and its skylights let sunlight stream over the restaurants, shops, and boutiques. I didn't visit often, but the Sand Shadow Café up here served the best kava in the city, no to mention those succulent rolls crammed with peppered meat and drenched in pizo sauces. We all had our weaknesses. So today I indulged mine while I pondered Scorch. What had she hidden in the Alcove? A person? If so, I had no clues as to who they were or what had happened to them.

The café was on a raised walkway above the Concourse, and I sat on the terrace outside so I could watch people go by in their colorful clothes, tunics fringed in tassels and blowsy trousers. The delicious smell of spices saturated the air. No wonder I was hungry. You could practically eat the mouth-watering aromas. Content, I sat back and enjoyed my meat roll.

A shadow fell across my table from behind. I stayed in the same position as if I hadn't noticed, but I tensed, ready to spring up and defend myself.

A tall woman with the look of a seasoned fighter walked around the table and sat across from me. She was my age, but without the advantages of age-delaying nanomeds. Gray showed at the temples of her black hair and lines creased the corners of her eyes. A gnarled scar ran along her neck, as if someone had tried to cut off her head. Given their spectacular failure, I doubted they were still alive. She wore dark trousers with a heavy belt and a muscle shirt that did nothing to hide her lean, well-built physique. Simple clothes, yes, but not cheap. They were designed from smart-cloth, able to warm or cool her body, clever enough to change color if needed, and supple enough to aid her movements. She wore the outfit with the casual disregard of someone who didn't care about its quality, a rare trait in the undercity. The years had changed her almost beyond recognition, but I would know her anywhere.

"Dig," I said.

She nodded. "Bhaaj."

"Met your punks."

She said only, "Yah. Dumb punks," but that was enough, an apology, undercity style. It was also her admission that yes, they were her punks, which meant she now ran the Kajada cartel. No surprise there, but I wished it weren't true.

"Long time," she said.

I nodded. How else could I answer? Dig was the last person I had seen before I enlisted. We had stood together by the exit from the undercity into the Concourse, and in all the years since, I had tried to forget our bitter argument that morning.

Today she said only, "You done with the army?"

"Yah," I said. "I work private."

"Heard." Her dark gaze remained impassive. "Whisper says Majda."

"ISC."

"So you're still military."

"Nahya." I wondered why she cared. "They just hired me."

She nodded. I waited, wondering what provoked her to come here in the open, which punkers avoided like the plague. It seemed a big deal just to apologize for her runners doing something stupid. She could have done that down deep.

"You," she finally said.

"Me?" I asked.

"Almost shot my jan," she said.

Ho! Did she mean "my jan" as in "my daughter"? I was Bhaajan because my mother had been Bhaaj. It was the sole piece of ID found with me as a newborn, a scrap of film with the words *She is the daughter of Bhaaj.* Had one of those punkers that jumped me been named Digjan?

"Which?" I asked.

"Had knife. Not gun."

Not the leader, then, but one of the other two girls. Yes, I remembered. The taller of those two had seemed familiar. Of course. She looked like Dig.

So Dig had a kid. No surprise there. She had always

valued family and would make sure her children knew their mother as Dig had never known hers. I wondered about the father. Undercity lovers ignored the elaborate courtship rituals followed in Cries. Young women approached young men with no fuss, and the fellows enjoyed their compromised honor as they pleased. Contrary to what the above-city believed, that didn't mean we valued our relationships less or that we didn't respect our men. Our code of honor placed great value on the ties people formed.

I would never forget how Dig and I had run laughing through the aqueducts like sisters, confident we ruled the undercity, though of course we hadn't ruled even our own misspent lives. The day I left for the army, angry words had flown between us, filled with a pain neither of us knew how to articulate. How could I walk away? I tried to tell her how much my meager education meant to me, the schooling I'd hacked from Cries, how it opened my eyes to the rest of the empire, but the terse dialect of the aqueducts left no way to express my wanderlust, not even to Dig.

I said only, "Digjan's father?"

"You don't know him." Her closed expression said *Stay out of my business* as clearly as if she held a gun on me.

I changed the subject. "You train Digjan?" She'd want her daughter to take over the cartel someday. Right, multi-generational drug cartels, just what the human race needed.

She spoke flatly. "No train."

"Why not?"

"So she can enlist."

That I hadn't expected. "Does she want that?"

"Mostly." Dig leaned forward, her face intent. "Get out."

I read her meaning from her body language. She didn't mean *get out of my business* this time, she meant she wanted her daughter out of the family business. Apparently I wasn't the only one here who didn't like what Dig did for a living.

"She has to want it enough," I said. "She'll have to work harder than the rest to survive."

"She's smart. Strong." After a moment, Dig added, "No punking."

Another surprise. Dig didn't let her daughter run drugs. Good. It was the smart choice.

"Keep her clean," I said. "No criminal record." Cries had no prisons. They sent convicts to colonies on the moon of another planet in the system. I could have seen Scorch in that miserable place, but not the stunned girl who had gaped at me in the canal.

"What else she need?" Dig asked.

"Got to pass tests," I said. "Reading, writing, numbers."

"Hacked her learning from the above-city. She can pass."

I hadn't expected Dig to school her daughter, not after our argument that day I left to enlist. If Digjan was like her mother, though, she would do well. Dig was damn smart.

I lapsed into full speech so I could give a better picture of what her daughter faced. "She'll have to go to the recruitment office in Cries. She won't have any problem with the physical tests." From what I'd seen of Digjan, she could probably outperform any above-city recruit. "If she can read, write, and do math, she should be all right for the other tests. And she should have a sponsor." Gods knew I could have used one when I enlisted.

"Sponsor?" Dig asked.

"Like a reference. It open doors." I paused. "She can give my name." I wouldn't sponsor a dealer, but I knew Dig. If she said her daughter never ran drugs, I trusted her word.

Dig nodded her thanks. Then she said, "Scorch."

I understood. Dig had come to pay her debt. Whatever acrimony lay between us, I had let her daughter go free and unharmed.

"Scorch had boxes," I said. "Crates. They're gone."

"Guns."

"Yah."

"They belong to Kajada now."

No surprise there. The cartel hadn't wasted any time moving in on Scorch's operation after I eliminated the competition. "Scorch planned to sell them. To the Traders, it looks like."

Dig tapped her temple. "Scorch was screwed here."

"Yah." I regarded her steadily. "You going through with the sale?"

Dig slammed the table with her palm. People around us turned to look. When they took in Dig's appearance, several got up to leave.

Dig spoke flatly. "Never." She had her other hand under the table, no doubt resting on some weapon hidden in her clothes. I had never been so glad to see someone ready to shoot me for insulting them. She wasn't selling to the Traders.

"Good," I said.

"Those guns belong to Kajada now."

That wasn't much better. "Got a war?" I asked dryly.

She met my gaze. "Time to clean out the Vakaar vermin."

Damn. If she went after the other cartel, the Vakaars, that meant trouble.

Dig stood up. "Bhaaj, eh." It was the undercity version of, "Good to see you, got to run."

"Wait," I said.

She stood there with one hand resting on her belt. A dart gun showed under her fingers.

I waited.

Dig sat back down, her expression closed. I had better make this quick.

"I heard someone put a food kitchen down here," I said.

She snorted. "You hear shit, Bhaaj. It's useless. Police set it up."

That wasn't the answer I expected. "You mean it actually exists?"

She turned in her seat and stretched out her arm, pointing up the Concourse. In the distance, a long, low building stood across the main throughway. "There." She stood up and added, "So."

With that, Dig left, her shadow following her until neither remained.

A chill walked its fingers up my back. Kajada was going after Vakaar. War was coming to the undercity.

XV

Dust Gangers

Displays throughout the Imperialate often showed images of Cries. It was good public relations: look at our beautiful, futuristic city. The wide streets were for pedestrians only. Designed in red tiles streaked with blue, they used stone that existed only in the Vanished Sea. The towers of Cries rose like obelisks honoring the architectural achievements of the human race. The few hover cars that flew above the city made clean arcs in the air, gleaming with wealth. Of course they never ran into each other, not in Cries, where nothing was ever out of place. You never saw wild kids out on joy rides, shrieking with laughter while they hung out the windows and dropped trinkets on annoyed pedestrians. The transit authority would say it was because you couldn't drive in the city until your twenty-fifth birthday. I would say it was because the kids with the guts to defy the rigid structure of life here were too busy dying in the dark under the glitzy city. Screw Cries.

Stop it, I told myself. Jak was right, we couldn't

expect the above-city to solve our problems. The rare times Cries offered help, they wanted to "fix" the undercity by making us like them. We had failed the mother who died in childbirth and we needed to fix that cause of that failure ourselves.

Although the undercity had no formal legal structures, we had plenty of unwritten laws. Adults like Gourd, who took responsibility for providing clean water, looked after all the children. Although few jobs existed, our population was sparse enough for most adults to find work. We learned trades undercity style, like the cyber-riders who exchanged their wizardry for whatever they desired. Some grew up to be crime bosses, like Jak, Scorch, and Dig. Charming company I kept.

Even so. Jak was no Scorch; he treated his people well and paid good wages. Who knew what his employees were doing now, though, with his casino hidden so well that even I had no idea where he stashed the place. Given that I was currently working for the military, the less Jak told me, the better. I couldn't reveal what I didn't know.

Cries, however, wasn't the poster child of the Imperialate propaganda machine. Its beauty was too stark. When it came to glossy testimonials to the human race, most broadcasters showed images of Selei City on Parthonia. Hell, even I liked living there. It was peaceful to my ravaged mind, which in that idyllic place could repress anything I wanted to forget. But it wasn't home. I had to acknowledge the truth. I couldn't run from Raylicon forever.

Today, I sat on a stone bench by a spacious boulevard in Cries. The sun beat down on the city and the desert beyond, which was visible in the distance between two widely spaced towers. Farther down the avenue, a couple strolled together. They were the only ones out during the midday sleep. I didn't feel like resting, though, so I commed the one person guaranteed to keep me awake.

The brusque voice rose from my comm. "Takkar here."

"It's Bhaajan," I said.

"Glad you deigned to acknowledge us," she said sourly.

"I'm filing today's report."

"You find anything?" she asked. "One more day, Major. Then we send in the troops."

"I finished the investigation." It wasn't true, but I'd found what they asked me to find. "The drug cartels have the guns. They lifted the weapons while we were bringing Prince Dayjarind to the palace."

Takkar swore with an expertise that could outshine any punker. "Which cartel? Kajada or Vakaar?"

I couldn't give her Dig's name, but it didn't matter. "I don't know. But whoever has them is about to attack the other cartel, and when they do, it'll be a fire bath." Kajada would win, given their shiny new weapons, but Vakaar would fight until the bitter finish. "The cartels are going to war."

"Well, shit," Takkar said.

"Yeah." That summed it up quite well.

"I'm sending in troops," Takkar said. "They'll wipe the goddamn ass of the aqueducts clean of all those punk vermin."

Charming. Maybe she wasn't as smart as I thought. Only one thing could unite the cartels: an invasion by ISC forces. If the army sent in troops, it would provoke Kajada and Vakaar into open warfare with the military, and the enraged drug bosses would take their combat into Cries. Nor was that the only reason to keep out the troops. Commander Braze wasn't the only Cries VIP with undercity ties. The last thing any of them wanted was for the military to declare open season on undercity crime. Takkar's method would get ugly fast, and civilians would die. A lot of them.

I said only, "Troops probably aren't the best idea."

The chief let out an angry breath. She didn't argue, though. After a moment, she said, "I'll report to Colonel Majda and we'll get back to you."

"I'll keep the line open."

"You do that," Takkar growled. "No more jammers."

"All right." I was too tired to argue.

Lying in front of a window-wall in a tower penthouse that looked over the desert, all that open space under the sky, would never feel real to me. Jak and I had spread a blanket on the plush carpet and made love while red light from the sunset bathed our bodies. He was like a fire demon rising from the darkness into this world of dying light.

Afterward we lay together, my back spooned against his front, the two of us gazing out the window-wall while the sunset filled the world with its fading light. The cloudless horizon burned deep crimson. When I had first come above ground at age fifteen, stepping out into that gift from the gods, I had stood stock still in amazement for a full five minutes under the red sky.

Then I had walked to the recruiting center.

I had worn my best clothes that day. They were still rags. I didn't tell the recruiter I was a dust rat, but she must have known. My only ID came from the orphanage where I had spent the first years of my life. As soon as she looked up my record, she must have known I ran away when I was three, back to the undercity. I hadn't been important enough for anyone to come after me.

The recruiter said I could enlist without a guardian's permission when I turned sixteen. She suggested I find a sponsor. Such a person did nothing overt, but the better positioned your sponsor, the better for you. Promotions came faster and postings were better. To this day, I wondered where she thought I'd find a sponsor. I had no one, so when I returned on my sixteenth birthday, I started on the lowest rung in the lowest category for an enlistee. It didn't matter. The universe changed for me that day I walked into the red light of sunset, and I never regretted those steps.

Jak bit at the nape of my neck. "Awake?"

"Yah," I said. "Just watching the light."

"Like fire."

I turned on my back to look at him. "When did you first see a sunset?"

He pushed up on his elbow. "Full sunset, all around? Don't think I remember."

"You must." It was a big deal for us. He wouldn't have forgotten.

It was a moment before he spoke. "I saw red light through the Concourse skylights. Got curious one day, when I was a kid. Walked up into the city. Cries was red. Everywhere. Bathed in that light." Softly he added, "That day, I promised myself I'd never be too poor to leave the aqueducts." In his normal voice, he said, "I started planning the Black Mark that night."

Strange, the effect of that light. It prodded me into uniform and him into crime. Ultimately, it had pushed us both toward what we wanted.

Jak stretched in the evening's light, long and lean on the blanket. Nice. Then he sat up, rubbing his neck. I didn't want to get up, but I still had work to do. I sat up too, and grabbed the clothes I'd been wearing earlier, before the sunset distracted us with its sensuous light.

We dressed in silence, but as we stood up, I said, "Jak."

He finished fastening up his trousers. "Yah?"

"What does Dig sell now? Still funk, dot-dope, bliss, and hack?"

"That's right. And node-bliss."

Node-bliss? "You mean bliss?"

"It's different than the usual. Softer." He grunted as he tugged on his black pullover. "Hell, it's so soft, you can't feel it at all."

It didn't surprise me. Bliss was one of the less addictive drugs. Kids used it above-city. Illegal, yes, but less serious than the hardcore monsters like funk or hack.

I pulled on my shoulder holster with its pulse gun. "Never heard of node-bliss."

"Doesn't do shit for me."

"You tried it?"

"Yah." He shrugged, all decked out in his dark leathers. "Whisper says it makes people go crazy, but I didn't feel squat. Nothing. Scorch sold it. Now that she's gone, probably it's gone, too."

Scorch? That was odd. I would have thought the cartel would stop her. They made fast work of anyone who poached on their territory. Hell, they were about to make fast work of each other.

"Dig and Hammer Vakaar are going to war," I said.

Jak had been looking at the sunset, but now he turned with a start. "Say what?"

"Dig has Scorch's guns." Probably Scorch's node-bliss, too, whatever that was. "She's going to kick Hammer's ass."

The light from outside cast a red glow across Jak's face. "Not good."

"Yah. Majda knows."

Anger flared in his gaze. "You turned in *Dig?*"

"No. I just told her the cartels had the guns." Quietly I added, "They have to know, Jak. All hell is going to break out down there. We need to get people to safety."

"The dust gangs will fight."

"We need to stop them."

"Stop them?" He snorted. "I don't think so. They're warriors."

I scowled at him. "They're kids. They should be worrying about going to proms or whatever, not which side of a drug war they're going to fight in."

"Oh, fuck that, Bhaajo."

"No, I don't want to fuck that." I smiled slightly. "Anyway, we already did, you and me."

He laughed and touched my cheek, the barest scrape of his rough fingertip. "Yah."

Gods. If someone could bottle his sexuality and sell it, she'd make billions. But I couldn't let him distract me. "We have to warn the aqueducts."

"Why?" He dropped his arm. "It's not our war."

"It's our code. Protect our own." The interconnected

ties in the undercity should have kept that mother from dying alone with her baby and small son. The authorities above-city didn't care. If the Chief Takkars had their way, they would wipe us out like an infestation. The aqueducts survived because we lived by a code. Protect. Every gang, punker, rider, and crime boss knew that code.

"I'm going down tonight," I said. "See if I can warn people. You come?"

It was a moment before he answered, but finally he said, "I'll pull together what I can. Meet me at the foyer exit from the Concourse, three hours."

I nodded. "Three hours."

During my previous searches of Scorch's operation, I'd looked for the guns or clues to what happened to them. Today I was searching for drugs. I walked the tangled pathways of the Maze methodically, looking for anything out of place. Eventually I neared the cave where Scorch had stored the guns, also the place where I had given that dust gang a tykado lesson.

Max, I thought. *Is anyone in the cavern up ahead?*

No one, Max thought. Then, **Yes, they are.** Then, **No.**

Which is it, yes or no?

It's hard to tell with all these rock formations. They cast sensor shadows.

Do you think that dust gang will come back?

It seems unlikely.

I had to agree. Trust didn't come easily here, and regardless of my origins, I was a stranger, a novelty that spurred them to ask come for one tykado lesson, but I doubted it would go any farther.

Have you ever heard of node-bliss? I asked.

You mean phorine? It's a prescription medicine.

I had never heard of phorine, either. *What does it do?*

It's a neural relaxant. Apparently it doesn't show up in routine exams.

That sounded odd. *Why not?*

To detect its use, you need to compare the user's neural map with their map when they aren't affected. Max paused. **I imagine that is a rather involved process.**

Jak said it didn't do anything for him.

I don't have any effects listed for it.

So what's the point of the stuff?

I can't say. I don't have any details.

It sounds like a scam. That would be like Scorch, to sell useless junk while she convinced her buyers they were doing some high-powered "neural relaxant."

Bhaaj, Max thought. **You asked me if anyone was in that storeroom.**

That's right. I was almost at the entrance. *Are you picking up someone?*

Yes. Max thought. **They are gathering.**

They? Maybe all four had come back. I walked into the cavern—and stopped stock still.

They stood waiting by the walls, the outcroppings, in front of me, children ranging in age from about six to young teens. Even as I counted twelve of them, a girl jumped down from a hiding place in the back and a young man stepped out from behind a ragged rock wall. The water-bottle girl stood in front with an older boy and girl, both about fourteen. The older girl was leanly muscled with lighter hair, brown more than black, that barely touched her shoulders. I recognized her, though it took me a moment to remember why. She had stood with the Oey dust gang that day they had let me pass in the canal. I remembered them in particular because their gang had include a cyber-rider, which was rare in the aqueducts, the youth with the Oey cyber-tracings on his arm. She nodded to me, a gesture I had used at her age, acknowledging our fight Trainer.

The older girl spoke. "Ready, all."

The group called out their answers. "Ready, all!"

Well damn. *Ready, all* meant they were ready to train. They stood waiting for my response. How the blazes did I answer? No simple *Sure, I can show you a few moves* would work here. If I accepted this unexpected trust they offered, I was agreeing to do more than teach them tykado. I was offering leadership. I couldn't make that promise, not when I had a life elsewhere. If I worked with them and then left Cries, it would betraying their trust. They had no idea they were asking me to make a much bigger decision, one that would tear apart my life. *You can never go home:* I had known, absorbed, lived that maxim for decades. I couldn't stay on Cries.

And yet . . . was it possible that here in front of me stood the glimmering of an answer to the broken pieces of the undercity? Like the light before dawn, a fledgling solution was coming to me.

That solution, however, demanded a sacrifice I couldn't make. I meant to tell them I had to leave. But somehow when I spoke, different words came out. In saying them, I made a decision, one that until this moment I hadn't realized I intended.

"Small ones here." I pointed to my left. "Older, bigger here." I pointed to the right.

The children moved, a jumbled shifting of position.

"Straight lines," I barked.

They snapped to attention, straightening out their lines. The Oey girl and the older boy remained at the front, assuming the position of leaders.

"Ready, all," I called to them.

"Ready, all!" They answered together, just as Jak, Dig, Gourd, and I had done with each other so many years ago, playing at being troops when we were small children, becoming more serious as we matured, four children supporting each other and our small circle of kin and kith. As unsettling as it was to hear those words from so many voices, it also felt familiar. Except this wasn't a game. I intended to ask more from them. If we did this right, perhaps they could form a network of support for the undercity, giving these young people a purpose beyond running and fighting. My only experience came from the army, and I doubted most of these kids were interested in ISC, but the discipline I had learned as a dust ganger had meshed well with my life in the military. Maybe I could give back to the aqueducts a little of what had helped me.

I raised my voice. "Ready to train?"

"Ready to train," they called in unison. They looked like they were enjoying themselves.

"Ready to honor the Code," I called.

They hesitated at this new addition to the routine. Then the older girl called, "Ready to honor the Code!"

They others immediately shouted after her. "Ready to honor the Code!"

"Protect," I said.

"Protect," they called.

"Live with honor."

"Live with honor!"

"Never abuse that honor."

"Never abuse that honor," they called. I had gone way off script, but they were caught up with it now.

"Ready?" I called.

"Dust rats, ready," they shouted.

"No!" The old anger surged in me, one that had become new again since I returned to Cries. "Not dust rats!"

They stared at me.

"Answer, ho!" I shouted.

They looked uncertain. Then Oey girl called, "Not dust rats!"

"Not dust rats!" the others said. Confusion showed on their faces. If I wanted to keep them with me, I had to give them something to call themselves, because I had just taken their identities.

I stepped up on a stump of rock. I didn't shout, but my voice carried throughout the cavern. "You are human. Rats are vermin. You aren't vermin. You are better than rats!"

They watched me, waiting to see what I would give them to replace what I had taken away. They weren't rats. They were better than that. What could I tell them?

What?

And then I knew.

"Lift your chins," I told them. "You are the dust knights."

They watched me with the hint of something on

their faces, a thing I wanted them to shout in defiance to the unforgiving city above.

Pride.

The Oey girl raised her voice, her words echoing in the cavern. "Dust knights, ready!"

The rest of the children shouted together. "Dust knights, ready!"

A chill went through me. The military said I had no Kyle abilities, but if any hint of precognition existed in my bones, it was whispering now of the future, of a time when a legendary movement would someday change the Imperialate, becoming a force for protection throughout the empire—a force born when a ragged group of impoverished children stood on a dying planet and shouted their name.

The Dust Knights of Cries.

BOOK III

The Phorine War

XVI

A Third Realm

The arched entrance to the Concourse was on the outskirts of Cries, beyond a terraced plaza. The entry stood at the top of the stairs that led down to the Concourse, which at its start lay only one story below ground level. The entrance was always open, with pennants snapping in the breezes and colored lights glowing on the arch at night. Gatekeepers looked after the entrance, welcoming visitors at an information kiosk at the bottom of the stairs. Beyond the kiosk, the Concourse stretched out in a wide avenue. Establishments lined the avenue, most at street level, though in a few places the shops and bistros were a few meters higher than the street, creating a terrace ideal for cafés with tables outside. A few lanes wandered off from the main avenue to areas with nightclubs. The main street sloped down in a gradual incline at first, but the ceiling stayed at ground level, until it was three stories above the street. Skylights up there let in sunlight, and police patrolled the area to ensure that tourists and above-city visitors were safe.

Exits from the Concourse into the true undercity were far different.

In one short hike, from gleaming entrance to ragged exit, the Concourse changed from a wonderland of lights and festive shops to a grungy alley. The street extended for over a kilometer, narrowing bit by bit, until at its end, it was no more than an uneven lane. The ceiling sloped down and a haze filled the air, coming from braziers in the market shacks, stoves where vendors were cooking their goods, and mist that formed when cooler air from the aqueducts below met the warmer Concourse. Aromas of cooking meat and pizo spice saturated the air. This was the only portion of the avenue my people visited. Technically the entire Concourse was part of the undercity, but only people in Cries believed that. No one in the aqueducts considered it part of our world. In fact, the police usually ran off any undercity intruders they caught on the boulevard.

Most exits from the Concourse to the aqueducts were hidden behind the rickety stalls that crusted the lower end of the street. Only one archway offered a visible exit. It stood at the very end of the street, with a sign that warned citizens not to venture beyond that point. Today I walked by that sign and into the rocky area beyond. We called this area the Foyer because it felt like the entrance to a house, a natural "room" hollowed out of the stone by whatever water had run through here in past ages. Jagged rock walls enclosed the area. On the far side, a walkway sloped downward, leading to the aqueducts. A street lamp shone at the head of the path, one of the few additions that Cries maintained for the aqueducts. I had always liked those lamps. They had an antique quality, not only the aged appearance of the metal, but also in the way the top curled around in a scrolled loop. A lamp hung by a chain from that curve.

Sometimes anthropologists from the university used this path to visit the aqueducts. I had known one in my youth, Professor Orin. The first time he came down, I followed him in secret, fascinated by the way he explored the niches and crannies in the walls. When a dust gang tried to mug him, it pissed me off that they interfered with my discovery. I had shouted at them from hiding places, throwing rocks and insults as if I were four gangers instead of one, until they decided Orin wasn't worth the trouble and went away. Orin was clearly flustered by the incident, which involved a lot of noise between people he mostly couldn't see, but he continued his research trip. I was so impressed when he didn't run back to Cries, I stayed with him the entire day, hidden and silent. After he left, I convinced Jak, Gourd, and Dig to help me protect him. Word of our taking him into our circle spread through the whisper mill, and after that people left Orin alone when he visited.

Orin had known I was following him. He lured me out with offers of cocoa sticks and water. He built enough trust that after a while I walked with him, talking about my life in my terse dialect. Eventually I led him to hidden artifacts. He let me work on his digs and he taught me the language of the above-city. I learned more from him about anthropology, the history of Cries, the world Raylicon, and our ancestors than I ever would have in a traditional school class.

Without realizing it, at least not at first, Orin stumbled on the only way to work with one of us. In the undercity, we hated charity. We made bargains.

My interactions with Orin benefited both him and me, so I didn't feel he was giving me charity or taking advantage of me.

I had loved those visits, better than any school. Formalized education would never work in the aqueducts. I couldn't imagine gangs or punkers sitting still for traditional classroom instruction. Sure, the cyberriders might try virtual classes, but they would spend more time screwing with the system than learning. Many of them already knew more about tech-mech and neural surgery than the teachers, knowledge they passed to their younger acolytes. They learned by doing, including on themselves. They were wizards, yes, but no safeguards existed beyond what they had worked out over the generations. If they ignored the safeties that time and experience had warned them to respect, they could pay a dear price. When they were at their best, however, no one could match them. They had also accumulated a body of arcane knowledge about biomech technology beyond anything known by even the best adepts in Cries.

I crossed the Foyer to the walkway that led to the canals, but instead of heading down to the aqueducts, I sat down on a truncated cone of rock. From there, I could look across the Foyer to the archway that opened onto the Concourse and the shacks clustered out there. Even as I watched, a boy snuck from the Concourse into the Foyer, smooth and stealthy, clutching meat sticks he had probably filched from a stall. He glanced at me as he ran by, headed to the aqueducts. After he disappeared around a curve of the path, the place was silent again.

"Heya," a voice rumbled.

I looked around. Jak was standing in the shadows nearby, near the wall.

"Heya," I said.

He came over and sat on a cone next to me. Some undercity gang had made these seats long ago, breaking off the top of rock formations and smoothing them into flat surfaces. The seats were in good condition because so few people used this exit. Above-city types didn't come here much and my people usually used hidden entrances to visit the Concourse.

"My circle is packing up," he told me. "Going to safety."

That was good news. His "circle" included the employees of the Black Mark and their families, also Gourd and the kids he looked after.

"I talked to some gangers and riders," I said. The newly minted dust knights, in fact. I had tasked them to spread the word: *Kajada and Vakaar are going to war. Take shelter.*

He nodded as he looked restlessly around the foyer. "Good."

"Jak."

"Hmm?" He had that jumpy quality that came when he couldn't concentrate. His fingers twitched where they rested on his legs. It was no wonder, given that anyone could see us sitting here. When he felt stressed or in danger, he preferred the shadows.

"How many children do you think live in the undercity?" I asked.

"Dunno. Thirty, maybe?" He shifted his weight. "Plus the punkers."

"I think it's more." I thought back my tykado session with the dust knights. "I saw fourteen today. Mostly gangers and a few riders. And that wasn't half of them, I'm sure."

"Don't see why it matters."

"That's a lot of children."

He was watching me now with a scrutiny I dreaded, because he always saw too much. "Did something happen?"

I didn't know how to tell him about the knights. Today I'd given them an unspoken promise that I would stay in Cries, but I wasn't ready to tell Jak. I wasn't even sure how I felt about it. So I changed the subject. "What about Braze, the commander who gambles in your club?"

He frowned at me. "What about her?"

"You got a lot of above-city types coming to the Black Mark."

"Sometimes." A dangerous smile quirked his lips. "You want dirt on the dandies?"

"No." Not that it wouldn't be useful, but this was about something else. "I wondered if other ISC officers go to your place."

"A few. Mostly Braze. Why?"

"We've all assumed Scorch was part of an offworld smuggling ring. Maybe we're wrong." I thought of how she murdered everyone connected to her operation. "She seemed obsessed with keeping her operation a secret."

"She had to. She had a Majda prince."

"Yah." It would be a long time before I stopped seeing the way she had slaughtered that guard in the desert. "But if she was involved with an offworld ring, she wouldn't have control over who knew her business. She couldn't do anything about them. That doesn't fit."

"You're saying ISC is wrong?"

"Could be." I grimaced, remembering Scorch's psychotic stare. "She had an obsessive need to stay in control. I can't see her agreeing to act as some minor cog in a big smuggling machine. It wouldn't give her enough control."

Jak was sitting completely still now. "Then where'd she get the guns?"

"Braze lost a lot in the Black Mark," I said. "More than she could pay, eh? She needed more credits, and fast, before you screwed with her. So she sold guns to Scorch."

"Braze fucked up," Jak said flatly. "That fault is hers. Not the Black Mark."

"Your casino enables gambling addicts."

He stood up, shifting his weight from foot to foot. "Got to go."

"No, you don't got to go," I growled. "You just don't like what I'm saying."

"Not argue this, Bhaajo."

I wished he wouldn't call me that when I was trying to be angry. I laid my hand on his vacated seat. "All right, let's leave it for now."

"Leave it for never," he muttered. But he sat again. "Why would Scorch want the weapons, if not for the smuggling ring?"

"I don't know. She could sell them to punkers."

He snorted. "Or kill them. Kajada, Vakaar, other bosses. Her rivals." His voice roughened. "Me."

"Not you." I would have strangled her first.

He spoke wryly. "She's a smuggler who smuggles guns to help her smuggle guns."

I wouldn't put it past her, but it still didn't fit.

"Dead people couldn't use those weapons, and she kept killing anyone who knew about her operation." I thought of the Alcove. "Maybe she was smuggling people."

"Prince Dayjarind."

"Him. Others." It still didn't explain the guns, though.

"What others?"

"I dunno. No one here but us dusters." The Traders would certainly want Dayj, but they had no use for us other undercity types. "I need to know more about Braze. Not what she does in the open, but in secret."

Jak turned on his slow, dark grin. "I should open the Black Mark again. See what goes on."

Gods. That grin of his was as potent as aged whiskey. "Yah," I murmured. "Let's see."

Lavinda was no less imposing when she was sitting down, but at least we could relax more than when we stood around in one of those alcoves overlooking the mountains. We were in the suite where I had stayed at the palace, seated at the same black lacquered table where I had drunk wine with Captain Krestone. It hit me hard. I'd missed Krestone.

Lavinda sipped her mug of kava. "You are an inordinately difficult person to find, Major."

"My apology." Normally I would have given her my spiel about why I needed secrecy, but I had told Chief Takkar I would be available and then I had gone shrouded. Lavinda had good reason for her annoyance.

However, she said only, "Takkar is concerned about the violence you think might break out in the aqueducts."

Interesting. Most people in Cries said "the slums." Aqueducts or canals were the names we used ourselves. "The cartels have been fighting for generations," I said. "With Scorch's weapons, they can ramp up their battles."

"It would help to know where they plan to fight."

"I don't know." Which was true. I had no idea.

Lavinda sounded frustrated. "We are getting nowhere in tracking those stolen guns."

"Don't laser carbines have chips you can trace?"

"That depends." She tapped her finger against her mug. "We assumed they were part of several shipments that disappeared last year, but tracing the chips in those carbines only led us to junk heaps. The smugglers had cut out the chips and thrown them in the waste."

Okay. This was my opening. "I'm not convinced these guns came from an offworld smuggling ring."

She was studying me closely. "Why not?"

Why indeed. I couldn't accuse an ISC officer without evidence, and I had none against Braze that wouldn't also implicate Jak. I chose my words with care. "I would suggest you do a search on chips for gun shipments that originated in Cries. Not stolen shipments, but weapons properly sent and supposedly delivered to military bases." The crates in the cavern had been recent issue. "Something within the last year."

Her voice turned icy. "Just exactly what are you implying?"

"I'm not implying anything," I said. "It's a suggestion. If it comes to nothing, that's all for the better." It would mean either Braze was smarter than I gave her credit for and had covered her tracks, or else I was an idiot with a stupid idea.

Lavinda took another swallow of her kava. I could almost feel her mind pressing against mine. I kept my thoughts shuttered.

After a moment, the colonel quit trying to spy on my mind, or at least the pressure receded. She set her mug on the table. "Anything else, Major?"

"Probably nothing," I said. "It looks like Scorch was also dealing fake drugs."

"Challenging the other cartels?" Dryly she said, "They probably wanted her dead, too."

That was the logical conclusion, but I didn't think so. "She wasn't dealing anything worth their time, I don't think. Just a phony designer drug. Supposedly it made some kids act crazy, but the only person I know who actually tried it told me that it had no effect at all."

"I'll note it in our files." She sounded preoccupied, still concerned with of smuggling and military treason rather than more minor issues. "Does this fake drug have a name?"

"I'm not sure," I said. "I heard it called node-bliss."

Lavinda froze, all of her attention suddenly on me. "What did you say?"

"Node-bliss." I didn't know what to make of her response. "Apparently it's slang for a drug called phorine."

"Gods almighty," she said. "Who the bloody hell is taking it?"

Her reaction hardly fit the legendary Majda restraint. "I'm not sure. The gangs maybe. Does it matter? From what I heard, it doesn't do anything."

She set her mug on the table and stood up. I watched her pace across the room. It had no windows, so when she reached a parchment wall painted with birds in red and gold plumage, she turned to me. "Thank you, Major. I will let you know if we need any more information."

Yah, right. I got up and stalked over to her. "I can't do the job you hired me to do if you hold back information."

Lavinda pushed her hand through her hair, mussing up the short locks. "You have no idea."

"So give me one."

"Phorine is a neural relaxant."

"I know that. I have no idea what it means."

"It affects a neurotransmitter called psiamine." She looked as if she were debating whether or not to continue. But she did go on. "It's an amino acid that psions carry. Psiamine allows psions to interpret the signals they receive from the brain waves of other people. The stronger the psion, the more phorine affects them. If she had given it to Dayj, the euphoria would have been almost unbearable and the withdrawal would probably have killed him."

"Good gods. Is he all right?"

"Yes, fine." More quietly, she added, "His body showed no trace of drugs."

"How is he?" One normally didn't ask after Majda princes, but she had brought him up.

"He is well." In a less formal voice, she said, "Happy, actually. He's more excited about college than any of us would have imagined. Parthonia University has agreed to admit him, contingent on his placement exams." She seemed bemused. "He is studying for them. It looks like he might do quite well. I'd never realized he spent so much time educating himself."

"I'm glad he's doing better." Another understatement. "As for the phorine, it might just be a rumor that Scorch was selling it."

"You said these rumors claimed people went crazy. What does that mean?"

"I've no clue." They were paying me to have a clue, but trying to fool them wouldn't achieve anything useful.

"Maybe they were in withdrawal," Lavinda said.

"It seems unlikely," I said. "They'd have to be psions. We're talking about people in the undercity here, not aristocrats with psi abilities or Abaj Tacalique warriors."

Lavinda rubbed her eyes, making no attempt to hide her fatigue. She seemed more willing to admit vulnerability than her sister, the General of the Pharaoh's Army. Lowering her arm, she said, "You're right, here on Raylicon the Kyle traits have survived mostly in the aristocracy and the Abaj. Those are our two most inbred populations. The royal Houses deliberately select for Kyle genes. That's one reason Dayj was betrothed to Roca Skolia. They're both powerful psions."

"And the Abaj Tacalique?"

"They don't reproduce," Lavinda said. "They clone themselves. They've been doing it for centuries. It's kept the Kyle traits strong in their gene pool." After a pause, she added, "It's also why they are dying out. It's difficult to clone psions."

I spoke wryly. "The last time I looked, I didn't see any aristocrats or Abaj warriors hanging around the aqueducts."

Lavinda smiled slightly, but then she stopped and stared at me. "Hell and damnation."

I blinked. "What?"

"Who *does* live in the undercity? The only other population on Raylicon that has been inbred for generations. Gods, maybe even millennia."

"You think we're breeding psions?" I felt silly even saying the words. "That can't be."

"Maybe not," she said. "But it's the population we missed, the one that until recently my people barely knew existed."

I didn't want to open up to her; it went against every grain of my undercity heart. But this was too important. "Children live there, run together, grow up, fall in love. They never leave. Adults find jobs in the aqueducts rather than in Cries. We've been having children for as long as Cries has existed, never mixing with the above-city." Had we unknowingly been producing the most sought after human resource known, the psions the Imperialate needed to survive?

"Never leaving," she murmured.

I didn't need telepathy to know her thought. "No," I said. "You can't go kidnapping our children or putting the adults in jail."

"Jail?" She seemed baffled. "No one is going to kidnap or imprison anyone, assuming they aren't breaking the law. We can help your people, bring them to live here in the city proper."

Now when we might have something they wanted, suddenly they cared. Screw that. "My people don't want to live in Cries. If you try to force it, they will fight you." I felt tired. "Colonel, we need to reach out to them. Let them choose. Make them want to come forward."

"Would they?"

It surprised me how easily she switched gears. Most Cries authorities would have reiterated their right to do what they wanted in the undercity. She asked a good question, and I wasn't sure I had an answer. After a moment, I said, "The aqueducts work on a barter system." Thievery, too, but that was better left out of this discussion. "My people won't take anything they perceive as charity. If we could find an exchange they could relate to, some might agree to Kyle testing."

She regarded me warily. "What sort of exchange?"

That was easy. "Food. Especially meat. That's hard to come by in the aqueducts." We could grow plants by modifying the dust and filtering water, but animals rarely survived down there. Humans were the only ones, and we weren't making such a great go of matters.

"You mean, offer them a meal?" She seemed bemused by the idea of food as currency.

"That's right." I doubted the gangs, riders, or punkers would trust such an agreement, but adults with children might agree.

"And then?"

"They let you test them. That's the bargain."

"I mean, after the tests." She considered me. "You say your people don't want charity, but everything else you say implies they need aid. So how do we give that aid?"

Good gods. Another offer to help. Although I resented that it took the possibility of psions in the undercity to stir her interest to this level, she had asked, and that mattered. I had promised her before that I would think about her questions. So how did I answer? I knew best what had worked for me. It wasn't for everyone, but it might offer a start.

"You could invite them to enlist," I said. "A few might take you up on it."

"We welcome recruits," Lavinda said. "What would encourage more to join?"

I paused, unsure how much to say. This could be a minefield. "If the army didn't make it so prohibitive for us."

Lavinda frowned at me. "We treat everyone the same. You came from the undercity and ended up as an officer. If others are willing to work hard, they can better themselves as well."

Yah, right. "If you think I was treated like everyone else, you're naïve."

Her voice cooled. "Take care, Major."

"With what?" I knew I should be cautious, but my old anger stirred. "The truth? I was ridiculed, humiliated, overlooked, given the worst of every assignment, and told I was worthless at every juncture. The only reason I succeeded is because I'm a cussed stubborn bullhead who would rather die trying than let them win. That's your egalitarian army, Colonel."

Incredibly, she didn't fire me for mouthing off. Instead she said, "So your army records say."

I blinked. "They do?"

"You never give up. That's one reason Vaj hired you."

I had nothing to say to that.

She spoke quietly. "Major, let us try this one step at a time."

"What do you suggest?"

"Just bring a few people in for testing. Let's see if anyone shows signs of the Kyle traits."

I wished this didn't feel like *Let's see if your people have value to mine.* Still, we needed to know if that value existed. Otherwise Cries could take advantage of us, rounding up psions the way they rounded up our children, except they would hang onto the psions much more tightly. If we became savvier, however, our value could become our currency. We could truly bargain with Cries.

I said only, "I thought psions were too rare to show up in a small sample."

"Very rare," Lavinda said. "The incidence of empaths in the general population is about one in a thousand. Telepaths are one in a million." After a moment, she added, "Prince Dayj's ability is one in a billion."

No wonder they protected him so fiercely. "Then why bother testing only a few people?"

"Their DNA can tell us a great deal. Kyle mutations are recessive. People often carry them without showing any traits."

Ah. I saw where she was going now. "So if the genes are more common in the undercity population, that implies psions are, too."

The colonel nodded. "A difference of even one percent would be like finding a mother lode."

That sounded like they were mining for ore. "They're people. Not a resource."

"Yes." She spoke quietly. "Major, I only want to do a few tests. They aren't invasive. As an exchange, we can offer a meal and a health check. Food, water, and medical help if they need it."

It was a reasonable bargain. I pushed back my natural distrust enough to say, "I'll see what I can do." No one would come to Cries for testing, but maybe I could figure out some workable compromise. This bargain might fall apart in mutual distrust, but we could at least try.

One step at a time.

XVII
Braze

Vice never stopped its wheels, not even with rumors of a drug war rustling through the whisper mill. Jak's casino was full to bursting tonight. I stood at a rail overlooking the main room and watched people in glittery clothes lose obscene amounts of money. Waiters eased their way among the crowd, serving drinks, food, and who knew what else. Bartenders listened to the woes of patrons who were tired of gambling, and exotic dancers gyrated in discreet alcoves. In the private rooms, some of those dancers were probably earning their pay in more intimate ways. Jak kept the lights dim, except for the shimmering walls and laser-drop drinks.

"Braze is here," a voice said at my side.

I looked up as Jak joined me at the rail. "Where?"

He indicated a table across the room. A holographic roulette sphere rotated in the air above the table, the orb filled with bouncing holo-balls. A brawny woman with muscular arms and a florid face was sitting at the table.

"Idiot," I muttered.

"That's rather ungracious," Jak murmured. "Braze is one of my favorite customers."

"Yah, because she's playing holo-roulette." I scowled at him. "I mean, come on, even a baby knows you can program that wheel to do whatever you want."

"I can't speak for the intellect of my customers," he purred. "I can only express my appreciation for their patronage."

"Aren't you the gracious one." Listening to him, you'd think his customers were contributing to a fund that supported the arts rather than losing their shirt to an undercity king of thieves.

His smile faded as he watched Braze place a bet at the table. A young man with a long gold fork scooped up Braze's glittering chip and deposited it in a niche on the table. The handsome fellow wore tight clothes that did nothing to hide his well-built physique, providing an effective distraction to the women at the table, including Braze, who was seated closest to him. She was going over the line, however, leering at him, patting his hip, making comments. The youth reddened, but kept doing his job, spinning the holo-sphere above the table.

Jak spoke into the comm in his wrist gauntlet. "Get someone over there and make sure she leaves him alone. No touching. If she keeps it up, take her away from the table."

A man's voice came out of the comm. "Got it, boss."

"Is Braze always that bad?" I asked after Jak thumbed off his comm.

"Yah," he muttered. "Someday I'm gonna kick her butt out of here."

So far this Braze hadn't struck me as someone bright enough to become an ISC commander. Either she had skills that weren't obvious or else she had some damn good connections.

"Gourd says Braze has a lot of contacts," I said.

"I've been checking," Jak said. "Looks like she knew Scorch."

"Think she realizes we suspect her?"

"I doubt it. I haven't said anything. You're the only other one who knows."

"I told Lavinda Majda." As Jak tensed, I added, "I only said I thought the stolen shipments originated on Raylicon. I didn't give names or reasons."

He scowled at me. "You're walking a narrow edge, Bhaaj."

"I have to. It's important."

"Why?"

"Node-bliss."

"What about it? The stuff is useless."

"Hardly. It's a Kyle drug. It only affects psions."

"Oh." After a moment, he added, "Well, I already knew I wasn't one."

"You said some kids took it and went crazy."

"Whisper says. Maybe it's true. Maybe not."

"I need to talk to them."

"You think we got empaths down here?"

"Maybe."

He took a moment to digest that thought. "I'll try to find them. I can't make any promises."

"Fair enough."

After that, we watched Braze gamble and get drunk. She was settling in for a long night.

✧ ✧ ✧

The soup kitchen wasn't actually called a soup kitchen. The sign on the front said Concourse Recreation Center. It wasn't a bad name. If they had called it anything that suggested charity, no one from the aqueducts would ever come here. Rec Center was nice and bland.

Watching Braze lose money had grown boring, so I left the Black Mark and went in search of the soup kitchen. Dig claimed the police ran this place, looking to lure in drug punkers so they could arrest them. I had no idea if that were actually true, but it didn't sound far-fetched. Even if the people here had no ulterior motives, my people would assume they did.

When I touched a panel by the entrance, the tall door swung inward. I walked into a large room, more of a hall, really. Tables were scattered to my right with a few game slates on them, and bedrolls lay piled against the wall. On my left, counters stretched out cafeteria style. Most were empty, but one had fresh vegetables on ice and hot food steaming in a few slots. Several rows of waters bottles stood on another counter. This was all free? Someone needed to kick some sense into the undercity. Charity or not, this looked worthwhile.

Then again, if my people did come here in any numbers, these supplies would go fast. A kitchen with free food wasn't a real solution. The undercity didn't want to be supported, the people wanted to make their own way, and Cries couldn't afford to support them even if we had been willing to accept charity.

Three people were sitting at table by the back wall, playing a board game. One of them looked up, a woman with yellow hair, a bit unusual in Cries where most everyone was dark, but not unheard of. She looked young, with a pleasant face and kind eyes. When she caught sight of me, she rose to her feet and headed over.

She smiled as she came up to me. "My greetings. Can I help you?"

"Who are you?" I asked. No, that was too blunt. I added, "Hello."

If she was offended, she gave no hint. "I'm Tanzia Harjan. Call me Tanzia, please." Her gaze took in my clothes, the high-quality cloth and expensive boots. "If you're looking for a place to eat, the Concourse has many good restaurants. You can get some pamphlets from the visitors center."

Good gods. She thought I was a tourist. "I'm not looking for a place to eat." I motioned at the room around us. "Do they come here?"

"Who?"

"Dust gangs. Cyber-riders. Punkers."

She hesitated. "You mean people from the undercity?"

"That's right."

"Almost never." Dryly she said, "The younger ones raid us every now and then. They steal food and water."

It didn't surprise me. I would have done the same if I was hungry. "They don't want charity."

She spoke carefully. "Ma'am, are you in the military?"

"How did you know?"

"The way you hold yourself." She went on as if she were plunging ahead and hoping she didn't offend me. "You dress well but you talk like you're from the aqueducts."

Huh. I hadn't realized my accent showed even

when I wasn't using dialect. And she said aqueducts, not slums. Point in her favor.

"Actually," I said, "I have a question for you."

"Yes?"

"If I bring some people here from below, can you give them a meal?" None of them would go to an office in Cries for Kyle testing, but a few might come here. "Just once, no strings attached."

"Of course. That's why we're here." She hesitated. "But how will you get them to come? We've been trying for two years with almost no success, except for the raids."

"They won't accept charity," I said. "It needs to be an exchange. You do something for them, they do something for you."

Her forehead furrowed. "For us? What do you mean?"

"For ISC, actually. The army wants to test them."

She scowled at me, the same kind of look I had given Cries authorities more than a few times in my youth. "Test them for what?"

"Psi," I said.

Confusion replaced her suspicion. "You mean tests to find empaths? In the *canals?*"

"Yah," I said. "In the canals." She didn't have to act so surprised.

"I'll check with my boss," she said, "but I'm pretty sure it would be fine."

"Who is your boss?"

"Second Level Gratar."

Second Level. It sounded like a rank in the Imperial Relief Allocation Services, a civilian group run by the government. "Are you IRAS?"

"Not me," she said. "I'm just a volunteer. But the IRAS set up this place."

"Ah." That made sense. They did a lot of charitable work.

"Who are you?" she asked.

"Bhaajan."

She waited. Then she said, "You're in the military?"

"No." Hearing how abrupt that sounded, I added, "I was. Army." I shifted my weight, uncomfortable with the questions. "Thank you for your help."

"Of course." She hesitated. "Can you really bring people from the aqueducts here?"

She looked as skeptical as I felt. Probably she thought I was some deluded good-doer who wandered in off the street. Who knew, maybe she was right. "I have no idea," I admitted. I thought of Braze gambling down in Jak's casino. "I have to go."

"Thank you for coming in." She seemed at a loss as to what to make of me. I didn't blame her. I felt the same way.

I left the Concourse Center and headed back to the aqueducts.

A ganger intercepted me before I reached the Black Mark. I was striding along the midwalk when she slipped out of the wall a few steps ahead. She was a dust knight, about fourteen, slender and long-legged, the girl who had struck me as a leader. I saw the signs of the future in her gaze, a sharp intelligence, her awareness of everything around her, and a kindness she probably tried to hide as a gang member. I had also noticed her because she stood with the Oey cyber-rider. I wasn't sure if he had adopted her name or he had adopted hers, but judging from what I had seen of them, it wouldn't be long before they shared more than a symbol. Gangers usually stayed with gangers, like Jak and me, and riders stayed with riders, but tradition rarely survived against the stronger force of love. Who knew, maybe they were setting a precedent, the first leaders in the knights, forging a new path for the undercity. Or maybe I was a deluded dreamer. But what the hell. I liked her.

"Heya," I said, slowing down.

"Got a message for you," she told me. "From Jak."

"Is Braze done for the night?" I asked.

"Yah, done. She's getting ready to leave."

We set off for the casino, jogging together along the midwalk. In places where it narrowed, she dropped behind me. In my youth, I wouldn't have let someone follow where I couldn't see them, but with all the sensors in my biomech, it made no difference; I knew what she was doing regardless of where she ran. In any case, I doubted she would attack. It wasn't only my intuition about her, though that played a big part in my decision to trust her. When the knights asked me to train them, they acknowledged me as one of their circle. It was an odd choice, given that I no longer lived here. I wouldn't have trusted an outsider. Then again, if I had thought someone could teach me tykado, I might have been willing to accept them on a limited basis.

As we descended into the deeper levels, we lost the spillover of light from the lampposts in the upper canals. I switched on my stylus and the sphere of light moved with us as we ran.

My companion kept up well, not at all out of breath.

So I said, "Bhaaj" and hit the heel of my hand against my abdomen. "Bhaajan."

She nodded to me. After a moment, she repeated my gesture. "Pat Sandjan."

So. Daughter of the sand. It was an act of trust for her to say her name; we never revealed them to outsiders. She hesitated before she said Sandjan, which made me think it was a nickname. Maybe someday she would tell me if she had inherited a second name. I used only Bhaajan because I knew nothing about my parents or true kin. I'd never chosen a nickname; why, I wasn't sure; maybe because I wanted to be someone's daughter even if I knew nothing else about the woman who died giving me birth.

Pat and I weren't alone. I caught rustles from the other side of the wall, hints of other runners. Every now and then I glimpsed one down in the canal or across on the other midwalk. They were training with us. We used to do that, me, Jak, Dig, and Gourd, jogging together. We hadn't thought anything about it; we just liked to run. It was what gangs did. It wasn't until I started winning marathons in the army that I realized what all that dashing about had done for me.

So we continued, our feet pounding the ground. We soon turned into a narrow tunnel. A few more turns and we reached the Black Mark. Pat went ahead, around a corner of the building, which was a hexagon tonight. I wondered how Jak always managed to fold up and hide an entire building so fast. One of these days, I'd convince him to let me help so I could see how he achieved that feat.

I stopped in front of the casino's wall and peered at the points of light glittering within the black surface.

They went too deep. The effect had to be holographic; those walls couldn't really be several meters thick.

"Heya, Bhaaj," a man said, his voice like whiskey.

I looked up to see Jak a few paces away. Pat had disappeared.

"Heya," I said. "Is Braze done?"

"Yah." He scowled. "She lost big."

"I thought you liked it when people lost big."

He shifted his feet like a runner impatient to take off. "Says she can't pay."

I walked with him around the building, squeezing between the walls and the surrounding rock formations. A few meters ahead, a horizontal line of light appeared in the darkness.

"Your casino has a leak," I said.

"It's the VIP exit." Jak stopped behind a rock column. "Private like."

Private, as in an exit for ISC officers who could be court-martialed if they were caught gambling. I joined him behind the column and switched off my stylus. The darkness became complete except for that glimmering line. With no other light here, it seemed as bright as a sun.

Jak's breath whispered across the nape of my neck. "Quiet here." His sensuous drawl wound around me. "Got ideas for the dark."

So did I, but this wasn't the time. "Got rocks for a brain," I muttered.

Jak laughed softly. "Need to get back inside. Braze'll be out soon."

I touched his hand where it rested on my shoulder. "See you."

"Yah," he murmured.

I didn't hear him leave, but I felt his departure as if it were loss of air behind me.

Up ahead, the line of light widened. A woman's gruff laugh scraped the night. "Andorian ale, Jak. Pure Andorian. Twenty cases. It's yours."

Jak's voice rumbled. "Might cover tonight's debt." He sounded good-natured, but I knew him too well to be fooled. He was pissed. He didn't want her ale, he wanted her credits. Even so. He served Andorian ale in his casino, and it didn't come cheap. Braze's offer might be worth what she lost. Which begged the question, why did an ISC officer have twenty crates of exorbitantly priced ale lying around, available to sell on the black market? You had to import it from offworld.

The line of light widened more, becoming an exit. Jak and Braze stood in the archway, their bodies silhouetted against the sparkling blackness beyond, where pinpoint holos glittered in the dark. Braze sounded drunk and horny. "You come with me," she said in a slurred voice. "C'mon, Jakie boy." She put her hand on the crouch of his pants. "You got it, hmm?"

I gritted my teeth, wondering how it would feel to break her oversized nose with my fist. Crunch. Yah, that would be good.

Jak deftly moved away her hand. "See you, Braze. My people will pick up the crates in the morning."

"Usual place," she mumbled.

"Yah." Jak stepped back into the casino. "The usual." He closed up the entrance, and the archway disappeared like a camera shutter snapping closed.

"Heh," Braze stood alone in the dark. In my IR vision, she was a hazy red glow.

Max, I thought. *Stealth mode on my boots.*

Done, Max thought. He sent commands to my ankle sockets, which connected to nanites in my boots. They would tweak the molecular structure of my footwear, softening or deforming the boots as needed to make my footfalls silent.

A glow formed around Braze, coming from a hand lamp. She set off in the direction opposite from where I stood. I waited a moment and then followed, silent and hidden.

Braze took a route with no obvious path, making her way between columns and walls riddled with holes. She was a large woman, most of that muscle. Probably she thought she was walking quietly, but to my augmented ears, she sounded like a herd of ruzik, the giant animals ridden by the Abaj Tacalique. Whatever race had stranded my ancestors on Raylicon had also bioengineered the ruzik using the DNA of several Earth species, including an animal called T-rex that died off eons ago. Apparently enough of its DNA survived to make new animals. So I prowled after Braze the T-rex.

I expected her either to go home, which meant I had wasted my time, or to meet her contacts in the Maze. She did neither. Instead she kept descending, deeper than smugglers usually ventured. They needed access to the surface to move their products, and we were below the canals now, in tunnels cool enough that my vision showed only the dimmest red. The aqueducts were warmer because they were closer to the surface; the cold here usually kept me from coming this deep.

Another light appeared ahead. I stepped behind

a tall outcropping and watched Braze approach the light, her body a bulky silhouette against its glow. She stopped and spoke, her voice barely audible.

Max, crank up my hearing, I thought.

Done.

"Twenty-five crates," Braze was saying. "And they better all be Andorian. I'll know if it's cheaper shit."

"Andorian ale?" a woman demanded. Her voice sounded like rusty hinges creaking on an antique door. "That wasn't in our bargain."

I knew that voice. But from where? It tugged my memory. I couldn't risk creeping any closer to see better. If either of she or Braze carried biomech in their bodies, they might hear.

"If you want the guns," Braze said, "then get me the ale."

"Fuck this," the other woman said.

"Fine," Braze told her. "I'm gone." She turned and headed in my direction.

I stayed hidden.

"Wait," the other woman said.

Braze paused, then slowly turned. "What?"

"Fifteen crates."

"I don't have time for this crap." Braze told her.

"Fifteen is better than none."

"Twenty-three."

"Twenty."

"Done," Braze said. "Plus a hundred thousand for the carbines."

So Braze was selling weapons. It didn't take a genius to figure out who wanted them. Yah, I recognized that rusty voice. Hammer Vakaar was hulking there in the shadows. She'd beaten the blazes out of me when we were kids, and in revenge, Dig had pummeled her into a pulp. Only she could best Hammer. The rancor between them had multiplied over the years, until gods only knew how much they hated each other now. If Hammer was buying carbines, that meant both cartels were armed with the best ISC had to offer, or the worst depending on your view. The war had just ramped up into disaster.

Braze and Vakaar talked a few more moments, working out where they would make their deliveries. I knew the place; it was near the Maze. Vakaar obviously intended to make a preemptive strike against the Kajadas, who had no idea their targets had turned the tables. Braze wrested a guarantee from Hammer that no fighting would begin until she left the undercity. After that all bets were off. Damn! That left me less than one hour to get out the warning. I couldn't turn off my jammer to comm anyone, not yet. The moment I lost my shroud, Hammer's spy tech would pick me up, and then I was dead.

As Braze and her contact parted ways, I caught a better glimpse of the other woman. Yah, that was Hammer, with her thick, short neck and large head. I froze, not even breathing.

When they were both gone, I took off.

The aqueducts passed in a blur as I ran. Other runners went with me, some visible, some not, but none could keep up with my enhanced speed. They were doing relays, sprinting hard for as long as they could, then passing the job to someone fresh.

I headed for the cavern where I had trained the dust knights earlier today. It was empty when I arrived. I slung off my pack, tore it open, and switched off the jammer. The moment I dropped my shroud, I became visible to everyone, including Chief Takkar. It was a risk, but I had no choice, and I was close enough to the surface now to set up a direct link. Takkar was my contact, but I had no time to deal with her. I thumbed my gauntlet comm and paged Lavinda Majda.

No answer.

Max, I thought. *Do I have the right link for Colonel Majda?*

It is one she used with you, he answered. **I don't know if—**

A familiar voice crackled from my comm. "Majda here."

"Colonel, this is Major Bhaajan." As I spoke, two dust knights dropped from the ceiling to the floor. I continued talking. "An illegal transfer of ISC guns is taking place right now in the aqueducts. When it finishes, Vakaar is going to attack Kajada. Both cartels are armed with tanglers and laser carbines."

Pat Sandjan and the Oey cyber-rider strode into the cave, breathing heavily from running. I nodded to them as I spoke to Lavinda. "We need your help," I told the colonel. "But not in the fighting. We need soldiers to protect our people."

Lavinda didn't miss a beat. "Major, if a battle is about to start under Cries, you damn well better bet I'm sending in soldiers to fight."

More of the knights were slipping into the cave, stepping out from behind rock formations or dropping from the ceiling. They stood watching me, the stranger in their midst doing the impossible, speaking directly to a Majda colonel.

"If you send troops against the cartels," I told her, "you'll have a bloodbath. Only one thing could make the cartels join forces when they're bent on annihilating each other. That's a common enemy. You. They won't care who gets in the way. If your people kill even one of the drug punkers, it will be even worse. The fighting will explode onto the Concourse, even above ground. Innocent people will die. Many of them. Families." I looked around at the knights. "Children."

She spoke firmly. "I will not stand by and do nothing."

"I'm not asking you to do nothing." I kept my voice calm so she would listen. "We need help. Send troops to protect our people." I thought fast. "Don't send them in uniform. Dress them as if they belong to the undercity. That won't fool anyone, but they'll be seen as less of a threat."

Silence.

Listen, please, I willed her. Takkar would tell me in no uncertain terms what I could do with my ideas, but with Lavinda I didn't know, except that she was undoubtedly notifying someone of my warning.

The colonel's voice crackled. "Major, what you are asking me to do amounts to standing by while the two cartels try to wipe each other out."

I sent a silent apology to Dig. She and I had chosen our paths, and however strong our bond, those roads had taken us apart forever. I just hoped it wasn't too late for her daughter. To Lavinda, I said, "It's the only way to keep them from wiping out everyone else."

"Wait," Lavinda said. "I'm getting a message." After a pause, her voice snapped out of my comm. "The Cries police tell me they would know if this war was brewing, and they say the slums are quiet."

Yah, right. "Colonel, trust me," I said. "I know how things work here. Trouble is coming." The dust knights were gathering around me, even more than the last time they had come here, all of them listening. I had to get these kids to safety. "Send protection, and let the cartels hammer it out between themselves."

"How many people live there beside the cartels?" Lavinda said. "About twenty?"

I stared at the comm. She thought only *twenty* other people lived here? Nearly twenty were just standing in this cave with me, and they were all children.

"It's a lot more than that," I said.

"Counting the drug runners, you mean," Lavinda said.

"No. I'm not counting them." The above-city had plenty of resources to monitor the canals. That they had no clue about how many people lived here spoke all too clearly about our value to them. Yet for all that I raged at Cries for ignoring my people while they lived in poverty beneath one of the wealthiest cities in the Imperialate, it wasn't only the above-city. We fiercely protected our isolation. We and Cries needed to find a way to work together.

"Colonel," I said. "Can you help us?"

"Are you sure this is what you want?" Lavinda asked. "Protection only?"

"Yes. I'm sure."

Lavinda exhaled. "Very well. We'll do it your way." She spoke grimly. "You better be right."

I let out a breath. "Thank you. Out here."

After I signed off, I turned my jammer on. The knights were waiting, their clothes gritty with red dust. I motioned them closer. Pat moved to the front with the older girl and boy I had pegged as leaders before. The Oey rider stood next to Pat, tall and fit, the silvery tracings of his high-tech tattoos swirling on his arms, as artistic as they were functional.

I nodded to the four of them and hit the heels of my palms together. "Bhaajan." They would give me their names or not, but only if they knew mine.

Pat spoke first. "Pat Sandjan," she said, not for my benefit, since I already knew, but to show the others she would reveal her name. Unexpectedly, she added, "Pat Cote."

Cote. It had to be her true name. It meant shelter, often for those who needed protection. It seemed apt for a dust knight who protected her circle. She also honored me by giving her full name.

The older girl next to Pat hit her palms together. "Runner."

The duster boy followed suit. "Rockson."

The Oey rider spoke, his voice resonant. "Biker." He glanced at Pat and nodded slightly to her. Then he turned back to me and added, "Tim Oey."

Another honor, his full name. His nickname, Biker, was a clever play on his status as a rider, a comparison to the sleek cycles people rode in the above-city, those gleaming, low to the ground vehicles that whizzed through the streets, the ultimate status symbol among Cries youth. His name implied he had the same status among the riders. Just as intriguing, Pat's dust gang took its name from a cyber-rider. It was no wonder she and Biker stood out as leaders; they weren't afraid to be different even if it meant breaking our unwritten traditions.

I spoke to the group. "You four will lead the knights."

They nodded their acceptance. None of them looked surprised.

Now for the rest of the kids. I had to phrase this in a way they would all accept, getting them out of danger without making them think I was asking them to hide. I spoke to all of them. "You are the knights. You must protect. Understand?"

They nodded, the youngest ones with wide, frightened gazes.

I raised my voice. "Protect!"

"Protect!" Their voices were ragged, hinting at fear. This wasn't training. This was the real thing.

"Got parents?" I asked. "How many of you?"

Three children waved their hands, cutting the air with a jerk.

Gods. Only *three* had parents? Who took care of these kids? I knew the answer, knew it from my own life. "Got sibs?" I asked. "How many?"

All of them waved this time, indicating they had brothers and sisters. They might not be related by blood to those they called their kin, but they were people the knights considered their circle, just as Gourd, Dig, and Jak had been my circle.

"Who rides the mesh waves?" I asked.

Six responded to that one, including Biker, all of them with silvery conduits in their clothes or skin, eyes lenses, artificial limbs, and who knew what else hidden under their rags. Six cyber-riders. Good. They could get out the news far faster than the others.

I regarded them all. "You are tasked with an important job. You must spread the word. All depends on you." It was true; they were the only ones who could give the warning in time. "Tell your families. Your sibs. Your circles. The cartel war is coming. You have heard this?"

"Yah," Biker said. "It's on the waves."

"And the whisper," Pat said.

Good. I was telling the knights something that only Hammer and Braze knew for certain. I didn't want the cartels to suspect these kids had spied on them. If rumors were already riding the waves, that was enough.

"Spread the word," I said. "Tell everyone: Go to ground." I raised my voice. "You are knights. It is up to you! Get your circles to safety." And in doing so, I hoped they would get themselves to safety as well. Making them responsible for the warning gave them a crucial task. Pat, Runner, Rockson, and Biker were older and full of the blazing energy that infused our youths. Left on their own, they would join the fighting. But they were also leaders. If they agreed to the role, the safety of these children would matter to them. They all became one large circle. These kids wouldn't be together if they weren't already attached through whatever complex relationships existed here. Taking responsibility for the safety of their circle could keep Biker, Pat, Runner, and Rockson from joining the fighting—

And from dying, for without guns, they couldn't survive against the armed cartels.

"Pat, Biker, Runner, Rockson," I said. "Command the knights."

"We'll take care of it," Biker said. The other three nodded.

I called out to the rest of the children. "Who are you?"

"Dust knights!" they shouted.

I motioned at the four leaders. "Follow your commanders!"

They turned to Pat and Biker. "Dust knights, ready!"

I spoke more quietly to the leaders. "It's up to you now."

They all nodded. Biker grinned at me. "Got speed."

"Good. Now go!"

With that, I left the cave and set off running through the Maze. *Gods help them.* Help the children. For I had another duty. I had to warn Dig. If I didn't, Vakaar would massacre Kajada, leaving Hammer free to take over the drug trade, making it even easier for her to wreck havoc with the bliss-disguised nightmares she sold. I could level the combat field. What happened then was up to them.

I just prayed the rest of our community survived their rampage.

XVIII
The Hidden

As I ran along a midwalk toward the Maze, I sent out my green beetle to find the closest Kajada punker. So of course it found the thug who had tried to blast me with a carbine yesterday. Bad luck, but I had no idea where to find Dig and no time to locate anyone else.

The punker is jogging on the midwalk of the canal to your left, Max told me. **Just on the other side of the wall that separates it from this canal.**

Good, I thought. *How do I get over there?*

My maps suggest a passage through the wall lies a few meters ahead.

I slowed as I approached an archway in the wall. Unlike many passages here, this one didn't come from damage to the ruins; it was a real entrance built by the ancient architects to provide access from one canal to the other. I stepped through the archway and walked down a short tunnel to the next canal. We were near enough to the Concourse that this one had a few street lamps.

Four gangers were clustered on the midwalk across

the canal, and a rider stood farther down, talking into a comm on her tech-mech arm. Spreading the warning, I hoped.

Looking in the other direction, I spied the Kajada punker up ahead, loping along the midwalk. I followed, easily gaining on her. When I was about ten meters away, she suddenly stopped and spun around, holding up a long blade that glittered.

I skidded to a halt and lifted my hands, palms facing her. The pulse revolver in my holster showed, of course, but I made no attempt to draw the weapon.

"What do you want?" she demanded.

"I need to talk to Dig."

"Fuck that."

"Fine," I said. "You give her the message. Tell her Vakaar has ISC guns. Hammer is going to attack. Fifteen minutes. Maybe less."

She stared at me. "Vakaar doesn't have shit."

I didn't have time for this posturing. "Vakaar has plenty of shit. Tanglers. Carbines. Tell Dig. You don't, Kajada dies. It's on you. GO!" With that, I took off again, running past her. She tried to threaten me with the knife, but I was already beyond her reach before she even finished turning.

Max, send the green beetle after her, I thought. *Let me know if she contacts Dig.*

She's running after you.

She won't catch me.

She turned into another tunnel. She's heading down-city.

I hoped that meant she was seeking out Dig. *Where's my red beetle?*

At the casino.

Has Jak folded up the place?

No.

Damn! But why would he fold? After being closed for a while, he was probably raking it in tonight. He had no idea what was up with the cartels.

I headed for the Black Mark.

Jak came around a bend, jogging toward me. How he knew I was coming, I couldn't have said, but he had always had a top-notch network. We stopped in front of each other, breathing heavily from the run.

"You got to close the Black Mark," I said.

"Why?" he asked. "Got a good night going."

"Braze sold ISC arms to Hammer. Vakaar is going after Kajada. Now."

He stared at me. "Shit."

"Yah."

He pulled me to a tunnel entrance behind a curtain of stone. As he moved, he tapped out a code on his belt. Light flickered on a slender conduit embedded in the leather, hardly noticeable. The better the tech, the smaller, and he could afford the best.

I squeezed with him into the hidden tunnel. "Are you warning the Mark?"

"Yah." He pulled me along a narrow passage lit only by my stylus.

"Where are we going?" I asked.

"Drug-bliss kid."

"You found one."

He spoke grimly. "More than one."

"Where?"

Jak drew me into a wider portion of he tunnel and pointed to a set of roughly hewn stairs on our left.

"Go see the family at top. They took in the baby and the boy you found. Say I sent you."

"You're going back to the Mark?"

"Yah," He kissed me, quick and fast, then took off running back the way we had come.

Well, so. No one had ever kissed me before I went into a fight before. I'd figure out how I felt about that later. Right now, I took the stairs two at a time. They wound around like a demented spiral staircase, some parts a natural progression of ledges, others hacked out by humans. In one place, I had to drop to my knees to push past an overhang blocking the way. On the other side, I kept going up and around. At the top, I stepped into a small foyer surrounded by rock. An opening stood across me, an archway tooled out of the stone like a work of art bordered by abstract carvings.

I walked over and stepped just inside the archway, unsure if I should go further. People lived here. The furniture was sculpted from rock formations with the same artistic beauty as the archway. Plush cushions softened them, embroidered with gold threads. Gorgeous tapestries hung on the walls, all woven in the undercity style, with glowing colors. They depicted scenes of canals and caves, shimmering in metallic threads, red, blue, green, gold, amber. Some showed fanciful depictions of how the aqueducts might have looked in ancient times, running with water.

"Heya," I called.

A man walked out of an inner doorway. He was holding a knife just as long and as ugly as the one the drug punker had brandished at me in the canal.

"How get here?" he demanded. Somewhere deeper in the home, a baby cried.

"Jak sent me," I said. "Said you took in the orphans I found."

His posture eased. "You're The Bhaaj?"

"Just Bhaajan." I wondered why he put "The" in front of my name.

He lowered his knife. "Come with."

I followed him through another sculpted archway and into a room with more tapestries on the walls. A lamp with an exquisite glass shade stood in one corner, its colors glowing red, blue, and gold. It was fastened to the wall and the shade was too high for a child to reach. The other corner sported a water desalination apparatus partially hidden by potted plants with blue and red flowers. They grew in modified canal dust. Hand woven rugs warmed the floor, their colors more subdued than the wall hangings, but their artistry just as exceptional. Toys were strewn everywhere, balls, dolls, and holo-readers. On my right, a curtain hung in the archway to another room. The place was uncommonly beautiful, and so utterly different from anything in Cries, it was hard to believe we all descended from the same culture.

"Nice," I said.

The man nodded.

The curtain rustled as a woman pushed it aside to enter the room. I recognized her as one of Jak's bartenders. She was holding the baby I had found in the tunnels, and it snuggled in her arms, cooing softly. The curtain fell back into place, then moved again, just enough to let a boy peek out at me. Pack Rat! He looked much less scared and much less dusty than the last time I had seen him. He smiled shyly, then let the curtain drop into place, hiding him.

I nodded to the woman. "Children doing better."

"Yah." She nuzzled the baby's head. "Was close for this one."

Behind her, the curtain shifted and a girl of about seven walked out. She stepped behind her mother and looked around her, watching me with large brown eyes.

"Three children?" I asked. That was counting the two orphans they had taken in.

"Four," the mother said.

The father spoke to me. "The older girl is a dust knight."

So that was why they recognized me. Their daughter must have been one of the three that indicated she had parents. The Cries authorities would undoubtedly cluck with concern about children living in caves, but a home like this could be a wonderful place to live.

I wondered, though, why their older daughter wasn't here. "Did she warn you?"

"Warn us?" the man asked. "About what?"

"The cartels are going to war," I said. "You stay here. Be safe. Don't go out." This home was well hidden. The cartels had no reason to come here. "She'll be home soon." I hoped to the gods that was true.

"We will stay," the man said.

"You come to see the blissers?" the woman asked.

"Yah." I hesitated, looking at her younger daughter, who seemed healthy, with clear eyes and well-brushed hair. Pack Rat finally came out of hiding and went to stand behind the girl. He was cleaned up, his face washed, his clothes fresh, the desperation gone from his gaze. It would be a long time before he forgot the nightmare of his mother's death, if ever, but with this family he might heal, as I had healed when I returned to the undercity from the orphanage. I had felt scorned and ignored above-city, worthless, or so I thought, until Jak, Gourd, and Dig became my family and the aqueducts became my home.

"Your children aren't blissers," I said.

"Not ours," the man said.

"We found them in a cave near here," the mother said.

The father spoke quietly. "Dying."

Was it a bad batch of the drug, or did phorine kill? "I come with," I said. "To see them."

"Yah, we go." The woman gave the baby to her daughter, who held it with practiced ease. Given that she had no younger siblings until a few days ago, she had probably held the babies of her friends. We all did that in the undercity, everyone looking after the children in our circle.

The woman took me to a tapestry across the room and pulled it aside to reveal a tunnel with polished sides. Someone had carved shelves into the wall at chest height and engraved their surfaces with graceful arabesques. As we entered the tunnel, she let the tapestry fall into place, leaving us in darkness. My ears ramped up, enough to hear someone run into the room we had just left. A girl spoke, out of breath, saying they should stay home, stay here, away from the canals. I recognized her voice; she was one of the older knights. I closed my eyes, hit with a wave of relief. Even if I hadn't come, this family would have heard the warning.

A light flared in the tunnel. The mother was holding a mesh cube that glowed with ads for various above-city vendors.

"Nice cube," I said.

She glanced at me. "Bought it on Concourse."

Bought. Not "found," which meant stolen, or "bargained for," which meant she traded for it in the undercity economy or on the black market. Bought meant purchased with above-city credits. Jak paid his employees in either credits or food and water, whatever they preferred, apparently enough that she could purchase amenities beyond what they needed for survival. It told me a lot about Jak, all of it good.

"Good work at the Black Mark?" I asked.

"Yah." She led down the finely tooled passage. "Enough for family."

I thought of the orphans she had taken in. "Got two more now."

"No worries." She raised the cube, letting more of its light fall across me. "Better to have children than cubes, heh?"

"Guess so." The orphans were fortunate to end up here. Then it hit me. This family had another potential source of income, something people from all over the Imperialate would pay a great deal for. I doubted it would occur to them; it wouldn't have to me when I lived here.

"Got good tapestries in your home," I said. "Glasswork, carvings, all of it. Nice."

"My husband makes them," she said.

Her husband was an artistic genius. And they were married. Although many couples here committed for life, most couldn't afford a marriage license or simply didn't fathom its purpose. We had our own ceremonies, none of which Cries recognized, but they meant more to us than a formal license. You also needed to go into Cries to get the license, which most of my people loathed doing. Some couldn't even take the light, their eyes had become so accustomed to the dark.

The Concourse, however, was more accessible. So I said, "Sell tapestries on Concourse," and waited for the explosion.

The woman swung around to me. "What! Crazy."

"Not crazy," I said. "Tourists will pay more for one tapestry than Jak pays in a tenday." At least they would if she and her husband knew they could get away with charging that much. "Your man can sell his carvings, too. And his glasswork."

"Got rocks in your head." She resumed her walk down the tunnel.

Rocks, pah. My people could make exquisite weavings, carvings, and glasswork, and nothing matched the haunting beauty of our music. Gods only knew how many were creating works that literally never saw the light of day. Tourists would pay huge sums for the arts of such an enigmatic, dangerous community. Beauty in the darkness. Yah, it would work. They would take the art home and talk about how they dared venture into the Cries undercity. Never mind that no one who actually lived undercity considered the tame, commercialized Concourse part of our world. Technically it belonged to us, and Cries vendors promoted it that way in their advertising.

"It's not crazy," I said as I followed her.

The woman just snorted. No matter. I'd work on the idea with both my people and Cries. Undercity vendors would need a license to set up a stall on the Concourse and that required a fee, not to mention approval by the city bureaucracy. It wouldn't be simple, but we were citizens of Cries and we had the right to file.

Somewhere in the distance, shouts reverberated, an echo that carried even to this secluded area, which was probably several kilometers away. The woman stopped, turning toward the noise.

"Cartels," I said. "Got to hurry. How far?"

"Not much." She glanced back at me. "These three, they took node-bliss only twice. After that, no more. They shook and jerked for days. Screamed. Cried. Begged for more."

If phorine induced a withdrawal that severe after only two doses, they must be powerful psions. "Are they all right now?" I asked.

"Some." The woman stepped into a crevice in the wall.

I followed her into a small room. More tapestries graced the wall, fluffy pallets with quilts lay on the floor, and a carved table was set with food and water.

Three people huddled on the beds. One was a young man. He lay on his side, curled in a fetal position, his arms wrapped around his stomach. An older teen in a clean tunic and loose pants sat on the pallet next to his, slouched against the wall, her knees drawn to her chest. A younger girl was sleeping on the bed next to hers.

"Heya," I murmured as I knelt next to the man. "Can you hear?"

He opened his eyes. "Yah," he whispered.

"Had bliss?"

"Before." He closed his eyes. "No more."

I looked around the room. The woman who had brought me here was preparing three plates of food at the table.

"How many days have they been here?" I asked.

She turned to me. "Three, maybe four. They had a terrible time."

The older girl spoke in a raspy voice. "Bliss gone."

I hated seeing them like this. "It was bad?"

"Very bad," she whispered.

I indicated the sleeping girl. "Is she okay?"

The man sat up slowly, as if he ached everywhere. "Better than us."

"The bliss didn't do so much for her," the older girl said.

Maybe the younger girl wasn't as strong of a psion. "Why is it gone?" I asked.

The girl fixed me with a cold stare. "Scorch dead."

"You bought from Scorch?"

"She gave it to us," the man said.

No way would Scorch provide free drugs, not without some ulterior motive. "What did you give her?"

The girl shrugged. "We moved crates for her."

As payment? Yah, right. Scorch had wanted them addicted. Why? Sure, she could make money off them once they were hooked, but given the low incidence of psions and the danger of pissing off the cartels, it didn't seem worth the bother.

"Anyone else do bliss?" I asked.

The older girl shrugged. "Not know."

"Scorch had a place for us to live," the man said. "To wait."

I suddenly felt ill. "Wait for what?"

"Visitors." He motioned toward the ceiling. "Away from Raylicon."

"Where was Scorch going to put you?" I asked, though I feared I already knew.

"Never saw," the girl rasped. "Never got to the Alcove. Scorch died."

I wanted to hit something. Scorch had meant to hide psions in the Alcove. Addicting them to phorine was nauseatingly brilliant. It not only let her find empaths and telepaths, it made them dependent on her, willing to do whatever she wanted. She hadn't been some minor cog in a weapons smuggling operation. Her sins had been even uglier. She intended to sell psions to the Traders.

"Scorch is fucked," I said. "Sell you into slavery."

The older girl scowled at me. "Lying."

"Not lying," I said flatly.

In the distance, a rumbling began, rising into thunder and then dying away, the noise of falling rock. I had to get out here, find out what was happening.

I stood up. "Stay here, yah?"

"Don't need to stay," the girl said defiantly. "Almost better."

"The cartels are fighting out there," I said. "Carbines, tanglers."

They all just looked at me. They knew better than to mess with the cartels, but they would never admit it out loud, especially not to me, the intruder who had cut off their phorine supply.

I looked around at them. "You feel?"

"Feel what?" the man asked.

"Thoughts," I said. "Moods."

The girl stiffened. "Not crazy!"

That had certainly hit a nerve. "Not crazy," I agreed. "But psion, yah?"

"Psion?" the man asked.

"Someone who feels moods," I said. "Maybe thoughts."

The man and the girl looked at each other. Neither denied my words.

"I'm tired," the man said. He lay back down and closed his eyes.

I looked at the woman who had brought me. She had left clean chamber pots in the corner and was holding the three that had been there.

"You all need to stay hidden," I told her.

The woman nodded. "We will stay."

Good. I had to go, however. I had work to do, and I was royally pissed. Scorch hadn't just broken the code we lived by, she had shattered it.

I wished I hadn't killed her, so I could kill her now.

XIX
Thunder

In the aqueducts, we fought guerilla style, hiding in ruins that were over five thousand years old. The cartels wouldn't care who they killed in their firestorm. Even if no one died, which seemed about as likely as no one cussing, the fighting could do serious damage to the aqueducts, an anthropological marvel unmatched by anything in our modern age.

Laser carbines didn't thunder, they hissed, but whatever the shot hit often exploded or collapsed as well as burned. Somewhere up ahead, rocks were crashing as walls toppled. I kept my pulse revolver up and ready as I eased through crevices in the walls, moving toward the noise.

Max, I thought. *Did that Kajada punker get my warning to Dig?*

Yes, he thought. **She reached Dig about ten minutes before the Vakaars attacked.**

Ten minutes was almost nothing, but it could be an eternity compared to no warning at all. I hoped it had been enough.

Toggle combat mode, I thought. Max would do it anyway the moment I started fighting, but I wanted the heightened senses it gave me now even though it meant my combat libraries might take over my actions if my node calculated I was in danger of getting whacked.

I eased out of a crevice, staying behind a column on the midwalk. A flash of light up ahead threw the canal into sharp relief, and then darkness descended again. I used my IR vision and thermal imaging to study the area, a mid-sized canal. Dust covered the midwalk, and the bittersweet stench of fused grit filled the air. Hiding places were everywhere, not only in the walls, but also in the ceiling crusted with small stalactites, and the canal floor, which was riddled with fallen rocks and columns that had toppled from the midwalk.

Three-dimensional battlefield, Max thought.

Unfortunately. *Send my beetles to monitor places I can't see, like the ceiling.*

A scrape came from behind me. I jerked around in time to see two figures in dark clothes sprint down the midwalk and dart into a crack in the wall. It was a good thing I moved, because a laser shot came from behind me at the same time, barely missing my body as it hit the wall. A fused chunk of rock flew out and struck my shoulder. Even as I stumbled, I was firing at whoever had used the laser. My node fine-tuned the shot based on its predictions of their location, and under the force of my shot, the wall exploded a few meters away. As rocks avalanched into the canal below, a woman tumbled with them, out of her hiding place, cussing as she fell.

"You're dead, Bhaaj," a woman said behind me.

I dodged the instant *before* she spoke. My enhanced ears picked up a noise and my node set me into motion. Even with all that, I barely leapt aside in time. Her shot whizzed so close, I smelled ionized air. She was above me, hidden in a crevice where the wall met the roof. I fired, and spinning projectiles from my gun flashed through the air.

The bullets tore apart her body. As blood dripped from the ceiling, I stared at the remains of her hiding place. No matter how many deaths I had caused or seen during combat, I never became inured to killing another human being. I hated it. But I hated dying even more.

I didn't recognize what was left of the woman, but I knew the insignia that showed on the remains of her sleeve: a line of light cutting through a red orb. Vakaar. It had probably once been a gang tag, but now it symbolized the cartel. It gave warning: they were after me. Maybe they had heard that I had warned Kajada about their attack, or Hammer might want me dead on principle, because Dig and I went way back. Whatever the reason, a Vakaar punker had just tried to whack me.

I stepped into a niche in the wall and stood still. In the distance, falling rocks crashed and rumbled and then petered into silence. I strained to pick up fainter noises, the scrapes that might come from snipers hiding in the rocks.

Max? I thought.

T* **end****

What?

No answer.

Well, damn. The EM pulse from my bullets must have affected my biomech. That wasn't supposed to happen; my web had safeties and backups, besides which, the EM pulse was confined to a volume of space about the size of a body. Still, no system was perfect. At least Max managed part of an answer. I hoped that meant he could fix the damage.

Yes, Max thought. **I'm mak**+ repairs.**

Good. You see anything with my beetles?

Fighting in this canal, up ahead.

Show me.

My perception shifted as he linked my optics to the beetle, so I saw what it saw. We were near the ceiling about one hundred meters down the midwalk. A man with a carbine lay stretched out up here on a hidden shelf, which from below probably looked like a flat part of the roof. The Vakaar insignia glinted on his gauntlets. Normally punkers didn't flaunt their symbols. Dig and Hammer were too smart to identify their people, which was probably why their cartels had survived when others disappeared. But today Vakaar was making a statement: *We own these canals.*

A woman stepped into view on the midwalk below, a tangler gripped in her hand. She wore no insignia, neither the Vakaar orb nor the Kajada ruzik. In fact, it looked like she had thrown on her clothes, her frayed tunic rumpled and her trousers with no belt or holster for her gun. Kajada, I'd wager, warned at the last minute that Vakaar was coming. The woman slipped behind a stone curtain and my beetle followed. Another man crouched back there, also Kajada, it looked like.

I recognized none of these people. True, I'd been gone for years, but even so, with all the punkers I had seen in the past few days, how could Dig be the only one I knew? More people lived here than I had realized. The aqueducts formed a huge network under the city, the Vanished Sea, and the ruins of ancient Cries. Although anthropologists had spent generations mapping the area, the city didn't consider our population worth the expense or risk of a census. Did *anyone* know how many people lived here? The police cared about the cartels and crime bosses, but no one bothered the gangs or riders as long as they kept off the Concourse. It was another reason the "Rec Center" was doomed to failure; even if my people wanted to go there, the police would stop them.

A scrape came from above. Following the sound, my beetle flew back to the man's hiding place in the ceiling. My fried systems still weren't working right, because the bot flew too close to his face. He stiffened and batted at the air. Damn! Although Raylicon had species of tiny flying reptiles, my beetle wouldn't pass a close inspection.

Max, get the bot away from him, I thought.

As the beetle darted away, the Vakaar man fired at the curtain where the Kajada punkers had hidden. The barrier collapsed in a blast of light, and fused rock rained over the midwalk. I twitched as if I had been there instead of a hundred meters away. Although the shot destroyed the curtain, no remains showed of the two punkers who had taken cover there. They must have moved on. That the sniper fired anyway could mean he didn't have sensors that located people. I doubted it, though. The cartels traded, stole, or smuggled plenty of tech-mech. More likely, my beetle spooked him.

Max, check the calibration for my bots, I thought. *Don't let them fly so close to the punkers.*

How do they identify a punker?

Good question. *Anyone in or near the fighting.* I hoped Colonel Majda kept her word about not sending troops to fight.

The Vakaar man dropped from his hiding place and landed in a crouch. He checked the area, kicking aside rock fragments that weren't fused to the ground or each other. Finally he climbed over the debris and took off down the midwalk, striding away from my location. When he was gone, I ran to the debris and searched for signs of human remains. I found none. Relieved, I clambered over the rocks and set off after the punker. Up ahead, in the distance, I could see him jogging. I doubted he had augmented hearing, since he didn't seem to realize I was following him. Somewhere farther down the canal, the rumble of an avalanche echoed in the canal.

My spinal node sent a direct thought to my mind, its voice eerily metallic compared to Max's more human tones: **Terminate target?** it asked.

No, just follow. My intention was to stop deaths, not cause them. Hell, I even wanted the punkers to survive. The percentage of adults in the undercity was already too low. We didn't need more of them whacked, leaving a community run by hungry children and pissed off adolescents.

My node took over my reflexes before I knew what happened, and I jumped off the midwalk the instant before a laser blasted the pathway. I landed on the canal floor in knee-deep dust, my legs bending, my hydraulics absorbing the impact. Powder swirled around me and the acrid stink of fused powder saturated the air, activating the filters in my nose. I sprinted down the canal, kicking up more dust, obstructing the view of whoever had fired. The jammer would shield me from their sensors—I hoped. Another shot hit the ground behind me. Damn! That was from the other side of the canal. I zigzagged in the clouds of powder. Shots came from the midwalks, the ceiling, the ground. The shooters were mostly firing at each other, but another blast hit the canal just meters ahead of me.

I crouched down, hiding under an outcropping with an overhang. *Max, can you tell who is shooting, and from where?*

A Vakaar is hiding in the canal floor to your right, he answered. **Another Vakaar is on the opposite midwalk and someone is in the ceiling above her—Vakaar I'd guess since he isn't attacking the punker below him. Two shooters on this side, identity unknown, probably Kajada.**

Got it. The dust was settling, so I edged farther under the overhang. Powder went up my nose and I choked.

Clearing obstruction, Max thought. The dust stopped bothering me as my filters broke the particles down into molecules my body could absorb.

A lightshow of shots suddenly crisscrossed the canal, flaring bolts that attacked the ground, the walls, and the columns that supported the aqueduct. Slagged rock flew everywhere, mixed with the swirling dust. I gagged on the stench of melted dust.

Goddamn it! I lifted my gun. *They're going to destroy the canal.*

If you start firing, they will locate and kill you, Max thought.

I'm not shooting at anyone. Damned if I didn't want to, though.

Good. Because you're the only one with a pulse revolver, and both sides probably want you dead.

Not Dig. I hoped.

True. But her people are unlikely to have the same compunctions about killing you.

Are you picking up anyone else in the area besides punkers?

Possibly, Max thought. **It's hard to tell with all the laser fire.** As if to punctuate his words, more shots flared in the canal. **I've picked up signs of two people hiding in the midwalk wall, neither with nanomed tech in their bodies, which means they probably aren't punkers.**

How do you know they're here if they have no meds for you to detect?

The red beetle went in close enough to pick up their heartbeats.

Can I reach them without being seen?

Maybe. I've mapped this area, but I don't know all the hidden passages. He paused. **Get to the canal wall closest to where you're hiding. You might fit into a hole there that might take put you into a tunnel that I think slopes up to the midwalk in the adjacent canal. From there, I think you can reach the trapped people.**

That's a lot of mights.

Yes. Unfortunately, it's the best I can do.

I peered through the dusty air. It felt sticky against my skin. Someone fired a shot that hit the ground a few meters beyond me, and partially melted debris plumed into the air. Under that cover, I sprinted for the canal wall, keeping low to the ground, scuffing up red dust. I doubted anyone noticed, given how much grit already filled in the air. I reached the wall—

And it didn't have a single damn hole.

Max! Where is the entrance? I crouched down, pressing against the wall. Any moment the dust would settle enough for someone to see me here.

Try to your right, Max thought.

I inched along, half blinded by grit, which was cooling into glassy sand that rained out of the air. My hand hit a cone of rock taller than my height. Reaching around it, I found a hole in the canal wall. Unfortunately, the cone was too close to the wall for me to squeeze past it into the opening.

Max, is this what you meant? I asked.

Yes. Apparently you won't fit.

Yah, brilliant deduction. I brought up my gun, waited until someone took another shot, and under that cover, I fired at the cone. Hopefully I also fried the sensors of anyone close enough to detect me. The cone broke apart while a new deluge of dust filled the air. As I squeezed into the hole, jagged edges of rock caught at my jacket and skin. The smart leather didn't tear, but a spike gauged my face and blood ran down my neck.

I'm sending meds through your bloodstream to treat your wounds, Max thought.

Yah, fine. I had no time to worry about injuries. I was crammed into a hole with no outlet in the middle of a battle. If the midwalk above me collapsed, it would crush me as flat as flint.

I turned around in the cavity, squeezing my way to the back. A vertical slit cut the rock there. I reached into the opening, but it was so narrow, I couldn't even get my elbow through. Some sort of open area lay beyond. I didn't have room to kick open the slit, which meant I had to fire my gun again, this time in a confined space. I flicked off the EM pulse so the close quarters wouldn't fry Max. Gritting my teeth, I waited until the noise out in the canal ratcheted up and then I fired, protecting my face with my arm. Debris blasted my body, ripping at my clothes and skin. A sliver of rock penetrated even my smart clothes and buried itself in my leg and something hard hit my temple. With a groan, I sagged forward and fell through the opening I had just created.

You should stop, Max thought. **Treat your wounds.**

Later. I climbed to my feet with my hand over my head. I barely had enough room to straighten up. *Just pray this place doesn't collapse on me.*

I wouldn't advise shooting anything else.

No kidding. I felt woozy and blood ran down my arm, but I was otherwise intact. My head bumped the roof when I walked forward, but I was able to make my way forward. The passage wasn't a tunnel so much as a natural warren of holes and jagged spaces. The air smelled better, less acrid that out in the canal. I reached a slope and climbed upward, my feet dislodging dirt and rocks.

Max, how did you know about this tunnel? I asked.

I mapped the area earlier by sending pulses of sound into the rock to find hollows.

Smart EI.

Thank you.

Got a suggestion for how I can get out?

Yes. Veer to your left and keep climbing.

I went left and soon spotted a line of light ahead, dim, gray, and welcome. When I reached the top of the incline, I stood up. Only two meters of flat, rocky ground separated me from that light. It came from a crack in the wall about two handspans wide and taller than my height.

Where are the beetles? I asked.

Monitoring the combat, Max thought.

I still heard the rumble of falling rock in the canal behind me. How much injury could these ruins take? They had lasted for millennia, but that was with relatively little use. If the one behind me collapsed, it could damage this canal as well.

Bring a beetle here, I thought. *I need its eyes.* I walked to the crack in the wall and stood to the side with my gun up and ready. The canal out there looked empty. It wasn't completely dark; diffuse light came from somewhere.

Here's the bot, Max thought.

The red beetle flew over my shoulder and hovered by my face. Max activated the red lights in its eyes and it blinked at me, glimmering. When Max turned off the lights, the bot became almost invisible. I barely saw it fly out into the canal.

I'm linking you to its eyes, Max thought.

I was suddenly flying over the canal, a wide one in good condition. The light came from a street lamp some distance up the midwalk. The city authority didn't maintain lamps any deeper than this canal, which lay only one level below the Concourse. I didn't think they realized people lived deeper than this.

I spoke to Max. *If the canal we just left collapses, what will that do to this one?*

I don't know. Weaken its supports, I suspect.

I wanted to throttle someone. Damn Dig and Hammer for putting their vendetta before the lives of our people, and damn Braze, for making the guns available. Dig had no clue what she had inherited from Scorch. She saw those weapons and turned greedy. She probably knew nothing about Scorch's phorine-saturated nightmare, selling our people to the Traders. I had no idea how many psions were in the undercity, but even if the three I had already met were the only ones, they would be a great find to the Trader Aristos. The Aristos would pay far more for psions than Scorch would ever have made on the guns.

I flew over the canal. In a throughway this central, people were usually out at all hours. Gangs would gather and make music or build dust sculptures. Children ran in packs. Riders played with their tech as they strode along, sending each other arcane messages only they understood. Tonight I saw no one. Good. The dust knights must have come through here.

I released my link with the beetle and became just Bhaaj again, hiding behind the wall. I stepped out on the midwalk with my gun drawn. *Max, can I reach those two people from here?*

The bot registers their heartbeats to your right, about twelve paces forward.

I walked forward with the wall on my right and stopped after twelve paces. About one handspan away, a crevice showed in the wall.

I believe they know you are here, Max thought. **Their heart rates have increased.**

They have any weapons?

I detect no tech-mech. They could have knives or similar.

So they weren't riders. It didn't surprise me, given how fast Biker could spread the word. The riders would know to avoid this canal. Normally they chose isolation over interacting with the rest of us, but Biker struck me as a leader who would reach out to all our people. He also ran with Pat's dust gang, which included his name, Tim Oey, in their insignia. It boded well for their spreading the warning. I hoped.

Here goes. With my gun up, I flicked on my stylus and shone it through the slit in the wall.

"Ai!" The frightened cry came from a girl. No one jumped out, however.

After a pause, I peered into the darkness. A man stood several paces back form the opening, and a small girl was hiding behind him with her eyes squeezed shut. The man had one arm up to shield his eyes and the other raised in a fist.

"I'm here to help," I said. "Come with. I'll take you away from the fight."

They stared at me, squinting as if I were holding a supernova.

"You cartel?" the man asked.

"Nahya," I said. My people had no word for someone who had left the undercity and then came back, so I just said, "I'm Bhaajan."

"Ah." The man lowered his arm. "The Bhaaj." He took the girl's hand and they stepped forward.

Max, I thought as I moved out of their way. *That's the second time someone has called me "The Bhaaj." Any idea what that means?*

It's your name.

Great. My EI was being wry. *They make it sound like a title.*

They have to call you something.

I suppose.

They eased sideways through the crack and stepped onto the midwalk. The girl looked about eight and the man was probably in his twenties. Their resemblance was unmistakable. Their skin was so light, it seemed translucent, like alabaster. They stood protecting their eyes, so I switched off my stylus, leaving us in only the dim light from the lamp down the midwalk.

The man lowered his hand. "Our thanks." The girl stopped squinting.

"Are you hurt?" I asked.

He shook his head. "We're fine."

I included my head toward the girl. "Your sister?"

"Daughter."

I nodded, acknowledging the bond, and motioned down the midwalk, toward the lamp. "We go that way. To safety."

Together, the thee of us headed toward the lamp. The midwalk was wide enough for all of us to walk abreast, which was rare in the canals. I stayed on the outside edge.

The girl spoke in a soft voice. "Got light."

"Yah," I murmured. As we passed under the street lamp, they both shaded their eyes.

"Where're you from?" I asked.

"The down-below," the man said. "Below the aqueducts."

I hadn't realized people lived that deep. "No light?"

"Not bright light." He motioned toward the streetlamp behind us. "Not like that."

If he thought that lamp was bright, they must live in almost total darkness. It could explain why they hadn't heard the warning, if they were that removed from our main population.

"Why come here?" I asked.

The girl lifted her chin. "Dust knights."

I blinked. "You know about the knights?"

"Came to join," the father said. He paused, then added, "If the knights got a place for us."

They had come up into the painful brightness to be dust knights. I felt a strange sensation building within, a sort of tension, but not exactly. Something was happening with the knights, I wasn't sure what, but it seemed good.

"Might have places," I said. "But know this. Knights live by a code. To be a knight, you must keep the code."

"We keep," the man said.

"Whisper says the code is tough," the girl told me earnestly.

I was surprised they had heard the code was tough, given that I had yet to figure out what it was, beyond "protect people." I thought of the cartels. "No drugs."

"No drugs," the man agreed. He sounded relieved.

"Protect dust gangers," the girl said.

"Protect cyber-riders," the man said.

"Protect families," the girl said.

"Train," the man said. "Learn discipline."

"Learn kicks!" The girl hopped on one leg while she kicked out with the other. It looked charming rather than fearsome, but it she was already that limber, she might someday become formidable at tykado.

The man smiled. "Learn to run," he told the girl.

The girl looked up at me. "Run long. Hard. Fast. Like The Bhaaj."

Before I could respond, the man added, "Learn to read. To write."

"Learn numbers," the girl said.

The man spoke quietly. "No killing. Unless you must, to defend your circle."

Good gods. Where had all that come from? No, I knew. It was bits and pieces of what I had said to the knights, to other people here, even to Dig. I hadn't formalized anything, but it sounded like what I would come up with if I decided to form a code.

"That's right," I said. "It's our code of honor."

"Stealing okay," the girl added.

It wasn't okay, actually, but I had deliberately left it out in my words to the knights. When you were starving, a code that forbade you to steal food was about as useful as trying to breathe when you were buried in dust. Before I included a ban against theft in the code, I had to find a workable alternative to feed people. The undercity was economically viable, yes, but just barely. We lived on an edge, and people fell over it all too often, into poverty.

Up ahead, a trio of adults jogged into view. They wore ragged clothes, as if they lived here, but they wouldn't fool anyone. Even from this far away, I could tell their outfits had no dust ingrained in the cloth, besides which, they moved together like a well-trained unit. They might as well have had "army" written all over them. Lavinda Majda had sent her troops.

"Ho!" The father stopped and pushed his daughter behind him. He must have hidden a knife in his clothes, because he now held a long blade with a honed edge that glinted.

"Wait." I laid my hand on his arm. "They may be friends."

"Not friends," he said. "Soldiers. Above-city."

"I'll talk with them. Stay here." I headed toward the trio, two women and a man.

As I drew nearer, I recognized the man, Major Duane Ebersole. I let out a breath. Him I trusted. The two women were active military. Duane had retired, but as far as Majda was concerned, that didn't matter. Once you had worn the uniform, they considered you theirs forever.

We met several hundred yards beyond where the father waited with his daughter. One of the women said, "Major Bhaajan?" She had dark hair pulled back from her face, and a holster showed under her jacket.

"That's right," I said. "Did Colonel Majda send you?"

Duane nodded and indicated the others. "We're one of four trios she sent here."

I tilted my head toward the man and the girl behind me. "Can you get them to safety?"

"We've set up a refuge to protect people," Ebersole said. "It's just below the Concourse."

"Good." The fighting wouldn't go that high, and it was a good distance from here. If any of these canals collapsed, the destruction wouldn't reach that part of the undercity. "They can't go anywhere with more light than here, though, unless they have lenses for their eyes."

"We'll take care of it." He looked past me to where the man and girl waited. "Will they come? No one here trusts us. We've had to round up some against their will."

It drilled rocks that they had to take people who protested. Even so. Better a pissed-off population than a dead one. "How many people have you gathered?" I asked.

"A big chunk of the population," one of the women said. "Aside from the cartels, that is."

I blinked at her. How had they rounded up a big chunk of our population and put them up by the Concourse? "How many?" I asked again.

"About eighteen," she answered. "Counting the two with you. Nine or ten children."

Eighteen people? And she thought that was a big chunk of our population? Good gods.

Duane spoke quietly. "More people live here."

I nodded, relieved at least one of them understood. "The rest are probably hiding." I led them to where the man waited with his daughter, but as we approached, the two stepped back.

I tilted my head at the soldiers and spoke to the father. "Friends. Take you to safety."

He stiffened. "No. Stay in aqueducts."

"Yah," I agreed. "Stay in aqueducts. A safer part."

The father stayed put, regarding me warily.

The girl peeked out from behind him, peering at the soldiers. "Got snap?" she asked.

I glanced at Duane. "Do you?"

"I don't understand her," he said.

"She wants to know if you have water." Sharing the bottles would be a gesture of good will.

"Oh. Yes, certainly." Duane pulled off his pack and took out a bottle. He knew to offer it to the father first, instead of the girl. "Would you like some?" he asked the man.

The father squinted at Duane. "What say?"

Duane tried again. "Would you like some water?" He spoke the above-city language of Cries beautifully, which meant the father could probably barely understand him.

When the father glanced at me, I said, "A bargain. Take their water. Go with them."

After an icy pause, the father thawed a bit and took the bottle. He handed it to his daughter, and her face lit up as she tore off the top. He accepted two more bottles from the other soldiers, then nodded to Duane in the undercity manner of accepting a bargain. "We go with."

"We'll make sure you're protected," Duane said. Awkwardly, he added, "Got protection." His undercity accent was terrible, but he tried, which meant far more than perfect words.

The man tilted his head, seeming more intrigued now than distrustful of Duane. He took his daughter's hand and they went with the soldiers.

As soon as they left, I headed the other way, deeper into the aqueducts, to see if anyone else was trapped. As I jogged along, the weapons fire in the other canal grew louder. A thunder of rocks crashed somewhere and I stopped, listening. Unlike the other falls, this one didn't fade into silence, but kept building.

The wall next to me began to shake.

Ho! I broke into a sprint just before the wall shattered. Up ahead, another part of the wall blew out, sending an avalanche of debris into the canal. I skidded to a stop a few meters away and spun around to look back the way I had come. The collapse behind me went all the way through to the other canal, leaving a giant hole. The battle was louder, and the flash of lasers in the other canal came again and again. A great crack sounded from above me, and I jerked up my head to see fissures running along the ceiling. I backed away, step by step, until I ran into the rock fall behind me. More fissures appeared in the ceiling.

"Gods almighty," I muttered.

You should get out of here, Max thought.

No kidding. I turned and clambered over the remains of the avalanche, going as fast as I could manage while rocks shifted under my feet and clattered into the canal. On the other side, I slid down to the midwalk. A groan of moving stone came from behind me and I looked back in time to see the roof over the midwalk bowing downward. It suddenly broke, and great chunks of red rock smashed down onto the midwalk. Dust flew everywhere, turning the air into a purplish haze.

Run! Max thought. **Get out of here!**

I raced away, down the midwalk. If even my supposedly emotionless EI was getting excited, I was in trouble. Up ahead, more of the wall crumbled, leaving another gaping hole through to the other canal. As I neared the debris, a woman scrambled through the opening. Laser fire flashed, just missing her head when she threw herself flat on the rocks. The beam flashed across this canal and hit the opposite wall. On this side, the rocks from the fall shifted under the woman and some tumbled into the canal. She scrambled down to the midwalk, jumped to her feet—

And it was Digjan, Dig's daughter.

She stood there, her hair a wild mane of black curls,

all hard muscles and a fierce scowl, a carbine clenched in her hands, and dust covering her clothes. A red cloth with the Kajada ruzik was tied around her bicep. Madly beautiful in a way the above-city would never understand, she looked like an ancient warrior. The Majdas might think of themselves as the heirs to the Ruby Empire, but in this moment, I had no doubt where the genes of those barbarian queens found expression.

She raised her carbine and sighted on me.

I whipped my gun up faster than she moved, but I had no intention of shooting her. I fired at her weapon instead. She was smarter than her friend, the girl whose carbine I had slagged, and even as she raised the gun, she threw herself to the side so that my bullet hit the rockslide behind her.

"Why shoot me?" I yelled. "I warned you all that Vakaar was coming."

Digjan jumped to her feet, her carbine still trained on me. "What the fuck do you want?"

"To get you out of here. If you're caught fighting for the cartel, your army career is done."

"Fuck the army."

I waved my gun at her. "What, you only know that one word? Fine, fuck the army. Give up."

"Shut up!" she shouted at me.

"Damn it, Digjan, I can sponsor you in the army. But not if you screw up here."

The ancient battle lust burned in her gaze, and I knew she was too far gone to reach. "Got a code," she said. "Protect Kajada. Kill Vakaar."

I clenched my gun. "Vakaar will kill you."

"I got no fear of measly Vakaars," she snarled. "Only loyalty to Kajada."

"No," a gravelly voice said. A woman pushed her way through the opening in the wall, and rubble cascaded around her as she stepped onto the midwalk.

Dig.

I stared at her, this woman who had been my closest friend until the day I left the undercity. She stood as tall as her daughter, with the same muscled physique and hair, that same antediluvian ferocity, but the decades had hardened her face and weathered it with scars.

"Go," she told her daughter. "No fight."

"No!" Digjan's expression blazed with energy. "I fight the Vakaars!" She lifted her gun in a salute to her mother. "For Kajada. Always."

Dig, who never showed emotion, watched her daughter as if her stone-cold heart were breaking. "Kajada values your loyalty above all else."

Digjan raised her chin. "Yah."

Quietly Dig said, "And Kajada releases you from your oath."

"What?" Her daughter stared at her in disbelief. "I won't desert you!"

A deeper, more ominous rumbling started somewhere far behind us, not in this canal, but in the one with the battle. Someone shouted, their voice panicked.

"Go," Dig told her daughter. "Go with Bhaaj."

Digjan's posture stiffened. "Only a coward would leave."

"You fought with honor," Dig said. "Great honor. Now go to a better life."

"I serve you," Digjan said.

"Serve what?" Dig demanded. The thunder of falling stone was growing louder. "Selling hack? Bliss? Funk? For what?"

"Make you queen of the undercity," Digjan told her.

"Queen of shit," Dig told her. "I want more for you."

"Don't want more!" Digjan shouted. But she looked confused, furious as much because she didn't know where to put her mother's words as because she wanted to fight. Great cracking noises were coming from the other canal, and fissures were opening in ceiling above us.

"Uh, we better go," I said.

Digjan never shifted her gaze from her mother. "I won't leave you."

Dig shook her gun. "Go! Now!" Behind her, more of the midwalk wall collapsed.

"We have to leave." I spun around—and froze. I could see through the many breaks in the midwalk wall into the next canal. Far in the distance, its roof was collapsing in a slow, relentless wave headed in our direction.

"Go with Bhaaj!" Dig shouted at her daughter. "That's my order!" She took off then, scrambling back through the breach in the wall.

Digjan hesitated only one moment. Then she spun around to me. "We go."

Go, yes, *but where?* Debris blocked us in both directions. As the other canal collapsed, it was taking what remained of the wall that separated it from this one and also the ceiling above that wall. The great wave of destruction rolled toward us with relentless speed.

I had to yell to be heard above the noise. "Down in the canal!"

Together, we half fell, half climbed down the rockslide left by the avalanche. At the bottom, we ran down the center of the canal, heading straight toward the oncoming destruction. Here in the middle we were far enough from the collapsing wall that we would escape the worst of the falling rocks—I hoped—when we ran past that wave shattering rock. Knee-deep dust hampered our stride, but I didn't use enhanced speed because Digjan couldn't keep that grueling pace.

More avalanches poured into the canal as the roof continued its collapse. The ceiling above us was intact, but rubble hurtled down into the canal from the collapsing wall. The wave approached us, we approached the wave, and when we finally ran by it, rocks thundered around us. When I stumbled, Dig hefted me to my feet. Mounds of rubble filled the canal, and we scrambled over them, grunting with exertion, choking on the dust-laden air.

A crack sounded directly above us.

I looked up with a jerk. Fissures were spreading across the ceiling everywhere now, not just above the midwalk.

"Run faster," I gasped at Digjan.

She tried, but she had reached her limit. Thunder roared behind us. Still running, I looked back. Damn! The roof of the entire aqueduct was falling, a new wave of destruction racing after us. In a few seconds, it would bury us in tons of rock.

I grabbed Digjan's arm and lunged into an enhanced sprint, literally dragging her forward. My biomech struggled to compensate for her added weight, and she struggled to keep her feet. Behind us, the thunder grew louder. We kept on, desperate, running, scrambling, falling, running, running, chased by tons of rock smashing into the canal.

It was several moments before I realized the thunder

was fading. I never paused and Digjan ran with me, gasping for breath. After a few more moments, the thunder stopped. We slowed to a normal run, and I let go of Digjan. Another few moments, and we reached a point where the canal was intact and no rubble blocked our way. Gulping in air, we turned around, walking backward, staring at what had once been a major canal in the undercity.

"Gods," I whispered.

For all the dust that filled the air, nothing could hide the devastation. Two canals had fallen, this one and the one where the battle had taken place. The collapse had only stopped where arches and supports reinforced the aqueducts. Whoever had designed this place had been a genius, able to limit the collapse even of two canals—but beyond those supporting buttresses, that miracle of architecture lay in ruins.

Digjan spoke in a hollow voice. "My mother."

"This wasn't enough to stop her." My voice cackled with all the dust. "Your mother is the orneriest hellcat I ever knew. If anyone could survive, it's her."

Digjan said nothing. We both knew the truth. If this collapse had moved as fast in Dig's direction as in ours, she couldn't have outrun it.

"Fighting must be done," Digjan said dully. "Fighters buried."

"Yah." Some may have survived, but I doubted it was many.

"Stupid," she said tiredly. Then she turned and headed down the canal.

I went with her.

XX

The Code

Lavinda Majda paced past the black lacquered table, her tread silent on the rug, her boots sinking into the blue pile. An untouched decanter of wine and two goblets sat on the table. I stood by the wall, too tense to sit. I could go to prison for what had happened today, the battle in the aqueducts. The air smelled faintly of expensive incense, just that barest hint of elegance, so different from the scorched smell of the canals.

The colonel stopped pacing and faced me, imposing in her uniform, her black hair pulled away from her face. "One of the trios I sent down there ended up in the fighting."

I tensed, fearing the worst. "What did they do?"

She spoke curtly. "They are soldiers. They fought." When I opened my mouth, she held up her hand. "In self-defense, Major. They were attacked. They left their attackers unconscious and Major Ebersole called for the medics. He said they found you a few minutes later."

Duane? That meant he had fought for his life only moments before I saw him. And he hadn't said a word. "Are they all right?"

"They're fine." Lavinda stood watching me, and I stood watching her. The silence stretched out until it felt like an elastic band pulled too tight, ready to break and hit me in the face. Then she said, "Major Ebersole agrees with your analysis. He believes that if my troops had deliberately engaged the cartels, the death toll and destruction would have been much worse."

I let out a breath. If her experts agreed with me, I might not go to trial after all. "Do you know how many died?"

Her laserlike focus never wavered. "We've found nine bodies so far. My people are working with yours to dig out the remains. At least fifteen cartel members were involved in the fighting. Maybe more. We can't tell for certain because they had shrouds." She scowled. "Stolen tech."

No surprise there. Military tech-mech was in big demand on the black market. I wanted to ask about Dig. Had they found her body? The question was burning a hole inside of me. But I kept my mouth shut. Digjan had gone to the refuge set up by the army, but she hadn't revealed she was the Kajada heir. I had no doubt she was helping the army dig out bodies. I just hoped she didn't have to unbury her mother.

Lavinda was waiting for a response, so I said, "Given what the cartels make off the drug trade, I'm not surprised they can afford black market tech."

Anger sharpened her voice. "Never mind if they destroy priceless ruins in their greed."

That was her biggest concern, the *ruins?* "And the people."

"Those people brought it on themselves."

I stiffened. One moment, I was almost ready to trust Lavinda, and the next she destroyed that trust. I had no polite response, so I said nothing.

After a moment, Lavinda said, "The problem with being an empath is that an ability to sense another person's mood doesn't tell you why they feel that way."

She was trying to read me again. Screw that. I safeguarded my mind like a warrior using a shield to fend off weapons.

"You're furious," Lavinda said. "Why?"

"I can't imagine why," I said coldly. "You just implied that losing the canals was a greater tragedy than the people who died."

Her voice hardened. "Cartel members died. Criminals who caused the destruction or deaths of untold numbers of people."

A part of me agreed, the darkness that took grim satisfaction in seeing the cartels decimate each other in their furious grab for power. But many people lived in the undercity, not just punkers, and however much I hated the cartels, their members were also human. In Dig's death, I had lost my oldest friend, the blood sister who stood at my side without fail no matter what happened. Lavinda might never understand why I felt as if Dig had saved my life that day she helped me escape the orphanage, but I knew.

I said only, "The cartels aren't the only people in the aqueducts."

"My troops found the civilians," she said. "As far as we know, they suffered no casualties."

By civilians, I assumed she meant people not involved in the battle. "How many?"

"Nineteen, mostly children or young adults." Lavinda rubbed her chin. "When you add that to the fifteen or so cartel members fighting in the canal, that comes to at least thirty-five. We hadn't realized so many people lived down there."

Thirty-five? I wanted to say, *How can you have no fucking clue?* But I kept my mouth shut. It wasn't only them. We didn't want Cries to notice us any more than they wanted to see the poverty beneath their gleaming city.

Lavinda spoke quietly. "Major, only a few days ago, you told me that you couldn't do your job if I withheld information from you."

"It's important." I would never have known about the phorine, for one.

"That works both ways."

I regarded her, silent.

The colonel scowled at me. "Put more bluntly, I can't do a damn thing if you clam up. Maybe we could help the undercity if we knew more of what your people need."

I took a deep breath. Only a moment ago, I wanted to rage that they did nothing for us. Now she offered an opening. What to say? Regardless of how clumsy I felt with words, I had to speak. She was offering me a chance to help my people. The Cries authorities would never let a crisis this big go unattended. They would send people to repair the ruins and investigate. How that process went could depend on what I said now to Lavinda.

I started with what I had intended to report anyway.

"I found three psions recovering from phorine withdrawal. They only took it twice, but they went through hell when their supply dried up."

She walked over to me. "Were they with the people my soldiers protected?"

"I don't think so. They were already hidden."

"We need to test them. Can you bring them here?"

"No." Even if I had been willing, which I wasn't, they would never agree to come.

She waited. When it became clear I intended to add nothing else, she said, "Major, if you won't reveal who they are, my troops will have to search the slums until we find them."

"If you threaten them that way, their people will hide them so well, you'll never find them."

I almost felt what she wanted to say: *We have the resources to find anyone.* The truth of that threat made it even worse, because Cries could have used those resources at any time to count how many people lived in the undercity. They never cared enough to make the effort. Now, when we had something they wanted, suddenly they were interested. The hell with them.

Lavinda spoke quietly. "Major, I would like to work as colleagues. Not adversaries."

I pushed my hand through my hair, which I had let loose around my shoulders now that the fighting was over. Getting angry was no solution. I had an opportunity here. I could do some good for my people, but if I wasn't careful, I could also end up causing them harm.

I started to pace, walking past the low table, wishing I had Lavinda's window so I could look at the mountains. Instead, I stopped in front of a tapestry on the wall. I knew this hanging. I had seen images of it in a museum article when I looked up the Majdas. It was considered priceless. Yet this masterpiece was a pale copy of what I had seen woven by the father in the undercity. His work had more richness, more detail, more technique. The arts of our ancestors had come down in the culture of my people undiluted, with a purity lost to the City of Cries.

I turned to Lavinda. "The undercity isn't a slum. It's true our population lives in poverty or on its edge. But we have a community unlike any other. The ruins aren't the only remnants of the ancient Cries that need protecting. So do my people, our culture, our lives." I regarded her steadily. "I fear that if your people come into our world, however well intentioned, you will destroy a remarkable community, one unlike any other, without realizing the damage you're doing."

"I want to help," Lavinda said, "not hurt."

"I know," I said softly.

She spoke with that intense concentration I recognized now as part of her personality. "We can bring the children without parents to the orphanage and maybe find them families in Cries or on the water farms outside the city. We can set up a Cries school to reeducate all your children. For the adults, we can register everyone from the undercity as citizens of Cries, offer them housing on the water farms or vocational training for jobs in the city, and help integrate them into our culture."

How could I answer? She had just described our worst fears.

Lavinda spoke with frustration. "Why not? Do your people *want* to live in squalor?"

Yah, squalor, right. I wanted to lash out, but I wrestled down my anger. If I answered badly, I would only hurt my own people and alienate someone who genuinely wanted to help. We needed help, yes, but at what price?

"Not squalor," I said, instinctively lapsing into the undercity dialect. "Got better."

"Do you mean they don't want squalor?" she asked. "Or that they don't live in squalor?"

"Don't live in," I said.

"What would you call the conditions my soldiers saw?" she demanded. "People in caves with no plumbing, no jobs, no easy mesh access."

"Call it undercity." I forced myself to speak her language. "It is a harsh life, yes, but also one of beauty and a freedom unlike anything in above-city." For all I knew, our preference for that life had become a genetic disposition. I had tried for years to deny that part of myself, to live an above-city life. In many ways I had succeeded, to the extent that I might never again live in the aqueducts, but this much I knew: they were still part of me at a level so basic, I could never separate that from what made me Bhaajan. Yes, I had left when I was sixteen, but it had been my choice, not imposed on me from the outside.

"If you try to change us to fit your way of life," I said, "it will destroy what makes us unique. What we value." I met her gaze. "And what we value has worth."

She seemed at a loss. "Then what help do you want?"

That was the crucial question. And who did the undercity have to answer on their behalf? Inarticulate me. I was no expert in diplomacy, negotiation, conflict resolution, or creative solutions to impossible problems.

I was just a retired soldier turned PI, rough around the edges, tending to stoicism. I could so easily fumble this opportunity, but as lacking as I might be, I was the only one here to negotiate an answer.

I started with something easy. "For one, help make it possible for business proprietors in the undercity to get a license for sales on the Concourse."

Lavinda looked startled. "The undercity has business owners?"

I gritted my teeth, then made myself relax and answer in a reasonable voice. "Yes. Certainly. And craftspeople. They could set up stalls or shops and participate legally in the Cries economy."

She raised an eyebrow. "Legally?"

Oh, great. I was one step away from telling her that a significant portion of the undercity economy consisted of theft, gambling, and illegally hacking the meshes. Smart move, Bhaaj.

"As opposed to the cartels," I said. Cries city already knew about them. Periodically the city authorities cracked down on the punkers, but usually they existed in an uneasy peace with the crime bosses, even partaking of their vices. That included Jak and his casino. He didn't kill people, but gambling could also become an addiction, one that had led Braze to supply weapons to the cartels.

"All the more reason to relocate people to Cries," she said. "So they don't turn to crime."

"My people don't want to live in Cries." I took a breath. "I've been thinking, a lot of ideas knocking around in my head. We talked before about the army. That's one solution. I'm thinking through other possibilities."

Her look tuned thoughtful. "What about sports?"

I blinked. "Sports?"

"My soldiers say the young people down there seem remarkably fit."

"Kids like to form teams and exercise together." That sounded so much more palatable than *They run in gangs and learn to beat each other up.*

"One of my sergeants noticed as much," Lavinda said. "She thinks some of those kids would kill on the ball court or track teams."

I almost choked on a groan. Yah, some punkers might literally commit murder if they were let loose in a sports contest with Cries athletes. Still, she had a point. If anything from Cries could draw interest among our youth, sports would do it. I'd have considered the idea if I hadn't wanted to join the army. We fought for fun as well as survival. Team sports weren't that different from gang battles, minus the bloodshed, and we were damn good at what we did. Hah! With some prep in tykado and track, our kids could wipe the floor with any above-city teams.

"It could work." I plunged ahead. "Our children need schooling, too, but what works in the above-city won't work for them."

Incredibly, she didn't tell me I was wrong and that our children just needed to shape up and adapt to the Cries schools and discipline, which was how everyone else had responded when I mentioned the problems with our education. Instead, she simply asked, "What would work?"

What indeed? An Earther had once told me about something called unschooling, a form of home school education where students didn't attend courses, real or virtual. Instead, they learned through their life experiences, including play, responsibilities, curiosity, interactions with kin and apprenticeships with mentors. That sounded similar to the undercity. Maybe I could find answers in their philosophies. We could invite mentors to visit the aqueducts, like Orin, who had let me help on his archeological digs. We'd have to ensure their safety. No one had bothered Orin because my gang protected him. How about the dust knights? They were already codifying my thoughts about learning. If I brought teachers to help, the knights would protect them. With the help of some adults, we might work out unschooling as part of the knight's training.

"Major?" Lavinda asked.

"I have some ideas," I said. "They're a bit rough."

"We can talk more when you've had chance to work on them." Lavinda spoke firmly. "But regardless, we need to test your people for Kyle traits as soon as possible."

"Why so fast?" Her pushing unsettled me.

"Major, good gods, we're talking about abilities rarer than one-tenth of one percent in the general human population. If that is different in the undercity, we need to know."

I didn't want to talk about psions. For some reason, every part of me resisted. But I had to. Even if the three I had already met were the only ones in the undercity, they deserved to hear whatever ISC might offer. I had seen in the military how psions with unshielded minds suffered, how they withdrew from human contact. If nothing else, ISC could teach them to protect their minds so they didn't crave phorine.

Without those shields, it was no wonder they lived in isolation, safe in the darkness.

Lavinda was watching me. "You told me before you would try to bring some people for testing. Are you saying differently now?"

"No, I'll keep my word." I'd even taken the first steps. "They might come to the Concourse Rec Center. Make it the bargain we talked about. For a meal and medical checkup, and they let your people test them."

She nodded. "Fair enough."

"But before I do this," I said, "you have to give me your word, on your honor as a Majda."

The moment she stiffened, I knew I had guessed right about the Majdas. They placed high value on their honor. I had no doubt they were brutally effective as politicians, military officers, and financial potentates, but they conducted their business according to their own code of integrity. She wouldn't like me demanding her word, but if she gave it, she would keep that promise. I hoped I was right, because I needed to trust them.

Lavinda spoke coldly. "My word on what?"

I met her gaze steadily. "That no matter what you discover in your tests, you won't force anyone who comes to the Center to stay. Offer them whatever you want, but if they say no, you let them go home."

For a moment she just looked at me. But finally she said, "Agreed."

"That's not all."

"You enjoy risks, don't you Major?"

I plunged ahead. "I need your word that you won't arrest anyone. No matter what you see, you won't take action." The riders, if any came, would be sporting stolen or mined tech-mech all over their bodies. Dust gangers would carry knives, dart throwers, maybe even stolen guns.

Lavinda scowled at me. "And why, pray tell, would I arrest any of these people?"

She had to know I wasn't going there. "I need your word. Or I can't ask anyone to show up."

The colonel was scrutinizing me again. I kept my mental barriers in place. After a moment, she let out a reluctant breath. "Very well. You have my word that we won't arrest, coerce, compel, or detain anyone you bring for testing. This one time, they have full sanctuary."

I hadn't realized how much I had tensed until my shoulders relaxed. "Thank you." I spoke carefully. "I can't promise anyone will come. They have trust problems with the above-city." To put it mildly. "But I'll do my best."

"It's a start." Lavinda extended her arm and I extended mine. We each grasped the other's elbows, shaking on our agreement. We had a bargain. It was a small thing, yes, a free meal for a few tests, but it was, as she said, a start.

I found Jak outside the entrance to the cave where I met with the dust knights. He stood leaning against a stone column, his arms crossed, watching me walk up the path.

"Heya." I grinned at him. "You come to join the knights?"

Jak shook his head. He had an odd expression. Not angry, not exactly. He looked... fierce? No, that wasn't right. He was hiding his mood, and unlike the inestimable Majdas, I was no empath.

"Something wrong?" I looked past him, peering into the cave. I didn't see anyone.

"Got no people there," he said.

Odd. The whisper mill would have let the knights know I was on my way. Then again, was it a surprise they stayed away? The cartel battle and the part I insisted they take may have alienated them. Or they may have decided my code was too much trouble. Disappointment washed over me. I hadn't planned to start the knights, but when they formed, it seemed like a good thing.

"Ah, well." I shrugged. "Got a lot to do anyway."

"No, you don't."

"I don't?"

"Come with." He indicated the path with slagged stalagmites where we had fought Scorch.

As I walked with Jak, I strained to listen for signs of people nearby. Dripping water somewhere muddled my reception. *Max,* I thought. *Can you tell if anyone is around?*

Maybe a rider or two, he thought. **No one else is close enough to detect heartbeats.**

"Why'd you come here?" I asked Jak. Nowadays he was far more interested in his casino than dust gangs.

"Dunno. Seemed a good idea."

I'd seen this mood before with him, closed and hard to read. It happened when we first made love, the day he lost a close friend, and the day I left for the army, all times with emotions he didn't want to talk about.

An unwelcome thought hit me. "Dig. They found her body."

"No, not yet." Jak took me toward another cave. I

went with him to the entrance—and stopped, frozen in place.

"The other cave was too small," Jak said.

People filled this one, a cavern twice as large as where we had trained before. More than twenty-five people had come, and others were probably hiding in the walls. Even as I formed that thought, a young woman dropped from the ceiling and stood in the back of the group, arms loose by her side, cyber implants showing in the circuitry that curled along her neck like a tattoo.

The children from before had all returned, including their leaders, Pat Sandjan and Biker from the Oey gang, along with Runner and Rockson. Both the father and daughter from the deep-down were also here, with lenses protecting their eyes. A gang in their late teens stood at my right, two young women and two young men, reminding me so much of Dig, Jak, Gourd, and myself, except these kids had scar patterns on their arms, a gang tat worked into their skin. Four adults had gathered by the wall on my left, half hidden in the shadows, men and women in their twenties, wary and impassive, their faces toughened by their years.

Everyone stood waiting to see what—if anything—I had to offer. This was pure undercity, no Cries influence. What would happen if we could harness the energy and self-imposed discipline of the gangers, the riders, and yes, even the punkers? I didn't have an answer, but as I walked into the cavern, I felt a chill. Something was happening here, something important, if I didn't screw it up.

Jak stood at my back. I knew he wasn't here to train. Whatever his reasons, his presence offered a show of support. He was taking a risk, because if my ideas fell apart, it would reflect badly on him. He was known throughout the undercity and a great deal of his influence came from his reputation, which had become so notorious that even the Majda police and their inimitable Chief Takkar knew about him. It meant a lot to me that he stayed.

I hadn't expected adults to show up. I couldn't work with them like with the kids. Then how? As an army officer, I had been in charge of many soldiers their age. A big difference existed with this group, however. Nothing required them to be here. This much was clear: whatever I did next would either earn their loyalty or turn them away.

I straightened up into military posture and paced in front of the group. Although I stopped in front of a line of children, I was looking over their heads at the four adults lounging by the wall. I couldn't see them clearly in the dim light, but I didn't think they were all gangers. For one, the rider who had dropped down from the ceiling had joined their group. I looked them over, and then I walked the other way, toward the gang of older teens. When I finished giving them the once-over, I went back to the center and considered the entire gathering.

"So," I said. "You think you're dust knights." I gave a snort. "Not that easy."

The younger children stood proud, because they knew they were already knights. I held back a smile at my seven-year-old knights. The teens I had asked to act as leaders were another story. They looked over the new people as if they were sizing up potential recruits, fourteen-year-olds appraising hardened gangers twice their age. Even so. They earned that right when they organized the knights to spread the warning about the cartels. The army trios had brought stragglers to safety, and I was grateful for their help, but it was the knights who had sent the population to ground. The only ones who missed the warning were the two Down-deepers I found during the battle, and they stood in front of me, hale and healthy instead of buried under tons of rubble.

I raised my voice. "You want to be dust knights? We aren't here to play. Knights train. Every day. They follow the Code. Got no time for the Code? You aren't a knight."

No one spoke, but the older gangers weren't lounging against the wall anymore. They looked pissed. At me.

I called out to the group, drill sergeant style. "Ready to follow the Code?"

The children who had already done this before shouted in unison. "Ready!"

"Ready to train," I said.

"Ready to train," they called back.

"Ready to honor to Code."

They didn't hesitate this time. "Ready to honor the Code."

"Dust knights protect!" I called. "Protect all!"

"Dust Knights protect!" They made their *Knights* sound like a title. "Protect all!"

"To live with honor!"

"To live with honor!"

"Never abuse that honor!"

"Never abuse that honor!"

I had ended the code at that point the last time, but now I added my own version of what the deep-down recruits had told me they heard.

"No drugs!" I said. "No bliss, funk, hack, dot. Nothing!"

Most of the younger children shouted, "No drugs!" but the older recruits just stared at me. The taller youth in the gang of older teens gave me an implacable gaze. Scars traced along his muscled biceps, a crisscross pattern of lines. All four of the gangs had those scars, but his were more extensive. He would be their leader. If he didn't agree to the code, none of them would.

I spoke to directly to him. "You want to be knights? Then swear to the Code. No Code, then you leave. Now." It was a harsh demand for a population where euphorics were as common as food, but if they wanted to be part of this, they had to make that vow. I didn't want drugs destroying what we were building.

The response came not from the scarred gang, but from the four adults across the cave. One of them came forward, not the rider, but the other woman. People jumped out of her way, stumbling back, clearing a path. I stiffened as she walked into the light. She was huge, taller even than me, and all huge muscles. A scar slashed across her face, and her left arm had embedded tech-mech that looked like it connected to her neural system. Those implants could give her an augmented strength as much as my own, at least for that arm. But she wasn't a rider. Her ragged clothes were scorched by fire. A laser shot couldn't have hit her directly or she wouldn't be here, but a backlash must have caught her. Damn. She was a punker from the battle.

I faced her with a hard gaze. If I showed any sign of weakness, that was it. The knights would never follow me if I couldn't stand up to the punkers. I didn't know if she was Vakaar or Kajada, but it didn't matter. Either she accepted the Code or she left. I didn't care squat about how large, intimidating, or violent of a killer I faced. If she didn't swear to the Code, she was out.

She stood there, staring at me, her gaze impassive. I stared back. After she considered me for several moments, she spoke in a gravelly voice, her words carrying throughout the cave.

"No drugs," she said.

Gods almighty. She had agreed. A sharp intake came from someone in the cave.

I nodded to her and the punker nodded back, each of us barely moving our heads. With that, we agreed to a pact as binding as my handshake with Lavinda. The punker stepped back, rejoining her group, two dust gangers and the rider. Probably the four of them had joined together after losing members of their own circles.

I spoke to the group as a whole. "No drugs!"

This time the call came from everyone, ragged but firm. "No drugs!"

"Dust Knights train! Every day!"

"Dust Knights train!" They all yelled with extra gusto. "Every day!"

Hah! They liked that one. Cries tykado teams, watch out. Training the knights would take some figuring out, given they were at such different levels and ages. I could set up groups, with the more advanced helping the less experienced. For the youngest, I didn't want them fighting so much as learning a way of life that would give them a sense of purpose and confidence.

Someday they might become martial arts wizards, but for now my intention was to provide a community they could depend on for guidance and support.

"Dust Knights learn!" I called. "Read. Write. Numbers."

That brought another hesitation. They didn't answer all at once, but one by one, and then in ragged groups, they did all call, "Dust Knights learn! Read! Write! Numbers!"

Okay, that one would be more difficult to implement. I still had to find a way to make that work, but we would figure out something.

I regarded them steadily. "Dust Knights don't lie!"

That brought an even bigger hesitation and more uneven response. "Dust Knights don't lie."

"What?" I shouted.

"Dust Knights don't lie!" they shouted.

"Never betray the Knights!" I shouted.

"Never betray the Knights!"

I stared at them all, my gaze hard, "Never murder!"

They looked back at me, silent. Most if not all of them had probably lost someone they loved to violence, including the cartel battle. If I swore them to an oath against murder, I was taking away their vengeance. They knew what I meant by murder; it didn't preclude killing in self-defense. Given how fast news traveled through the whisper, they would all know by now that I had killed a Vakaar punker yesterday. But if I didn't make the ban on murder part of the Code, I could be creating an army of assassins by giving them such rigorous military training.

My voice carried throughout the cavern. "Dust Knights never murder." Even if they agreed now, I would eventually lose some of them to that demand. That changed nothing of my intent. "Swear to the Code," I said. "Or leave."

Pat Sandjan and Biker answered together, clear and firm. "Never murder."

No one else spoke. No one else moved. Nothing. Gods only knew what would happen to the Oey knights if the oath ended here. They had courage, for they had just put the survival of their circle in jeopardy.

The gang leader the scarred arms abruptly spoke, the youth who had watched me with such hostility before. He met my gaze and spoke in a deep voice. "Never murder."

A ragged call went through the group. "Never murder."

"Dust Knights never murder!" I shouted at them.

"Dust Knights never murder!" they shouted back, all of them this time.

"Dust Knights, ready!"

"Dust Knights, ready!"

So it was done. The Dust Knights of Cries had a Code. I let out a silent breath and spoke more normally. "Let's get started, then."

The group shifted, people moving, relaxing, preparing to work. I grouped them by age. The girl from Down-deep looked panicked when I moved her father, so I put them on the edges of their respective groups, which left them right next to each other. I warmed everyone up with calisthenics, giving simpler versions to the younger children. For today, we all worked together, training in an underground cavern lit only by my light stylus.

Teaching tykado wasn't my only purpose. I hoped

becoming a part of this group would give them a sense of accomplishment that extended to the rest of their lives. Through the Knights, I could introduce new ideas. I wanted them to know they had choices, that they didn't have to spend their lives stealing, wasting away in the dark, clawing at each other for the limited resources. True change wouldn't come from outside, from charity kitchens or the above-city forcing our children into their schools. It started here, from within.

Maybe the Knights could become a source of stability in the aqueducts. It had already started, with the warning they spread about the cartel. The undercity couldn't keep its autonomy if we didn't police ourselves. The cartel battle had stirred up too much attention. Unless we strengthened our community from within, the above-city would come in and try to do it themselves, injuring our way of life without realizing what they were taking. Maybe I was a fool to believe I could help just by teaching people how to do tykado, but it was worth a try.

A part of me wanted to run from this, to return to my easy life in Selei City and leave the darkness behind. But the undercity would be with me no matter where I went, and I could no longer escape that truth.

XXI
Negotiation

The plunk of water never stopped in the Grotto. Drip. Pause. Drip. Big drops fell from the ceiling and plopped into the pool. Intermittent but ceaseless, they had fallen since before I was born and they would continue long after we all were gone. I sat on a rock stump and turned on my stylus, creating a small bubble of light in the darkness.

I expected Gourd, but it was Jak who walked out of the shadows, coming around the lake, his black clothes a part of the darkness.

"Heya," I said.

"Heya." He sat on the ledge where Gourd had sat the last time.

"Good fighting," I said, thinking of the training session today. "Had my back. Thanks."

"Eh. You got good scrap there."

I smiled. We had called ourselves scrap as kids, half meaning our rough-tumble bouts and half that we were made of scrap metal.

Jak's smiled flickered, then vanished. "Got a good thing there, Bhaaj. The Knights."

I wondered why he sounded angry. "Could be. We'll see."

He met my gaze. "Will we?"

I didn't know how to respond to his real question, which wasn't about the Knights, so I said, "Yah. See what happens."

"That all you'll see?"

He wasn't going to let me off. So I said, "Nahya." I reached out and touched his arm. "See what's good here."

His grin returned in full, wicked force. "See what's trouble, eh?"

Ho! That grin of his was more potent than any hack. I scowled. "Yah. Plenty of trouble."

He just smiled. It was enough. In the millennia past, when women had led armies across the stars, empires could have fallen over a man like him. An Earther once told me about a prince whose face launched a thousand ships into war. The Earther swore the legend referred to a woman named Helen of Troy, not a man, but I hadn't believed her, even if Earthers had once lived in patriarchal cultures and somehow survived. Jak could have inspired a thousand ships and then some.

So okay, the love of my life was also, as Takkar so kindly put it, a disreputable undercity kingpin. But he was my kingpin. Darkness and light. He wasn't Dig, whose trade had torn apart lives. He catered to other vices, gambling and sex, but he also supported the undercity. He paid his employees well, found them medical care, and used his network to support people, as he had done for the children I found with their dead mother. Jak was no saint, nor would he ever be, but the good in him also went deep, for all that he denied that particular truth.

All I said was, "Gourd's not coming?"

"He's making water."

We all had our roles, Gourd, Jak, Dig, and me. But now we were three instead of four. "Jak."

He regarded me, wary from whatever he heard in my tone. "Yah?"

"I have to report Braze." I was the only witness who could provide evidence that an ISC officer had supplied the cartels with weapons. Both sides, for gods' sake.

"Can't," he said flatly.

"Won't mention the Black Mark."

"You won't have evidence without that."

I rubbed my eyes, tired after the long day. He was right. Braze had sold the weapons to pay off her gambling debts. If I testified to that, I would implicate Jak.

"You got my word," I told him. "I won't mention the Black Mark."

"Then the military has no case."

"Probably not. But they'll have enough to look harder." I could cast suspicion on Braze. What they did about it was their decision.

"You got to give your word," he said. "No mention of the Black Mark. No hint."

"You got my word."

He nodded, accepting the promise.

"Now you give me your word," I said.

He tensed. But that was how matters worked. A bargain. I gave my oath, he gave his.

"For what?" he asked.

"About the Black Mark."

He regarded me warily. "What about it?"

"It makes gambling addicts."

His scowl deepened. "It's just cards and dice, Bhaaj. It makes nothing."

"It makes problems. Not with everyone, sure. But some."

"What, you want me to promise no gambling?" He snorted, not bothering to dignify the idea with his refusal.

"Promise me this," I said. "You won't let the gambling destroy people."

"That's their responsibility. Not mine."

"You own the Black Mark. That gives you responsibility."

"I don't know what the hell you expect," he growled.

I wasn't sure myself. I sat thinking. "You got a bar, a badass drinks too much, the bartender shuts her down. Refuses that last drink. Sends her home."

"I can't shut down my gamblers."

"The Black Mark is yours. You can do whatever you want."

He glared at me. But after a moment, he said, "I'll give it a think."

I nodded. If he said he'd think about it, he would come up with something. He couldn't solve the problems of gambling addiction any more than a bartender sending a drunk home would solve the problems of alcoholism. But it might help.

Beyond Jak, three figures were taking form out of the shadows. He looked around, following my gaze. The trio walked into the light: Pat Sandjan Oey; the youth with the scars who led the dust gang of older teens; and the towering adult punker who had scared the blazes out of everyone. As they came over, Jak stood up and melted away into the shadows.

The trio sat on rock stumps around mine. I hadn't requested them in particular, just put out the word that I wanted the leaders. I left it up to the knights to decide on those leaders, because their choice would tell me a lot about who they would follow. I knew I could work with Pat, but I was less sure about these other two.

I tapped the heels of my hand together. "Bhaajan."

The youth with the scars hit his hand together. "Ruzik."

I nodded to him. Ruzik, after the powerful reptilian mounts ridden by the Abaj Tacalique. A good, strong name.

The punker considered me with a cold gaze. Her voice sounded like a growl, but I suspected that was just the way she naturally spoke. She said, "Dark Singer."

Well, shit. "Singer" meant someone who sung death to her victims. An assassin. "Dark" was a rank, not a name. It indicated that among her circle, she had the most kills. I had no doubt she had composed more than a few songs, including in the recent battle. I was screwed.

Yet she had also sworn to the Code of the Dust Knights. And her gang sent her as their leader, though none of them were punkers. Seeing a rider in a gang was unusual enough, I had never known a punker to ran with a dust gang. You never left the cartel, not if you valued your life. So why was Singer here? Maybe she wanted out of the cartel and finally had the chance. More likely, she intended to rebuild whichever one she came from, recruiting from among the gangs and riders. Learning tykado could make her even more brutally effective.

Had I been Chief Takkar, I'd have thrown her in prison. But I was Bhaajan, so I instead I said, "You're a Knight."

"Yah." She made that one word a challenge.

"Knights don't sing," I said. "Don't shoot, sniff, or hack."

Her gaze never wavered. "Got Code."

I had to make a choice. So I called on my intuition about people, which could mean zilch but had served me well in the past. I chose to believe she came to the knights because she wanted to change her life, not because she intended to build a new cartel. I hoped to the gods I was right.

I considered the three of them. "We got an offer. A bargain."

Pat looked intrigued. "What for what?"

I answered carefully. "The who is easier than the what. It's not like any other bargain."

Ruzik frowned. "Why not?"

"It's with the above-city."

Singer spat to the side. "The hell with that."

"The army wants to test us for psi," I said.

"Psi?" Ruzik's forehead furrowed. "What is that?"

"Someone who feels moods," Pat said. "Hears thoughts."

"Lying," Singer said. "The army wants to finish wiping out the cartels."

"They gave their word," I said. "They'll just test us, nothing else."

"They want to round us up, yah?" Ruzik demanded. "Send us to prison."

"Nahya," I said. "Just test. Then we can leave."

"Leave what?" Pat asked. "Where is the test?"

"The Concourse Rec Center," I said.

"Fuck that," Singer said.

"The police won't touch any of us," I said. "I have that promise."

"A lie," Ruzik stated.

"No. Is true," I told him.

Singer gave me an incredulous look. "Says who?"

"Majda," I said. "Colonel Lavinda Majda."

They all stared at me.

"Bullshit," Singer said.

Pat motioned at my gauntlet comm. "We all heard her jack with Majda on that."

I wasn't sure where "jack" came from, but probably it meant she and the other knights had heard me warning Lavinda about the cartel battle. "That's right," I said. "Talk with Majda."

Singer considered Pat. Beneath her perpetually hostile gaze, I thought I saw something else. Respect. She had seen a fourteen-year-old girl stand up and swear to a part of the Code that no one else would accept, not at first. That took guts.

Singer turned back to me. "Majda sent in soldiers during our fight."

"Majda also gave her word," I said. "No army interference in the battle."

Singer just sat, cold and unsmiling. The rest of us waited. Only she could accept or reject that claim. The moment stretched out, longer and colder.

Then she spoke in her gravelly voice. "It's true. They didn't interfere."

My shoulders relaxed a fraction. "Will you do the bargain? And bring the others?"

Ruzik snorted. "Those tests are useless."

"Maybe not," I said. "People here maybe have psi."

"Never seen it," Ruzik told me. "Hear thoughts? Stupid, eh."

"Maybe you've never seen it," I said, "but if anyone tests positive, the army will offer good bargains."

Singer suddenly spoke, sharp and angry. "Bargains like node-bliss? Fuck them."

So she knew about node-bliss. I hadn't thought the cartels were selling it, mainly because they hadn't cracked down on Scorch, and they would have if she encroached on their territory. "Is that what you want? Node-bliss?"

"I don't want shit," she told me. "I'm done with it."

Good gods. That sounded like she had *taken* the drug. The image of Singer as a psion was hard to credit. Still, if the drug did nothing to her, why the vehement reaction? She was in a lot better shape than the users I had seen in the cave, but she'd had more time to recover, and I didn't doubt she was stronger than all of us here combined.

Pat spoke. "Say we take these tests. What's the bargain?"

"Food and fresh water," I said. "A good meal."

They sat taking that in. Singer said, "Don't like it."

"Yah," Pat said. "I don't trust them."

Ruzik squinted at me. "They got meat?"

I almost smiled, remembering Jak. In our youth, he had craved steak, especially during that growth spurt he went through at sixteen. I hadn't cared much, but I had grown more slowly, if that made a difference. It was hard to say. We had always managed to find enough food, and Jak was as sharp as a honed knife, so I doubted malnutrition had affected him. Well, probably not. Gods knew, he could be a stubborn, hardheaded man, always hyperactive, but he probably would have been that way no matter what. Regardless, he had always loved big, juicy steaks.

"They got meat," I told Ruzik. "Plenty."

He tried to look disinterested, but I recognized the signs. He wanted that steak.

"We can't go on the Concourse," Pat said. "Cops chase us away."

"They won't for this," I said.

Pat just snorted.

"They'll feed everyone?" Ruzik asked.

"Everyone," I said. "Big steaks."

Singer spoke in a rough voice. "They feed baby, too?"

She had a child? *That* I didn't expect. Maybe she was asking for someone else in her circle.

"Baby, too." I thought back to my talk with Lavinda. "They'll also bring doctors, to do health checks." I had seen so many times how becoming a parent or guardian could prod people to change their lives, striving to create a future for the child they looked after.

"What is a doctor?" Ruzik asked.

"Healer," I said.

Pat frowned. "Not sick."

They could all use checkups and vitamin meds, but they wouldn't believe that. I needed a better argument. "Listen," I said. "We *all* should walk Concourse. Hold our heads high." The old anger stirred within me. "It is our undercity, including the Concourse. We have a right to be there. If enough of us come, they can't run us off."

The three of them just looked at me. If my little speech had any effect, they showed no sign.

"Just give it a think." I motioned upward. "Meet me in the Foyer tomorrow, noon, when the sun reaches the top of its travel." People here paid little attention to sunrise or sunset, which we couldn't see, but it was easy to steal mesh access and get the exact moment of any day.

They continued to look at me.

"We'll go to Rec Center," I said. "Have a meal, fresh water, do the tests, come home."

No response.

I tried again. "You don't have to come. But tell the others, yah? Let them choose."

"Maybe tell about the steak," Ruzik allowed.

Neither Pat or Singer spoke. They didn't refuse, either, though. I wasn't optimistic, but it could have gone a lot worse.

We would see what happened.

XXII

Into the Light

I found Ruzik waiting in the Foyer by the archway that opened onto the Concourse. That was it. Only Ruzik. No one else.

He nodded to me, framed in the archway. Beyond him, the Concourse stretched away into the smoky air, a narrow lane fading into the haze.

A rustle came from a ledge above us. A girl swung into view and dropped next to Ruzik, landing easily on her feet. I recognized her as a member of his gang. She wore a large knife in a sheath on her leather belt. I didn't want them coming armed, but if I told her to lose the blade, I had no doubt neither she nor Ruzik would come. Two people wasn't many, but it was better than none.

Max, I thought. *Is it noon?*

Three minutes past, he answered.

In the malleable time of the undercity, three minutes wasn't much. *We'll wait a bit more.*

Ruzik and the girl stood together, looking at the Concourse. The scar patterns on their arms glinted in the misty light trickling through the archway. They stood close, every now and then one of them brushing the other, and I figured they were lovers. The aroma of frying spice-rolls drifted around us, coming from stalls on the Concourse. A calculating gleam appeared in the girl's eyes. If I didn't get moving soon, I was going to lose them when they went out prowling to filch spice-rolls.

I tried to contain my agitation. Surely someone else would come.

No one else was in sight anywhere, however, except for a vendor standing in the market stall closest to the archway. Mist hazed the other stalls. They probably had vendors as well, but I saw no customers, not this close to the exit.

Ruzik's girlfriend stepped out into the Concourse, glancing around as if sizing up potential marks. When she turned back to Ruzik, he glowered at her. "Meat is better than spice," he said.

She frowned, but she came back to rejoin him.

We should start for the Rec Center, Max thought. **They won't wait much longer.**

Yah, it looks like it. I stepped toward them, and the girl turned with a start, but her gaze went past my shoulder. When I followed her look, my pulse jumped.

Across the Foyer, a group was coming up the walkway from the undercity, the family with the father who wove those incredible tapestries. The mother was carrying the baby they had adopted and Pack Rat walked at her side, holding her hand. Their two daughters flanked their father, including the older girl in the Dust Knights. Nor was it only them. The three psions they nursed through the phorine withdrawal had also come, the youth and the two girls. The trio looked exhausted and emaciated, but they walked with a steady step.

Ruzik and his girlfriend joined me, watching the newcomers with unabashed fascination. The older girl in the phorine trio glowered at them.

The mother came over to me. "Heya."

I nodded to her, a thanks for their coming. "We were just going."

We all headed to the archway. I moved ahead to make sure I emerged from the haze first at this end of the Concourse. Lavinda knew we were coming, so no one should stop us, but we had no guarantees. I was wearing above-city clothes, nothing overt, but with an expensive cut that sent a message: *I belong here by your own rules.* I loathed the unwritten "rules" that forbade my people to walk the Concourse, but I knew how to use them.

"Wait," a voice called behind us.

I turned to look. Someone was in the Foyer, hidden in shadows. Puzzled, I went through the group clustered behind me and under the archway. Digjan stood there in the Foyer, her gaze defiant, fierce in her torn black shirt, dark trousers, and a chain belt. A sheathed knife hung from a loop of her belt—and she gripped a laser carbine in one hand. The pinpoint light on its power unit shone with a full charge, casting blue light over the rocks. Hell and damnation. If Digjan walked out there with a carbine, all bets were off.

She glared at me, her gaze a challenge. "I come with."

I hadn't expected this. She had to be going through hell with the fighting and her mother. No one had found Dig's body yet. Digjan's presence was an act of trust, even given the carbine. I had to make a decision: let her bring the gun or tell her no. She wouldn't come without her weapon, and if I turned her back, the others would probably leave as well. But the moment she stepped out there with stolen ISC property, all hell could break loose. I didn't want anyone hurt, neither my people nor any Cries citizens.

I tapped on my gauntlet comm. I only had to wait a moment before a woman's voice snapped into the air. "Colonel Majda here."

Digjan stared at me in disbelief. Ruzik swore under his breath, but his girlfriend's voice was perfectly distinct as she said, "What the fuck is she doing?"

"Colonel," I said into my comm. "We're coming out."

"You're late," Lavinda said. "Is there a problem?"

I kept my gaze on Digjan as I spoke to Lavinda. "I need you to swear. I need your word that no one I bring will be arrested, detained, or penalized in any manner."

"I've already given you my word," Lavinda said.

"I want to make sure." I never took my gaze off Digjan, who needed to hear this. "No matter what or who you see."

Lavinda said, "You have my word, Major."

I exhaled. "Good. We're coming. Out here." I tapped off the comm. Then I spoke to Digjan. "I need your word that you won't threaten or shoot anyone."

She scowled at me. "They attack, I protect us."

"Yah," I said. "But we made a bargain. They agreed no attack. You must agree, too."

Her fist clenched the gun so tightly, her knuckles turned white. But she gave a brusque nod. "Agreed." For one moment, her impassive mask slipped, revealing a hint of her fear and the anguish she hid. It lasted the barest second and then vanished, her expression once more unreadable.

I nodded to her as if I hadn't seen, showing respect. We had a bargain. It was time to go.

But wait. Someone was coming up the path behind Dig, someone *large,* eight feet tall—no, it was two people, a small boy riding on a man's shoulders, the two of them coming into the lamplight. Well, hell. It was Jak. He was carrying a boy of about five in tattered trousers and shirt, and another boy walked at his side, a fellow about nine or ten. The child on his shoulders laughed as Jak's steps jostled him.

I smiled as Jak came up beside Digjan. "Heya," I said. "Got babies."

He reddened. "Not mine."

"Not baby," the older boy stated.

"They're dust rats," Digjan said. "They got no family."

"Dust Knights," Ruzik told her. "Not rats."

I peered past Jak, but no one else was coming up the path. People might be hiding in the spaces that networked these walls, curious, but not enough to come into the open. Even so. We had sixteen people, more than I expected. And Jak! I grinned, and he scowled. He had no intention of letting anyone think he was soft, not the notorious Mean Jak, but that wouldn't stop him from giving these boys a free meal.

"So," I said. "We go."

Ruzik's girlfriend said, "Yah. Go together. Hold head high. This is *our* Concourse."

I felt a curious sensation then, hearing her repeat my words, as if something moved inside of me. The others nodded, except for the mother holding the baby. She looked tired.

I went over to the mother and tilted my head at the baby. "I can carry her."

With undisguised relief, she handed me the child. The baby gave an annoyed cry of protest and stared at me with large eyes. I wondered if she recognized me as the person who found her in the cave. Probably not. I had held babies in my youth, those of my friends, but it had been years. The infant gurgled and settled into the crook of my arm. Belatedly, I realized it would make a statement that the first person who walked out of the haze would be a woman carrying a child. That spoke to a woman's power, a symbol of her authority among our peoples both above and below city. It also meant we came without threat, for we didn't bring our children into danger. That I came dressed as someone from the above-city would also serve as protection for the infant.

It hit me then; our group was mostly children. Four adults, twelve kids. The police would look terrible if they moved against children who were simply taking a walk, even those forbidden to enter the Concourse. Good. It might help offset their reaction to Digjan and her damn laser carbine. Ruzik and his girlfriend hardly looked innocuous, either, especially with that dagger the girl wore. Ruzik undoubtedly also had one hidden on his person. Neither they nor Digjan had come to fight, but if they felt threatened, that could change. I hoped I was right about Lavinda, that she would keep her word.

Pack Rat was looking up at me. "Come with you," he said.

I smiled at him. "You remember me?"

"Yah." He jumped, mimicking one of my tykando moves.

I glanced at the mother. "Is okay?"

"Is good," she said.

I offered my hand, but Pack Rat drew himself up as if he were an adult, albeit a small one, and shook his head. I took a breath and walked under the archway. He stayed at my side, both of us stepping into the smoky haze that filled this end of the Concourse. I heard the others following, but I was too tense to turn and look, as if the act of my needing to see if they came with us would be enough to make them leave.

Pack Rat gazed around with wide eyes at the market stalls clustering on either side. Tassels hung from their eaves. Streamers were wrapped around the poles that held up their canvas roofs or flapping in erratic gusts of air created by vents farther up the Concourse. Down here, the paltry currents weren't enough to clear out the haze. Time and smoke had dimmed the stalls, fading their panels into dusty red hues.

The counters fronting the stalls were piled high with goods, most of it junk, but some worthwhile salvage. Vendors stood behind their goods, watching us. Most days they would be chattering, calling out to their rare customers or joshing each other. Today they just stared, grizzled men, burly women, and sellers too green to have stalls on better parts of the Concourse. The few pedestrians had stepped back between the stalls, giving us space. Everyone looked baffled. Nothing like this had happened before, that denizens of the undercity walked boldly into the light, coming *en masse,* or at least as much mass as sixteen people could muster. None of the vendors looked happy. Several tapped their wrist comms and spoke urgently to whoever they had contacted. Probably the police.

Just let us get there, I thought. *Let us reach the Center without any trouble.*

Was that directed at me? Max asked.

No. I do have a something you can do, though. I took the green beetle out of my jacket. I hadn't brought my gun, jammer, or pack, nothing except this bot. *Connect me to the beetle. I want to see if Colonel Majda came.* I opened my hand and the bot soared away, into the air.

Connecting, Max thought.

Suddenly I was seeing through the eyes of the beetle. I flew up the Concourse, close to the ceiling. I was aware of the alley where I was walking, but just barely. The scene I viewed as the beetle came through much more vividly, showing the Concourse three stories below.

Go closer to the Rec Center, I thought. *That's where Lavinda would be if she came.*

I soared higher. The Concourse widened into a street and then a boulevard. Air currents flowed more strongly here. The haze thinned and the stalls brightened, yellow pavilions with blue tassels hanging from their eaves. Cafes appeared, at first no more than glorified stalls, but farther up they became fancier bistros. A few people were out walking, and others sat on the terraces of cafés, sipping kava. It was a low volume time. Many people slept at noon, given the forty hours of daylight on Raylicon, which was why I had chosen this time. No crowds, but it wasn't night either, so the police wouldn't think we were prowling around in the dark.

Farther up the Concourse, upscale clubs appeared. It was too early for nightlife, but a few young people congregated here. The Concourse was perfect for the younger crowds from Cries, just risqué enough for them to feel as if they were doing something illicit, though in truth it was perfectly safe. Above-city types rarely ventured off the Concourse, given all the warnings about the undercity. It was true, if they came to the aqueducts, they could get mugged. Rich kids sometimes risked it anyway. They thought it was exciting, a good story for their friends. The gangers just wanted them to go away, preferably without their belongings, especially any food, fresh water, tech-mech, or jewelry the muggers could sell on the black market. Every now and then you heard rumors of an affair between undercity and above-city lovers, but those never seemed to end well.

The Rec Center lay ahead. A long, low building the color of a pale sky, it stood bathed in the sunshine pouring through a skylight above the building. The tall doors were shut. Bad choice. If we made it this far, the closed entrance would look unwelcoming. Two cops were outside, both armed with carbines. Just lovely. Greet the people you asked to trust you with the same guns that had just devastated their home. Not that we were any better, with Digjan and the gangers coming armed.

No sign of Lavinda, though. *Try farther up,* I thought.

The Concourse continued to widen as I sailed onward, as large as two boulevards now. I wondered why they put the Rec Center in a place that was so inaccessible to the aqueducts. Probably because of its size. They would have done better to locate a smaller structure near the end of the Concourse. That was where the kids came out to prowl, like Ruzik and his girlfriend. They might actually hang out at the Center if it was easier to visit.

I found Colonel Majda, Max thought.

Show me.

The bot backtracked to where several cafés lined the Concourse across from the Rec center, set on a terrace higher than the street. Lavinda was standing at a rail there with Chief Takkar and Major Duane Ebersole. The colonel's bars glinted on the shoulders of Lavinda's uniform, Duane wore his black trousers and shirt, and Takkar had on her usual police digs, with a pulse gun on her hip.

As I came within range, I heard Ebersole saying, "—the police know their orders not to shoot."

Lavinda looked around the Concourse. "It all seems quiet."

"I thought she said they were coming," Takkar spoke curtly. "I don't see squat."

That was odd. They should be able to see us. *Max, show me the end of the Concourse.*

My view shifted as the beetle turned toward the distant end of the Concourse, about a kilometer away, where the narrowed lane disappeared into a white haze. I couldn't see squat, either. Although the beetle had some IR capability, the haze down there was the same temperature as its surroundings, and the bot couldn't do enough thermal imaging to distinguish anyone.

"I see them," Lavinda said. "A woman with a child, it looks like."

"It's Bhaajan with two kids," Takkar said.

Max, magnify my vision, I thought.

My view became clearer. Yes, now I saw the woman,

me in fact, which was weird. Seeing myself coming out of the mist, I finally understood why people always knew I had been a military officer. I had that distinctive walk, an upright carriage and sense of readiness. I hadn't realized I moved that way. It was softened a bit because I was carrying a baby, with a small boy walking at my side. Pack Rat looked flustered, but also amazed by his surroundings. If it hadn't been for his ragged clothes, we could have passed for a tourist family.

"I guess two is better than none," Takkar said.

Duane Ebersole spoke. "No, there's more with her."

Three people came into view behind me, Ruzik, his girlfriend, and the other girl in their gang. The fourth member of their gang strode out from between two stalls, probably after using one of the hidden Concourse entrances. They all wore knives now, and they walked abreast in a line. I could tell they were nervous, but if I hadn't known them, I would have seen only four gangers striding along the street.

"Good gods," Lavinda said. "Are those drug runners?"

"Most of the runners are dead," Ebersole said. "That's probably a dust gang."

"They better keep those knives sheathed," Takkar growled. "Or I'll have them in the clink faster than you can say fuck it all to hell."

"Captain." Lavinda sounded irritated. "You have my orders. Neither your force nor the Cries police will do anything to these people."

"And if they attack someone?" Takkar demanded. "You want me just to stand by?"

"You use nonlethal force." Lavinda spoke quietly. "Let's just hope it doesn't come to that."

You and me both, I thought.

Another group was forming out of the haze, but I couldn't see them clearly. At my thought, the beetle flew in closer. Ah! It was Jak with the two boys, the family, and the three bliss addicts. The older daughter in the family walked on the outside of her kin like a bulwark between the family and the Concourse. A protector. A knight.

"That looks like all of them," Ebersole said. I could barely hear him, I was so far away.

"I think so—no, wait," Lavinda said. "There's more."

What? There weren't more. Or were there? Led by Pat Oey, a gaggle of children was coming out of the haze. Pat guided them, tall and graceful in her strength, like a warrior protecting her tribe. No wonder she was late; rounding up so many kids could take time. If the circle she led included that many children, then at only fourteen years of age, she was already a well-established leader in the undercity. Rockson, another leader in the Knights, appeared with more children, many with gaunt faces and hollowed gazes. A large man walked in their midst, towering. Gourd! Who was he carrying? The woman was so emaciated, she looked like a skeleton with skin pulled tight over her bones. But she was alive. Her eyes stayed open as her head lolled against his chest.

As I flew closer, more people materialized out of the haze. Biker had brought the cyber-riders, including the adults and trans-folk, the true wizards, geniuses who rode the mesh-waves in support of the undercity, using a finesse no one in Cries could match. Another wave appeared, led by the father and daughter from the Down-deep. Every person in their group had alabaster skin and wore eye lenses or visors, protection against what, for them, had to be the unbearably brilliant light of the Concourse. Yet here they were, walking into sunlight—the first time in years, maybe even in generations, that anyone from that deep below Cries had come out of the dark.

When I saw who came behind them, I inhaled sharply. I knew that looming woman, her muscled frame, her menacing walk. Dark Singer. She had a carbine slung over her right shoulder and a tangler on her hip. Black gauntlets surrounded her wrists, both with dart throwers, their tips surely dipped in poison. She did nothing to hide the Vakaar insignia on her gauntlets, the slash of white across a dark orb.

She held a baby in her left arm.

The child was about a year old, looking around at what it probably experienced as a chaos of colors and smells. Emotions built inside of me, so many mixed together, fear for the safety of these people and incredulity that so many came. I finally recognized the strongest, an emotion unlike any we usually felt below. Triumph. It was bittersweet, for so much pain came with these people. This had gone far beyond what I had asked of them. They were a full procession, adults and children in rags, many too thin, but none cowed. In their silence, they were making a statement, loud and undeniable. *This is our city, too. We have the right to be here.*

The final wave formed out of the haze.

Singer's gang appeared first, then Digjan and the other two punkers in her trio, striding like the violent queens who once ruled the Raylicon desert. Today they came armed with carbines and tanglers instead of swords, and the procession they defended was far different than the armies of our ancient history. When I saw them clearly, I knew why this group came last. They brought the dying. Gangers and punkers together carried crude stretchers, each supporting a crumpled fighter from the battle. An older dust Knight helped a punker who was hopping on one leg, using a metal rod for his crutch. A heavily pregnant girl walked with the two of them, holding her huge belly with one arm. I thought of the mother I had found dead with her baby a few days ago. Then I thought of another mother so many years ago—a girl named Bhaaj who had died alone—and my eyes burned with the tears I had never learned how to shed.

Police patrolled the procession from end to end. Tourists retreated to shops or cafés. Gawkers lined the rail where Lavinda stood with Chief Takkar and Major Duane Ebersole. Everyone stared, their disbelief plain. I wasn't sure if our numbers shocked them or that so many of us came in rags, gaunt and scarred. *See what you've ignored,* I thought. *See the crime Cries has let go for years, centuries, maybe even millennia.*

A sudden motion caught the attention of the beetle, and it whipped around to show me a woman running across the Concourse toward the Center. *Follow her,* I thought.

The beetle flew above the runner, who turned out to be Tanzia, the volunteer who worked at the Center. When she reached the building, she grabbed the handles on the double doors and heaved them outward, calling out an order: *Stay open!*

I followed her inside. The building looked the same as the first time I had come here, with three people playing a board game across the room, two men and a woman. Today, however, several doctors and psi-testers were also setting up med stations, and extra rows of water bottles waited on the closest counter.

A man in a white IRAS uniform ran into the Center. With no pause, he grabbed a cart by the wall, shoved it to the counter with the bottles, and swept them onto the cart.

Tanzia shouted to the trio playing the board game, "Get more food! Hurry!"

As they jumped to their feet, the woman called out, "What are you doing?"

Tanzia went to her, gulping in air from her run. "We need more supplies."

"How much?" one of the men asked.

"All of it!" Tanzia said.

"I hardly think so," the woman said. "We have supplies meant to last a year down there."

Tanzia met her gaze. "And it won't be enough."

Major Ebersole jogged into the Center and joined the IRAS officer, helping him tear down the counter. "Even with this gone," Ebersole said, "no way will we have enough space. We'll have to feed and treat some of them outside."

In the midst of it all, one of the Center volunteers was walking through the semi-organized chaos toward the open door, his face puzzled.

Follow, I thought.

As the man stepped outside, he whispered, "Saints almighty." The bot followed him—and I saw the full procession.

It filled the length of the Concourse.

We had been wrong. All of us. I had been so smug

thinking Lavinda had no idea how many of us lived in the undercity. I was no better. It wasn't thirty people, not ninety, not two hundred and ninety. According to my node, nearly four hundred people were walking up the Concourse, and stragglers were still feeding into the procession. I counted at least fifteen with carbines, and many wore knives. Saints only knew how many had tanglers. Either there were more punkers than any of us had realized, or the gangs had taken up their arms after the battle.

As we neared the Center, soldiers ran to the building from the other direction, farther up the Concourse. Lavinda must have commed them for extra supplies. Some carried tables or crates, and others were rolling in extra med stations. Police stood everywhere, monitoring the procession with their gauntlet sensors.

I released my link with the beetle—and I was suddenly in my own body again, leading the procession. We had reached the Center, and I was walking past the med stations that the frazzled volunteers were setting up outside. I slowed as I entered the building, and the procession poured around me, children staring around with unabashed curiosity, adults taking it in with warier gazes. People reached for the snap-bottles that volunteers offered and headed toward the counters where food steamed and fruits and vegetables were piled in slots. The mother of the baby took him out of my arms with a nod of thanks. She hurried back to her family, and Pack Rat went with her, holding her hand.

The volunteers served the children first, then the adults. Children settled on the floor with their plates piled high, doing what we had always done when the opportunity presented itself, which was chowing down with gusto. Volunteers were opening bedrolls. Gourd laid the emaciated woman he was carrying on a pallet while a medic attached lines to her body and a doctor shouted for fluid pacs. Other medics helped the gangs and punkers set down their stretchers with the casualties from the battle. The Center had too few volunteers—no way could they deal with all these people—

Except the Knights were helping. They had assigned themselves to sections in the procession, and they were making sure their groups received food and water in an orderly manner.

A tall woman walked into the Center, a steady figure amid the chaos. Lavinda. She came over to me, her step firm, her face calm, but I knew her enough well to see she was in shock. She stopped next to me and we stood together in the middle of the room.

"You brought them," the colonel said.

She was a master of understatement today. I tried to answer, but I couldn't.

Lavinda looked around. "We'll provide medical attention and food first, before the tests."

I found my voice. "That would be good."

She turned a hard stare on Digjan and the other two punkers with her. They stood near the door, their faces hard as they looked across the room. I followed their gaze and my stomach clenched.

Singer was standing on the other side of the hall with her baby in one arm. She wasn't doing anything other than waiting for her turn with the medic examining the youngest children. She didn't have to do squat. Just waiting there, she was everyone's worst fear of the undercity, huge, scarred, tattooed with a cartel insignia, the carbine large on her shoulder and the tangler glinting at her waist. People avoided her as if she were an explosive ready to detonate. But no one challenged her. Lavinda had given her word that anyone could receive medical care, and that included even the baby of the undercity's most notorious cartel assassin.

Singer looked around the room as if she were on reconnaissance. Her gaze raked over the Kajada punkers and she froze with the eerie stillness I had seen in troops before they went to battle.

"Time to intervene," Lavinda said in a low voice. "We can't risk trouble." She tapped the *on* panel of her gauntlet comm. "This could turn into a riot."

"Wait," I said. Singer had sworn to the Code of the Dust Knights, as incongruous as it seemed. When her gaze came to rest on me, I lifted my chin the way I had when I demanded she swear to the Code or leave.

Singer considered me. Then she left the line and stalked forward. People jumped aside, some of them stumbling backward to get out of her way as fast as possible.

She went to a table someone had heaped with fruit. Only a few succulent red orbs remained. A volunteer was carrying another crate forward, but Singer ignored him as she swept the last fruit to the floor. While children ran after the scattered orbs, Singer pulled the table to where I stood with Lavinda. She regarded us impassively. Then she slid the carbine off her shoulder, its strap scraping along her giant bicep. With her gaze on Lavinda and with her curious baby in her other arm, she grasped the gun's stock, flipped it over, and thunked the weapon on the table. She pulled the tangler out of the frayed holster on her belt and set it next to the carbine. With that done, she looked across the room at the Kajada punkers, her challenge obvious. Then she strode back to the line of people waiting to see the harried doctor who was checking the babies. No one argued when she resumed the same place in line where she had stood before.

Everyone was watching us. I met Digjan's stare and tilted my head. She knew what I meant. She stood there, her face thunderous, and I felt sure she would turn away. Noise filled the room, the hum of equipment, the clack of utensils, but we paid no attention. I could almost feel her anger.

Digjan walked forward.

Lavinda stayed at my side, but she didn't interfere. When Digjan reached the table, she threw a hostile glance toward Singer, who was watching us. Then Digjan pulled off her carbine and set it next to Singer's guns. With no more ado, she strode back to her place by the wall.

What followed next felt surreal, and it could only happen on this day where everything had turned upside down. They all came forward, all the punkers and gangers, and one by one they piled their guns in front of Lavinda. They were making a statement for each other that had nothing to do with the colonel, finally agreeing, after the carnage of battle, that at least for today, it was time to stop killing. I knew what they meant, but I also knew what I hoped Lavinda would see. They were returning stolen property.

These kids weren't the ones who had smuggled the guns; Commander Braze hijacked them, Scorch bought them from Braze, and Dig stole them from Scorch. Lavinda was no fool; she knew these fighters hadn't come here to give up their weapons. I doubted they had returned all the guns; tanglers were easier to hide than carbines, and far fewer of those lay in the heap on the table. No matter. They had returned the visible weapons. Digjan probably didn't realize it, but the moment she laid her carbine on the table, she made her hopes to join the army a possibility again. Instead of flaunting stolen ISC property in front of a colonel, she had recovered it in service of the army. At least, I hoped Lavinda would be willing to spin it that way.

The chaos of our arrival was calming. More volunteers arrived, carting in supplies. Children were laughing, especially the younger ones, who must have thought this was the most amazing lark, free food and a parade, all with more friends to play with than they had seen before. Somewhere a baby wailed and a boy grunted as a doctor gave him an air-syringe shot. The testers were working now, too, doing Kyle exams. A boy and girl ran through the Center, knocking over chairs. Before the harried volunteers could object, one of the Dust Knights grabbed both kids, admonishing them to behave. Everywhere, the Knights quietly organized the crowd, undertaking duties I hadn't given them, though I would have if I'd realized the need. They kept the children reasonably well behaved, a feat probably no one else here could have managed. The Knights were part of the undercity, and the other children listened in a way they wouldn't do for the Cries authorities.

I spoke to Lavinda, indicating the three recovering

bliss users, who had sat in one corner while they nibbled at meat rolls. "You should test them for Kyle traits. They were addicted to phorine."

Lavinda beckoned to Duane Ebersole, who was seated at a nearby table, administering tests to a young man. Duane glanced at us, then offered a snap-bottle to the youth. The kid shrugged, but the moment Duane left the table, the boy took the bottle and downed its sparkling water in gulps.

When Duane came over, Lavinda indicated the phorine users. "Make sure you check them."

He nodded. "I'll take them next."

"Can you tell if anyone here is a psion?" I asked.

Duane glanced at me, then at the colonel.

"Go ahead," Lavinda said.

"I can't give specifics yet," he said, "but we have a rough idea." He took a breath. "Of the twenty-four people I've so far tested, eight are empaths. One is a telepath."

Lavinda stared at him. "What did you say?"

Duane met her gaze, and I could see the shock underlying his outward calm. "My results are the same as what the other testers are recording." He motioned at the room teeming with people. "Colonel, *one-third* of these folks are empaths. Five percent of them are telepaths."

"That's impossible," Lavinda said. "Did you check your equipment?"

"Thoroughly. We all have." He let out a breath. "The results are genuine."

I had no idea what to say. Over thirty percent empaths, when in the general population, empaths were at best one-tenth of one percent. That meant the undercity had three hundred times more empaths than normally found among human beings. And five percent telepaths? If only one in a million people were telepaths, that meant the undercity rate was *fifty-thousand* times the normal occurrence among humans.

I spoke in a low voice, finally understanding. "Our ancestors went under the city because their minds couldn't take the flood of human emotions drowning them in Cries." Yes, I saw. The isolation protected us. Over the ages, deep within the canals, my ancestors had lived, loved, and interbred, concentrating the psionic traits of ancient Raylicon.

Lavinda spoke quietly. "I don't know if this is the greatest crime ever committed here or our greatest miracle."

Both, I thought.

A silence fell over the Center. Conversations died down and even the small children went silent as people looked toward the doorway. I turned—and stiffened.

A woman had walked into the room. She resembled the drug punkers, but in the way that a grown desert-lion resembled its cubs. This was no throwback to the barbarian queens of our past, this was the real thing. She stood as tall as Lavinda, as muscled as Singer, as scarred as Ruzik, and as implacable as Scorch. She looked like she had been through hell. Her clothes were burned, her right arm was obviously broken in several places, and gashes covered her body, crusted with dried blood, purpled by bruises. She held a primed carbine in her hand, ready to shoot, with the snout pointed at the ceiling. She had a tangler in her other hand, also drawn, pointing at the floor between mine and Lavinda's feet. She stood there like an avenging demon come to exact her price for the devastation of her empire.

Dig had survived.

The soldiers did what, for them, was the only logical action. Two moved to guard the table with the guns, preventing anyone from retrieving them. That meant Dig was the only openly armed cartel member in a room with both Vakaars and Kajadas. Either the cartels had been larger than we thought or not as many had died as the army believed, because I counted the insignia of at least five Vakaars, including Singer, and four Kajadas, including Digjan. Right now, with one violent sweep of her carbine, Dig could slaughter the surviving Vakaars before they had a chance to move. The soldiers would fire, but I had no doubt Dig had better biomech than any of us. She could move fast enough to achieve her goal before she died. That she would kill many other people in the process wouldn't stop her if she were furious enough over the destruction of her cartel.

Lavinda tapped her comm and spoke in a low, fast voice. "Takkar, get me a unit—"

"No." I laid my hand on her wrist and prayed people didn't get court-martialed for touching Majda royalty without permission.

Lavinda moved away her arm, but she stopped speaking.

"Colonel?" Takkar's voice came out of the comm. "A unit of what?"

With her gaze on Dig, Lavinda said, "Wait, Captain."

Dig continued watching us. I tilted my head toward the wall where her daughter stood with the other two Kajada punkers. Dig glanced that way, and Digjan nodded to her mother, her body tensed. Dig inclined her head, and I understood her unspoken message to her daughter. *Wait.*

We all waited. The soldiers in the room kept their hands on their guns.

Dig walked forward, limping badly. It looked like only sheer determination kept her going. She came on, approaching Lavinda and me. One of the soldiers stepped closer to Lavinda, but the colonel shook her head and the soldier stopped. Everyone was watching that carbine Dig had aimed at the ceiling and the tangler pointed between our feet.

Dig approached steadily despite her limp, but I knew what it cost her. I knew her tells. She was in excruciating pain. Gods only knew what had happened to her when the canal collapsed or how long she had been down there before she crawled free.

She didn't come directly to us. Instead she went to the table with the guns. A soldier stood in front of the piled weapons, blocking her way. She looked at him, her face hard. We all tensed as she lowered her carbine—

And handed it to the soldier.

Gods above. Had that actually happened? I watched with disbelief as Dig also gave him her tangler. I hoped the people here realized the freaking miracle they had just witnessed, that Dig Kajada willingly surrendered her weapons.

Dig turned and spoke to Lavinda in her rasping voice, her words strained and careful, for she was doing her best to use above-city speech rather than undercity dialect.

"Colonel," Dig said, "I understand that anyone who

comes here, for this one day, has got sanctuary. No matter who they are."

I could almost feel how badly Lavinda wanted to deny those words, how much she wanted to clap Dig into the technological version of irons.

The colonel said only, "That is correct."

Dig tapped a panel on her gauntlet and spoke into her comm. "Bring them."

In response, a Center volunteer from outside walked through the sunlight streaming into the center—and he brought with him three children, a boy and two girls ranging in age from about six to twelve. Canal dust covered them, their clothes crusted with blue and red powder as if an avalanche had buried them. Bruises and gashes covered their skin, but none of them looked seriously hurt. Someone had protected them from a rock fall, and though I couldn't have said how I knew, I had no doubt that person had thrown her own body across theirs, taking the brunt of the rocks.

Digjan inhaled sharply, and the children glanced at her. The smallest, the boy, gave a cry of recognition and started toward her, but the volunteer holding his hand drew him back. Instead, he brought the children to us and they all stood there with Dig.

"These are my children," Dig told Lavinda. "Do I have your word that you will treat them as you treat everyone else here?"

"Yes," Lavinda said. "You have my word."

Dig continued in her ragged above-city speech. "They were taken by Vakaar during the combat and caught in the collapse of the canals. I ask that you see to their medical condition. Feed them." She took a rattling breath. "And you test them for the emotion and thought hearing. All of them. Completely."

"We will do that," Lavinda said. "For you, too, if you wish."

Dig nodded. Then her eyes rolled back into her head and she collapsed like a great stone column in the aqueducts crashing to the ground.

"Dig," I shouted, dropping to my knees next to her body.

People were running to us. Digjan called her mother's name, and then she was at my side, crouched next to Dig. Medics pushed their way past us and lifted up the cartel queen. I followed as they carried her to a pallet at one of the medical stations. People were everywhere, hooking Dig to monitors, paramedics calling, the doctor injecting her with gods only knew what.

"She's failing," someone yelled.

I stood back with Digjan, barely breathing while the medics worked. Gourd came up on Digjan's other side and Jak stood with me. I felt as if I was seeing it through a haze, everything slowed down.

A voice cut through the chaos, low, rasping, unmistakable. "Fuck that, let me die in peace."

I didn't know whether to laugh or cry. I grabbed Digjan's arm and we pushed our way forward. As we knelt next to the pallet where Dig was hooked up to monitors and lines, Gourd and Jak crouched on the other side. Dig's other daughters knelt by Jak, near their mother, and the boy squeezed between the two of them.

Dig looked up at her oldest daughter. Then she looked at me. She took Digjan's hand and crossed it with mine, laying her daughter's palm on top of my knuckles. She spoke to Digjan, her words barely audible. "You see this Bhaajan person? Great pain in my ass."

"Stop talking," Digjan told her. "You need to rest. Recover."

Dig scowled. "Not argue with me, just once, Daughter." She shook our joined hands. "Bhaaj is a great ass pain, yah. Bhaaj is also good. You be like her, Digjan. *Like her.* Not me."

Digjan gripped her hand. "You won't die."

Dig glowered at her. "You won't argue." She glanced at me. "Always, this jan argues." Her voice was fading and her eyes closed, but nothing hid her satisfaction as she said, "Vakaar is gone."

"Hammer is dead?" Digjan asked.

"I kill." Dig opened her eyes. "Your father is avenged."

Digjan's voice cracked. "Mother—"

"No more cartel," Dig told her. "You take it over, I'll come back from the dead and whoop your damn ass."

"Don't die," Digjan whispered.

"Little son, little jans." Dig reached for her other children and they clutched her fingers. Dig let out a breath, sighed once, and closed her eyes. The monitors stopped beeping and gave that horrible siren scream of death.

I was vaguely aware of the medics pushing me away so they could work on Dig. I rose to my feet and stumbled back, but nothing changed. The machines kept up their death wail. Digjan and her sisters and brother stayed with their mother until the other two Kajada punkers drew them away. The medics pulled a sheet over Dig, covering her entire body, including her head. Digjan was kneeling on the ground, rocking back and forth, holding her brother and sisters.

The other punkers knelt with them, holding Digjan and the children.

I couldn't take it anymore. Dig had been a monster. Why was I breaking apart? I spun around and strode away from them all. I was aware of Lavinda in front of me. She was trying to say something, but I couldn't hear. I shook my head and kept going. What could I say? Oh sorry, Colonel, I neglected to tell you that my oldest friend, the blood sister I swore my life to when I was three years old, also happened to be one of the undercity's worst criminals.

I walked into the light streaming through the doorway. Then I was outside, among the others who had come up from the undercity. Many had crowded around the door, watching the scene unfold. They parted and I strode past them, past the doctors treating patients, past the testers doing exams. Soon I was running in long strides that took me away from the Center. I had to escape. I followed side streets that wound between market stalls, then went farther, past shops closed for the noon sleep, until the sounds of the Center faded behind me. When I reached the wall of the Concourse, I sank down with my back against the white stone barrier, an empty shop on either side, and sat with my knees drawn up to my chest and my forehead on my knees.

A rustle came from nearby. I looked up to see Jak settling next to me. Gourd dropped down on my other side. We sat there together, leaning against one another.

"Damn Dig," I whispered.

"A greater ass pain even than Bhaaj." Jak's ironic tone was ruined when his voice cracked.

I gave a ragged laugh that threatened to end with a sob. "Yah."

"She argued even more than Digjan," Gourd said.

"She saved my life more than once," I said.

"Dig was my first," Gourd said. "Good first."

"You're Digjan's father?" I asked. That didn't fit with what I had just heard.

He shook his head. "Dig and me, we were just kids. Later she had a bigger love."

"Same father, all four children," Jak said. "Vakaar killed him."

So the cartel war had been about more than drugs. Dig was avenging the death of her children's father. I put my forehead back on my knees and closed my eyes. Too much had happened. So many emotions, so much grief and triumph, pain and joy, fighting, killing and birth, children laughing and children dying, starvation and freedom, the freedom simply to stand in the sunlight. I couldn't absorb it all, even comprehend what it felt like to walk up the Concourse with four hundred people following me. I didn't know whether to mourn or rejoice. My mind couldn't hold all these emotions. I was drowning.

The knees of my trousers must have taken a spill from the water in someone's snap-bottle. Those weren't tears on my face, sliding down my cheeks, soaking into my clothes.

We sat there, me and Gourd and Mean Jak clumped together. Jak put his arm around my shoulders and I put mine around his waist. Gourd put his big arm over Jak's on my shoulders, and I put my other one around Gourd's waist.

And then we did what dust rats never did.

We cried.

XXIII
The Children

I had expected, when I received a summons to the palace, to meet Lavinda in her office or one of those round alcoves with tall windows that were like polished jewel boxes. Instead, the pilot who picked me up at the penthouse landed his flyer in a vast garden behind the palace, a place of many plants on terraces. After he left, I stood on the highest terrace at the end of a path paved in stones that were a wimpy purple color.

Lavender, Max thought.

What? I couldn't concentrate.

The color of the stones. It's called lavender.

Yah, good. I was trying with no success to stop feeling nervous. The garden was far more lush than anything that grew naturally in this desert. The few trees were sculptures. The one nearest to where I stood looked like a great flying lizard, its leafy wings outstretched, its double trunk like two legs braided around each other. A fountain burbled beyond it, and flowers bloomed everywhere, big orchids, blue, pink, and red. The terraced gardens descended in huge steps to a meadow below, and beyond the meadow, the mountains rose into the sky.

I couldn't see on the other side of the palace, but I knew the mountains there descended down to the desert. On that side, I could have seen Cries in the distance, but here I saw nothing except blue and red peaks with no foliage. A stark view, yes, but spectacularly beautiful in its barren majesty. I needed that view today. The sight eased the ragged edges of my mind. It was hard to believe only a day had passed since we of the undercity walked the Concourse and changed the history of Cries.

After a while, I wondered what had happened to Lavinda. I had never known her to be late. Just as I was about to go in search of her, footsteps sounded behind me. I turned—and blinked. Four guards were approaching along the path from the palace. A man walked in their midst. It wasn't Lavinda who had come to see me, but her husband.

Prince Paulo wore simple clothes, no gems or gold, just a blue shirt and dark trousers. As he drew closer, I realized the cloth was imported Haverian silk, a fabric woven by tinarian spiders on the planet Haveria. I had never actually seen anyone wealthy enough to wear clothes made from that silk. What unsettled me even more, though, was that he didn't have on his robe. Within the palace, Majda men didn't have to go robed, but they also didn't usually talk to outsiders.

When Paolo reached me, I bowed, acutely self-conscious. "My greetings, Your Highness."

"Major." He lifted his hand, indicating a bench under the tree. "Would you care to sit?"

"Uh, yah, sure," Gods, I sounded like an idiot.

Majda men did that to me. Their mere presence was enough to leave us mere mortals tongue-tied.

We settled on the bench, he on one end and me on the other, with two of his guards standing behind the bench, the third on the side next to Paolo, and the fourth a few meters to the front, checking out the terraces, as if gods forbid, a tiny flying lizard might trespass on the Majda prince he guarded. I couldn't think of anything intelligent to say, so I waited.

"I often come to this garden to think," Paolo said. "I find it soothing."

"It's beautiful." I couldn't imagine why I was here.

"The army architects sent me their records of the collapsed canals," Paolo said. "Along with reports from the university detailing the historical value and structure of the ruins."

It seemed bizarre they would send him all that information, but what did I know? I said only, "Part of two canals fell." Wryly I added, "They made a lot of noise."

He smiled. "I imagine so. Have you had a good look at them since then?"

"Several times." I was still puzzled. "Why do you ask?"

"The engineers could rebuild them," he said, "but they don't feel they can do the canals justice. Repairing a ruin that ancient is no easy task."

I wondered why he cared. Then it hit me. Good gods. "You're going to direct the repair."

"Why does that surprise you?"

I had expected the Anthropology Department at the university to spearhead the work. The canals were marvels, and of course Cries would want them preserved. But no one would expect a prince of the realm to do the job, especially one of Paolo's standing. Were I a diplomat with expertise in verbal nuance, I could have soft-pedaled my response, but I was just inarticulate me. So I said, "I'm surprised you agreed to fix a slum, even one with historical value. You're one of the top architects in the Imperialate. And you live in seclusion."

"I saw the records of your procession on the Concourse." His voice had an odd sound, as if it were hollowed out. "We have much to answer for."

"We?"

"Majda. Cries. Anyone who stood by and did nothing when we could have helped."

I couldn't answer. That touched too close to the scorched places in my heart. The irony was that my people would shy away from his help, wary of royalty setting their hand onto our lives. But the Majdas weren't what I expected. Yes, they were wealthy and privileged, and they took their lives for granted, oblivious to the bitter truths of life below their shimmering city. The gap between their sphere and ours was so big, we might never truly understand each other. Yet both Lavinda and her husband were willing to try bridging that gap.

I had to say something. This wasn't the time for undercity silence. "Having you design the repair means a great deal."

He inclined his head, a response not so different from how we acknowledged such statements in the undercity. Then he said, "I can't, however, visit the ruins."

"Can you work from holographic recordings?"

"If they are done well." He considered me. "I need someone who knows the canals to make the recordings."

That couldn't be what it sounded like. "Are you asking me?"

"If you have the time." With a look of apology, he added, "It will be a lot of work. But you would be compensated."

"I'm just a private investigator. Another architect would be a better choice."

"It is not the training." He stopped as if searching for the right words. "What you see in the undercity, Major, cannot be learned. No architect I know could go down there and give me a true picture, not in the way someone who understands the aqueducts could provide. For me to do justice to the repair, I need to know those canals as they are seen by someone who loves them."

Love? That was nuts. I didn't even like the aqueducts. Except that was lie, and if it had taken me too long to admit that truth, the least I could do was acknowledge it now.

After a moment, Paolo said, "My apology if I gave offense."

"No. No, you didn't." I took a breath. "Yes, I accept."

His smile flashed. "Thank you."

I nodded to him, undercity style. We had a bargain.

Paolo glanced behind us. Following his gaze, I saw a tall woman in a green uniform waiting by the palace, partially hidden by the vines hanging off a latticed arch in the garden.

Paolo stood up, and I rose as well. When I bowed from the waist, he inclined his head to me. He took his leave then, his guards falling in around him. The woman came forward, but she didn't stop to talk when they passed on the pathway, though it looked like they exchanged a greeting. It seemed oddly formal for a husband and wife, but then, much of what the Majdas did seemed too formal to me. The woman walked through the lattice archway—and I stiffened. It wasn't Lavinda.

The Majda queen had come to see me.

Vaj walked to the bench where I stood, imposing in her general's uniform and long-legged gait. She nodded to me the same way that Paolo had done, but she somehow made it intimidating.

"Major," she said.

"My greetings, General." I was glad for the cool breezes in the mountains, because otherwise I would have been sweating despite the nanomeds in my body that were supposed to moderate such reactions.

She motioned at the bench and we both sat down. "Paolo said you accepted the job."

"Yes, I did."

Vaj gazed out over the terraces. I didn't have the sense she was deliberately remaining silent, but rather that she wanted to think and felt inclined to do it while we were sitting here. After a moment she turned back to me. "We didn't expect what you discovered about this woman Scorch."

I hadn't either. "I don't think she had much interest in smuggling weapons. She only became involved because it gave her a contact among the Traders."

"Yes, that appears to be the case." Her voice took on a darker quality. "She found psions by addicting them to phorine. She controlled them by limiting the supply of the drug. She planned to sell them to the Traders."

I didn't miss her phrasing: *Planned. Not did.* "Then she hadn't yet?"

"From what we've determined, she was setting up the first sale when you killed her." The general's voice was ice. "Hers would have been the ultimate crime, because we had no idea, none of us, that the people she planned to sell even existed."

Scorch had known, damn her greedy little soul. As much as I might resent that it took this discovery to make the powers in Cries care about us, I hated far more the future Scorch would have created with her greed. I hated Scorch. I didn't much like myself, either, for the fierce satisfaction I felt in having killed her, but I was glad I had ended her miserable egomaniacal life.

At the moment, however, my feelings were irrelevant. I had a greater concern. Cries had taken notice of the undercity, big-time. "What do you plan to do?" I asked. "Now that you know about my people?"

She spoke in her perfect Iotic accent with that dusky voice. "I imagine my solutions will be different than what you might suggest."

That wasn't what I wanted to hear. But I had to deal with this, because if I didn't, the general would go ahead with her own plans. "What are your solutions?"

"For one, we must get those children a better life." She spoke firmly. "We can build special schools in Cries and board them until they reach their majority. We will rehabilitate the adults to fit into society, to speak and dress properly, and live in normal homes. We can teach them appropriate vocations so they can make a living." She went on, inexorable. "We'll offer the psions training so they can use their abilities and learn what they can do for the military and government."

I couldn't speak, I could only stare at her. No, I couldn't look. If I stayed another moment, something inside me would explode and I would antagonize the most powerful human being in the Imperialate after the Pharaoh and the Imperator.

I got up and walked to the edge of the terrace. I wanted to cross my arms over my abdomen and bend over, a posture I had often taken as a child when I was hurt. I couldn't do that here, I couldn't do anything to show weakness. I stared at the mountains and understood why Lavinda liked rooms with windows, because the sight of those peaks with their powerful serenity, enduring for long before we came to this world, was all that kept me calm.

Gradually my pulse slowed. I finally turned to the general. She had walked to another part of the terrace, giving me room, her gaze on the mountains. When I moved, she turned to me and I went over to her. She didn't seem surprised by my reaction. Although she couldn't have been back on Raylicon for long, I had no doubt she had already talked with Lavinda.

I spoke evenly. "If you institute that program for the undercity, my people will fight you with their every breath. The children will run away from your schools and think of it as escaping prison. They will leave again and again no matter how many times you round them up, and if you lock them up, they will do anything to escape, even risk their lives. The adults will use whatever jamming tech they can smuggle, steal, or salvage to take their kin so deep and far below the canals and the Vanished Sea, you will never find them all. You will destroy an irreplaceable community, probably the only of its kind in existence, and multiply an already grueling death rate, all in an attempt to control people who will never agree to live the way you want."

Her gaze never wavered. "We're offering life," she said coldly. "Over half those people who came to the Center were undernourished. Some were starving. Others were injured, bones broken and never properly set, birth defects never treated, the mineral levels in their bodies dangerously high. From what my people tell me, yours have no formal education or medical care, and no homes other than caves. Major, many of those people live well below the poverty level."

What, you just noticed? I held back my anger, shielding my mind. General Majda hadn't created this situation, and I wouldn't help anyone by losing my temper.

I spoke calmly. "My people have struggled with poverty for centuries. Millennia, even." We had no formal accounts, only oral legends handed down from generation to generation, but some of those stories were ancient, from a time before modern Cries existed. "We need to treat the causes of the problems, not ignore them by wiping out the culture."

"I cannot fathom," Vaj said, "why anyone would die for the right to live in a slum. Don't your people want to improve their station?"

I gritted my teeth, then made myself stop. "Improve by whose definition? The undercity isn't a slum. It's a unique world with its own beauty, just as the beauty of Cries is stark compared to a paradise like Selei City on the world Parthonia. People in Selei City see life here as 'barbaric,' but no one would ever suggest retraining the people of Cries so they would act like people in Selei City and work in vocational jobs there." Let the proud Majda chew on that noisome idea. "The undercity has an ancient history. Our culture, language, way of life—it has *value.*" I somehow kept my voice even. "That my people are crushed under the weight of poverty is true. It shouldn't be such a choice—live in poverty or destroy an ancient culture." I lifted my hands, then let them drop. "The cartels shattered two canals. Your brother-in-law is going to rebuild them with as much care as it takes to remain true to the nature of those ruins. Why would we do any less for the people who live there? The changes need to come from within the undercity, with my people and yours working together."

I stopped then, unable to say more. That was one of the longest speeches I had ever given. I had no idea if I was making headway, but she seemed angry, at least as much as I could read of her guarded expression. She turned to look at the mountains with her hands clasped behind her back. Apparently Lavinda and I weren't the only ones who found the scene calming. Great. We could all take turns staring. Maybe then we wouldn't want to punch each other.

After several moments, Vaj said, "My sister Lavinda has offered a suggestion."

I regarded her warily. "Yes?"

The general turned back to me. "That your people choose a representative, someone who will provide an interface between Cries and the undercity. My people would try working with that representative to find solutions that are acceptable to both of our communities."

I exhaled with relief. "I think that would be a good idea."

"I am willing to agree to this on a trial basis," Vaj said, "with one condition."

"Yes?"

She spoke in a dry voice. "Major, you are the nightmare of any leader who has ever dealt with a disenfranchised population."

Where had that come from? I had no suitable answer, at least not one I could say to royalty, so I kept my mouth shut.

"The success story," she continued. "The striver who rises above poverty and leads a rewarding life. Of course, it's what we want to believe everyone can do."

She wasn't making sense. "Why is that a nightmare?" It was how the above-city ignored our problems, by saying I was an example of how we could better ourselves if we tried, which meant our problems were our own fault. I had heard that over and over in the military, until I wanted to throttle those who said my people "earned" their poverty through laziness, lack of character, and inferior genetics.

"The nightmare," she said, "is when the golden daughter returns and incites her people to unrest." She shook her head. "That procession you led yesterday could have easily turned into a riot. The way those people followed you may be one of the greatest acts of trust I've ever seen. They see you as a leader, someone who can move them to action."

For flaming sake. "General, I have no wish to incite—"

Vaj stopped me by holding up her hand. "Perhaps not. But I have concerns."

"So your condition is that I leave Cries?" Now, after I had finally admitted to myself that I needed to stay.

"No," Vaj said. "My condition is that you become the undercity representative who works with my people."

I blinked. "Why?"

"Because any decision you make as that representative, any activity you encourage your people to take, will directly affect the changes you are working for on their behalf." She paused, intent on me. "If you want me to refrain from implementing my plans, Major, then give me reason to trust that your ideas will work better."

Put that way, it made sense. She had just given me a powerful incentive to seek peaceful change. I had no desire to start riots or whatever, but she had a point. Violence could easily erupt if the under and above cities interacted more, especially given that the undercity was now armed with some serious artillery. The weapons the punkers and gangers had returned or that the army had dug out of the collapsed canal only constituted about half of the guns I had seen in Scorch's storeroom. The rest were still down in the aqueducts.

"All right," I said. "I agree."

She didn't nod. Instead she said, "I have two questions for you, before we make it final."

"Yes?"

Her gaze hardened. "You had a rather dramatic reaction to the death of the Kajada cartel queen. Then you disappeared for nearly an hour from the Center. Why?"

That was blunt. But I understood. In her view, the distance from "agitator who leads demonstration" to "cartel sympathizer" probably wasn't much. "She and I were friends as children, long before she took over the cartel." I stopped, hit with the confusing ache that came whenever I thought of Dig. "That whole day was intense, especially her death. I needed some time. I went to a secluded part of the Concourse and sat for a while with two friends."

Vaj didn't look surprised, but I couldn't tell if she believed me. "Her oldest daughter left with her brother and sisters right after they were tested. I understand the daughter took her siblings to an undercity family that had already agreed to care for them."

It didn't surprise me that Dig had made arrangements for her children in case anything happened to her. In her line of work, that was the only rational choice. From what I had seen of Digjan, I had no doubt she was fiercely protective of her brother and sisters. Nor did it surprise me that they had left the Concourse. Our people had trickled back to the aqueducts throughout the day, until no one remained at the Center. Not one person had accepted an offer from the military for Kyle training, at least not yet. Whether anyone would eventually, I couldn't tell.

"I'm sure the children will be well taken care of," I said, hoping the general wasn't about to ask me to turn in Dig's kids. I would have to refuse, which could destroy the precarious balance in this negotiation we were trying to conduct.

Vaj was still studying me. "The oldest, the one you called Digjan, came to the army recruiting center today and enlisted."

Ho! "You mean, she went through with it?"

"So you did know."

"I've offered to sponsor her."

"Yes, she wrote that on her documents. We noted it with her other sponsor."

Other sponsor? "Who is that?"

The general spoke dryly. "It seems my sister Lavinda has taken an interest."

Saints almighty. Majda royalty and a colonel in the Pharaoh's Army? Digjan's enlistment had just gone from the bottom of the heap to the top. Doors would open everywhere for her. I found it hard to credit, though. Did Lavinda feel guilt about what she had seen yesterday? I could envision her helping Digjan enlist, but sponsoring her was another matter altogether. It implied she had a far greater investment in the daughter of a drug queen than I'd ever have expected.

"Why would she do that?" I asked.

"Because we don't want her to join the army," Vaj said. "We're sending her to the Dieshan Military Academy."

My mouth dropped open. I closed it and said, "That's for Jagernauts." They were the elite of the ISC elite, the legendary psibernetic fighter pilots. The Academy had thousands of applicants every year from the best programs across an empire and accepted only twenty or thirty as cadets.

Vaj started walking and I went with her along a path in the garden. "This girl Digjan," Vaj said. "She has one of the highest psi ratings of the people we tested. Genetically, her mother's DNA has many of the markers, but unpaired." She glanced at me. "You know Kyle traits are recessive?"

I nodded. "My understanding is that you need the DNA from both parents to be a psion."

"That's right." She took a side path that headed deeper into the garden. "Her father must have also carried many Kyle mutations, because she manifests many of the traits."

I could see how that made her a prime candidate for a Jagernaut, but she needed a lot more than raw ability. "Won't she have to pass entrance exams?" For acceptance into the academy, she would need to beat some of the most accomplished young people in the Imperialate.

"She has a remarkable education," Vaj said.

"You're kidding."

She spoke wryly. "That was the recruiter's response too. But we've given her many tests. She repeatedly scores in the top percentiles. She was quite blunt about hacking the city meshes and stealing her education. Her mother insisted, apparently from the day the girl could speak."

That was the last response I expected. Dig had scorned my attempts to learn. She told me it was a waste of time. I couldn't tell the General of the Pharaoh's Army that, so instead I said, "I'm glad she did well."

"Apparently it had something to do with whatever you told her mother the day you enlisted."

I didn't want to recall the argument with Dig that day I left. It hurt too much. But if it had led to this, then some good had come out of those wrenching words.

"So you think she can pass the Academy exams?" I asked.

"With preparation." Vaj shrugged. "She'll have no problem with the physical tests. That girl is in incredible shape. We found no signs that she ever suffered from malnutrition."

I spoke dryly. "I doubt her mother ever lacked the money to buy food." Dig had often raided her family's stores to feed Gourd, Jak, and me. It was one reason we hadn't suffered malnutrition. I also had to admit that spending the first three years of my life in an orphanage where I was fed properly gave me a better start on life than most undercity children.

"Her mother left her an ugly legacy," Vaj said. "And yet—"

I waited. Then I said, "And yet?"

The general exhaled. "Digjan Kajada has no trace of drugs in her body. No indication she ever used them, not even according to our most sophisticated exams. She's cleaner than many of the kids who come in from Cries. She's never been arrested, never caught drug running, never netted when the police rounded up cartel members. The closest she ever came to an arrest was when she walked onto the Concourse yesterday holding that gun." She glanced at me. "Which she returned."

I suspected Vaj didn't believe any more than I did that Digjan wanted to return the gun. But regardless, Digjan had put her weapon on the table, and the army was willing to let that be enough.

I let my shoulders relax, feeling a hint of closure finally, after all these years. "Digjan is a strong young woman. She'd make a good Jagernaut." It was a far better use of her abilities than inheriting her mother's cartel.

Then I remembered I wasn't in the clear yet. "You said you had two questions."

Vaj looked up with a start, as if she had been lost in her thoughts. "Oh. Yes. What is a Dust Knight?"

Damn! I didn't want them interfering with the Knights. That was ours and ours alone, purely undercity. I had to tell her something, though, and the words needed some truth, because she was too savvy to fool.

"It's a sort of club," I said. "The kids agree to a code where they don't lie, do drugs, or fight to hurt people. In return, I teach them some moves and philosophies from tykado."

"Ah, yes." Vaj still looked preoccupied. "Lavinda thought sports would be a good outlet."

We walked for a while through the garden, along a bluestone path under the pale sky of Raylican. Small winged reptiles flew over the flowers like tiny ruziks taken flight. Lost in her own thoughts, Vaj seemed to have forgotten me.

We were strolling by a gold-tiled pond when she spoke again. "Almost every organ in her body was damaged, even crushed."

I glanced up. "Ma'am?"

"The Kajada drug queen." Vaj met my gaze. "Apparently the Vakaar queen tried to kill her children. They were caught in the collapse of the ruins and Kajada protected them with her body. Somehow, she and the children dug their way out. It took them more than a day. Then Kajada took them to the Center. You know the rest."

I stared at her. "With internal injuries that serious? She should have been dead!"

"Yes, she should have." Vaj stopped by a lattice heavy with red vines. "I have heard of superhuman feats performed by parents protecting their children, but until I saw the records from yesterday, I had never witnessed such."

Well, Dig never did anything halfway. She protected her three younger children from being crushed by rocks and her oldest daughter from being crushed by her life. If it hadn't been for Dig, I knew Jak, Gourd, and I would have been worse off growing up. Yet she had also plagued Cries with gruesome drug trade. I doubted I would ever sort out how I felt about her, all that love and anger mixed together. But Digjan had escaped, and her siblings would, too. I'd make sure of that.

A quartet of male guards was approaching us through the garden. Odd. Usually they came with one of the princes. They were alone now, though.

Vaj inclined her head toward the guards. "Go with them."

"All right," I said, puzzled. Then I realized Paolo and I had a great deal to work out for the aqueducts.

As I joined Paolo's guards, however, Vaj said, "Major."

I turned back to her. "Yes?"

She stood like a tall statue. "You didn't get tested yesterday."

"It wasn't necessary. I had a Kyle workup in the army." I shrugged, the way I had back then. "I have no psi ability." She should know that already, given that she had looked at my records.

"The tests didn't say you have no ability," Vaj told me. "They said you didn't manifest any."

"Isn't that the same thing?"

"If the testers had been certain you had no ability, they would have given you a rating of zero." She paused. "They didn't give you any rating."

"I thought psi traits always showed up on tests."

"Usually." She had an odd look, deep and quiet.

"Unless you repress them so much that you barely feel them yourself."

This made no sense. "Why would I do that?"

"Perhaps to protect your mind." Softly she said, "From a life that was killing everyone around you."

I felt hot, then cold. I didn't want to have this conversation. "I'm sure I have no abilities."

"Perhaps not," Vaj said. "However, one of the analysts who examined you in the army suggested testing you further as an empath. Also for precognitive dreams."

No. My dreams were just dreams. My thoughts were ordinary. I had absolutely no desire to be an empath. I had enough trouble dealing with my own emotions. I couldn't take on any others.

After I was silent for a while, Vaj nodded, acknowledging the end of the conversation. Then, incredibly, she smiled. It was only slight, barely an upward curve of her lips, but it was still a smile. She raised her hand, a gesture of respect. "Go well, Major."

"Thank you." I lifted my hand. "And you."

We parted then, she returning to the palace and me to meet with the architect who would try to repair the injuries to a world in the darkness.

The guards didn't take me to see Paolo.

We went to an alcove tiled like a sunrise, with a border along the floor like the horizon of the desert. Above it, the wall shaded from rose hues into lighter blue. Across the room, a man sat at a similarly tiled table next to a tall window. He was studying holos above the table, images about the physics of Higgs bosons. Sun streamed in through the window, glistening on his black hair, his face, his broad shoulders, and his clothes, velvet and Haverian silk, with diamonds on the shirt cuffs. The scene was so arresting that I froze just inside the door, causing one of the guards to bump into me. He stopped after hitting my shoulder, and I couldn't move.

Beauty wasn't power. I'd read my share on that subject in my officer training classes, where they made damn sure we would know how to treat everyone in our command fairly and didn't do something stupid that could get the army sued for harassment or swamped in scandal. I read the bulleted outlines they had given us, and then out of curiosity I looked up the scholarly works. I'd never forgotten how, in my youth, I could wheedle food out of Concourse vendors because they thought I was pretty. It became one of many techniques in my bag of tricks for How To Eat, along with numerous methods of petty theft. The articles pointed out the obvious, that beauty was an illusory "power" dependent on physical characteristics that weren't permanent and said nothing about a person's worth or character. It rarely lasted. That was certainly true in the undercity, where most of us had gaunt faces, scars, or the pockmarks of disease by the time we were adults. Either that, or we were dead and didn't give a whack about power dynamics.

In Raylicon's past, women had attained power through war, wealth, and work. Men were "powerful" if women found them desirable, but once they were owned, they had no say in their lives. That wasn't power, it was possession, and even I could see it was wrong. Yes, I knew the scholarship, and I knew its truth, but in this moment none of that mattered, because Dayjarind Majda had, by his mere presence, rendered me utterly powerless.

I had seen holos of him and I had seen him after we rescued him from Scorch, but I had never seen him like this, at his best, contentedly sitting in the sun reading his books. He was the singularly most devastating man I had ever met, and if he had asked me to prostrate myself on the floor right then and babble like an idiot, I would have done it. So okay, I was an idiot. Sue me. It would have been worth it for these few moments in his presence.

All he did, however, was motion me over to the table. "Major, please join me." Then he smiled, and I could have died in ecstasy.

My heart continued to beat, however, so instead of expiring, I went over and sat across from him at the table.

"My glittings," I said. Gods, I was a moron today. "Uh, greetings, that is. My greetings. Your Higgness. Your Highness, I mean."

Dayj was kind enough not to laugh. "My greetings, Major." He tapped a square on the table and the holos disappeared. "It's good to see you." He seemed delighted to say those words. I supposed he didn't have much chance to use them, given his lack of visitors.

"Are you studying?" I asked.

"For my placement tests. The university is sending an examiner from Parthonia. She'll be here in a few days." He grinned at me. "If I pass, and I think I will, then I'm off to university."

I almost lost him after the grin, but I caught enough to understand. "That's wonderful."

We sat in awkward silence. Then I said, "Did you want to see me about something?"

He hesitated. "What happened in the aqueducts, the

fighting and destruction, is my fault. I feel I should make amends, but I have no idea how to do so."

Good gods. "How could it be your fault?"

"My foolish trip to the canals started the chain of events that made it possible for the cartel to steal the weapons, which started the fighting."

"That's not your fault."

He spoke dryly. "Really? Scorch would have just given those carbines and tanglers to the Kajada cartel out of the goodness of her heart?"

"Uh, well, no."

"If I had never gone there," he said, "Kajada couldn't have stolen the guns, Vakaar wouldn't have felt the need to arm themselves in response, the canals would still be intact, and people would be alive who are dead now."

"Dayj, you can't blame yourself for the violence of the cartels." I shook my head. "Without you, we wouldn't have learned Scorch's plans. You prevented one of the worst crimes in the history of this planet. She could have sold psions for years, feeding off the undercity, decimating us, giving the Traders the advantage over our military they've sought for centuries, and we would never have known." I spoke firmly. "Raylicon and the Imperialate owe you an incalculable debt of gratitude."

He grimaced. "I didn't do anything except act stupid."

"You had the courage to break the rules. It shook up everything. When the dust settled, the world had changed." Gently I said, "For the better."

He sat for a while, taking that in. Then he said, "I hadn't seen it in those terms."

"You should. Because they're true." If Scorch had killed or sold him, it would have been a different story, but his family had acted fast enough that he sat here preparing for college exams instead of living as a slave.

Dayj smiled. "You're a good person, Major."

That was embarrassing, because I knew better. I had good in me, yes. Most people did, even Dig, maybe even Scorch. But darkness also lived in my heart. Yet despite everything that had happened to Dayj, he still saw the good in people. I hoped he always kept a portion of that innocence, for it was worth more than all the wealth of the Majdas.

A wide plaza stretched out from the outskirts of Cries in two shallow terraces, all blue and gray stone. A fountain bubbled on the upper terrace. Even from this far away, I could hear children laughing as they splashed in the water.

The entrance to the Concourse lay beyond the terraces, an archway wide enough for several people to walk through together. The stairs inside descended to the boulevard, which at this end was only one story underground. The sun had spent the last hour setting, and the archway glowed with lights, blue and gold, sparkling in the fading day.

I was walking next to a retaining wall, headed for the archway, when a boy came alongside me, an above-city child of about eight, clean and new in his sports clothes.

I smiled at him. "My greetings, sir."

"Are you The Bhaaj?" A lock of floppy brown hair fell into his eyes and he pushed it back.

It startled me to hear the odd title spoken in an above-city accent. I slowed to a stop and sat on the wall so my height was equal to his. "I'm just Bhaaj. What can I do for you?"

He regarded me earnestly. "I want to join the Dust Knights."

Good gods. This young fellow had probably never even seen a stalagmite, let alone been to the undercity. "Where did you hear about the Knights?"

He smiled, a flash of healthy teeth. "My cousin's brother has a girlfriend who heard about it from a boy at her school who snuck down to the canals." He straightened up, pulling back his shoulders. "Dust Knights follow the Code. Protect and train. Do good."

Well, I hoped they would do good. It seemed a small thing, that this charming fellow wanted to join the Knights—except he came from the above-city, from the world of magic and privilege. Until this moment, everything that had happened, everything we had done, had revolved around the undercity coming to an accommodation with Cries. It hadn't occurred to me that someone from Cries might want to come to us.

I couldn't take this nice kid to the aqueducts. He wouldn't last five minutes. Maybe, though, we could work out a program at the Rec Center where the children could do a sport together, both above- and undercity teams. I didn't know if anyone would show up besides this boy, but it was worth a try. It was certainly a better way to introduce undercity youth to above-city culture than Vaj's draconian idea of forcing our children into state schools.

"Tell you what," I said. "If you're still interested in five days, come to the Rec Center in the morning, tenth hour. I'll meet you and we'll talk." I needed time to put some ideas together.

"You're sure?" he asked.

"Absolutely," I said.

"Good!" He stepped onto the wall and jumped off with a yell.

A chill swept over me, and I had the oddest sense, as if I saw a time centuries beyond this day, an age when the Knights had become a legend that served an empire. They were revered throughout the Imperialate, a secret order of protectors even more difficult to join than the Jagernauts, an order based in an exquisite, mythical place hidden beneath the oldest city in the Imperialate.

The chill went away as fast as it came, and I was once again sitting in a warm evening on the edge of Cries. I snorted at my ridiculous imagination, and the boy laughed at the undignified sound.

"Tomi," a woman called. "Come on. Time for dinner."

Looking back, I saw a woman walking across the plaza toward us. I grinned at Tomi. "Better get going. Knights have to eat their cabbage-roots to stay strong."

"I hate cabbage-roots," he announced. He waved and took off, running toward his mother.

I resumed my walk to the Concourse, thinking. I had to prepare for my meeting with the Majdas reps. Tomorrow I would go to various offices in Cries to see if I could arrange market licenses for undercity vendors. The office staff would resist the idea, of course, but I would keep at it until I wore them down. I could be annoyingly persistent.

I would also talk to the directors of the Rec Center. If we could arrange a less conspicuous annex near the end of the Concourse, our young people might go there. And I'd look up Orin at the university. It would be good to see him. Even if he no longer went to the aqueducts, he might know who did. Perhaps I could convince them to work as mentors with our children in return for the kids acting as guides to the canals. I could check with the engineers, too, to see if they'd work with the cyber-riders. It would take some mega-tech to lure out the riders, and engineers were less likely than anthropologists to enter the undercity, but you never knew.

So I pondered as I walked the Concourse. Even if only a few of my ideas succeeded, it was a start. Or so I hoped. I might be setting myself up for a lot of work with little chance of success. No matter. It was worth the effort. We had caught the attention of the above-city, and incredibly, at least for now, they were willing to work with us.

Tonight, though, I didn't want to think anymore. I was on my way to meet someone more tempting than any ruins, tech, or Majda prince. I was going to spend the evening with my disreputable kingpin. Thoughts about changing the world could wait until tomorrow.

Characters & Family History

Boldface names refer to Ruby psions. All Ruby psions use **Skolia** as their last name. The **Selei** name indicates the direct line of the Ruby Pharaoh. Children of **Roca** and **Eldrinson** take Valdoria as a third name. The del prefix means "in honor of," and is capitalized if the person honored is (or was) a Triad member. Most names are based on world-building systems drawn from Mayan, North African, and Indian cultures. The family tree below corresponds to the time of the Lightning Strike books, which take place roughly 123 years after the events of *Undercity*.

= marriage

~

Lahaylia Selei (Ruby Pharaoh: deceased)	=	**Jarac** (Imperator: deceased)

Lahaylia and **Jarac** founded the modern-day Ruby Dynasty. **Lahaylia** was created in the Rhon genetic project. Her lineage traces back to the ancient Ruby Dynasty that founded the Ruby Empire.

Lahaylia and **Jarac** have two daughters, **Dyhianna Selei** and **Roca.**

~

Dyhianna (Dehya)	=	(1)	William Seth Rockworth III (separated)
	=	(2)	**Eldrin Jarac Valdoria**

Dehya is the Ruby Pharaoh. She married William Seth Rockworth III as part of the Iceland Treaty between the Skolian Imperialate and Allied Worlds of Earth. They had no children and later separated. The dissolution of their marriage would negate the treaty, so neither the Allieds nor Imperialate recognize their divorce. Her second marriage is to Eldrin, a member of the Ruby Dynasty. *Spherical Harmonic* tells the story of what happened to **Dehya** after the Radiance War.

Dehya and **Eldrin** have two children, **Taquinil Selei** and **Althor Vyan Selei. Taquinil** is an extraordinary genius and an untenably sensitive empath. He appears in *The Radiant Seas*, *Spherical Harmonic*, and *Carnelians*.

~

Althor Vyan	=	**Akushtina (Tina) Selei Santis Pulivok**

Althor and **Tina** appear in *Catch the Lightning*, which was expanded and rewritten into the eBook duology *Lightning Strike, Book I* and *Lightning Strike, Book II.* **Althor Selei** is named after his uncle, **Althor Valdoria** (who is named after his father, **Eldrinson Althor Valdoria**, the "King of Skyfall").

The short story "Avo de Paso" tells of how **Tina** and her cousin Manuel go to the New Mexico desert to grieve the death of Tina's mother. It appears in the anthologies *Redshift*, ed. Al Sarrantino, and *Fantasy: The Year's Best, 2001*, eds. Robert Silverberg and Karen Haber.

~

Roca = (1) Tokaba Ryestar (deceased)
= (2) Darr Hammerjackson (divorced)
= (3) **Eldrinson Althor Valdoria**

Roca is the sister of the Ruby Pharaoh. She is in the direct line of succession to the Ruby throne and to all three titles of the Triad. She is also the Foreign Affairs Councilor of the Assembly, a seat she won through election rather than as an inherited title. A ballet dancer turned diplomat, she appears in most of the Ruby Dynasty novels, in particular *Skyfall*.

Roca and Tokaba Ryestar had one child, **Kurj** (Imperator and Jagernaut). **Kurj** married Ami when he was a century old, and they had one child named Kurjson. **Kurj** appears in *Skyfall, Primary Inversion*, and *The Radiant Seas*, and with more minor roles in many of the other books.

Although no records exist of **Eldrinson's** lineage, it is believed he descends from the ancient Ruby Dynasty. He is a bard, farmer, and judge on the planet Lyshriol (also known as Skyfall). His spectacular singing voice is legendary among his people, a genetic gift he bequeathed to his sons Eldrin and Del-Kurj. The novel *Skyfall* tells how **Eldrinson** and **Roca** met. They have ten children:

Eldrin (Dryni) Jarac (bard, opera singer, consort to Ruby Pharaoh, Lyshriol warrior)

Althor Izam-Na (engineer, Jagernaut, Imperial Heir)

Del-Kurj (Del) (rock singer, Lyshriol warrior, twin to **Chaniece**)

Chaniece Roca (runs Valdoria family household, twin to **Del-Kurj**)

Havyrl (Vyrl) Torcellei (farmer, doctorate in agriculture)

Sauscony (Soz) Lahaylia (military scientist, Jagernaut, Imperator)

Denric Windward (teacher, doctorate in literature)

Shannon Eirlei (Blue Dale archer)

Aniece Dyhianna (accountant, Rillian queen)

Kelricson (Kelric) Garlin (mathematician, Jagernaut, Imperator)

~

Eldrin appears in *The Final Key, Triad, The Radiant Seas, Spherical Harmonic, The Ruby Dice, Diamond Star, Carnelians,* and *Lightning Strike, Book II/Catch the Lightning*. See also **Dehya**.

~

Althor Izam-Na = (1) Coop and Vaz
= (2) Cirrus (former provider to Ur Qox)

Althor is one of the three Imperial scions Kurj chose as his possible heir, along with Soz and Kelric. He distinguished himself as a Jagernaut in the J-Forces of Imperial Space Command. He has two daughters: **Aliana Miller Azina**, born to a Trader taskmaker, and Eristia Leirol Valdoria, born to Syreen Leirol, a Skolian actress turned linguist. Coop and Vaz have a son, Ryder Jalam Majda Valdoria, with **Althor** as co-father. Vaz and Coop appear in *Spherical Harmonic*. **Althor** and Cirrus also have a son. Althor and Coop appear in *The Radiant Seas*.

~

Del-Kurj, often considered the renegade of the Ruby Dynasty, is a rock singer who rose to fame on Earth after the Radiance War. His story is told in *Diamond Star*, which is accompanied by a soundtrack cut by the rock band Point Valid with Catherine Asaro. The songs on the CD are all from the book. **Del** also appears in *The Quantum Rose, Schism, Carnelians*, and the novella "Stained Glass Heart."

~

Chaniece is Del's twin sister. They come as close to sharing a mind as two Rhon empaths can do without becoming one person. **Chaniece** appears in *Diamond Star, Schism*, and *The Quantum Rose*.

~

Havyrl (Vyrl) = (1) Liliara (Lily) **Torcellei** (deceased)
= (2) Kamoj Quanta Argali

Vyrl is a farmer who married his childhood sweetheart Lily and stayed on Skyfall for most of his life, until he became a pawn in the political intrigue following the Radiance War. He is also an accomplished dancer. The story of **Havyrl** and Lily appears in "Stained Glass Heart," in the anthology *Irresistible Forces*, ed. Catherine

Asaro, 2004. The story of **Havyrl** and Kamoj appears in *The Quantum Rose*, a science-fiction retelling of *Beauty and the Beast* which won the 2001 Nebula Award. An early version of the first half was serialized in *Analog*, May–July/August 1999.

~

Sauscony (Soz) = (1) Jato Stormson (divorced)
Lahaylia = (2) Hypron Luminar (deceased)
= (3) **Jaibriol Qox** (aka **Jaibriol II**)

Soz is one of the three Imperial scions Kurj chose as his possible heir, along with Althor and Kelric. A strategic genius, she became the greatest military leader known in the Skolian Imperialate. The story of her time as a cadet at the Dieshan Military Academy is told in *Schism*, *The Final Key*, and "Echoes of Pride" (*Space Cadets*, ed. Mike Resnick, 2006). *The Final Key* tells of the first Skolian-Trader war and Soz's part in that conflict. The story of Soz's rescue of colonists from the world New Day is told in the novelette "The Pyre of New Day" (*The Mammoth Book of SF Wars*, ed. Ian Whates and Ian Watson, 2012). How **Soz** and Jato met appears in the novella, "Aurora in Four Voices" (*Analog*, December 1998). **Soz** and **Jaibriol**'s stories appear in *Primary Inversion* and *The Radiant Seas*. They have four children: **Jaibriol III, Rocalisa, Vitar,** and **del-Kelric.**

Jaibriol Qox Skolia (aka **Jaibriol III**) Emperor of the Trader Empire = Tarquine Iquar (Trader Empress, Finance Minister, and Aristo queen of the Iquar Line)

Jaibriol III, the eldest child of **Soz** and **Jaibriol II**, becomes the emperor of the Eubian Concord, also known as the Trader Empire. As such, he must hide his true identity, that he is also an heir to the Ruby Throne. The story of how **Jaibriol III** becomes Emperor at age seventeen is told in *The Moon's Shadow*. The story of how Jaibriol and his uncle Kelric deal with each other as the leaders of opposing empires appears in *The Ruby Dice* and *Carnelians*. **Jaibriol III** also appears in *The Radiant Seas* as a child and as a teenager.

~

Denric is a teacher. He accepts a position on Sandstorm, an impoverished colony, to run a school for the children there. His harrowing introduction to his new home appears in the story, "The Edges of Never-Haven" (*Flights of Fantasy*, ed. Al Sarrantino). He also appears in *The Quantum Rose*.

~

Shannon is the most otherworldly member of the Ruby Dynasty. He inherited the rare genes of a Blue Dale Archer from his father, **Eldrinson**. He left home at age sixteen and sought out the Archers, believed to be extinct. He appears in *Schism, The Final Key, The Quantum Rose*, and as a child in "Stained Glass Heart."

~

Aniece = Lord Rillia

Aniece is the most business-minded of the Valdoria children. Although she never left her home world Lyshriol, she earned an MBA and became an accountant. Lord

Rillia rules a province including the Rillian Vales, Dalvador Plains, Backbone Mountains, and Stained Glass Forest. **Aniece** decided at age twelve that she would marry Rillia, though he was much older, and she kept at her plan until she achieved her goal. **Aniece** and Rillia appear in *The Quantum Rose.*

~

Kelricson (Kelric) Garlin	=	(1) Corey Majda (deceased)
	=	(2) Deha Dahl (deceased)
	=	(3) Rashiva Haka (Calani trade)
	=	(4) Savina Miesa (deceased)
	=	(5) Avtac Varz (Calani trade)
	=	(6) Ixpar Karn
	=	(7) Jeejon (deceased)

Kelric is one of the three Imperial scions Kurj chose as his possible heir, along with **Soz** and **Althor**. He is a major character in *Carnelians, The Ruby Dice*, "The Ruby Dice" (novella, *Baen's Universe 2006*), *Ascendant Sun, The Last Hawk*, and the novelette "Light and Shadow" (Analog, April 1994). He also appears in *The Moon's Shadow, Diamond Star,* "A Roll of the Dice" (*Analog*, July/August 2000), and as a toddler in "Stained Glass Heart" (*Irresistible Forces*, ed. Catherine Asaro, 2004).

Kelric and Rashiva have one son, Jimorla Haka, who becomes a renowned Calani. **Kelric** and Savina have one daughter, **Rohka Miesa Varz,** who becomes the Ministry Successor in line to rule the Estates of Coba.

~

The novella "Walk in Silence" (*Analog*, April 2003) tells the story of Jess Fernandez, an Allied Starship Captain from Earth, who deals with the genetically engineered humans on the Skolian colony of Icelos.

The novella "The City of Cries" (*Down These Dark Spaceways*, ed. Mike Resnick) tells the story of Major Bhaaj, a private investigator hired by the House of Majda to find Prince Dayj Majda after he disappears.

The novella "The Shadowed Heart" (*Year's Best Paranormal*, ed. Paula Guran, and *The Journey Home*, ed. Mary Kirk) is the story of Jason Harrick, a Jagernaut who barely survives the Radiance War.

Time Line

Circa BC 4000	Group of humans moved from Earth to Raylicon
Circa BC 3600	Rise of the Ruby Dynasty
Circa BC 3100	Raylicans launch their first interstellar flights. Rise of the ancient Ruby Empire.
Circa BC 2900	Ruby Empire declines
Circa BC 2800	Last interstellar flights. Ruby Empire collapses.
Circa AD 1300	Raylicans begin to regain lost knowledge
AD 1843	Raylicans regain interstellar flight
AD 1871	Aristos found Eubian Concord (aka Trader Empire)
AD 1881	Lahaylia Selei born
AD 1904	Lahaylia Selei founds Skolian Imperialate
AD 2005	Jarac born
AD 2111	Lahaylia Selei marries Jarac
AD 2119	Dyhianna Selei born

AD 2122	Earth achieves interstellar flight with the inversion drive
AD 2132	Allied Worlds of Earth formally established
AD 2144	Roca born
AD 2169	Kurj born
AD 2203	Roca marries Eldrinson Althor Valdoria (*Skyfall*)
AD 2204	Eldrin Jarac Valdoria born (*Skyfall*)
	Jarac Skolia, Patriarch of the Ruby Dynasty, dies (*Skyfall*)
	Kurj becomes Imperator (*Skyfall*)
	Death of Lahaylia Selei, the first modern Ruby Pharaoh, followed by the ascension of Dyhianna Selei to the Ruby Throne
AD 2205	Major Bhaajan hired by the House of Majda ("The City of Cries" and *Undercity*)
	Bhaajan establishes the Dust Knights of Cries (*Undercity*)
AD 2206	Althor Izam-Na Valdoria born
AD 2207	Del-Kurj (Del) and Chaniece Roca born
AD 2209	Havyrl (Vyrl) Torcellei Valdoria born
AD 2210	Sauscony (Soz) Lahaylia Valdoria born
AD 2211	Denric Windward Valdoria born
AD 2213	Shannon Eirlei Valdoria born
AD 2215	Aniece Dyhianna Valdoria born
AD 2219	Kelricson (Kelric) Garlin Valdoria born
AD 2220	Eldrin and Dehya marry

AD 2221 Taquinil Selei born

AD 2223 Vyrl and Lily elope at age fourteen and create a political crisis ("Stained Glass Heart")

AD 2227 Soz enters Dieshan Military Academy (*Schism* and "Echoes of Pride")

AD 2228 First declared war between Skolia and Traders (*The Final Key*)

AD 2237 Jaibriol II born

AD 2240 Soz meets Jato Stormson ("Aurora in Four Voices")

AD 2241 Kelric marries Admiral Corey Majda

AD 2243 Corey Majda assassinated ("Light and Shadow")

AD 2255 Soz leads rescue mission to colony on New Day ("The Pyre of New Day")

AD 2258 Kelric crashes on Coba (*The Last Hawk*)

AD 2259 Soz and Jaibriol II go into exile (*Primary Inversion* and *The Radiant Seas*)

AD 2260 Jaibriol III born, aka Jaibriol Qox Skolia (*The Radiant Seas*)

AD 2263 Rocalisa Qox Skolia born (*The Radiant Seas*)

Althor Izam-Na Valdoria meets Coop ("Soul of Light")

AD 2269 Vitar Qox Skolia born (*The Radiant Seas*)

AD 2273 del-Kelric Qox Skolia born (*The Radiant Seas*)

AD 2274 Aliana Miller Azina born (*Carnelians*)

AD 2275	Jaibriol II captured by Eubian Space Command (ESComm) and forced to become puppet emperor of the Trader empire (*The Radiant Seas*)
	Soz becomes Imperator of the Skolian Imperialate (*The Radiant Seas*)
AD 2276	Radiance War begins, also called the Domino War (*The Radiant Seas*)
AD 2277	Traders capture Eldrin (*The Radiant Seas*)
	Radiance War ends (*The Radiant Seas*)
AD 2277–8	Kelric returns home and becomes Imperator (*Ascendant Sun*)
	Jaibriol III becomes the Trader emperor (*The Moon's Shadow* and *The Radiant Seas*)
	Dehya stages coup in the aftermath of the Radiance War (*Spherical Harmonic*)
	Imperialate and Eubian leaders meet for preliminary peace talks (*Spherical Harmonic*)
	Jason Harrick crashes on the planet Thrice Named ("The Shadowed Heart")
	Vyrl goes to Balumil and meets Kamoj (*The Quantum Rose*)
	Vyrl returns to Skyfall and leads planetary act of protest (*The Quantum Rose*)
AD 2279	Althor Vyan Selei born (the second son of Dyhianna and Eldrin)

	Del sings "The Carnelians Finale" and nearly starts a war (*Diamond Star*)
AD 2287	Jeremiah Coltman trapped on Coba ("A Roll of the Dice" and *The Ruby Dice*)
	Jeejon dies (*The Ruby Dice*)
AD 2288	Kelric and Jaibriol Qox sign peace treaty (*The Ruby Dice*)
AD 2289	Imperialate and Eubian governments meet for peace negotiations (*Carnelians*)
AD 2298	Jess Fernandez goes to Icelos ("Walk in Silence")
AD 2326	Tina and Manuel return to New Mexico ("Ave de Paso")
AD 2328	Althor Vyan Selei meets Tina Santis Pulivok (*Catch the Lightning*; also the duology *Lightning Strike, Book I* and *Lightning Strike, Book II*)

Taken together, *Lightning Strike, Book I* and *Lightning Strike, Book II* are similar to the story told in *Catch the Lightning*, but substantially rewritten and expanded for the eBook release.

The eBook version of *Primary Inversion* is rewritten from the original and considered by the author as the best version.

LOIS McMASTER BUJOLD

The Best-Selling Vorkosigan Saga

"One of SF's outstanding talents . . . an outstanding series." —*Booklist*

Shards of Honor
trade pb • 978-1-4767-8110-5 • $16.00

Barrayar
trade pb • 978-1-4767-8111-2 • $16.00

The Warrior's Apprentice
trade pb • 978-1-4767-8130-3 • $16.00

Cetaganda
pb • 0-671-87744-5 • $7.99

Miles, Mystery and Mayhem
pb • 0-7434-3618-0 • $7.99
Contains *Cetaganda, Ethan of Athos* and "Labyrinth" in one volume.

Brothers in Arms
pb • 1-4165-5544-7 • $7.99

Mirror Dance
pb • 0-671-87646-5 • $7.99

Memory
pb • 0-671-87845-X • $7.99

Miles in Love
hc • 1-4165-5522-6 • $19.00
trade pb • 1-4165-5547-1 • $14.00
Contains *Komarr, A Civil Campaign* and "A Winterfair Gift" in one volume.

Komarr
hc • 0-671-87877-8 • $22.00
pb • 0-671-57808-1 • $7.99

A Civil Campaign
hc • 0-671-57827-8 • $24.00
pb • 0-671-57885-5 • $7.99

Diplomatic Immunity
hc • 0-7434-3533-8 • $25.00
pb • 0-7434-3612-1 • $7.99

Cryoburn
hc • 978-1-4391-3394-1 • $25.00

Captain Vorpatril's Alliance
trade pb • 978-1451639155 • $15.00

Gentleman Jole and the Red Queen
hc • 978-1-4767-8122-8 • $27.00

Falling Free
pb • 1-4165-5546-3 • $7.99

IF YOU LIKE... YOU SHOULD TRY...

DAVID DRAKE
David Weber
Tony Daniel
John Lambshead

DAVID WEBER
John Ringo
Timothy Zahn
Linda Evans
Jane Lindskold
Sarah A. Hoyt

JOHN RINGO
Michael Z. Williamson
Tom Kratman
Larry Correia
Mike Kupari

ANNE MCCAFFREY
Mercedes Lackey
Lois McMaster Bujold
Liaden Universe® by Sharon Lee & Steve Miller
Sarah A. Hoyt
Mike Kupari

MERCEDES LACKEY
Wen Spencer
Andre Norton
James H. Schmitz

LARRY NIVEN

Tony Daniel

James P. Hogan

Travis S. Taylor

Brad Torgersen

ROBERT A. HEINLEIN

Jerry Pournelle

Lois McMaster Bujold

Michael Z. Williamson

HEINLEIN'S "JUVENILES"

Rats, Bats & Vats series by Eric Flint & Dave Freer

Brendan DuBois' *Dark Victory*

David Weber & Jane Lindskold's Star Kingdom Series

Dean Ing's *It's Up to Charlie Hardin*

David Drake & Jim Kjelgaard's *The Hunter Returns*

HORATIO HORNBLOWER OR PATRICK O'BRIAN

David Weber's Honor Harrington series

David Drake's RCN series

Alex Stewart's *Shooting the Rift*

HARRY POTTER

Mercedes Lackey's Urban Fantasy series

JIM BUTCHER

Larry Correia's The Grimnoir Chronicles

John Lambshead's *Wolf in Shadow*

TECHNOTHRILLERS

Larry Correia & Mike Kupari's Dead Six Series
Robert Conroy's *Stormfront*
Eric Stone's *Unforgettable*
Tom Kratman's Countdown Series

THE LORD OF THE RINGS

Elizabeth Moon's *The Deed of Paksenarrion*
Shattered Shields ed. by Schmidt and Brozek
P.C. Hodgell
Ryk E. Spoor's Phoenix Rising series

A GAME OF THRONES

Larry Correia's *Son of the Black Sword*
David Weber's fantasy novels
Sonia Orin Lyris' *The Seer*

H.P. LOVECRAFT

Larry Correia's Monster Hunter series
P.C. Hodgell's Kencyrath series
John Ringo's Special Circumstances Series

ZOMBIES

John Ringo's Black Tide Rising Series
Wm. Mark Simmons

GEORGETTE HEYER

Lois McMaster Bujold
Catherine Asaro
Liaden Universe® by Sharon Lee & Steve Miller
Dave Freer

DOCTOR WHO

Steve White's TRA Series

Michael Z. Williamson's *A Long Time Until Now*

HARD SCIENCE FICTION

Ben Bova

Les Johnson

Charles E. Gannon

Eric Flint & Ryk E. Spoor's Boundary Series

Mission: Tomorrow ed. by Bryan Thomas Schmidt

GREEK MYTHOLOGY

Pyramid Scheme by Eric Flint & Dave Freer

Forge of the Titans by Steve White

Blood of the Heroes by Steve White

NORSE MYTHOLOGY

Northworld Trilogy by David Drake

Pyramid Power by Eric Flint & Dave Freer

URBAN FANTASY

Mercedes Lackey's SERRAted Edge Series

Larry Correia's Monster Hunter International Series

Sarah A. Hoyt's Shifter Series

Sharon Lee's Carousel Series

David B. Coe's Case Files of Justis Fearsson

The Wild Side ed. by Mark L. Van Name

DINOSAURS

David Drake's *Dinosaurs & a Dirigible*

David Drake & Tony Daniel's *The Heretic* and *The Savior*

HISTORY AND ALTERNATE HISTORY

Eric Flint's Ring of Fire Series
David Drake & Eric Flint's Belisarius Series
Robert Conroy
Harry Turtledove

HUMOR

Esther Friesner's *Chicks 'n Chaimail*
Rick Cook
Spider Robinson
Wm. Mark Simmons
Jody Lynn Nye

VAMPIRES & WEREWOLVES

Larry Correia
Wm. Mark Simmons
Ryk E. Spoor's *Paradigm's Lost*

WEBCOMICS

Sluggy Freelance... John Ringo's Posleen War Series
Schlock Mercenary...John Ringo's Troy Rising Series

NONFICTION

Hank Reinhardt
The Science Behind The Secret by Travis Taylor
Alien Invasion by Travis Taylor & Bob Boan
Going Interstellar ed. By Les Johnson